...A.. Award (twice), and the RT Book Re...
...hievement Award for 'a body of work which makes us
... teaches us about love'. Marion adores her family, her
...vak, her dog, and lying on the beach with a book someone
...e has written. Heaven!

...my Woods took the scenic route to becoming an author.
...he's been a bookkeeper, a high school English teacher and a
...laims specialist, but now that she makes up stories for a
...iving, she's never giving it up. She grew up in Austin, Texas,
...d lives there with her wonderfully goofy, supportive
...hand and a spoiled rescue dog. Amy can be reached on
...ebook, Twitter and her website, www.amywoodsbooks.com

...rese Beharrie has always been thrilled by romance. Her
...e of reading established this, and now she gets to write
...y-ever-afters for a living and about all things romance in
...blog at theresebeharrie.com. She married a man who
...antly exceeds her romantic expectations and is an infinite
...e of inspiration for her romantic heroes. She lives in
...e Town, South Africa, and is still amazed that her dream
...ng a romance author is a reality.

Summer of Love

MARION LENNOX
AMY WOODS
THERESE BEHARRIE

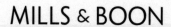
MILLS & BOON

First Published in Great Britain 2019
by Mills & Boon, an imprint of HarperCollins*Publishers*
1 London Bridge Street, London, SE1 9GF

SUMMER OF LOVE © 2019 Harlequin Books S. A.

His Cinderella Heiress © 2016 Marion Lennox
An Officer And Her Gentleman © 2016 Amy Woods
The Millionaire's Redemption © 2017 Therese Beharrie

ISBN: 978-0-263-27664-0

0719

HIS CINDERELLA HEIRESS

MARION LENNOX

To Mitzi. My shadow.

CHAPTER ONE

A WOMAN WAS stuck in his bog.

Actually, Finn Conaill wasn't sure if this land was part of the estate, but even if this wasn't the property of the new Lord of Glenconaill he could hardly ignore a woman stuck in mud to her thighs.

He pulled off the road, making sure the ground he steered onto was solid.

A motorbike was parked nearby and he assumed it belonged to the woman who was stuck. To the unwary, the bike was on ground that looked like a solid grass verge. She'd been lucky. The wheels had only sunk a couple of inches.

She'd not been so lucky herself. She was a hundred yards from the road, and she looked stuck fast.

'Stay still,' he called.

'Struggling makes me sink deeper.' Her voice sounded wobbly and tired.

'Then don't struggle.'

Of all the idiot tourists… She could have been here all night, he thought, as he picked his way carefully across to her. This road was a little used shortcut across one of County Galway's vast bogs. The land was a sweep of sodden grasses, dotted with steel-coloured washes of ice-cold water. In the distance he could see the faint outline of Castle Glenconaill, its vast stone walls seemingly merging into the mountains behind it. There'd been a few tough sheep on the road from the village, but here there was nothing.

There was therefore no one but Finn to help.

'Can you come faster?' she called and he could hear panic.

'Only if you want us both stuck. You're in no danger. I'm coming as fast as I can.'

Though he wouldn't mind coming faster. He'd told the housekeeper at the castle he'd arrive mid-afternoon and he was late already.

He spent considerable time away from his farm now, researching farming methods, investigating innovative ideas, so he had the staff to take care of the day-to-day farming. He'd been prepared to leave early this morning, with his manager more than ready to take over.

But then Maeve had arrived from Dublin, glamorous, in designer clothes and a low-slung sports car. She looked a million light years away from the woman who'd torn around the farm with him as a kid—who once upon a time he was sure he wanted to spend his life with. After a year apart—she'd asked for twelve months 'to discover myself before we marry'—what she'd told him this morning had only confirmed what he already knew. Their relationship was over, but she'd been in tears and he owed her enough to listen.

And then, on top of everything else, there'd been trouble lambing. He'd bottle-fed Sadie from birth, she was an integral part of a tiny flock of sheep he was starting to build, and he hadn't had the heart to leave until she was safely delivered.

Finally he'd tugged on clean trousers, a decent shirt and serviceable boots, and there was an end to his preparation for inheriting title and castle. If the castle didn't approve, he'd decided, it could find itself another lord.

And now he was about to get muddy, which wasn't very lordly either.

At least he knew enough of bogland to move slowly, and not get into trouble himself. He knew innocuous grassland often overlaid mud and running water. It could give way at any moment. The only way to tread safely was to look for rocks that were big enough to have withstood centuries of sodden land sucking them down.

After that initial panicked call, the woman was now silent and still, watching him come. The ground around her was a mire, churned. The bog wasn't so dangerous that it'd suck her down like quicksand, but it was thick and claggy so, once she'd sunk past her knees, to take one step after another back to dry land would have proved impossible.

He was concentrating on his feet and she was concentrating on watching him. Which he appreciated. He had no intention of ending up stuck too.

When he was six feet away he stopped. From here the ground was a churned mess. A man needed to think before going further.

'Thank you for coming,' she said.

He nodded, still assessing.

She sounded Australian, he thought, and she was young, or youngish, maybe in her mid to late twenties. Her body was lithe, neat and trim. She had short cropped, burnt-red curls. Wide green eyes were framed by long dark lashes. Her face was spattered with freckles and smeared with mud; eyeliner and mascara were smudged down her face. She had a couple of piercings in one ear and four in the other.

She was wearing full biker gear, black, black and black, and she was gazing up at him almost defiantly. Her thanks had seemed forced—like *I know I've been stupid but I defy you to tell me I am.*

His lips twitched a little. He could tell her anything he liked—she was in no position to argue.

'You decided to take a stroll?' he asked, taking time to assess the ground around her.

'I read about this place on the Internet.' Still he could hear the defiance. Plus the accent. With those drawn-out vowels, she had to be Australian. 'It said this district was famous for its quaking bogs but they weren't dangerous. I asked in the village and the guy I asked said the same. He said if you found a soft part, you could jump up and down and it bounced. So I did.'

His brows lifted. 'Until it gave way?'

'The Internet didn't say anything about sinking. Neither did the guy I asked.'

'I'd imagine whoever you asked assumed you'd be with someone. This place is safe enough if you're with a friend who can tug you out before you get stuck.'

'I was on my bike. He knew I was alone.'

'Then he'd be trying to be helpful.' Finn was looking at the churned-up mud around her, figuring how stuck she truly was. 'He wouldn't be wanting to disappoint you. Folk around here are like that.'

'Very helpful!' She glowered some more. 'Stupid bog.'

'It's a bit hard to sue a bog, though,' he said gently. 'Meanwhile, I'll fetch planks from the truck. There's no way I'll get you out otherwise. I've no wish to be joining you.'

'Thank you,' she said again, and once more it was as if the words were forced out of her. She was independent, he thought. And feisty. He could see anger and frustration—and also fury that she was dependent on his help.

She was also cold. He could hear it in the quaver in her voice, and by the shudders and chattering teeth she was trying to disguise. Cold and scared? But she wasn't letting on.

'Hold on then,' he said. 'I'll not be long. Don't go any-where.'

She clamped her lips tight and he just knew the effort it was taking her not to swear.

To say Jo Conaill was feeling stupid would be an under-statement. Jo—Josephine on her birth certificate but no-where else—was feeling as if the ground had been pulled from under her. Which maybe it had.

Of all the dumb things to do…

She'd landed in Dublin two nights ago, spent twenty-four hours fighting off jet lag after the flight from Sydney, then hired a bike and set off.

It was the first time she'd ever been out of Australia and she was in Ireland. Ireland! She didn't feel the least bit Irish, but her surname was Irish and every time she looked in the mirror she felt Irish. Her name and her looks were her only connection to this place, but then, Jo had very few connections to anything. Or anyone.

She was kind of excited to be here.

She'd read about this place before she came—of course she had. Ireland's bogs were legion. They were massive, mysterious graveyards of ancient forests, holding trea-sures from thousands of years ago. On the Internet they'd seemed rain-swept, misty and beautiful.

On her lunch break, working as a waitress in a busy café on Sydney Harbour, she'd watched a You Tube clip of a couple walking across a bog just like this. They'd been jumping up and down, making each other bounce on the spongy surface.

Jumping on the bogs of Galway. She'd thought maybe she could.

And here she was. The map had shown her this road, describing the country as a magnificent example of undis-turbed bog. The weather had been perfect. The bog looked amazing, stretching almost to the horizon on either side of her bike. Spongy. Bouncy. And she wasn't stupid. She had stopped to ask a local and she'd been reassured.

So she'd jumped, just a little at first and then venturing further from the road to get a better bounce. And then the surface had given way and she'd sunk to her knees. She'd struggled for half an hour until she was stuck to her thighs. Then she'd resigned herself to sit like a dummy and wait for rescue.

So here she was, totally dependent on a guy who had the temerity to laugh. Okay, he hadn't laughed out loud but she'd seen his lips twitch. She knew a laugh when she saw one.

At least he seemed…solid. Built for rescuing women from bogs? He was large, six-two or -three, muscular, lean and tanned, with a strongly boned face. He was wearing moleskin trousers and a khaki shirt, open-necked, his sleeves rolled above the elbows to reveal brawny arms.

He was actually, decidedly gorgeous, she conceded. Definitely eye candy. In a different situation she might even have paused to enjoy. He had the weathered face and arms of a farmer. His hair was a deep brown with just a hint of copper—a nod to the same Irish heritage she had? It was wavy but cropped short and serviceable. His deep green eyes had crease lines at the edges—from exposure to weather?

Or from laughter.

Probably from laughter, she decided. His eyes were laughing now.

Eye candy or not, she was practically gritting her chattering teeth as she waited for him. She was totally dependent on a stranger. She, Jo Conaill, who was dependent on nobody.

He was heading back, carrying a couple of short planks, moving faster now he'd assessed the ground. His boots were heavy and serviceable. Stained from years of work on the land?

'I have a bull who keeps getting himself bogged near the water troughs,' he said idly, almost as if he was talking to himself and not her. 'If these planks can get Horace out, they'll work for you. That is if you don't weigh more than a couple of hundred pounds.'

Laughter was making his green eyes glint. His smile, though, was kind.

She didn't want kind. She wanted to be out of here.

'Don't try and move until they're in place,' he told her. 'Horace always messes that up. First sign of the planks and he's all for digging himself in deeper.'

'You're comparing me to a bull?'

He'd stooped to set the planks in place. Now he sat back on his heels and looked at her. Really looked. His gaze raked her, from the top of her dishevelled head to where her leather-clad legs disappeared into the mud.

The twinkle deepened.

'No,' he said at last. 'No, indeed. I'll not compare you to a bull.'

And he chuckled.

If she could, she'd have closed her eyes and drummed her heels. Instead, she had to manage a weak smile. She had to wait. She was totally in this man's hands and she didn't like it one bit.

It was her own fault. She'd put herself in a position of dependence and she depended on nobody.

Except this man.

'So what do they call you?' He was manoeuvring the planks, checking the ground under them, setting them up so each had a small amount of rock underneath to make them secure. He was working as if he had all the time in the world. As if she did.

She didn't. She was late.

She was late and covered in bog.

'What would who call me?' she snapped.

'Your Mam and Daddy?'

As if. 'Jo,' she said through gritted teeth.

'Just Jo?'

'Just Jo.' She glared.

'Then I'm Finn,' he said, ignoring her glare. 'I'm pleased to meet you, Just Jo.' He straightened, putting his weight on the planks, seeing how far they sank. He was acting as if he pulled people out of bogs all the time.

No. He pulled bulls out of bogs, she thought, and that was what she felt like. A stupid, bog-stuck bovine.

'You're Australian?'

'Yes,' she said through gritted teeth, and he nodded as if Australians stuck in bogs were something he might have expected.

'Just admiring the view, were we?' The laughter was still in his voice, an undercurrent to his rich Irish brogue, and it was a huge effort to stop her teeth from grinding in frustration. Except they were too busy chattering.

'I'm admiring the frogs,' she managed. 'There are frogs in here. All sorts.'

He smiled, still testing the planks, but his smile said he approved of her attempt to join him in humour.

'Fond of frogs?'

'I've counted eight since I've been stuck.'

He grinned. 'I'm thinking that's better than counting sheep. If you'd nodded off I might not have seen you from the road.' He stood back, surveyed her, surveyed his planks and then put a boot on each end of the first plank and started walking. The end of the planks were a foot from her. He went about two-thirds along, then stopped and crouched. And held out his hands.

'Right,' he said. 'Put your hands in mine. Hold fast. Then don't struggle, just let yourself relax and let me pull.'

'I can...'

'You can't do anything,' he told her. 'If you struggle you'll make things harder. You can wiggle your toes if you like; that'll help with the suction, but don't try and pull out. If you were Horace I'd be putting a chain under you but Horace isn't good at following orders. If you stay limp like a good girl, we'll have you out of here in no time.'

Like a good girl. The patronising toerag...

He was saving her. What was she doing resenting it? Anger was totally inappropriate. But then, she had been stuck for almost an hour, growing more and more furious with herself. She'd also been more than a little bit frightened by the time he'd arrived. And cold. Reaction was setting in and she was fighting really hard to hold her temper in check.

'Where's a good wall to kick when you need it?' Finn asked and she blinked.

'Pardon?'

'I'd be furious too, if I were you. The worst thing in the world is to want to kick and all you have to kick is yourself.'

She blinked. Laughter and empathy too? 'S...sorry.'

'That's okay. Horace gets tetchy when he gets stuck, so I'd imagine you're the same. Hands—put 'em in mine and hold.'

'They're covered in mud. You won't be able to hold me.'

'Try me,' he said and held out his hands and waited for her to put hers in his.

It felt wrong. To hold this guy's hands and let her pull... Jo Conaill spent her life avoiding dependence on anyone or anything.

What choice did she have? She put out her hands and held.

His hands were broad and toughened from manual work. She'd guessed he was a farmer, and his hands said she was right. He manoeuvred his fingers to gain maximum hold and she could feel the strength of him. But he was wincing.

'You're icy. How long have you been here?'

'About an hour.'

'Is that right?' He was shifting his grip, trying for maximum hold. 'Am I the first to come along? Is this road so deserted, then?'

'You're not a local?'

'I'm not.' He was starting to take her weight, sitting back on his heels and leaning backward. Edging back as the planks started to tilt.

The temptation to struggle was almost irresistible but she knew it wouldn't help. She forced herself to stay limp.

Channel Horace, she told herself.

'Good girl,' Finn said approvingly and she thought: *What—did the guy have the capacity to read minds?*

He wasn't pulling hard. He was simply letting his weight tug her forward, shifting only to ease the balance of the planks. But his hold was implacable, a steady, relentless pull, and finally she felt the squelch as the mud eased its grip. She felt her feet start to lift. At last.

He still wasn't moving fast. His tug was slow and steady, an inch at a time. He was acting as if he had all the time in the world.

'So I'm not a local,' he said idly, as if they were engaged in casual chat, not part of a chain where half the chain was stuck in mud. 'But I'm closer to home than you are.'

He manoeuvred himself back a little without lessening his grip. He was trying not to lurch back, she realised. If he pulled hard, they both risked being sprawled off the planks, with every chance of being stuck again.

He had had experience in this. With Horace.

'Horace is heavier than you,' he said.

'Thanks. Did you say…two hundred pounds?'

'I did, and I'm thinking you're not a sliver over a hundred and ninety. That's with mud attached,' he added kindly. 'What part of Australia do you come from?'

'S... Sydney.' Sometimes.

'I've seen pictures.' Once more he stopped and readjusted. 'Nice Opera House.'

'Yeah.' It was hard to get her voice to work. He'd released her hands so he could shift forward and hold her under her arms. Once more he was squatting and tugging but now she was closer to him. Much closer. She could feel the strength of him, the size. She could feel the warmth of his chest against her face. The feeling was...weird. She wanted to sink against him. She wanted to struggle.

Sinking won.

'We...we have great beaches too,' she managed and was inordinately proud of herself for getting the words out.

'What, no mud?'

'No mud.'

'Excellent. Okay, sweetheart, we're nearly there. Just relax and let me do the work.'

He had her firmly under the arms and he was leaning back as she forced herself to relax against him. To let him hold her...

The feeling was indescribable—and it worked!

For finally the mud released its grip. Even then, though, he was still in control. He had her tight, hauling her up and back so that she was kneeling on the planks with him, but she wasn't released. He was holding her hard against him, and for a moment she had no choice but to stay exactly where she was.

She'd been stuck in mud for an hour. She was bone-chillingly cold, and she'd been badly frightened. Almost as soon as the mud released her she started to shake.

If he didn't hold her she could have fallen right off the

planks. No, she *would* have fallen. She felt light-headed and a bit sick.

He held and she had to let him hold. She needed him.

Which was crazy. She didn't need anyone. She'd made that vow as a ten-year-old, in the fourth or fifth of her endless succession of foster homes. She'd yelled it as her foster mother had tried to explain why she had to move on yet again.

'It's okay,' she'd yelled. 'I don't need you. I don't need anyone.'

Her foster mother had cried but Jo hadn't. She'd learned to never let herself close enough to cry.

But now she was close, whether she willed it or not. Her rescuer was holding her in a grip so strong she couldn't break it even if she tried. He must be feeling her shaking, she thought, and part of her was despising herself for being weak but most of her was just letting him hold.

He was big and warm and solid, and he wasn't letting her go. Her face was hard against his chest. She could feel the beating of his heart.

His hand was stroking her head, as he'd stroke an injured animal. 'Hey there. You're safe. The nasty bog's let you go. A nice hot bath and you'll be right back to yourself again. You're safe, girl. Safe.'

She hadn't been unsafe, she thought almost hysterically, and then she thought maybe she had been. If he hadn't come... Hypothermia was a killer. She could have become one of those bog bodies she'd read about, found immaculately preserved from a thousand years ago. They'd have put her in a museum and marvelled at her beloved bike leathers...

'There was never a chance of it,' Finn murmured into her hair and his words shocked her into reaction.

'What?'

'Freezing to your death out here. There's sheep wandering these bogs. I'm thinking a farmer'll come out and check them morn and night. If I hadn't come along, he would have.'

'But if you're not…if you're not local, how do you know?' she demanded.

'Because the sheep I passed a way back look well cared for, and you don't get healthy sheep without a decent shepherd. You were never in real danger.' He released her a little, but his hands still held her shoulders in case she swayed. 'Do you think you can make it back to the road?'

And then he frowned, looking down at her. 'You're still shaking. We don't want you falling into the mud again. Well, this is something I wouldn't be doing with Horace.'

And, before she could even suspect what he intended, he'd straightened, reached down and lifted her into his arms, then turned towards the road.

She froze.

She was close to actually freezing. From her thighs down, she was soaking. She'd been hauled up out of the mud, into this man's arms, and he was carrying her across the bog as if she weighed little more than a sack of flour.

She was powerless, and the lifelong sense of panic rose and threatened to drown her.

She wanted to scream, to kick, to make him dump her, even if it meant she sank into the bog again. She couldn't do anything. She just…froze.

But then, well before they reached the road, he was setting her down carefully on a patch of bare rock so there was no chance she'd pitch into the mud. But he didn't let her go. He put his hands on her shoulders and twisted her to face him.

'Problem?'

'I…no.'

'You were forgetting to breathe,' he said, quite gently. 'Breathing's important. I'm not a medical man, but I'd say breathing's even more important than reaching solid ground.'

Had her intake of breath been so dramatic that he'd heard it—that he'd felt it? She felt ashamed and silly, and more than a little small.

'You're safe,' he repeated, still with that same gentleness. 'I'm a farmer. I've just finished helping a ewe with a difficult lambing. Helping creatures is what I do for a living. I won't hurt you. I'll clean the muck off you as best I can, then put your bike in the back of my truck and drive you to wherever you can get yourself a hot shower and a warm bed for the night.'

And that was enough to make her pull herself together. She'd been a wimp, an idiot, an absolute dope, and here she was, making things worse. This man was a Good Samaritan. Yeah, well, she'd had plenty of them in her life, but that didn't mean she shouldn't be grateful. He didn't need her stupid baggage and he was helping her. Plus he was gorgeous. That shouldn't make a difference but she'd be an idiot not to be aware of it. She made a massive effort, took a few deep breaths and tugged her dignity around her like a shield.

'Thank you,' she managed, tilting her face until she met his gaze full-on. Maybe that was a mistake. Green eyes met green eyes and something flickered in the pit of her stomach. He was looking at her with compassion but also…something else? There were all sorts of emotions flickering behind those eyes of his. Yes, compassion, and also laughter, but also…empathy? Understanding?

As if he understood what had caused her to fear.

Whatever, she didn't like it. He might be gorgeous. He might have saved her, but she needed to be out of here.

'I can take care of myself from here,' she managed. 'If you just walk across to the road, I'll follow in your footsteps.'

'Take my hand,' he said, still with that strange tinge of understanding that was deeply unsettling. 'You're shaky and if you fall that's time wasted for both of us.'

It was reasonable. It even made sense but only she knew how hard it was to place her hand in his and let him lead her back to the road. But he didn't look at her again. He watched the ground, took careful steps then turned and watched her feet, making sure her feet did exactly the same.

Her feet felt numb, but the leathers and biker boots had insulated her a little. She'd be back to normal in no time, she thought, and finally they stepped onto the glorious solid road and she felt like bending down and kissing it.

Stupid bogs. The Irish could keep them.

Wasn't she Irish? Maybe she'd disinherit that part of her.

'Where can I take you?' Finn was saying and she stared down at her legs, at the thick, oozing mud, and then she looked at her bike and she made a decision.

'Nowhere. I'm fine.' She forced herself to look up at him, meeting his gaze straight on. 'Honest. I'm wet and I'm dirty but I don't have far to go. This mud will come off in a trice.'

'You're too shaken to ride.'

'I *was* too shaken to ride,' she admitted. 'But now I'm free I'm not shaking at all.' And it was true. Jo Conaill was back in charge of herself again and she wasn't about to let go. 'Thank you so much for coming to my rescue. I'm sorry I've made you muddy too.'

'Not very muddy,' he said and smiled, a lazy, crooked smile that she didn't quite get. It made her feel a bit…melting. Out of control again? She didn't like it.

And then she noticed his feet. His boots were still clean. Clean! He'd hauled her out of the bog and, apart from a few smears of mud where he'd held her, and the fact that his hands were muddy, he didn't have a stain on him.

'How did you do that?' she breathed and his smile intensified. 'How did you stay almost clean?'

'I told you. I'm an old hand at pulling creatures out of trouble. Now, if you were a lamb I'd take you home, rub you down and put you by the firestove for a few hours. Are you sure I can't do that for you?'

And suddenly, crazily, she wanted to say yes. She was still freezing. She was still shaking inside. She could have this man take her wherever he was going and put her by his fireside. Part of her wanted just that.

Um…not. She was Jo Conaill and she didn't accept help. Well, okay, sometimes she had to, like when she was dumb enough to try jumping on bogs, but enough. She'd passed a village a few miles back. She could head back there, beg a wash at the pub and then keep on going.

As she always kept going.

'Thank you, no,' she managed and bent and wiped her mud-smeared hands on the grass. Then she finished the job by drying them on the inside of her jacket. She gave him a determined nod, then snagged her helmet from the back of her bike. She shoved it onto her head, clicked the strap closed—only she knew what an effort it was to make her numb fingers work—and then hauled the handles of her bike around.

The bike was heavy. The shakiness of her legs wouldn't quite support…

But there he was, putting her firmly aside, hauling her bike around so it was facing the village. 'That's what you want?'

'I…yes.'

'You're really not going far?'

'N… No. Just to the village.'

'Are you sure you'll be fine?'

'I'm sure,' she managed and hit the ignition and her bike

roared into unsociable life. 'Thank you,' she said again over its roar. 'If I can ever do anything for you…'

'Where will I find you?' he asked and she tried a grin.

'On the road,' she said. 'Look for Jo.'

And she gave him a wave with all the insouciance she could muster and roared off into the distance.

CHAPTER TWO

As CASTLES WENT, it seemed a very grand castle. But then, Finn hadn't seen the inside of many castles.

Mrs O'Reilly, a little, round woman with tired eyes and capable, worn hands, bustled into the dining room and placed his dinner before him. It was a grand dinner too, roast beef with vegetables and a rich gravy, redolent of red wine and fried onions. It was a dinner almost fit for…a lord?

'There you are, My Lord,' the housekeeper said and beamed as she stood back and surveyed her handiwork. 'Eh, but it's grand to have you here at last.'

But Finn wasn't feeling grand. He was feeling weird.

My Lord. It was his title. He'd get rid of it, he decided. Once the castle was sold he didn't need to use it. He wasn't sure if he could ever officially abandon it but the knowledge of its existence could stay in the attic at the farm, along with other family relics. Maybe his great-great-great-grandson would like to use it. That was, if there ever was a great-great-great-grandson.

He thought suddenly of Maeve. Would she have liked to be My Lady? Who knew? He was starting to accept that he'd never known Maeve at all. Loyalty, habit, affection—he'd thought they were the basis for a marriage. But over the last twelve months, as he'd thrown himself into improving the farm, looking at new horizons himself, he'd realised it was no basis at all.

But Maeve's father would have liked this, he thought, staring around the great, grand dining room with a carefully neutral expression. He didn't want to hurt the housekeeper's feelings, but dining alone at a table that could fit twenty, on fine china, with silver that spoke of centuries of use, the family crest emblazoned on every piece, with a vast silver epergne holding pride of place in the centre of the shining mahogany of the table… Well, it wasn't exactly his style.

He had a good wooden table back at his farm. It was big enough for a man to have his computer and bookwork at one end and his dinner at the other. A man didn't need a desk with that kind of table, and he liked it that way.

But this was his heritage. His. He gazed out at the sheep grazing in the distance, at the land stretching to the mountains beyond, and he felt a stir of something within that was almost primeval.

This was Irish land, a part of his family. His side of the family had been considered of no import for generations but still…some part of him felt a tug that was almost like the sensation of coming home. Finn was one of six brothers. His five siblings had left their impoverished farm as soon as they could manage. They were now scattered across the globe but, apart from trips to the States to check livestock lines, or attending conferences to investigate the latest in farming techniques, Finn had never wanted to leave. Over the years he'd built the small family plot into something he could be proud of.

But now, this place…why did it feel as if it was part of him?

There was a crazy thought.

'Is everything as you wish?' Mrs O'Reilly asked anxiously.

He looked at her worried face and he gazed around and

thought how much work must have gone into keeping this room perfect. How could one woman do it?

'It's grand,' he told her, and took a mouthful of the truly excellent beef. 'Wonderful.'

'I'm pleased. If there's anything else…'

'There isn't.'

'I don't know where the woman is. The lawyer said mid-afternoon…'

He still wasn't quite sure who the woman was. Details from the lawyers had been sparse, to say the least. 'The lawyer said you'd be expecting me mid-afternoon too,' he said mildly, attacking a bit more of his beef. Yeah, the epergne was off-putting—were they tigers?—but this was excellent food. 'Things happen.'

'Well,' the woman said with sudden asperity, 'she's Fiona's child. We could expect anything.'

'You realise I don't know anything about her. I don't even know who Fiona is,' he told her and the housekeeper narrowed her eyes, as if asking, *How could he not know?* Her look said the whole world should know, and be shocked as well.

'Fiona was Lord Conaill's only child,' she said tersely. 'His Lady died in childbirth. Fiona was a daughter when he wanted a son, but he gave her whatever she wanted. This would have been a cold place for a child and you can forgive a lot through upbringing, but Fiona had her chances and she never took them. She ran with a wild lot and there was nothing she wanted more than to shock her father. And us… The way she treated the servants… Dirt, we were. She ran through her father's money like it was water, entertaining her no-good friends, having parties, making this place a mess, but His Lordship would disappear to his club in Dublin rather than stop her. She was a spoiled child and then a selfish woman. There were one too many parties, though. She died of a drug overdose ten years ago, with only His Lordship to mourn her passing.'

'And her child?'

'Lord Conaill would hardly talk of her,' she said primly. 'For his daughter to have a child out of wedlock... Eh, it must have hurt. Fiona threw it in his face over and over, but still he kept silent. But then he wouldn't talk about you either and you were his heir. Is there anything else you'll be needing?'

'No, thank you,' Finn said. 'Are you not eating?'

'In the kitchen, My Lord,' she said primly. 'It's not my place to be eating here. I'll be keeping another dinner hot for the woman, just in case, but if she's like her mother we may never hear.'

And she left him to his roast beef.

For a while the meal took his attention—a man who normally cooked for himself was never one to be ignoring good food—but when it was finished he was left staring down the shining surface of the ostentatious table, at the pouncing tigers on the epergne, at his future.

What to do with this place?

Sell it? Why not?

The inheritance had come out of the blue. Selling it would mean he could buy the farms bordering his, and the country down south was richer than here. He was already successful but the input of this amount of money could make him one of the biggest primary producers in Ireland.

The prospect should make him feel on top of the world. Instead, he sat at the great, grand dining table and felt... empty. Weird.

He thought of Maeve and he wondered if this amount of money would have made a difference.

It wouldn't. He knew it now. His life had been one of loyalty—eldest son of impoverished farmers, loyal to his parents, to his siblings, to his farm. And to Maeve.

He'd spent twelve months realising loyalty was no basis for marriage.

He thought suddenly of the woman he'd pulled out of the bog. He hoped she'd be safe and dry by now. He had a sudden vision of her, bathed and warmed, ensconced in a cosy pub by a fire, maybe with a decent pie and a pint of Guinness.

He'd like to be there, he thought. Inheritance or not, right now maybe he'd rather be with her than in a castle.

Or not. What he'd inherited was a massive responsibility. It required...more loyalty?

And loyalty was his principle skill, he thought ruefully. It was what he accepted, what he was good at, and this inheritance was enough to take a man's breath away. Meanwhile the least he could do was tackle more of Mrs O'Reilly's excellent roast beef, he decided, and he did.

If she had anywhere else to go, she wouldn't be here. *Here* scared her half to death.

Jo was cleaned up—sort of—but she was still wet and she was still cold.

She was sitting on her bike outside the long driveway to Castle Glenconaill.

The castle was beautiful.

But this was no glistening white fairy tale, complete with turrets and spires, with pennants and heraldic banners fluttering in the wind. Instead, it seemed carved from the very land it was built on—grey-white stone, rising to maybe three storeys, but so gradually it gave the impression of a vast, long, low line of battlements emerging from the land. The castle was surrounded by farmland, but the now empty moat and the impressive battlements and the mountains looming behind said this castle was built to repel any invader.

As it was repelling her. It was vast and wonderful. It was…scary.

But she was cold. And wet. A group of stone cottages were clustered around the castle's main gates but they all looked derelict, and it was miles back to the village. And she'd travelled half a world because she'd just inherited half of what lay before her.

'This is my ancestral home,' she muttered and shivered and thought, *Who'd want a home like this?*

Who'd want a home? She wanted to turn and run.

But she was cold and she was getting colder. The wind was biting. She'd be cold even if her leathers weren't wet, she thought, but her leathers were wet and there was nowhere to stay in the village and, dammit, she had just inherited half this pile.

'But if they don't have a bath I'm leaving,' she muttered.

Where would she go?

She didn't know and she didn't care. There was always somewhere. But the castle was here and all she had to do was march across the great ditch that had once been a moat, hammer on the doors and demand her rights. One hot bath.

'Just do it,' she told herself. 'Do it before you lose your nerve entirely.'

The massive gong echoed off the great stone walls as if in warning that an entire Viking war fleet was heading for the castle. Finn was halfway through his second coffee and the sound was enough to scare a man into the middle of next week. Or at least spill his coffee. 'What the…?'

'It's the doorbell, My Lord,' Mrs O'Reilly said placidly, heading out to the grand hall. 'It'll be the woman. If she's like her mother, heaven help us.' She tugged off her apron, ran her fingers through her permed grey hair, took a quick peep into one of the over-mantel mirrors and then tugged at the doors.

The oak doors swung open. And there was…

Jo.

She was still in her bike gear but she must have washed. There wasn't a trace of mud on her, including her boots and trousers. Her face was scrubbed clean and she'd re-applied her make-up. Her kohl-rimmed eyes looked huge in her elfin face. Her cropped copper curls were combed and neat. She was smiling a wide smile, as if her welcome was assured.

He checked her legs and saw a telltale drip of water fall to her boots.

She was still sodden.

That figured. How many bikers had spare leathers in their kitbags?

She must be trying really hard not to shiver. He looked back at the bright smile and saw the effort she was making to keep it in place.

'Good evening,' she was saying. She hadn't seen him yet. Mrs O'Reilly was at the door and he was well behind her. 'I hope I'm expected? I'm Jo Conaill. I'm very sorry I'm late. I had a small incident on the road.'

'You look just like your mother.' The warmth had disappeared from the housekeeper's voice as if it had never been. There was no disguising her disgust. The house-keeper was staring at Jo as if she was something the cat had just dragged in.

The silence stretched on—an appalled silence. Jo's smile faded to nothing. *What the…?*

Do something.

'Good evening to you too,' he said. He stepped forward, edging the housekeeper aside. He smiled at Jo, summoning his most welcoming smile.

And then there was even more silence.

Jo stared from Mrs O'Reilly to Finn and then back again. She looked appalled.

As well she might, Finn conceded. As welcomes went, this took some beating. She'd been greeted by a woman whose disdain was obvious, and by a man who'd seen her at her most vulnerable. Now she was looking appalled. He thought of her reaction when he'd lifted her, carried her. She'd seemed terrified and the look was still with her.

He thought suddenly of a deer he'd found on his land some years back, a fawn caught in the ruins of a disused fence. Its mother had run on his approach but the fawn was trapped, its legs tangled in wire. It had taken time and patience to disentangle it without it hurting itself in its struggles.

That was what this woman looked like, he thought. Caught and wanting to run, but trapped.

She was so close to running.

Say something. 'We've met before.' He reached out and took her hand. It was freezing. Wherever she'd gone to get cleaned up, it hadn't been anywhere with a decent fire. 'I'm so glad you're…clean.'

He smiled but she seemed past noticing.

'You live here?' she said with incredulity.

'This is Lord Finn Conaill, Lord of Castle Glenconaill,' the housekeeper snapped.

Jo blinked and stared at Finn as if she was expecting two heads. 'You don't look like a lord.'

'What do I look like?'

'A farmer. I thought you were a farmer.'

'I am a farmer. And you're an heiress.'

'I wait tables.'

'There you go. We've both been leading double lives. And now… It seems we're cousins?'

'You're not cousins,' Mrs O'Reilly snapped, but he ignored her.

'We're not,' he conceded, focusing only on Jo. 'Just distant relations. You should be the true heir to this whole place. You're the only grandchild.'

'She's illegitimate,' Mrs O'Reilly snapped and Finn moved a little so his body was firmly between Jo and the housekeeper. What was it with the woman?

'There's still some hereabouts who judge a child for the actions of its parents,' he said mildly, ignoring Mrs O'Reilly and continuing to smile down at Jo. 'But I'm not one of them. According to the lawyer, it seems you're Lord Conaill's granddaughter, marriage vows or not.'

'And…and you?' *What was going on?* She had the appearance of street-smart. She looked tough. But inside… the image of the trapped fawn stayed.

'My father was the son of the recently deceased Lord Conaill's cousin,' Finn told her. He furrowed his brows a little. 'I think that's right. I can't quite get my head around it. So that means my link to you goes back four generations. We're very distant relatives, but it seems we do share a great-great-grandfather. And the family name.'

'Only because of illegitimacy,' Mrs O'Reilly snapped.

Enough. He turned from Jo and faced Mrs O'Reilly square-on. She was little and dumpy and full of righteous indignation. She'd been Lord Conaill's housekeeper for years. Heaven knew, he needed her if he was to find his way around this pile but right now…

Right now he was Lord Conaill of Castle Glenconaill, and maybe it was time to assume his rightful role.

'Mrs O'Reilly, I'll thank you to be civil,' he said, and if he'd never had reason to be autocratic before he made a good fist of it now. He summoned all his father had told him of previous lords of this place and he mentally lined his ancestors up behind him. 'Jo's come all the way from Australia. She's inherited half of her grandfather's estate and for now this castle is her home. *Her* home. I therefore expect you to treat her with the welcome and the respect her position entitles her to. Do I make myself clear?'

There was a loaded silence. The housekeeper tried glaring but he stayed calmly looking at her, waiting, his face impassive. He was Lord of Glenconaill and she was his housekeeper. It was time she knew it.

Jo said nothing. Finn didn't look back at her but he sensed her shiver. If he didn't get her inside soon she'd freeze to death, he thought, but this moment was too important to rush. He simply stood and gazed down at Mrs O'Reilly and waited for the woman to come to a decision.

'I only...' she started but he shook his head.

'Simple question. Simple answer. Welcome and respect. Yes or no.'

'Her mother...'

'Yes or no!'

And finally she cracked. She took a step back but his eyes didn't leave hers. 'Yes.'

'Yes, what?' It was an autocratic snap. His great-great-grandfather would be proud of him, he thought, and then he thought of his boots and thought: *maybe not*. But the snap had done what he intended.

She gave a frustrated little nod, she bobbed a curtsy and finally she answered him as he'd intended.

'Yes, My Lord.'

What was she doing here? If she had to inherit a castle, why couldn't she have done it from a distance? She could have told the lawyer to put up a For Sale sign, sell it to the highest bidder and send her a cheque for half. Easy.

Why this insistence that she had to come?

Actually, it hadn't been insistence. It had been a strongly worded letter from the lawyer saying decisions about the entire estate had to be made between herself and this unknown sort-of cousin. It had also said the castle contained possessions that had been her mother's. The lawyer suggested that decisions would be easier to make with her here, and the estate could well afford her airfare to Ireland to make those decisions.

And it had been like a siren song, calling her...home?

No, that was dumb. This castle had never been her home. She'd never had a home but it was the only link she had to anyone. She might as well come and have a look, she'd thought.

But this place was like the bog that surrounded it. The surface was enticing but, underneath, it was a quagmire. The housekeeper's voice had been laced with malice.

Was that her mother's doing? Fiona? Well, maybe invective was to be expected. Maybe malice was deserved.

What hadn't been expected was this strong, hunky male standing in the doorway, taking her hand, welcoming her—and then, before her eyes, turning into the Lord of Glenconaill. Just like that. He'd been a solid Good Samaritan who'd pulled her out of the bog. He'd laughed at her—which she hadn't appreciated, but okay, he might have had reason—and then, suddenly, the warmth was gone and he was every bit a lord. The housekeeper was bobbing a curtsy, for heaven's sake. What sort of feudal system was this?

She was well out of her depth. She should get on her bike and leave.

But she was cold.

The lawyer had paid for her flight, for two nights' accommodation in Dublin and for the bike hire—he'd suggested a car or even a driver to meet her, but some things were non-negotiable. Two nights' accommodation and the bike was the extent of the largesse. The lawyer had assumed she'd spend the rest of her time in the castle, and she hadn't inherited anything yet. Plus the village had no accommodation and the thought of riding further was un-bearable.

So, even if she'd like to ride off into the sunset, she wasn't in a position to do it.

Plus she was really, really cold.

Finn…Lord of Glenconaill?…was looking at her with eyes that said he saw more than he was letting on. But his gaze was kind again. The aristocratic coldness had dis-appeared.

His gaze dropped to the worn stone tiles. There was a puddle forming around her boots.

'I met Miss Conaill down the bog road,' he said, smiling at her but talking to the housekeeper. 'There were sheep on the road. Miss Conaill had struck trouble, was off her bike, wet and shaken, and I imagine she's still shaken.' He didn't say she'd been stuck in a bog, Jo thought, and a surge of gratitude made her almost light-headed. 'I of-fered to give her a ride but, of course, she didn't know who I was and I didn't know who she was. I expect that's why you're late, Miss Conaill, and I'm thinking you're still wet. Mrs O'Reilly, could you run Miss Conaill a hot bath, make sure her bedroom's warm and leave her be for half an hour? Then there's roast beef warm in the oven for you.'

His voice changed a little, and she could hear the return of the aristocrat. There was a firm threat to the house-keeper behind the words. 'Mrs O'Reilly will look after you, Jo, and she'll look after you well. When you're warm and fed, we'll talk again. Meanwhile, I intend to sit in your grandfather's study and see if I can start making sense of this pile we seem to have inherited. Mrs O'Reilly, I de-pend on you to treat Jo with kindness. This is her home.'

And there was nothing more to be said. The house-keeper took a long breath, gave an uncertain glance up at…her Lord?…and bobbed another curtsy.

'Yes, My Lord.'

'Let's get your gear inside,' Finn said. 'Welcome to Castle Glenconaill, Miss Conaill. Welcome to your inheritance.'

'There's no need for us to talk again tonight,' Jo managed. 'I'll have a bath and go to bed.'

'You'll have a bath and then be fed,' Finn said, and there was no arguing with the way he said it. 'You're welcome here, Miss Conaill, even if right now it doesn't feel like it.'

'Th…thank you,' she managed and turned to her bike to get her gear.

If things had gone well from there they might have been fine. She'd find her bedroom, have a bath, have something to eat, say goodnight and go to bed. She'd talk to the lawyer in the morning. She'd sign whatever had to be signed. She'd go back to Australia. That was the plan.

So far, things hadn't gone well for Jo, though, and they were about to get worse.

She had two bags—her kitbag with her clothes and a smaller one with her personal gear. She tugged them from the bike, she turned around and Finn was beside her.

He lifted the kitbag from her grasp and reached for the smaller bag. 'Let me.'

'I don't need help.'

'You're cold and wet and shaken,' he told her. 'It's a wise woman who knows when accepting help is sensible.'

This was no time to be arguing, she conceded, but she clung to her smaller bag and let Finn carry the bigger bag in.

He reached the foot of the grand staircase and then paused. 'Lead the way, Mrs O'Reilly,' he told the housekeeper, revealing for the first time that he didn't know this place.

And the housekeeper harrumphed and stalked up to pass them.

She brushed Jo on the way. Accidentally or on purpose, whatever, but it seemed a deliberate bump. She knocked the carryall out of Jo's hand.

And the bag wasn't properly closed.

After the bog, Jo had headed back to the village. She'd have loved to have booked a room at the pub but there'd been a No Vacancies sign in the porch, the attached cobwebs and dust suggesting there'd been no vacancies for years. She'd made do with a trip to the Ladies, a scrub under cold water—no hot water in this place—and an attempt at repair to her make-up.

She'd been freezing. Her hands had been shaking and she mustn't have closed her bag properly.

Her bag dropped now onto the ancient floorboards of Castle Glenconaill and the contents spilled onto the floor.

They were innocuous. Her toiletries. The things she'd needed on the plane on the way over. Her latest project...

And it was this that the housekeeper focused on. There was a gasp of indignation and the woman was bending down, lifting up a small, clear plastic vial and holding it up like the angel of doom.

'I knew it,' she spat, turning to Jo with fury that must have been building for years. 'I knew how it'd be. Like mother, like daughter, and why your grandfather had to leave you half the castle... Your mother broke His Lordship's heart, so why you're here... What he didn't give her... She was nothing but a drug-addicted slut, and here you are, just the same. He's given you half his fortune and do you deserve it? How dare you bring your filthy stuff into this house?'

Finn had stopped, one boot on the first step. His brow snapped down in confusion. 'What are you talking about?'

'Needles.' The woman held up the plastic vial. 'You'll find drugs too, I'll warrant. Her mother couldn't keep away from the stuff. Dead from an overdose in the end, and here's her daughter just the same. And half the castle left to her… It breaks my heart.'

And Jo closed her eyes. *Beam me up*, she pleaded. Where was a time machine when she needed one? She'd come all this way to be tarred with the same brush as her mother. A woman she'd never met and didn't want to meet.

Like mother, like daughter… What a joke.

'I'll go,' she said in a voice she barely recognised. She'd sleep rough tonight, she decided. She'd done it before— it wouldn't kill her. Tomorrow she'd find the lawyer, sign whatever had to be signed and head back to Australia.

'You're going nowhere.' The anger in Finn's voice made her eyes snap open. It was a snap that reverberated through the ancient beams, from stone wall to stone wall, worthy of an aristocratic lineage as old as time itself. He placed the kitbag he was holding down and took the three steps to where the housekeeper was standing. He took the vial, stared at it and then looked at the housekeeper with icy contempt.

'You live here?' he demanded and the woman's fury took a slight dent.

'Of course.'

'Where?'

'I have an apartment…'

'Self-contained?'

'I…yes.'

'Good,' he snapped. 'Then go there now. Of all the cruel, cold welcomes…' He stared down at the vial and his mouth set in grim lines. 'Even if this was what you thought it was, your reaction would be unforgivable, but these are sewing needles. They have a hole at the end, not through the middle. Even if they were syringes, there's a score of reasons why Miss Conaill would carry them other than drug addiction. But enough. You're not to be trusted to treat Miss Conaill with common courtesy, much less kindness. Return to your apartment. I'll talk to you tomorrow morning but not before. I don't wish to see you again tonight. I'll take care of Miss Conaill. Go, now.'

'You can't,' the woman breathed. 'You can't tell me to go.'

'I'm Lord of Glenconaill,' Finn snapped. 'I believe the right is mine.'

Silence. The whole world seemed to hold its breath.

Jo stared at the floor, at her pathetic pile of toiletries and, incongruously, at the cover of the romance novel she'd read on the plane. It was historical, the Lord of the Manor rescuing and marrying his Cinderella.

Who'd want to be Cinderella? she'd thought as she read it, and that was what it felt like now. Cinderella should have options. She should be able to make the grand gesture, sweep from the castle in a flurry of skirts, say, *Take me to the nearest hostelry, my man, and run me a hot bath...*

A hot bath. There was the catch. From the moment Finn had said it, they were the words that had stuck in her mind. Everything else was white noise.

Except maybe the presence of this man. She was trying not to look at him.

The hero of her romance novel had been...romantic. He'd worn tight-fitting breeches and glossy boots and intricate neckcloths made of fine linen.

Her hero had battered boots and brawny arms and traces of copper in his deep brown hair. He looked tanned and weathered. His green eyes were creased by smiles or weather and she had no way of knowing which. He looked far too large to look elegant in fine linen and neckcloths, but maybe she was verging on hysterics because her mind had definitely decided it wanted a hero with battered boots. And a weathered face and smiley eyes.

Especially if he was to provide her with a bath.

'Go,' he said to Mrs O'Reilly and the woman cast him

a glance that was half scared, half defiant. But the look Finn gave her back took the defiance out of her.

She turned and almost scuttled away, and Jo was left with Finn.

He didn't look at her. He simply bent and gathered her gear back into her bag.

She should be doing that. What was she doing, staring down at him like an idiot?

She stooped to help, but suddenly she was right at eye level, right…close.

His expression softened. He smiled and closed her bag with a snap.

'You'll be fine now,' he said. 'We seem to have routed the enemy. Let's find you a bath.'

And he rose and held out his hand to help her rise with him.

She didn't move. She didn't seem to be able to.

She just stared at that hand. Big. Muscled. Strong.

How good would it be just to put her hand in his?

'I forgot; you're a wary woman,' he said ruefully and stepped back. 'Very wise. I gather our ancestors have a fearsome reputation, but then they're your ancestors too, so that should make me wary as well. But if you can cope with me as a guide, I'll try and find you a bedroom. Mind, I've only just found my own bedroom but there seem to be plenty. Do you trust me to show you the way?'

How dumb was she being? Really dumb, she told herself, as well as being almost as offensive as the woman who'd just left. But still she didn't put her hand in his. Even though her legs were feeling like jelly—her feet were still icy—she managed to rise and tried a smile.

'Sorry. I…thank you.'

'There's no need to thank me,' he said ruefully. 'I had the warm welcome. I have no idea what bee the woman has in her bonnet but let's forget her and find you that bath.'

'Yes, please,' she said simply and thought, despite her wariness, if this man was promising her a bath she'd follow him to the ends of the earth.

CHAPTER THREE

JO HAD A truly excellent bath. It was a bath she might well remember for the rest of her life.

Finn had taken her to the section of the castle where Mrs O'Reilly had allocated him a bedroom. He'd opened five doors, looking for another.

At the far end of the corridor, as far from Finn's as she could be, and also as far from the awesome bedroom they'd found by mistake—it had to have been her grandfather's—they'd found a small box room containing a single bed. It was the only other room with a bed made up, and it was obvious that was the room Mrs O'Reilly wanted her to use.

'We'll make up another,' Finn had growled in disgust—all the other rooms were better—but the bed looked good to Jo. Any bed would look good to Jo and when they'd found the bathroom next door and she'd seen the truly enormous bathtub she'd thought she'd died and gone to heaven.

So now she lay back, up to her neck in heat and steam. Her feet hurt when she got in, that was how cold they were, but the pain only lasted for moments and what was left was bliss.

She closed her eyes and tried to think of nothing at all.

She thought of Finn.

What manner of man was he? He was… what…her third cousin? Something removed? How did such things work? She didn't have a clue.

But they were related. He was…family? He'd defended her like family and such a thing had never happened to her.

He felt like…home.

And that was a stupid thing to think. How many times had she been sucked in by such sweetness?

'You're so welcome. Come in, sweetheart, let's help you unpack. You're safe here for as long as you need to stay.'

But it was never true. There was always a reason she had to move on.

She had to move on from here. This was a flying visit only.

To collect her inheritance? This castle must be worth a fortune and it seemed her grandfather had left her half.

She had no idea how much castles were worth on the open market but surely she'd come out of it with enough to buy herself an apartment.

Or a Harley. That was a thought. She could buy a Harley and stay on the road for ever.

Maybe she'd do both. She could buy a tiny apartment, a place where she could crash from time to time when the roads got unfriendly. It didn't need to be big. It wasn't as if she had a lot of stuff.

Stuff. She opened her eyes and looked around her at the absurd, over-the-top bathroom. There was a chandelier hanging from the beams.

A portrait of Queen Victoria hung over the cistern, draped in a potted aspidistra.

Finn had hauled open the door and blanched. 'Mother of… You sure you want to use this?'

She'd giggled. After this whole appalling day, she'd giggled.

In truth, Finn Conaill was enough to make any woman smile.

'And that's enough of that,' she said out loud and splashed

her face and then decided, dammit, splashing wasn't enough, she'd totally submerge. She did.

She came up still thinking of Finn.

He'd be waiting. 'Come and find me when you're dry and warm,' he'd said. 'There's dinner waiting for you somewhere. I may have to hunt to find it but I'll track it down.'

He would too, she thought. He seemed like a man who kept his promises.

Nice.

And Finn Conaill looked sexy enough to make a girl's toes curl. And when he smiled…

'Do Not Think About Him Like That!' She said it out loud, enunciating each word. 'You've been dumb enough for one day. Get tonight over with, get these documents signed and get out of here. Go buy your Harley.'

Harleys should be front and foremost in her mind. She'd never thought she'd have enough money to buy one and maybe now she would.

'So think about Harleys, not Finn Conaill,' she told herself as she reluctantly pulled the plug and let the hot water disappear. 'No daydreaming. You're dry and warm. Now, find yourself some dinner and go to bed. And keep your wits about you.'

But he's to be trusted, a little voice said.

But the old voice, the voice she knew, the only voice she truly trusted, told her she was being daft. *Don't trust anyone. Haven't you learnt anything by now?*

He heard her coming downstairs. Her tread was light but a couple of the ancient boards squeaked and he was listening for her.

He strode out to meet her and stopped and blinked.

She was wearing jeans and an oversized crimson sweater. She'd lost the make-up. Her face was a smatter of freckles and the rest seemed all eyes. She'd towelled her hair dry but it was still damp, the short curls tightly sprung, coiling as much as their length allowed.

She was wearing some kind of sheepskin bootees which looked massively oversized on her slight frame. She was flushed from the heat of her bath, and she looked like a kid.

She was treading down the stairs as if Here Be Dragons, and it was all he could do not to move forward and give her a hug of reassurance.

Right. As if that'd go down well. Earlier he'd picked her up when she needed to be picked up and she'd pretty near had kittens.

He forced himself to stay still, to wait until she'd reached the bottom. Finally she looked around for where to go next and she saw him.

'Hey,' he said and smiled and she smiled back.

It was a pretty good smile.

And that would be an understatement. This was the first time he'd seen this smile full on, and it was enough to take a man's breath away.

He had to struggle with himself to get his voice to sound prosaic.

'Kitchen?' he managed. 'Dining room's to the left if you like sitting with nineteen empty chairs and an epergne, or kitchen if you don't mind firestove and kettle.'

'Firestove and kettle,' she said promptly but peered left into the dining room, at its impressive size and its even more impressive—ostentatious?—furnishings. 'This is nuts. I have Queen Victoria in my bathroom. Medieval castle with interior decorator gone mad.'

'Not quite medieval, though the foundations might be. It's been built and rebuilt over the ages. According to Mrs O'Reilly, much of the current decorating was down to your mother. Apparently your grandfather kept to himself, the place gathered dust and when she was here she was bored.'

'Right,' she said dryly, looking askance at the suits of armour at the foot of the stairs. 'Are these guys genuine?'

'I've been looking at them. They're old enough, but there's not a scratch on them. Aren't they great?' He pointed to the sword blades. 'Note, though, that the swords have been tipped to make them safe. The Conaills of Glen-conaill seem to have been into making money, not war. *To take and to hold* is their family motto.' He corrected himself. '*Our* family creed.'

'Not my creed,' she said dryly. 'I don't hold onto anything. Did you say dinner?'

'Kitchen this way. I used your bath time to investigate.' He turned and led her through thick wooden doors, into the kitchen beyond.

It was a truly impressive kitchen. A lord's kitchen.

A massive firestove set into an even larger hearth took up almost an entire wall. The floor was old stone, scrubbed and worn. The table was a vast slab of timber, scarred from generations of use.

The stove put out gentle heat. There was a rocker by the stove. Old calendars lined the walls as if it was too much trouble to take them down in the new year—simpler to put a new one up alongside. The calendars were from the local businesses, an eclectic mix of wildlife, local scenery and kittens. Many kittens.

Jo stopped at the door and blinked. 'Wow.'

'As you say, wow. Sit yourself down. Mrs O'Reilly said she'd kept your dinner hot.' He checked out the firestove, snagged a tea towel and opened the oven door.

It was empty. *What the heck?*

The firestove had been tamped for the night, the inlet closed. The oven was the perfect place to keep a dinner warm.

He closed the oven door and reconsidered. There was

an electric range to the side—maybe for when the weather was too hot to use the firestove? Its light was on.

The control panel said it was on high.

He tugged open the oven door and found Jo's dinner. It was dried to the point where it looked inedible.

'Uh oh,' he said, hauling it out and looking at it in disgust. And then he looked directly at Jo and decided to say it like it was. 'It seems our housekeeper doesn't like you.'

'She's never met me before tonight. I imagine it's that she doesn't...she didn't like my mother.'

'I'm sorry.'

'Don't be. I didn't like my mother myself. Not that I ever met her.'

He stared down at the dinner, baked hard onto the plate. Then he shrugged, lifted the lid of the trashcan and dumped the whole thing, plate and all, inside.

'You realise that's probably part of a priceless dinner set?' Jo said mildly.

'She wouldn't have served you on that. With the vitriol in the woman it's a wonder she didn't serve you on plastic. Sit down and I'll make you eggs and bacon. That is...' He checked the fridge and grinned. 'Eureka. Eggs and bacon. Would you like to tell me why no one seems to like your mother?'

'I'll cook.'

'No,' he said gently. 'You sit. You've come all the way from Australia and I've come from Kilkenny. Sit yourself down and be looked after.'

'You don't have to...'

'I want to, and eggs and bacon are my speciality.' He was already hauling things out of the fridge. 'Three eggs for you. A couple—no, make that three for me. It's been a whole hour since dinner, after all. Fried bread? Of course, fried bread, what am I thinking? And a side of fried tomato so we don't die of scurvy.'

So she sat and he cooked, and the smell of sizzling bacon filled the room. He focused on his cooking and behind him he sensed the tension seep from her. It was that sort of kitchen, he thought. Maybe they could pull the whole castle down and keep the kitchen. The lawyer had told him they needed to decide what to keep. This kitchen would be a choice.

'*To take and to hold*. Is that really our family creed?' Jo asked into the silence.

'*Accipere et Tenere*. It's over the front door. If my schoolboy Latin's up to it…'

'You did Latin in school?'

'Yeah, and me just a hayseed and all.'

'You're a hayseed?'

He didn't mind explaining. She was so nervous, it couldn't hurt to share a bit of himself.

'I have a farm near Kilkenny,' he told her. 'I had a short, terse visit from your grandfather six months back, telling me I stood to inherit the title when he passed. Before that I didn't have a clue. Oh, I knew there was a lord way back in the family tree, but I assumed we were well clear of it. I gather our great grandfathers hated each other. The title and all the money went to your side. My side mostly starved in the potato famine or emigrated, and it sounded as if His Lordship thought we pretty much got what we deserved.'

He paused, thinking of the visit with the stooped and ageing aristocrat. Finn had just finished helping the team milk. He'd stood in the yard and stared at Lord Conaill in amazement, listening to the old man growl.

'He was almost abusive,' he told Jo now. 'He said, "Despite your dubious upbringing and low social standing, there's no doubt you'll inherit my ancient title. There's no one else. My lawyers tell me you're the closest in the male line. I can only pray that you manage not to disgrace our name." I was pretty much gobsmacked.'

'Wow,' Jo said. 'I'd have been gobsmacked too.' And then she stared at the plate he was putting down in front of her. 'Double wow. This is amazing.'

'Pretty impressive for a peasant.' He sat down with his own plate in front of him and she stared at the vast helping he'd given himself.

'Haven't you already eaten?'

'Hours ago.' At least one. 'And I was lambing at dawn.'

'So you really are a farmer.'

'Mostly dairy but I run a few sheep on the side. But I'll try and eat with a fork, just this once.' He grinned at her and then tackled his plate. 'So how about you? Has your grandfather been firing insulting directions at you too?'

'No.'

Her tone said, *Don't go there,* so he didn't. He concentrated on bacon.

It was excellent bacon. He thought briefly about cooking some more but decided it had to be up to Jo. Three servings was probably a bit much.

Jo seemed to focus on her food too. They ate in silence and he was content with that. Still he had that impression of nervousness. It didn't make sense but he wasn't a man to push where he wasn't wanted.

'Most of what I know of this family comes from one letter,' Jo said at last, and he nodded again and kept addressing his plate. He sensed information was hard to get from this woman. Looking up and seeming expectant didn't seem the way to get it.

'It was when I was ten,' she said at last. 'Addressed to my foster parents.'

'Your foster parents?'

'Tom and Monica Hastings. They were lovely. They

wanted to adopt me. It had happened before, with other foster parents, but they never shared the letters.'

'I see.' Although he didn't. And then he thought, *Why not say it like it is?* 'You understand I'm from the peasant side of this family,' he told her. 'I haven't heard anything from your lot before your grandfather's visit, and that didn't fill me in on detail. So I don't know your history. I'd assumed I'd just be inheriting the title, and that only because I'm the next male in line, no matter how distant. Inheriting half this pile has left me stunned. It seems like it should all be yours, and yet here you are, saying you've been in foster homes...'

'Since birth.' Her tone was carefully neutral. 'Okay, maybe I do know a bit more than you, but not much. I was born in Sydney. My mother walked out of the hospital and left me there, giving my grandfather's name as the only person to contact. According to the Social Welfare notes that I've now seen—did you know you can get your file as an adult?—my grandfather was appalled at my very existence. His instructions were to have me adopted, get rid of me, but when my mother was finally tracked down she sent a curt letter back saying I wasn't for adoption; I was a Conaill, I was to stay a Conaill and my grandfather could lump it.'

'Your grandfather could lump it?'

'Yeah,' she said and rose and carried her plate to the sink. She ran hot water and started washing and he stood beside her and started wiping. It was an age-old domestic task and why it helped, he didn't know, but the action itself seemed to settle her.

'It seemed Fiona was a wild child,' she told him at last. 'She and my grandfather fought, and she seemed to do everything she could to shock him. If I'd been a boy I'm guessing she would have had him adopted. My grandfather might have valued a boy so having him adopted away from the family might have hurt him more than having an illegitimate grandchild. But I was just a girl so all she could do to shock him was keep me as a Conaill and grind it into his face whenever she could. So Social Welfare was left with him as first point of contact and I went from foster home to foster home. Because I'd been in foster care for ever, though, there was always the possibility of adoption. But every time any of my foster parents tried to keep me, they'd contact my grandfather and eventually he'd talk to Fiona—and she would refuse. It seemed she wanted to keep me in my grandfather's face.'

'So it was all about what was between Fiona and her father. Nothing about you.'

'It seems I was the tool to hurt him.' She shrugged and handed him the scrubbed frying pan. 'Nothing else. Why he's left me anything… I don't understand.'

'I suspect he ran out of options,' Finn told her. He kept his attention on the pan, not on her. 'I was the despised poor relation who stood to inherit the title whether he willed it to me or not. You were the despised illegitimate granddaughter. I imagine it was leave everything to us or leave it to a cats' home—and there's no sign that he was fond of cats.' He gazed around the kitten-adorned walls. 'Except in here, but I doubt the kitchen was his domain.'

'I guess.' She let the water run away and watched it swirl into the plughole. 'Isn't it supposed to swirl the other way?'

'What?'

'I'm in a different hemisphere. Doesn't the water go round in opposite directions?'

'What direction does it go round in Australia?'

'I have no idea.'

'You've never looked?'

'It's not the sort of thing you notice.'

'We could check it out on the Internet.'

'We could,' she conceded. 'Or we could go to bed.' And then she paused and flushed. 'I mean...' She stopped and bit her lip. 'I didn't...'

'You know, despite the fact that your mother was a wild child, I'm absolutely sure you didn't just proposition me,' he said gently and handed her the dishcloth to wipe her hands. 'You're tired, I'm tired and tomorrow we have a meeting with the lawyer and a castle to put on the market. That is, unless you'd like to keep it.'

She stared at him. 'Are you kidding? What would I do with a castle?'

'Exactly,' he said and took the dishcloth back from her and hung it up, then took her shoulders in his hands and twisted her and propelled her gently from the room. 'So tomorrow's for being sensible and we might as well start now. Bedtime, Jo Conaill. Don't dream of bogs.'

'I wouldn't dare,' she told him. 'I've been stuck in some pretty scary places in my time but the bog's the worst. Thank you for pulling me out.'

'It was my pleasure,' he told her. 'And Jo...'

'Yes?' He'd let her go. She was out of the door but glancing back at him.

'I'm glad I've inherited with you. If we have to be dissolute, unwanted relatives, it's good that it's two of us, don't you think?'

'I guess.' She frowned. 'I mean...we could have done this on our own.'

'But it wouldn't have been as much fun,' he told her. 'Tomorrow promises to be amazing. How many times in your life do you inherit a castle, Jo Conaill?' Then, as she didn't answer, he chuckled. 'Exactly. Mostly none. Go to bed, Jo, and sleep thinking of fun. Tomorrow you wake up as Lady of the Castle Glenconaill. If we have to inherit, why not enjoy it?'

'I'm not a Lady...'

'You could be,' he told her. 'Okay, neither of us belong,

but tomorrow, just for a little, let's be Lord and Lady of all we survey. We might even Lord and Lady it over Mrs O'Reilly and if she gives us burnt toast for breakfast it's off with her head. What do you say?'

She gazed at him, dumbfounded, and then, slowly, her face creased into a smile again.

It really was a beautiful smile.

'Exactly,' he told her. 'Tomorrow this is our place. It's where we belong.'

'I don't belong.'

'Yes, you do,' he told her. 'Your grandfather and your mother no longer hold sway. Tomorrow you belong here.'

'I guess I could pretend…'

'There's no pretence about it. Tomorrow you belong right here.'

She met his gaze. Everything that needed to be said had been said but just for a moment she stayed. Just for a moment their gazes locked and something passed between… Something intangible. Something strong and new and… unfathomable.

It was something he didn't understand and it seemed she didn't either. She gazed at him for a long moment and then she shook her head, as if trying to clear a mist she'd never been in before. As if trying to clear confusion.

'Goodnight,' she said in a voice that was decidedly unsteady.

'Goodnight,' he told her and finally she left.

He stood where he was.

Surely she hadn't guessed that he'd had a crazy impulse to walk across and kiss her?

And surely her eyes hadn't said that that kiss might have been welcome?

His bedroom was magnificent, almost as magnificent as the one the old Lord had slept in. He lay in the vast four-poster bed and thought of the cramped cots he and his brothers had shared as kids, of the impoverished farm his parents had struggled to keep, of a childhood lacking in anything but love.

But he thought of Jo and he knew he'd been lucky. She'd told him little, and yet there was so much behind her words that he could guess. A childhood of foster homes, and anyone who wanted to keep her being unable to do so.

She looked tough on the surface but he didn't need to scratch very deep before seeing scars.

She was…intriguing.

And that was something he shouldn't be thinking, he decided. Wasn't life complicated enough already?

'No.' He said it suddenly, out loud, and it surprised even him. His life wasn't complicated. He'd fought to make their parents' farm prosper. His father had died when he was in his teens and his brothers were younger. His mother had had no choice but to let him have his head. He'd set about changing things, firstly trying to keep them all from starving but in the end relishing the challenge. None of his brothers had had any inclination to stay on an impoverished farm. They'd gone on to have interesting, fulfilling careers but farming seemed to be in Finn's blood. By the time his mother died, twenty years later, the farm was an excellent financial concern.

And then there'd been Maeve, the girl next door, the woman he'd always assumed shared his dreams. The woman he'd thought he'd marry.

'You're loyal to a fault.' Sean, his youngest brother, had thrown it at him on his last visit home. 'You took on the farm when you were little more than a kid and practically hauled us all up. You gave up your dreams for us. You never let our mam down. You've managed to make a go of the farm, and that's great, but Maeve—just because you promised eternal love when you were ten years old doesn't mean you owe her loyalty for life. She doesn't want this life. I'm thinking half what she thought was love for you was loyalty to her dad, but there's more to life than loyalty. She's seen it. So should you.'

Sean was right. The last twelve months had taught him that what he thought of as love was simply loyalty to a friend, loyalty to a way of life, loyalty to his vision of his future.

So where did his future lie now?

He thumped the pillow and then, when it didn't result in immediate sleep, he tossed back the covers and headed to the window. It was a vast casement window, the stone wall almost two feet thick.

Beneath the window the land of Glenconaill stretched away to the moonlit horizon, miles of arable land reaching out to the bogs and then the mountains beyond.

If he'd inherited the whole thing...

'You didn't. This place is money only,' he muttered and deliberately drew the great velvet curtains closed, blocking out the night. 'Don't you be getting any ideas, Lord Finn of Glenconaill.'

And at the sound of his title he grinned. His brothers would never let him live it down. All now successful businessmen in their own rights, they'd think it was funny.

And Maeve...well, it no longer mattered what Maeve thought. He'd accepted it over the last few months and this morning's visit had simply confirmed it. Yes, she was in a mess but it wasn't a mess of his making. Their relationship was well over.

Had she faced her father or gone back to Dublin?

It was none of his business.

He headed back to bed and stared up at the dark and found himself thinking of the wide acres around Castle Glenconaill.

And a girl sleeping not so far from where he lay. A woman.
A woman named Jo.

By the time Jo came downstairs, the massive dining room
was set up for breakfast. The housekeeper greeted her with
a curt, 'Good morning, miss. Lord Conaill's in the dining
room already. Would you like to start with coffee?'

It was pretty much your standard Bed and Breakfast
greeting, Jo decided, and that was fine by her. Formal
was good.

She walked into the dining room and Finn was there,
reading the paper. He was wearing a casual shirt, sleeves
rolled past his elbows. Sunbeams filtered through the massive windows at the end of the room. He looked up at her
as she entered and he smiled, his deep green eyes creasing
with pleasure at the sight of her—and it was all a woman
could do not to gasp.

Where was formal when she needed it?

'Did you sleep well?' he asked and somehow she found
her voice and somehow she made it work.

'How can you doubt it? Twelve hours!'

'So you'd be leaving the jet lag behind?'

'I hope so.' She sat at the ridiculous dining table and
gazed down its length. Mrs O'Reilly had set places for
them at opposite ends. 'We'll need a megaphone if we
want to communicate.'

'Ah, but I don't think we're supposed to communicate.
Formality's the order of the day. You're the aristocratic
side of the family. I'm the peasant.'

'Hey, I'm on the wrong side of the blanket.'

'Then I'm under the bed, with the rest of the lint bun-
nies.'

She choked. The thought of this man as a lint bunny...

Mrs O'Reilly swept in then with coffee and placed
it before her with exaggerated care. 'Mr O'Farrell's just

phoned,' she told Finn, stepping back from the table and wiping her hands on her skirt as if she'd just done something dirty. 'He's the lawyer for the estate. He's been staying in Galway and he can be here in half an hour. I can ring him if that's not satisfactory.'

Finn raised his brows at Jo. 'Is that satisfactory with you?'

'I...yes.'

'We can see him then,' Finn told her. 'In Lord Conaill's study, please. Could you light the fire?'

'The drawing room would be...'

'The study, please,' Finn said inexorably and the woman stared at him.

Finn gazed calmly back. Waiting.

For a moment Jo thought she wouldn't answer. Finally she gave an angry tut and nodded.

'Yes, My Lord.'

'Mrs O'Reilly?'

'Yes.'

'You haven't asked Miss Conaill what she'd like for breakfast.'

'Toast,' Jo said hurriedly.

'And marmalade and a fruit platter,' Finn added. 'And I trust it'll be up to the excellent standard you served me. You do realise you burned Miss Conaill's dinner last night?'

He was holding the woman's gaze, staring her down, and with a gaze like that there was never any doubt as to the outcome.

'I'm sorry, My Lord. It won't happen again.'

'It won't,' Finn told her and gave a curt nod and went back to his newspaper.

The woman disappeared. Jo gazed after her with awe and then turned back to Finn. He was watching her, she found. He'd lowered his paper and was smiling at her, as if giving the lie to the gruff persona she'd just witnessed.

And it was too much. She giggled. 'Where did you learn to be a lord?' she demanded. 'Or is that something that's born into you with the title?'

'I practice on cows,' he said with some pride. 'I've had six months to get used to this Lordship caper. The cows have been bowing and scraping like anything.' He put his paper down and grinned. 'Not my brothers so much,' he admitted. 'They haven't let me live it down since they heard. Insubordination upon insubordination. You've never seen anything like it.'

'Do you guys share the farm?' She held her coffee, cradling its warmth. The dining room had an open fire in the hearth, the room was warm enough, but the sheer size of it was enough to make her shiver.

'I own my parents' farm outright, but it wasn't much of an inheritance when I started. My brothers all left for what they saw as easier careers and they've done well. Me? I've put my heart and soul into the farm and it's paid off.'

'You're content?'

He grinned at that. 'I'm a lord. How can I not be content?'

'I meant with farming.'

'Of course I am. I don't need a castle to be content. Cows are much more respectful than housekeepers.'

'I'm sure they are,' she said, thinking the man was ridiculous. But she kind of liked it.

She kind of liked him.

'No wife and family?' she asked, not that it was any of her business but she might as well ask.

'No.' He shrugged and gave a rueful smile. 'I've had a long-term girlfriend who's recently decided long-term is more than long enough. See me suffering from a broken heart.'

'Really?'

'Not really.' He grinned. 'I'll live.'

And then Mrs O'Reilly came sniffing back in with toast and he followed her every move with an aristocratically raised eyebrow until she disappeared again. It was a bit much for Jo.

'You do the Lord thing beautifully.'

'You should try.'

'Not me. I'm inheriting what there is to inherit and then I'm out of here.'

'Maybe that's wise,' Finn said thoughtfully. 'From all accounts, your grandpa wasn't the happiest of men. Maybe being aristocratic isn't all it's cut out to be.'

'But being content is,' she said softly. 'I'm glad… I'm glad, Finn Conaill, that you're content.'

The lawyer arrived just as Mrs O'Reilly finished clearing breakfast. Jo had had half a dozen emails from this man, plus a couple of phone calls from his assistant. She'd checked him out on the Internet. He was a partner in a prestigious Dublin law firm. She expected him to be crusty, dusty and old.

He turned up in bike leathers. He walked in, blond, blue-eyed, his helmet tucked under one arm, a briefcase by his side, and she found herself smiling as she stood beside Finn to greet him. There were things she'd been dreading over this meeting. Being intimidated by the legal fraternity was one of them, but this guy was smiling back at her, dumping his gear, holding out his hand in greeting. A fellow biker.

'Whose is the bike?' he asked.

'Mine,' she said. 'Hired in Dublin.'

'You should have let me know. My father would disapprove but I know a place that hires vintage babies. Or there are places that hire Harleys. We could have set one up for you.'

'You're kidding. A Harley?' She couldn't disguise the longing.

'No matter. After this morning, I imagine you'll be able to buy half a dozen Harleys.' He glanced at Finn and smiled. 'And yours will be the Jeep?'

And there it was, the faintest note of condescension. Jo got it because she was used to it, and she glanced up at Finn's face and she saw he got it too. And his face said he was used to it as well.

The lawyer's accent was strongly English. She'd read a bit of Ireland's background before she came. The lawyer would be public school educated, she thought. Finn…not so much. But she watched his face and saw the faint twitch at the edges of his mouth, the deepening of the creases at his eyes and thought, *He's amused by it.*

And she thought, *You'd be a fool to be condescending to this man.*

'I'm the Jeep,' he conceded.

'And the new Lord Conaill of Glenconaill,' the lawyer said and held out his hand. 'Congratulations. You're a lucky man.'

'Thank you,' Finn said gravely. 'I'm sure every Irishman secretly longs for his very own castle. I might even need to learn to eat with a fork to match.'

He grinned to take any offence from the words and Jo found herself grinning back. This man got subtle nuances, she thought, but, rather than bristling, he enjoyed them. She looked from Finn to the lawyer and thought this farmer was more than a match for any smart city lawyer.

'Lord Conaill and I have just been having breakfast,' she said. 'Before he takes me on a tour of the estate.'

'You know you're sharing?'

'And that's what you need to explain,' Finn said and they

headed into her grandfather's study, where John O'Farrell of O'Farrell, O'Farrell and O'Lochlan spent an hour explaining the ins and outs of their inheritance.

Which left Jo...gobsmacked.

She was rich. The lawyer was right. If she wanted, she could have half a dozen Harleys. Or much, much more.

The lawyer had gone through each section of the estate, explaining at length. She'd tried to listen. She'd tried to take it in but the numbers were too enormous for her to get her head around. When he finally finished she sat, stunned to silence, and Finn sat beside her and she thought, *He's just as stunned as I am.*

Unbelievable.

'So it's straight down the middle,' Finn said at last. 'One castle and one fortune.'

'That's right and, on current valuations, they're approximately equal. In theory, one of you could take the castle, the other the fortune that goes with it.' The lawyer looked at Jo and smiled. He'd been doing that a bit, not-so-subtle flirting. But then he decided to get serious again and addressed Finn.

'However, if you did have notions of keeping the castle, of setting yourself up as Lord of Glenconaill and letting Miss Conaill take the rest, I have bad news. This place is a money sink. My father has been acting as financial adviser to Lord Conaill for the last forty years and he knows how little has been spent on the upkeep of both castle and land. He's asked me to make sure you know it. The cosmetic touches have been done—Lord Conaill was big on keeping up appearances and his daughter insisted on things such as central heating—but massive capital works are needed to keep this place going into the future. Lord Conaill told my father he thought your own farm is worth a considerable amount but, in my father's opinion, if you wished to keep the castle, you'd need considerably more.

And, as for Miss Conaill…' he smiled again at Jo '… I suspect this lady has better things to do with a fortune than sink it into an ancient castle.'

Did she?

A fortune…

What would the likes of her do with a fortune?

Finn wasn't speaking. He'd turned and was looking out of the massive casement window to the land beyond.

He'd need time to take this in, she thought. They both would. This was…massive. She tried to think of how it would affect her, and couldn't. She tried to think of how it would affect Finn, but watching his broad shoulders at the window was making things seem even more disconcerting.

So focus on something else. Anything.

'What about Mrs O'Reilly?' she found herself asking, and the lawyer frowned.

'What about her?'

'It's just…there's no mention of her in the will and she seems to have been here for ever. She knew my mother.'

Finn turned and stared at her. She kept looking at the lawyer.

'I believe she has,' the lawyer said. 'There has been… discussion.'

'Discussion?'

'She rang after the funeral,' the lawyer admitted. 'Her husband was the old Lord's farm manager and she's maintained the castle and cared for your grandfather for well over thirty years. My father believes she's been poorly paid and overworked—very overworked as the old Lord wouldn't employ anyone else. My father believes she stayed because she was expecting some sort of acknowledgement in the will. She knew the castle was to be left to you, My Lord,' he told Finn. 'But it would have been a shock to hear the remainder was to be left to a granddaughter he'd never seen.'

He hesitated then but finally decided to tell it how it was. 'The old Lord wasn't without his faults,' he told them. 'My father said he wouldn't be surprised if he'd made promises to her that he had no intention of keeping. It gave him cheap labour.'

'And now?' Jo asked in a small voice.

'Her husband died last year. The place is without a farm manager and I wouldn't imagine you'll be having ongoing use for a housekeeper. She'll move out as soon as you wish.'

'But she's been left nothing? No pension? Nothing at all?'

'No.'

'That sucks,' Jo said.

'She doesn't like you,' Finn reminded her, frowning.

'It still sucks. She took care of my grandfather?'

'I believe she did,' the lawyer told her. 'For the last couple of months he was bedbound and she nursed him.'

'And she hated my mother, so she can't be all bad. How much would a cottage in the village and a modest pension be? Actually, you don't even need to tell me. Work it out and take it from my half.'

'She burned your dinner!' Finn expostulated.

Jo shrugged and smiled. 'If I thought she'd just inherited my home I might have burned her dinner.'

'She called your mother a drug addict.'

'My mother *was* a drug addict.' She turned back to the lawyer. 'Can you set it up?'

'Of course, but…'

'Take it from both sides,' Finn growled. 'We both have a responsibility towards her and we can afford to be generous. A decent house and a decent pension.'

'There's no need…' Jo started.

'We're in this together,' he said.

The lawyer nodded. 'It seems reasonable. A pension

and a local cottage for Mrs O'Reilly will scarcely dent what you'll inherit.

'Well, then,' he said, moving on. 'Irish castles with a history as long as this sell for a premium to overseas buyers looking for prestige. If you go through the place and see if there's anything you wish to keep, we can include everything else with the sale. I'd imagine you don't wish to stay here any longer than you need. Would a week to sort things out be enough? Make a list of anything you wish to keep, and then I'll come back with staff and start cataloguing. You could both have your inheritance by Christmas.' He smiled again at Jo. 'A Harley for Christmas?'

'That'd be…good,' Jo said with a sideways look at Finn. How did he feel about this? She felt completely thrown.

'Excellent,' Finn said and she thought he felt the same as she did.

How did she know? She didn't, she conceded. She was guessing. She was thinking she knew this man, but on what evidence?

'Jo, let me know when you've finished up here,' the lawyer was saying. 'We can advance you money against the estate so you can stay somewhere decent in Dublin. I can lend you one of my bikes. I could take you for a ride up to Wicklow, show you the sights. Take you somewhere decent for dinner.'

'Thanks,' she said, though she wasn't all that sure she wanted to go anywhere with this man, with his slick looks and his slick words.

'And you'll be imagining all the cows you can buy,' he said jovially to Finn and she saw Finn's lips twitch again.

'Eh, that'd be grand. Cows… I could do with a few of those. I might need to buy myself a new bucket and milking stool to match.'

He was laughing but the lawyer didn't get it. He was

moving on. 'Welcome to your new life of wealth,' he told them. 'Now, are you both sure about Mrs O'Reilly?'

'Yes.' They spoke together, and Finn's smile deepened. 'It's a good idea of Jo's.'

'Well, I may just pop into the kitchen and tell her,' the lawyer told them. 'I know she's been upset and, to be honest, my father was upset on her behalf.'

'But you didn't think to tell us earlier?' Finn demanded.

'It's not my business.' He shrugged. 'What you do with your money is very much your own business. You can buy as many milking stools as you want. After the castle's sold I expect I won't see you again. Unless…' He smiled suggestively at Jo. 'Unless you decide to spend some time in Dublin.'

'I won't,' Jo said shortly and he nodded.

'That's fine. Then we'll sell this castle and be done with it.'

CHAPTER FOUR

WHAT HAD JUST happened seemed too big to get their heads around. They farewelled the lawyer. They looked at each other.

'How many people do you employ on your farm?' Jo asked and he smiled. He'd enjoyed the lawyer's attempt at condescension and he liked that Jo had too.

'Ten, at last count.'

'That's a lot of buckets.'

'It is and all.'

'Family?' she asked.

'My parents are dead and my brothers have long since left.' He could tell her about Maeve, he thought, but then— why should he? Maeve was no longer part of his life.

'So there's just you and a huge farm.'

'Yes.'

'But you're not wealthy enough to buy me out?'

He grinned at that. 'Well, no,' he said apologetically. 'Didn't you hear our lawyer? He already has it figured.'

He tried smiling again, liking the closeness it gave them, but Jo had closed her eyes. She looked totally blown away.

'I need a walk.'

And he knew she meant by herself. He knew it because he needed the same. He needed space to get his head around the enormity of what had just happened. So he nodded and headed outside, across the castle grounds, past the dilapidated ha-ha dividing what had once been gardens from the fields beyond, and then to the rough ground where sheep grazed contentedly in the spring sunshine.

The lawyer's visit had thrown him more than he cared to admit, and it had thrown him for two reasons.

One was the sheer measure of the wealth he stood to inherit.

The second was Jo. Her reaction to Mrs O'Reilly's dilemma had blown him away. Her generosity...

Also the smarmy lawyer's attempt to flirt with her. Finn might have reacted outwardly to the lawyer with humour but inwardly...

Yeah, inwardly he'd have liked to take that smirk off the guy's face and he wouldn't have minded how he did it.

Which was dumb. Jo was a good-looking woman. It was only natural that the lawyer had noticed and what happened between them was nothing to do with Finn.

So focus on the farm, he told himself, but he had to force himself to do it.

Sheep.

The sheep looked scrawny. How much had their feed been supplemented during the winter? he asked himself, pushing all thoughts of Jo stubbornly aside, and by the time he'd walked to the outer reaches of the property he'd decided: not at all.

The sheep were decent stock but neglected. Yes, they'd been shorn but that seemed to be the extent of animal husbandry on the place. There were rams running with the ewes and the rams didn't look impressive. It seemed no one really cared about the outcome.

There were a couple of cows in a small field near the road. One looked heavily in calf. House cows? He couldn't imagine Mrs O'Reilly adding milking to her duties and both were dry. The cows looked as scrawny as the landscape.

Back home in Kilkenny, the grass was shooting with

its spring growth. The grass here looked starved of nutrients. It'd need rotation and fertiliser to keep these fields productive and it looked as if nothing had been done to them for a very long time.

He kept walking, over the remains of ancient drainage, long blocked.

Would some American or Middle Eastern squillionaire pay big bucks for this place? He guessed they would. They'd buy the history and the prestige and wouldn't give a toss about drainage.

And it wasn't their place. It was...*his*?

It wasn't, but suddenly that was the way he felt.

This was nuts. How could he feel this way about a place he hadn't seen before yesterday?

He had his own farm and he loved it. His brothers had grown and moved on but he'd stayed. He loved the land. He was good at farming and the farm had prospered in his care. He'd pushed boundaries. He'd built it into an excellent commercial success.

But this... Castle Glenconaill... He turned to look at its vast silhouette against the mountains and, for some reason, it almost felt as if it was part of him. His grandfather must have talked of it, he thought, or his father. He couldn't remember, but the familiarity seemed bone-deep.

He turned again to look out over the land. What a challenge.

To take and to hold...

The family creed seemed wrong, he decided, but *To hold and to honour...* That seemed right. To take this place and hold its history, to honour the land, to make this place once more a proud part of Irish heritage... If he could do that...

What was he thinking? He'd inherited jointly with a woman from Australia. Jo had no reason to love this place and every reason to hate it. And the lawyer was right; even with the wealth he now possessed, on his own he had no hope of keeping it. To try would be fantasy, doomed to disaster from the start.

'So sell it and get over it,' he told himself, but the ache to restore this place, to do something, was almost overwhelming.

He turned back to the castle but paused at the ha-ha. The beautifully crafted stone wall formed a divide so stock could be kept from the gardens without anything as crass as a fence interfering with the view from the castle windows. But in places the wall was starting to crumble. He looked at it for a long moment and then he couldn't resist. Stones had fallen. They were just…there.

He knelt and started fitting stone to stone.

He started to build.

To hold and to honour… He couldn't hold, he decided, but, for the time he was here, he would do this place honour.

Jo thought about heading outside but Finn had gone that way and she knew he'd want to be alone. There was silence from the kitchen. Mrs O'Reilly was either fainting from shock or trying to decide whether she could tell them they could shove their offer. Either way, maybe she needed space too.

Jo started up towards her bedroom and then, on impulse, turned left at the foot of the staircase instead of going up.

Two massive doors led to what looked like an ancient baronial hall. She pushed the doors open and stopped dead.

The hall looked as if it hadn't been used for years. Oversized furniture was draped with dustsheets and the dustsheets themselves were dusty. Massive beams ran the length of the hall, and up in the vaulted ceiling hung gener-

ations of spider webs. The place was cold and dank and…
amazing.

'Like something out of Dickens,' she said out loud and
her voice echoed up and up. She thought suddenly of Miss
Havisham sitting alone in the ruins of her bridal finery
and found herself grinning.

She could rent this place out for Halloween parties.
She could…

Sell it and go home.

Home? There was that word again.

And then her attention was caught. On the walls…tap-
estries.

Lots of tapestries.

When she'd first entered she'd thought they were paintings but now, making her way cautiously around the edges
of the hall, she could make out scores of needlework art-
works. Some were small. Some were enormous.

They were almost all dulled, matted with what must
have been smoke from the massive blackened fireplace
at the end of the room. Some were frayed and damaged.
All were amazing.

She fingered the closest and she was scarcely breathing.

It looked like…life in the castle? She recognised the
rooms, the buildings. It was as if whoever had done the
tapestries had set themselves the task of recording everyday life in the castle. Hunting. Formal meals with scores
of overdressed guests. Children at play. Dogs…

She walked slowly round the room and thought, *These
aren't from one artist and they're not from one era.*

They were the recording of families long gone.

Her family? Her ancestors?

It shouldn't make a difference but suddenly it did. She
hated that they were fading, splitting, dying.

Her history…

And Finn's, she thought suddenly. In her great-great-grandfather's era, they shared a heritage.

Maybe she could take them back to Sydney and restore them.

Why? They weren't hers. They'd be bought by whoever bought this castle.

They wouldn't be her ancestors, or Finn's ancestors. They'd belong to the highest bidder.

Maybe she could keep them.

But Jo didn't keep *stuff*, and that was all these were, she reminded herself. *Stuff*. But still… She'd restored a few tapestries in the past and she wasn't bad at it. She knew how to do at least step one.

As she'd crossed the boundaries of the castle last night she'd crossed a creek. No, a stream, she corrected herself. Surely in Ireland they had streams. Or burns? She'd have to ask someone.

But meanwhile it was spring, and the mountains above Castle Glenconaill must surely have been snow-covered in winter. The stream below the castle seemed to be running full and free. Clear, running water was the best way she knew to get soot and stains from tapestries, plumping up the threads in the process.

She could try with a small one, she decided, as her fingers started to itch. She'd start with one of the hunting scenes, a brace of pheasants without people or place. That way, if she hurt it, it wouldn't matter. She could start with that one and…

And nothing. She was going home. Well, back to Australia.

Yeah, she was, but first she was getting excited. First, she was about to clean a tapestry.

Finn had placed a dozen rocks back in their rightful position and was feeling vaguely pleased with himself. He'd decided he should return to the castle to see what Jo was doing—after all, they were here for a purpose and repairing rock walls wasn't that purpose—and now here she was, out in the middle of the stream that meandered along the edge of the ha-ha.

What was she doing? Those rocks were slippery. Any minute now she'd fall and get a dunking.

'Hey!'

She looked up and wobbled, but she didn't fall. She gave him a brief wave and kept on doing what she was doing.

Intrigued, he headed over to see.

She was messing with something under water.

The water would be freezing. She had the sleeves of her sweater pulled up and she'd hauled off her shoes. She was knee-deep in water.

'What's wrong?'

She kept concentrating, her back to him, stooped, as if adjusting something under water. He stood and waited, more and more intrigued, until finally she straightened and started her unsteady way back to the shore.

'Done.'

He could see green slime attached to the rocks underneath the surface. She was stepping gingerly from rock to rock but even the ones above the surface would be treacherous.

He took a couple of steps out to help her—and slipped himself, dunking his left foot up to his ankle.

He swore.

'Whoops,' Jo said and he glanced up at her and she was grinning. 'Uh oh. I'm sorry. I'd carry you if I could but I suspect you're a bit heavy.'

'What on earth are you doing?'

'Heading back to the castle. All dry.' She reached the shore, jumping nimbly from the last rock, then turned and proffered a hand to him. 'Can I help?'

'No,' he said, revolted, and her smile widened.

'How sexist is that? Honestly…'

'I was trying to help.'

'There's been a bit of that about,' she said. 'It's not that I don't appreciate it; it's just that I hardly ever need it. Bogs excepted.'

'What were you doing?' He hauled himself out of the water to the dry bank and surveyed his leg in disgust. His boot would take ages to dry. Jo, on the other hand, was drying her feet with a sock and tugging her trainers back on. All dry.

'Washing tapestries,' she told him and he forgot about his boots.

'Tapestries…?'

'The hall's full of them. You should see. They're awesome. But they're filthy and most of them need work. I've brought one of the small ones here to try cleaning.'

'You don't think,' he asked cautiously, 'that soap and water might be more civilised?'

'Possibly. But not nearly as much fun.'

'Fun…' He stared at his leg and she followed his gaze and chuckled.

'Okay, fun for me, not for you. I'm obviously better at creeks than you are.'

'Creeks…'

'Streams. Brooks. What else do you call them? Whatever, they'll act just the same as home.' She gestured to the surrounding hills, rolling away to the mountains in the background. 'Spring's the best time. The water's pouring down from the hills; it's running fast and clean and it'll wash through tapestries in a way nothing else can, unless I'm prepared to waste a day's running water in the castle. Even then, I wouldn't get an even wash.'

'So you just lie it in the stream.' He could see it now, a

square of canvas, stretched underwater and weighed down by rocks at the edges.

'The running water removes dust, soot, smoke and any burnt wool or silk. It's the best way. Some people prefer modern cleaning methods, but in my experience they can grey the colours. And, as well, this way the fibres get re-hydrated. They plump up almost as fat as the day they were stitched.'

'You're intending to leave it here?'

'I'll bring it in tonight. You needn't worry; I'm not about to risk a cow fording the stream and sticking a hoof through it.'

'And then what will you do?' he asked, fascinated.

'Let it dry and fix it, of course. This one's not bad. It has a couple of broken relays and warps but nothing too seri-ous. I'll see how it comes up after cleaning but I imagine I'll get it done before I leave. How's the stone wall going?'

To say he was dumbfounded would be an understate-ment. This woman was an enigma. Part of her came across tough; another part was so fragile he knew she could break. She was wary, she seemed almost fey, and here she was calmly setting about restoring tapestries as if she knew exactly what she was talking about.

He was sure she did.

'You saw me working?' he managed and she nodded.

'I walked past and you didn't see me. It feels good, doesn't it, working on something you love. So…half a yard of wall fixed, three or four hundred yards to go? Reckon you'll be finished in a week?' She clambered nimbly up the bank and turned and offered a hand. 'Need a pull?'

'No,' he said, and she grinned and withdrew her hand.

And he missed it. He should have just taken it. If he had she would have tugged and he would have ended up right beside her. Really close.

But she was smiling and turning to head back to the castle and it was dumb to feel a sense of opportunity lost.

What was he thinking? Life was complicated enough without feeling…what he was feeling…

And that's enough of that, he told himself soundly. It behoved a man to take a deep breath and get himself together. This woman was…complicated, and hadn't he decided on the safe option in life? His brothers had all walked off the land to make their fortunes and they'd done well. But Finn… He'd stayed and he'd worked the land he'd inherited. He'd aimed for a good farm on fertile land. A steady income. A steady woman?

Like Maeve. That was a joke. He'd thought his dreams were her dreams. He'd known her since childhood and yet it seemed he hadn't known her at all.

So how could he think he knew Jo after less than a day?

And why was he wondering how he could know her better?

'So do you intend to keep the suits of armour?' Jo asked and he struggled to haul his thoughts back to here and now. Though actually they were here and now. They were centred on a slip of a girl in a bright crimson sweater and jeans and stained trainers.

If Maeve had come to the castle with him, she'd have spent a week shopping for clothes in preparation.

But his relationship with Maeve was long over—apart from the minor complication that she wouldn't tell her father.

The sun was on his face. Jo was by his side, matching his stride even though her legs were six inches shorter than his. She looked bright and interested and free.

Of course she was free. She was discussing the fate of two suits of armour before she climbed back on her bike and headed back to Australia.

'I can't see them back on the farm,' he admitted.

'Your farm is somewhere near a place called Kilkenny,' she said. 'So where is that? You head down to Tipperary and turn…?'

'North-east. I don't go that way. But how do you know of Tipperary?'

'I looked it up on the map when I knew I was coming. There's a song… *It's a Long Way to Tipperary*. I figured that's where I was coming. A long way. And you farm cows and sheep?'

'The dairy's profitable but I'd like to get into sheep.'

'It's a big farm?'

'Compared to Australian land holdings, no. But it's very profitable.'

'And you love it.'

Did he love it?

As a kid he certainly had, when the place was rundown, when everywhere he'd looked there'd been challenges. But now the farm was doing well and promising to do better. With the money from the castle he could buy properties to the north.

If he wanted to.

'It's a great place,' he said mildly. 'How about you? Do you work at what you love?'

'I work to fund what I love.'

'Which is?'

'Tapestry and motorbikes.'

'Tell me about tapestry,' he said, and she looked a bit defensive.

'I didn't just look up the Internet and decide to restore from Internet Lesson 101. I've been playing with tapestries for years.'

'Why?' It seemed so unlikely…

'When I was about ten my then foster mother gave me a tapestry do-it-yourself kit. It was a canvas with a painting of a cat and instructions and the threads to complete it. I learned the basics on that cat, but when I finished I thought the whiskers looked contrived. He also looked smug so I ended up unpicking him a bit and fiddling. It started me drawing my own pictures. It works for me. It makes me feel…settled.'

'So what do you do the rest of the time?'

'I make coffee. Well. I can also wait tables with the best of them. It's a skill that sees me in constant work.'

'You wouldn't rather work with tapestries?'

'That'd involve training to be let near the decent ones, and training's out of my reach.'

'Even now you have a massive inheritance?'

She paused as if the question took concentration. She stared at her feet and then turned and gazed out at the grounds, to the mountains beyond.

'I don't know,' she admitted. 'I like café work. I like busy. It's kind of like a family.'

'Do they know where you are?'

'Who? The people I work with?'

'Yes.'

'Do you mean if I'd sunk in a bog yesterday would they have cared or even known?' She shrugged. 'Nope. That's not what I mean by family. I pretty much quit work to come here. Someone's filling in for me now, but I'll probably just get another job when I go back. I don't stay in the same place for long.'

'So when you said family…'

'I meant people around me. It's all I want. Cheerful company and decent coffee.'

'And you're stuck here with me and Mrs O'Reilly and coffee that tastes like mud.'

'You noticed,' she said approvingly. 'That's a start.'

'A start of what?' he asked mildly and she glanced sharply up at him as if his question had shocked her. Maybe it had. He'd surprised himself—it wasn't a ques-

tion he'd meant to ask and he wasn't sure what exactly he
was asking.

But the question hung.

'I guess the start of nothing,' she said at last with a
shrug that was meant to be casual but didn't quite come
off. 'I can cope with mud coffee for a week.'

'All we need to do is figure what we want to keep.'

'I live out of a suitcase. I can't keep anything.' She said
it almost with defiance.

'And the armour wouldn't look good in a nice modern
bungalow.'

'Is that what your farmhouse is?'

'It is.' The cottage he'd grown up in had long since dete-
riorated past repair. He'd built a large functional bungalow.

It had a great kitchen table. The rest…yeah, it was functional.

'I saw you living somewhere historic,' Jo said. 'Thatch
maybe.'

'Thatch has rats.'

She looked up towards the castle ramparts. 'What about
battlements? Do battlements have rats?'

'Not so much.' He grinned. 'Irish battlements are possibly a bit cold even for the toughest rat.'

'What about you, Lord Conaill? Too cold for you?'

'I'm not Lord Conaill.'

'All the tapestries in the great hall…they're mostly from
a time before your side of the family split. This is your
history too.'

'I don't feel like Lord Conaill.'

'No, but you look like him. Go in and check the tapestries. You have the same aristocratic nose.'

He put his hand on his nose. 'Really?'

'Yep. As opposed to mine. Mine's snub with freckles,
not an aristocratic line anywhere.'

And he looked at her freckles and thought…it might not be the Conaill nose but it was definitely cute.

He could just…

Not. How inappropriate was it to want to reach out and touch a nose? To trace the line of those cheekbones.

To touch.

He knew enough about this woman to expect a pretty firm reaction. Besides, the urge was ridiculous. Wasn't it?

'I reckon your claim to the castle's a lot stronger than mine,' she was saying and he had to force his attention from her very cute nose to what they were talking about.

They'd reached the forecourt. He turned and faced outward, across the vast sweep of Glenconaill to the mountains beyond. It was easier talking about abstracts when he wasn't looking at the reality of her nose. And the rest of her.

'Your grandfather left the castle to two strangers,' he told her. 'We're both feeling as if we have no right to be here, and yet he knew I was to inherit the title. He came to my farm six months ago and barked the information at me, yet there was never an invitation to come here. And you were his granddaughter and he didn't know you either. He knew we'd stand here one day, but he made no push to make us feel we belong. Yet we do belong.'

'You feel that?'

'I don't know,' he said slowly. 'It's just…walking across the lands today, looking at the sheep, at the ruined walls, at the mess this farmland has become, it seems a crime that no push was made…'

'To love it?' She nodded. 'I was thinking that. The tapestries… A whole family history left to disintegrate.' She shrugged. 'But we can't.'

'I guess not.' He gazed outward for a long moment, as though soaking in something he needed to hold to. 'Of course you're right.'

'If he'd left it all to you, you could have,' Jo said and he shrugged again.

'Become a Lord in fact? Buy myself ermine robes and employ a valet?'

'Fix a few stone walls?'

'That's more tempting,' he said and then he grinned. 'So your existence has saved me from a life of chipping at cope stones. Thank you, Jo. Now, shall we find out if Mrs O'Reilly intends to feed us?'

And Jo thought…it felt odd to walk towards Castle Glenconaill with this man by her side.

But somehow, weirdly, it felt right.

'What are you working on at the moment?' Finn asked and she was startled back to the here and now.

'What?'

'You're carrying sewing needles. I'm not a great mind, but it does tell me there's likely to be sewing attached. Or do you bring them on the off chance you need to darn socks?'

'No, I…'

'Make tapestries? On the plane? Do you have a current project and, if so, can I see?'

She stared up at him and then stared down at her feet. And his feet. One of his boots was dripping mud.

Strangely, it made him seem closer. More human.

She didn't show people her work, so why did she have a sudden urge to say…?

'Okay.'

'Okay?' he said cautiously.

'It's not pretty. And it's not finished. But if you'd really like to see…'

'Now?'

'When your foot's dry.'

'Why not with a wet foot?'

'My tapestry demands respect.'

He grinned. 'There speaks the lady of the castle.'

'I'm not,' she said. 'But my tapestry's up there with anything the women of this castle have done.' She smiled then, one of her rare smiles that lit her face, that made her seem…

Intriguing? No, he was already intrigued, he conceded. Desirable?

Definitely.

'Are you sure?' she asked and he caught himself. He'd known this woman for how long?

'I'm very sure,' he told her. 'And, lady of the castle or not, your tapestry's not the only thing to deserve respect. I will take my boot off for you.'

'Gee, thanks,' she told him. 'Fifteen minutes. My bedroom. See you there.'

And she took off, running across the forecourt like a kid without a trouble in the world. She looked…free.

She looked beautiful.

Fifteen minutes with his boot off. A man had to get moving.

The tapestry was rolled and wrapped in the base of her kitbag. He watched as she delved into what looked to be the most practical woman's pack he'd ever seen. There were no gorgeous gowns or frilly lingerie here—just bike gear and jeans and T-shirts and sweaters. He thought briefly of the lawyer and his invitation to dinner in Dublin and found himself smiling.

Jo glanced up. 'What?'

'Is this why you said no to our lawyer's invite? I can't see a single little black dress.'

'I don't have a use for 'em,' she said curtly.

'You know, there's a costume gallery here,' he said and she stared.

'A costume gallery?'

'A store of the very best of what the Conaills have worn for every grand event in their history. Someone in our past has decided that clothes need to be kept as well as paintings. I found the storeroom last night. Full of mothballs and gold embroidery. So if you need to dress up…'

She stared at him for a long moment, as if she was almost tempted—and then she gave a rueful smile and shook her head and tugged out the roll. 'I can't see me going out to dinner with our lawyer in gold embroidery. Can you? But if you want to see this…' She tossed the roll on the bed and it started to uncurl on its own.

Fascinated, he leaned over and twitched the end so the whole thing unrolled onto the white coverlet.

And it was as much as he could do not to gasp.

This room could almost be a servant's room, it was so bare. It was painted white, with a faded white coverlet on the bed. There were two dingy paintings on the wall, not very good, scenes of the local mountains. They looked as if they'd been painted by a long ago Conaill, with visions of artistic ability not quite managed.

But there was nothing 'not quite managed' about the tapestry on the bed. Quite simply, it lit the room.

It was like nothing he'd ever seen before. It was colour upon colour upon colour.

It was fire.

Did it depict Australia's Outback? Maybe, he thought, but if so it must be an evocation of what that could be like. This was ochre-red country, wide skies and slashes of river. There were wind-bent eucalypts with flocks of white cockatoos screeching from tree to tree… There were so many details.

And yet not. At first he could only see what looked like burning: flames with colour streaking through, heat, dry. And then he looked closer and it coalesced into its separate parts without ever losing the sense of its whole.

The thing was big, covering half the small bed, and it wasn't finished. He could see bare patches with only vague pencil tracing on the canvas, but he knew instinctively that these pencil marks were ideas only, that they could change.

For this was no paint by numbers picture. This was… Breathtaking.

'This should be over the mantel in the great hall,' he breathed and she glanced up at him, coloured and then bit her lip and shook her head.

'Nope.'

'What do you do with them?'

'Give them to people I like. You can have this if you want. You pulled me out of a bog.'

And once more she'd taken his breath away.

'You just…give them away?'

'What else would I do with them?'

He was still looking at the canvas, seeing new images every time he looked. There were depths and depths and depths. 'Keep them,' he said softly. 'Make them into an exhibition.'

'I don't keep stuff.'

He hauled his attention from the canvas and stared at her. 'Nothing?'

'Well, maybe my bike.'

'Where do you live?'

'Where I can rent a room with good light for sewing. And where my sound system doesn't cause a problem. I like my music loud.' She shrugged. 'So there's another thing I own—a great speaker system to plug into my phone. Oh, and toothbrushes and stuff.'

'I don't get it.' He thought suddenly of his childhood, of his mother weeping because she'd dropped a plate belonging to her own mother. There'd been tears for a ceramic thing. And yet…his focus was drawn again to the tapestry. That Jo could work so hard for this, put so much of herself in it and then give it away…

'You reckon I need a shrink because I don't own stuff?' she asked and he shook his head.

'No. Though I guess…'

'I did see someone once,' she interrupted. 'When I was fifteen. I was a bit…wild. I got sent to a home for trouble-some adolescents and they gave me a few sessions with a psychoanalyst. She hauled out a memory of me at eight, being moved on from a foster home. There was a fire en-gine I played with. I'd been there a couple of years so I guess I thought it was mine. When I went to pack, my fos-ter mum told me it was a foster kid toy and I couldn't take it. The shrink told me it was significant, but I don't need a fire engine now. I don't need anything.'

He cringed for her. She'd said it blithely, as if it was no big deal, but he knew the shrink was right. This woman was wounded. 'Jo, the money we're both inheriting will give you security,' he said gently. 'No one can take your fire engine now.'

'I'm over wanting fire engines.'

'Really?'

And she managed a smile at that. 'Well, if it was a truly excellent fire engine…'

'You'd consider?'

'I might,' she told him. 'Though I might have to get my-self a Harley with a trailer to carry it. Do Harleys come with trailers? I can't see it. Meanwhile, is it lunchtime?'

He checked his watch. 'Past. Uh oh. We need to face Mrs O'Reilly. Jo, you've been more than generous. You don't have to face her.'

'I do,' she said bluntly. 'I don't run away. It's not my style.'

Mrs O'Reilly had made them lunch but Finn wasn't sure how she'd done it. Her swollen face said she'd been weep-ing for hours.

She placed shepherd's pie in front of them and stood back, tried to speak and failed.

'I can't...' she managed.

'Mrs O'Reilly, there's no need to say a thing.' Jo reached for the pie and ladled a generous helping onto her plate. 'Not when you've made me pie. But I do need dead horse.'

'Dead horse?' Finn demanded, bemused, and Jo shook her head in exasperation.

'Honestly, don't you guys know anything? First, dead horse is Australian for sauce and second, shepherd's pie without sauce is like serving fish without chips. Pie and sauce, fish and chips, roast beef with Yorkshire pud... What sort of legacy are you leaving for future generations if you don't know that?'

He grinned and Mrs O'Reilly sniffed and sniffed again and then beetled for the kitchen. She returned with four different sauce bottles.

Jo checked them out and discarded three with disgust.

'There's only one. Tomato sauce, pure, unadulterated. Anything else is a travesty. Thank you, Mrs O'Reilly, this is wonderful.'

'It's not,' the woman stammered. 'I was cruel to you.'

'I've done some research into my mother over the years,' Jo said, concentrating on drawing wiggly lines of sauce across her pie. 'She doesn't seem like she was good to anyone. She wasn't even good to me and I was her daughter. I can only imagine what sort of demanding princess she was when she was living here. And Grandpa didn't leave you provided for after all those years of service from you and your husband. I'd have been mean to me if I were you too.'

'I made you sleep in a single bed!'

'Well, that is a crime.' She was chatting to Mrs O'Reilly as if she were talking of tomorrow's weather, Finn thought. The sauce arranged to her satisfaction, she tackled her pie with gusto.

Mrs O'Reilly was staring at her as if she'd just landed from another planet, and Finn was feeling pretty much the same.

'A single bed's fine by me,' she said between mouthfuls. 'As is this pie. Yum. Last night's burned beef, though…that needs compensation. Will you stay on while we're here? You could make us more. Or would you prefer to go? Finn and I can cope on our own. I hope the lawyer has explained what you do from now on is your own choice.'

'He has.' She grabbed her handkerchief and blew her nose with gusto. 'Of course…of course I'll stay while you need me but now… I can have my own house. My own home.'

'Excellent,' Jo told her. 'If that's what you want, then go for it.'

'I don't deserve it.'

'Hey, after so many years of service, one burned dinner shouldn't make a difference, and life's never about what we deserve. I'm just pleased Finn and I can administer a tiny bit of justice in a world that's usually pretty much unfair. Oh, and the calendars in the kitchen…you like cats?'

'I…yes.'

'Why don't you have one?'

'Your grandfather hated them.'

'I don't hate them. Do you hate them, Finn?'

'No.'

'There you go,' Jo said, beaming. 'Find yourself a kitten. Now, if you want. And don't buy a cottage where you can't keep one.'

She was amazing, Finn thought, staring at her in silence. This woman was…stunning.

But Jo had moved on. 'Go for it,' she said, ladling more pie onto her fork. 'But no more talking. This pie deserves all my attention.'

* * *

They finished their pie in silence, then polished off apple tart and coffee without saying another word.

There didn't seem any need to speak. Or maybe there was, but things were too enormous to be spoken of.

As Mrs O'Reilly bustled away with the dishes, Jo felt almost dismayed. Washing up last night with Finn had been a tiny piece of normality. Now there wasn't even washing up to fall back on.

'I guess we'd better get started,' Finn said at last.

'Doing what?'

'Sorting?'

'What do we need to sort?' She gazed around the ornate dining room, at the myriad ornaments, pictures, side tables, vases, stuff. 'I guess lots of stuff might go to museums. You might want to keep some. I don't need it.'

'It's your heritage.'

'Stuff isn't heritage. I might take photographs of the tapestries,' she conceded. 'Some of them are old enough to be in a museum too.'

'Show me,' he said and that was the next few minutes sorted. So she walked him through the baronial hall, seeing the history of the Conaills spread out before her.

'It seems a shame to break up the collection,' Finn said at last. He'd hardly spoken as they'd walked through.

'Like breaking up a family.' Jo shrugged. 'People do it all the time. If it's no use to you, move on.'

'You really don't care?'

She gazed around at the vast palette of family life spread before her. Her family? No. Her mother had been the means to her existence, nothing more, and her grandfather hadn't given a toss about her.

'I might have cared if this had been my family,' she told him. 'But the Conaills were the reason I couldn't have a family. It's hardly fair to expect me to honour them now.'

'Yet you'd love to restore the tapestries.'

'They're amazing.' She crossed to a picture of a family group. 'I've been figuring out time frames, and I think this could be the great-great-grandpa we share. Look at Great-Great-Grandma. She looks a tyrant.'

'You don't want to keep her?'

'Definitely not. How about you?' she asked. 'Are you into family memorabilia?'

'I have a house full of memorabilia. My parents threw nothing out. And my brothers live very modern lives. I can't see any of this stuff fitting into their homes. I'll ask them but I know what their answers will be. You really want nothing but the money?'

'I wanted something a long time ago,' she told him. They were standing side by side, looking at the picture of their mutual forebears. 'You have no idea how much I wanted. But now…it's too late. It even seems wrong taking the money. I'm not part of this family.'

'Hey, we are sort of cousins.' And, before she knew what he intended, he'd put an arm around her waist and gave her a gentle hug. 'I'm happy to own you.'

'I don't…' The feel of his arm was totally disconcerting. 'I don't think I want to be owned.' And this was a normal hug, she told herself. A cousinly hug. There was no call to haul herself back in fright. She forced herself to stand still.

'Not by this great-great-grandma,' he conceded. 'She looks a dragon.' But his arm was still around her waist, and it was hard to concentrate on what he was saying. It was really hard. 'But you need to belong somewhere. There's a tapestry somewhere with your future on it.'

'I'm sure there's not. Not if it has grandmas and grandpas and kids and dogs.' Enough. She tugged away because it had to be just a cousinly hug; she wasn't used to hugs and she didn't need it. She didn't! 'I'm not standing still long enough to be framed.'

'That's a shame,' he told her, and something in the timbre of his voice made her feel…odd. 'Because I suspect you're worth all this bunch put together.'

'That's kissing the Blarney Stone.'

He shrugged and smiled and when he smiled she wanted that hug back. Badly.

'I'm not one for saying what I don't mean, Jo Conaill,' he told her. 'You're an amazing woman.'

'D…don't,' she stammered. For some reason the hug had left her discombobulated. 'We're here to sort this stuff. Let's start now.'

And then leave, she told herself. The way she was feeling… The way she was feeling was starting to scare her.

The size of the place, the mass of furnishings, the store of amazing clothing any museum would kill for—the entire history of the castle was mind-blowing. It was almost enough to make her forget how weird Finn's hug made her feel. But there was work to be done. Figuring out the scale of their inheritance would take days.

Underground there were cellars—old dungeons?—and storerooms. Upstairs were 'living' rooms, apartment-sized chambers filled with dust-sheeted furniture. Above them were the bedrooms and up a further flight of stairs were the servants' quarters, rooms sparsely furnished with an iron cot and dresser.

Over the next couple of days they moved slowly through the place, sorting what there was. Most things would go straight to the auction rooms—almost all of it—but, by mutual consent, they decided to catalogue the things that seemed important. Detailed cataloguing could be done later by the auctioneers but somehow it seemed wrong to sell everything without acknowledging its existence. So they moved from room to room, taking notes, and she put the memory of the hug aside.

Though she had to acknowledge that she was grateful for his company. If she'd had to face this alone...

This place seemed full of ghosts who'd never wanted her, she thought. The costume store on its own was enough to repel her. All these clothes, worn by people who would never have accepted her. She was illegitimate, despised, discarded. She had no place here, and Finn must feel the same. Regardless of his inherited title, he still must feel the poor relation.

And he'd never fit in one of these cots, she thought as they reached the servants' quarters. She couldn't help glancing up at him as he opened the door on a third identical bedroom. He was big. Very big.

'It'd have to be a bleak famine before I'd fit in that bed,' he declared. He glanced down at the rough map drawn for them by Mrs O'Reilly. 'Now the nursery.'

The room they entered next was huge, set up as a schoolroom as well as a nursery. The place was full of musty furniture, with desks and a blackboard, but schooling seemed to have been a secondary consideration.

There were toys everywhere, stuffed animals of every description, building blocks, doll's houses, spinning tops, dolls large and small, some as much as three feet high. All pointing to indulged childhoods.

And then there was the rocking horse.

It stood centre stage in the schoolroom, set on its own dais. It was as large as a miniature pony, crafted with care and, unlike most other things in the nursery, it was maintained in pristine condition.

It had a glossy black coat, made, surely, with real horse hide. Its saddle was embellished with gold and crimson, as were the bridle and stirrups. Its ears were flattened and its dark glass eyes stared out at the nursery as if to say, *Who Dares Ride Me?*

And all around the walls were photographs and paintings, depicting every child who'd ever sat on this horse, going back maybe two hundred years.

Jo stared at the horse and then started a round of the walls, looking at each child in turn. These were beautifully dressed children. Beautifully cared for. Even in the early photographs, where children were exhorted to be still and serious for the camera or the artist, she could see their excitement. These Conaills were the chosen few.

Jo's mother was the last to be displayed. Taken when she was about ten, she was dressed in pink frills and she was laughing up at the camera. Her face was suffused with pride. *See*, her laugh seemed to say. *This is where I belong.*

But after her…nothing.

'Suggestions as to what we should do with all this?' Finn said behind her, sounding cautious, as if he guessed the well of emotion surging within. 'Auction the lot of them?'

'Where are you?' she demanded in a voice that didn't sound her own.

'Where am I where?'

'In the pictures.'

'You know I don't belong here.'

'No, but your great-great-grandfather…'

'I'm thinking he might be this one,' Finn said, pointing to a portrait of a little boy in smock and pantaloons and the same self-satisfied smirk.

'And his son's next to him. Where's your great-grand-father? My great-grandpa's brother?'

'He was a younger son,' Finn said. 'I guess he didn't get to ride the horse.'

'So he left and had kids who faced the potato famine instead,' Jo whispered. 'Can we burn it?'

'What, the horse?'

'It's nasty.'

Finn stood back and surveyed the horse. It was indeed…

nasty. It looked glossy, black and arrogant. Its eyes were too small. It looked as if it was staring at them with disdain. The poor relations.

'I'm the Lord of Glenconaill,' Finn said mildly. 'I could ride this nag if I wanted.'

'You'd squash it.'

'Then you could take my photograph standing over a squashed stuffed horse. Sort of a last hurrah.'

She tried to smile but she was too angry. Too full of emotion.

'How can one family have four sets of Monopoly?' Finn asked, gazing at the stacks of board games. 'And an Irish family at that? And what were we doing selling Bond Street?'

'They,' she snapped. 'Not we. This is not us.'

'It was our great-great-grandpa.'

'Monopoly wasn't invented then. By the time it was, you were the poor relation.'

'That's right, so I was,' he said cheerfully. 'But you'd have thought they could have shared at least one set of Monopoly.'

'They didn't share. Not this family.' She fell silent, gazing around the room, taking in the piles of…stuff. 'All the time I was growing up,' she whispered. 'These toys were here. Unused. They were left to rot rather than shared. Of all the selfish…' She was shaking, she discovered. Anger that must have been suppressed for years seemed threatening to overwhelm her. 'I hate them,' she managed and she couldn't keep the loathing from her voice. 'I hate it all.'

'Even the dolls?' he asked, startled.

'All of it.'

'They'll sell.'

'I'd rather burn them.'

'What, even the horse?' he asked, startled.

'Everything,' she said and she couldn't keep loathing

from her voice. 'All these toys… All this sense of entitle-ment… Every child who's sat on this horse, who's played with these toys, has known their place in the world. But not me. Not us. Unless your family wants them, I'd burn the lot.'

'My brothers have all turned into successful business-men. My nieces and nephews have toys coming out their ears,' Finn said, a smile starting behind his eyes. There was also a tinge of understanding. 'So? A bonfire? Ex-cellent. Let's do it. Help me carry the horse downstairs.'

She stared, shocked. He sounded as if her suggestion was totally reasonable. 'What, now?'

'Why not? What's the use of having a title like mine if I can't use some of the authority that comes with it? Back at my farm the cows won't so much as bow when I walk past. I need to learn to be lordly and this is a start.' He looked at the horse with dislike. 'I think that coat's been slicked with oils anyway. He'll go up like a firecracker.'

'How can we?'

'Never suggest a bonfire if you don't mean it,' he said. 'There's nothing we Lords of Glenconaill like more than a good burning.' He turned and stared around at the assort-ment of expensive toys designed for favoured children and he grimaced. 'Selling any one of these could have kept a family alive for a month during the famine. If there was a fire engine here I'd say save it but there's not. Our ances-tors were clearly people with dubious taste. Off with their heads, I say. Let's do it.'

CHAPTER FIVE

THE NURSERY WAS on the top floor and the stairway was narrow. The horse went first, manoeuvred around the bends with Finn at the head and Jo at the tail. Once downstairs, Finn headed for the stables and came back with crumbling timber while Jo carted more toys.

While they carried the horse down she was still shaking with anger. Her anger carried her through the first few armfuls of assorted toys but as Finn finished creating the bonfire and started helping her carry toys she felt her anger start to dissipate.

He was just too cheerful.

'This teddy looks like he's been in a tug of war or six,' Finn told her, placing the teddy halfway up the pyre. 'It's well time for him to go up in flames.'

It was a scruffy bear, small, rubbed bare in spots, one arm missing. One ear was torn off and his grin was sort of lopsided.

She thought of unknown ancestors hugging this bear. Then she thought of her mother and hardened her heart. 'Yes,' she said shortly and Finn cast her a questioning glance but headed upstairs for another load.

She followed, carting down a giraffe, two decrepit sets of wooden railway tracks and a box of blocks.

The giraffe was lacking a bit of stuffing. He was lopsided.

He was sort of looking at her.

'It's like the French Revolution,' Finn told her, stacking them neatly on his ever-growing pyre. 'All the aristocracy off to the Guillotine. I can just imagine these guys saying, "Let them eat cake".'

But she couldn't. Not quite.

The horse was sitting right on top of the pile, still looking aristocratic and nasty. The teddy was just underneath him. It was an old teddy. No one would want that teddy.

She was vaguely aware of Mrs O'Reilly watching from the kitchen window. She looked bemused. She wasn't saying anything, though.

These toys were theirs now, to do with as they wanted, Jo thought with a sudden stab of clarity. Hers and Finn's. They represented generations of favoured children, but now…were she and Finn the favoured two?

She glanced at Finn, looking for acknowledgement that he was feeling something like she was—anger, resentment, sadness.

Guilt?

All she saw was a guy revelling in the prospect of a truly excellent bonfire. He was doing guy stuff, fiddling with toys so they made a sweeping pyre, putting the most flammable stuff at the bottom, the horse balanced triumphantly at the top.

He was a guy having fun.

'Ready?' he asked and she realised he had matches poised.

'Yes,' she said in a small voice and Finn shook his head.

'You'll have to do better than that. You're the lady of the castle, remember. It's an autocratic "Off with their heads", or the peasants will sense weakness. Strength, My Lady.'

'Off with their heads,' she managed but it was pretty weak.

But still, she'd said it and Finn looked at her for a long

moment, then gave a decisive nod and bent and applied match to kindling.

It took a few moments for the wood to catch. Finn could have put a couple of the more flammable toys at the base, she thought. That would have made it go up faster. Instead he'd left a bare spot so the fire would have to be strongly alight before it reached its target.

The teddy would be one of the first things to catch, she thought. The teddy with the missing ear and no arm. And an eye that needed a stitch to make his smile less wonky.

She could...

No. These were favoured toys of favoured people. They'd belonged to people who'd rejected her. People who'd given her their name but nothing else. People who'd made sure she had nothing, and done it for their own self-ish ends.

The teddy... One stitch...

The flames were licking upward.

The giraffe was propped beside the teddy. There was a bit of stuffing oozing out from his neck. She could...

She couldn't. The fire was lit. The thing was done.

'Jo?' Finn was suddenly beside her, his hand on her shoulder, holding her with the faintest of pressure. 'Jo?'

She didn't reply. She didn't take her eyes from the fire.

'You're sure you want to do this?' he asked.

'It's lit.'

'I'm a man who's into insurance,' he said softly and she looked down and saw he was holding a hose.

A hose. To undo what she needed to do.

The teddy...

Even the evil horse...

She couldn't do it. Dammit, she couldn't. She choked back a stupid sob and grabbed for the hose. 'Okay, put it out.'

'You want the fire out?'

'I'll do it.'

'You'll wet the teddy,' he said reproachfully. 'He'll get hypothermia as well as scorched feet. Trust me, if there's one thing I'm good at it's putting out fires.'

And he screwed the nozzle and aimed the hose. The water came out with satisfactory force. The wood under the teddy hissed and sizzled. Flames turned to smoke and then steam.

The teddy was enveloped with smoke but, before she realised what he intended, Finn stomped forward in his heavy boots, aimed the hose downward to protect his feet, then reached up and gathered the unfortunate bear.

And the giraffe.

He played the water for a moment longer until he was sure that no spark remained, then twisted the nozzle to off and turned back to her.

He handed her the teddy.

'Yours,' he said. 'And I know I said I have too much stuff, but I'm thinking I might keep the giraffe. I'll call him Noddy.'

She tried to laugh but it came out sounding a bit too much like a sob. 'N... Noddy. Because...because of his neck?'

'He's lost his stuffing,' Finn said seriously. 'He can't do anything but nod. And Teddy's Loppy because he's lopsided. He looks like he's met the family dog. One side looks chewed.'

'It'd be the castle dog. Not a family dog.'

'Ah, but that's where you're wrong,' he said, softly now, his gaze not leaving her face. As if he knew the tumult of stupid emotions raging within her. 'These people rejected us for all sorts of reasons but somehow they still are family. Our family. Toe-rags most of them, but some will have been decent. Some will have been weak, or vain or silly, and some cruel and thoughtless, but they were who they were. This…' he waved to the heap of toys spared from the flames '…this is just detritus from their passing.'

'Like us.'

'We're not detritus. We're people who make decisions. We're people who've spared a nursery full of toys and now need to think what to do with them.' He looked doubtfully at his lopsided giraffe. 'You did say you could sew.'

'I… I did.'

'Then I'll ask you to fix him so he can sit in my tool-shed and watch me do shed stuff. Maybe Loppy can sit on your handlebars and watch you ride.'

'That'd be silly.'

'Silly's better than haunted.'

She stared at the pile of ancient toys, and then she turned and looked up at the castle.

'It's not its fault.'

'It's not even the horse's,' Finn said gently. 'Though I bet he collaborated.'

'He'd probably sell for heaps.'

'He would. I didn't like to say but there's been one like him in the window of the antique shop in the village at home. He has a three hundred pound price tag.'

'Three hundred… You didn't think to mention that when I wanted to burn him?'

'I do like a good bonfire.'

She choked on a bubble of laughter, emotion dissipating, and then she stared at the horse again. Getting sensible. 'We could give him away. To a children's charity or something.'

'Or we could sell him to someone who likes arrogant horses and give the money instead,' Finn told her. 'Think how many bears we could donate with three hundred pounds. Kids need friends, not horses who only associate with the aristocracy.'

There was a long silence. Mrs O'Reilly had disappeared

from her window, no doubt confused by the on-again off-again bonfire. The sun was warm on Jo's face. In the shelter of the ancient outbuildings there wasn't a breath of wind. The stone walls around her were bathed in sunshine, their grey walls softened by hundreds of years of wear, of being the birthplace of hundreds of Conaills, of whom only a few had been born with the privilege of living here.

'I guess we can't burn the whole castle because of one arrogant grandfather and one ditzy mother,' she said at last, and Finn looked thoughtful. Almost regretful.

'We could but we'll need more kindling.'

She chuckled but it came close to being a sob. She was hugging the teddy. Stupidly. She didn't hug teddies. She didn't hug anything.

'I suppose we should get rational,' she managed. 'We could go through, figure what could make money, sell what we can.'

'And make a bonfire at the end?' he asked, still hopefully, and her bubble of laughter stayed. A guy with the prospect of a truly excellent bonfire…

'The sideboards in the main hall are riddled with woodworm,' she told him, striving for sense. 'Mrs O'Reilly told me. They'd burn well.'

'Now you're talking.'

She turned back to the pile of unburned toys and her laughter faded. 'You must think I'm stupid.'

'I'm thinking you're angry,' Finn told her. He paused and then added, 'I'm thinking you have cause.'

'I'm over it.'

'Can you ever be over not being wanted?'

'That's just the trouble,' she said, and she stared up at the horse again because it was easier looking at a horse than looking at Finn. He seemed to see inside her, this man, and to say it was disconcerting would be putting it mildly. 'I *was* wanted. Three separate sets of foster parents wanted to adopt me but the Conaills never let it happen. But I'm a big girl now. I have myself together.'

'And you have Loppy.'

'I'll lose him. I always lose stuff.'

'You don't have to lose stuff. With the money from here you can buy yourself a warehouse and employ a storeman to catalogue every last teddy.' He gestured to the pile. 'You can keep whatever you want.'

'I don't know…what I want.'

'You have time to figure it out.'

'So what about you?' she demanded suddenly. 'What do you want? You're a lord now. If you could…would you stay here?'

'As a lord…' He sounded startled. 'No! But if I had time with these sheep…'

'What would you do with them?' she asked curiously, and he shrugged and turned and looked out towards the distant hills.

'Someone, years ago, put thought and care into these guys' breeding. They're tough, but this flock's different to the sheep that run on the bogs. Their coats are finer. As well, their coats also seem repellent. You put your hand through a fleece and you'll find barely a burr.'

'Could you take some back to your farm? Interbreed?'

'Why would I do that? Our sheep are perfect for the conditions there. These are bred for different conditions. Different challenges.' And he gazed out over the land and she thought he looked…almost hungry.

'You'd like a challenge,' she ventured and he nodded.

'I guess. But this is huge. And Lord of Glenconaill… I'd be ridiculous. Have you seen what the previous lords wore in their portraits?'

She grinned. 'You could ditch the leggings.'

'And the wigs?'

'Hmm.' She looked up at his gorgeous thatch of dark

brown hair, the sun making the copper glints more pronounced, and she appeared to consider. 'You realise not a single ancestor is showing coloured hair. They wore hats or wigs or waited until they'd turned a nice, dignified white.'

'So if I'm attached to my hair I'm doomed to peasantry.'

'I guess.'

'Then peasantry it is,' he said and he smiled and reached out and touched her copper curls. 'I don't mind. I kind of like the company.'

And then silence fell. It was a strange kind of silence, Jo thought. A different silence. As if questions were being asked and answered, and thought about and then asked again.

The last wisps of leftover smoke were wafting upwards into the warm spring sunshine. The castle loomed behind them, vast and brooding, as if a reminder that something immeasurable was connecting them. A shared legacy.

A bond.

This man was her sort-of cousin, Jo thought, but the idea was a vague distraction, unreal. This man was not her family. He was large and male and beautiful. Yet he felt...

He felt unlike any of the guys she'd ever dated. He felt familiar in a sense that didn't make sense.

He felt...terrifying. Jo Conaill was always in control. She'd never gone out with someone who'd shaken that control, but just standing beside him...

'It feels right,' Finn said and she gazed up at him in bewilderment.

'What feels right?'

'I have no idea. To stand here with you?'

'I'm leaving.'

'So am I. We have lives. It's just...for here, for now... it feels okay.' He paused but there was no need for him to continue. She felt it too. This sense of...home.

What was she thinking? Home wasn't here. Home wasn't this man.

'My home's my bike,' she said, out of nowhere, and she said it too sharply, but he nodded as if she'd said something that needed consideration.

'I can see that, though the bike's pretty draughty. And there's no bath for when you fall into bogs.'

'I don't normally fall into bogs.'

'I can see that too. You're very, very careful, despite that bad girl image.'

'I don't have a bad girl image.'

'Leathers and piercings?' He smiled down at her, a smile that robbed his words of all possible offence. And then he lifted her arm to reveal a bracelet tattoo, a ring of tiny rosebuds around her wrist. 'And tattoos. My nieces and nephews will think you're cool.'

'Your nieces and nephews won't get to see it.'

'You don't want to meet them?'

'Why would I want to?'

'They're family, too.'

'Not my family.'

'It seems to me,' he said softly, 'that family's where you find it. And it also seems that somehow you've found it. Your hair gives you away.'

'If we're talking about my red hair then half of Ireland has it.'

'It's a very specific red,' he told her. 'My daddy had your hair and I know if I've washed mine nicely you can see the glint of his colour in mine.' And he lifted a finger and twisted one of her short curls. His smile deepened, an all-enveloping smile that was enough to make a woman sink into it. 'Family,' he said softly. 'Welcome to it, Jo Conaill. You and your teddy.'

'I don't want…'

'Family? Are you sure?'

'Y…yes.'

'That's a big declaration. And a lonely one.' He turned so he was facing her, then tilted her chin a little so her gaze was meeting his. 'I might have been raised in poverty, but it seems to me that you've been raised with the more desperate need. Does no one love you, Jo Conaill?'

'No. I mean…' Why was he looking at her? Why was he smiling? It was twisting something inside her, and it was something she'd guarded for a very long time. Something she didn't want twisting.

'I won't hurt you, Jo,' he said into the stillness and his words made whatever it was twist still more. 'I promise you that. I would never hurt you. I'm just saying…'

And then he stopped…saying.

Finn Conaill had been trying to work it out in his head. Ever since he'd met her something was tugging him to her. Connecting.

It must be the family connection, he'd thought. Or it must be her past.

She looked stubborn, indecisive, defiant.

She looked afraid.

She'd taken a step back from him and she was staring down at the bear in her arms as if it was a bomb about to detonate.

She didn't want family. She didn't want home.

And yet…

She wanted the teddy. He knew she did.

By now he had some insight into what her childhood must have been. A kid alone, passed from foster family to foster family. Moved on whenever the ties grew so strong someone wanted her.

Learning that love meant separation. Grief.

Learning that family wasn't for her.

A cluster of wild pigeons was fussing on the cobblestones near the stables. Their soft cooing was a soothing background, a reassurance that all was well on this peaceful morning. And yet all wasn't well with this woman before him. He watched her stare down at the teddy with something akin to despair.

She wanted the teddy. She wanted…more.

Only she couldn't want. Wanting had been battered out of her.

She was so alone.

Family… The word slammed into his mind and stayed. He'd been loyal to Maeve for so many years he couldn't remember and he'd thought that loyalty was inviolate. But he'd known Jo for only three days, and somehow she was slipping into his heart. He was starting to care.

'Jo…' he said into the silence and she stared up at him with eyes that were hopelessly confused, hopelessly lost.

'Jo,' he said again.

And what happened next seemed to happen of its own volition. It was no conscious movement on his part, or hers.

It was nothing to do with them and yet it was everything.

He took the teddy from her grasp and placed it carefully on the ground.

He took her hands in his. He drew her forward—and he kissed her.

Had he meant to?

He didn't have a clue. This was unchartered territory.

For this wasn't a kiss of passion. It wasn't a kiss he'd ever experienced before. In truth, in its beginning it hardly felt like a kiss.

He tilted her chin very gently, with the image of a wild creature strongly with him. She could pull away, and he half expected her to. But she stayed passive, staring mutely up at him before his mouth met hers. Her chin tilted with the pressure of his fingers and she gazed into his eyes with an expression he couldn't begin to understand. There was a sort of resigned indifference, an expression which should have had him stepping back, but behind the indifference he saw a flare of frightened...hope?

He didn't want her indifferent, and it would be worse to frighten her. But the hope was there, and she was beautiful and her mouth was lush and partly open. And her eyes invited him in...

It was the gentlest of kisses, a soft, tentative exploration, a kiss that understood there were boundaries and he wasn't sure where they were but he wasn't about to broach them.

His kiss said *Trust me.* His kiss matched that flare of hope he was sure he'd seen. His kiss said, *You're beautiful and I don't understand it but something inside is drawing me to you.* And it said, *This kiss is just the beginning.*

Her first reaction was almost hysterical. Her roller coaster of emotions had her feeling this was happening to someone other than her.

But it was her. She was letting the Lord of Glenconaill kiss her.

Was she out of her mind?

No. Of course she wasn't. This was just a kiss, after all, and she was no prude. She was twenty-eight years old and there'd been men before. Of course there had. Nothing serious—she didn't do serious—but she certainly had fun. And this man was lovely. Gorgeous even. She could take him right now, she thought. She could tug him to her bed, or maybe they should use his bed because hers was ridiculously small. And then she could tear off his gear and see his naked body, which she was sure would be excellent, and she was sure the sex would be great...

Instead of which, her lips were barely touching his and her body was responding with a fear that said, *Go no fur-*

ther. Go no further because one thing she valued above all others was control, and if she let this man hold her…

Except he was holding her. His kiss was warm and strong and true.

True? What sort of description was that for a kiss?

But then, in an instant, she was no longer thinking of descriptions. She wasn't thinking of anything at all. The kiss was taking over. The kiss was taking her to places she'd never been before. The kiss was…mind-blowing.

It was as if there'd been some sort of shorting to her brain. Every single nerve ending was snapped to attention, discarding whatever it was they'd been concentrating on and rerouting to her mouth. To his mouth. To the fusing of their bodies.

To the heat of him, to the strength, to the feeling of solid, fierce desire. For this was no cousinly kiss. This wasn't even a standard kiss between man and woman or if it was it wasn't something Jo had ever experienced before.

She was losing her mind. No, she'd lost it. She was lost in his kiss, melting, moulding against him, opening her lips, savouring the heat, the taste, the want—and she wanted more.

Her body was screaming for more. That was what all those nerve endings were doing—they'd forgotten their no doubt normally sensible functions and they were screaming, *This is where you're meant to be. Have. Hold.*

This is your…your…

No.

Whatever it was, whatever her body had been about to yell, she was suddenly closing down in fright. She was tugging away, pushing, shoving back. He released her the instant she pushed. She stood in the silent courtyard and stared at him as if he had two heads.

He didn't have two heads. He was just a guy. Just a stranger who happened to be vaguely related.

He was just the guy who'd saved her teddy.

She stared down at the bear at her feet, gasped and stooped to grab it. But Finn was before her, stooping to pick it up before she did. Their gaze met on the way up, and he handed over the bear with all solemnity.

'Was that why we stopped?' he asked. 'Because you'd dropped your bear?'

'Don't…don't be ridiculous.'

'Then don't look scared. Sweetheart, it was just a kiss.'

'I'm not your sweetheart.'

'No.'

'And I couldn't care less about the teddy.' But she did, she realised.

Why?

Because Finn had offered to burn it for her?

Because Finn had saved it?

The stupid twisting inside her was still going on and she didn't understand it. She didn't want it. It felt as if she was exposing something that hurt.

'We can give these things to charity,' she managed. 'That'd be more sensible than burning.'

'Much more sensible,' he agreed. Then he picked up the giraffe. 'I'll still be keeping this lad, though. No one would be wanting a stuffed giraffe with a wobbly neck.'

'I'll mend him for you.'

'That would be a kindness. But he's still not going to charity. How about Loppy?'

'I guess… I'm keeping him as well.' She was still wary, still unsure what had just happened. Still scared it might happen again.

'Then here's a suggestion,' he said, and the cheerful ordinariness was back in his voice, as if the kiss had never happened. 'There's a trailer in the stables. I'll hook it up and cart these guys—with the exception of Loppy and Noddy—into the village before the night dew falls. That'll stop us needing to cart them upstairs again. Meanwhile, you do some mending or take a walk or just wander the parapets and practice being Lady of the Castle. Whatever you want. Take some space to get to know Loppy.'

'I…thank you.' It was what she needed, she conceded. Space.

'Take all the time you need,' Finn said and then his smile faded and the look he gave her was questioning and serious. 'We're here until the documents can be signed. We do need to figure if there's anything in this pile to keep. But Jo…'

'Y… Yes?'

'Never, ever look at me again as if you're afraid of me,' he told her. 'We can organise things another way. I can stay in the village, or you can if that makes you feel safer. Whatever you like. But I won't touch you and I won't have you scared of me.'

'I'm not.'

'Yes, you are,' he said gently. 'And it needs to stop now.'

It took a couple of hours to link the trailer, pack the toys and cart them into the village. In truth, it was wasted time—there was so much in the castle to be sorted and dispersed that taking one load to the local charity shop was a speck in the ocean.

But he knew Jo needed him to leave. He'd kissed her, he'd felt her respond, he'd felt the heat and the desire—and then he'd felt the terror.

He wasn't a man to push where he wasn't wanted. He wasn't a man who'd ever want a woman to fear him.

And then there was the complication of Maeve and her father's expectations. He was well over it. The whole thing made him feel tired, but Maeve had left loose ends that needed to be sorted and they needed to be sorted now.

He was almost back at the castle but somehow he didn't

want to be taking the complication of Maeve back there. He pulled to the side of the road and rang.

'Finn.' Maeve's voice was flat, listless. Normally he'd be sympathetic, gently pushing her to tell him what was happening but today things felt more urgent.

'Have you told him?'

'I can't. I told you I can't. That's why I came to see you. Finn, he'll be so upset. He's wanted us to marry for so long. He's already had a heart attack. It'll kill him.'

'That's a risk you have to take. Keeping the truth from your father any longer is dumb.'

'Then come and tell him with me. You can placate him. He's always thought of you as his son.'

'But I'm not his son,' he said gently. 'Maeve, face it.'

'Give me another week. Just a few more days.'

'By the time I come home, Maeve.' His voice was implacable. 'It has to be over.'

There was a moment's pause. Then... 'Why? You've met someone else?' And, astonishingly, she sounded indignant.

And that was what he got for loyalty, he thought grimly. An ex-fiancée who still assumed he was hers.

'It's none of your business, Maeve,' he told her and somehow forced his voice back to gentleness. 'Whatever I do, it's nothing to do with you.'

He disconnected but he stayed sitting on the roadside for a long time.

Loyalty...

It sat deep with him. Bone-deep. It was the reason he couldn't have walked away from his mam and brothers when his dad died. It would have been far easier to get a job in Dublin, fending for himself instead of fighting to eke out an existence for all of them. But the farm was his home and he'd fought to make it what it was, supporting his family until the need was no longer there. And by then the farm felt a part of him.

And Maeve? Maeve was in the mix too. She'd been an only child, his next door neighbour, his friend. Her father dreamed of joining the two farms together, and Finn's loyalty to that dream had always been assumed.

Maeve had smashed that assumption. He should be sad, he thought, but he wasn't. Just tired. Tired of loyalty?

No.

He could see the castle in the distance, solid, vast, a piece of his heritage. A piece of his country's heritage. Could old loyalties change? Shift?

His world seemed out of kilter. He wasn't sure how to right it but somehow it seemed to have a new centre.

A woman called Jo?

It was too soon, he told himself. It was far too soon, but for now…for now it was time to return to the castle.

Time to go…to a new home?

CHAPTER SIX

Jo SEEMED TO spend the next three days avoiding him as much as she could. The tension between them was almost a physical thing. The air seemed to bristle as they passed, so they spent their time doing what their separate skills required, separately.

Finn took inventory of the farm, working his way through the flocks of sheep, looking at what needed to be done before any sale took place. Inside the castle, the personal stuff was deemed to be Jo's, to do with what she wanted. She, after all, was the granddaughter of the house, Finn said firmly. She wanted none of it—apart from one battered bear—but things needed to be sorted.

She had three categories.

The first contained documents that might be important and photographs she decided to scan and file electronically in case someone in the future—not her—needed to reference them.

The second was a list of the things that seemed to go with the castle—the massive furnishings, the tapestries, the portraits.

The third contained items to be sold or given to museums. That included the storeroom full of ancient clothes. At some point in the far distant past, one of their ancestors had decided the amazing clothes worn on ceremonial occasions by generations of Conaills were worth preserving. A storeroom had been made dry and mothproof. The clothes smelled musty and were faded with age but they were still amazing.

'A museum would kill for them,' Jo told Finn.

He'd come in to find her before dinner. She was on the storeroom floor with a great golden ballgown splayed over her knees. The white underskirt was yellowed with age, but the mass of gold embroidery worked from neckline to hem made it a dazzle of colour.

'Try it on,' Finn suggested and Jo cast him a look that was almost scared. That was what he did to her, he thought ruefully. One kiss and he had her terrified.

'I might damage it.'

'I will if you will,' he told her. He walked across to a cape that would have done Lord Byron proud. 'Look at this. Are these things neckcloths? How do you tie them? I'd have to hit the Internet. I'm not sure of the boots, though— our ancestors' feet seems to have been stunted. But if I can find something… Come on, Jo. We're eating dinner in that great, grand dining room. Next week we'll be back to being Finn the Farmer and Jo the Barista. For tonight let's be Lord and Lady Conaill of Castle Glenconaill. Just for once. Just because we can.'

Just because we can. The words echoed. She looked up at him and he could see the longing. Tattoos and piercings aside, there was a girl inside this woman who truly wanted to try on this dress.

'Dare you,' he said and she managed a smile.

'Only if you wear tights.'

'Tights?'

'Leggings. Breeches. Those.' She pointed to a pair of impossibly tight pants.

'Are you kidding? I'll sing falsetto for ever.'

'Dare you,' she said and suddenly she was grinning and so was he and the thing was done.

* * *

He was wearing a magnificent powder-blue coat with gilt embroidery, open to just above his knees. He'd somehow tied an intricate cravat, folds of soft white linen in some sort of cascade effect that was almost breathtaking. He looked straight out of the pages of the romance novel she'd read on the plane. His dark hair was neat, slicked, beautiful. And he was wearing breeches.

Or pantaloons? What were they called? It didn't matter. They clung to his calves and made him look breathtakingly debonair. He looked so sexy a girl's toes could curl.

She forced herself to look past the sexy legs, down to his shoes. They looked like slippers, stretched but just on. More gilt embroidery.

More beauty.

'If you're thinking my toes look squashed you should feel everything else,' he growled, following her gaze. 'How our ancestors ever fathered children is beyond me. But Jo...' He was staring at her in incredulity. 'You look... beautiful.'

Why that had the power to make her eyes mist she had no idea. He was talking about the clothes, she told herself. Not her.

'You're beautiful already,' he told her, making a lie of her thoughts. 'But that dress...'

She was wearing the dress he'd seen on her knee and why wouldn't she? This was a Cinderella dress, pure fantasy, a dress some long ago Conaill maiden had worn to a ball and driven suitors crazy. She'd have to have had warts all over her not to drive suitors crazy, Jo thought. This dress was a work of art, every inch embellished, golden and wondrous. It was almost more wondrous because of the air of age and fragility about it.

But it fitted her like a glove. She'd tugged it on and it had slipped on her like a second skin. The boned bodice pushed her breasts up, cupping them so their swell was accentuated. She'd powdered her curls. She'd found a tiara in her grandfather's safe, and a necklace that surely wasn't diamonds but probably was. There were earrings to match.

She, too, was wearing embroidered dancing slippers. She needed a ball, she thought, and then she thought, no, she had enough. She had her beautiful gown.

She had her Prince Charming.

And oh, those breeches…

'Our ancestors would be proud of us,' Finn told her and offered his arm, as befitted the Lord of the Castle offering his arm to his Lady as they approached the staircase to descend to the dining hall.

She hesitated only for a moment. This was a play, she told herself. It wasn't real.

This was a moment she could never forget. She needed to relax and soak it in.

She took his arm.

'Our ancestors couldn't possibly not be proud of us,' she told him as they stepped gingerly down the stairs in their too-tight footwear. But it wasn't her slippers making her feel unsafe, she thought. It was Finn. He was so big. He was so close.

He was so gorgeous.

'Which reminds me…' He sounded prosaic, but she suspected it was an effort to make himself sound prosaic. She surely couldn't. 'What are we going to do with our ancestors?'

'What do you mean?'

'All the guys who wore these clothes. All the pictures in the gallery.'

'I guess…they'll sell with the castle. They can be someone else's ancestors.'

'Like in Gilbert and Sullivan? Do you know *The Pirates of Penzance*?' He twirled an imaginary moustache

and lowered his voice to that of a raspy English aristocrat. 'Major General Stanley, at your service,' he said,
striding ahead down the staircase and turning to face up
to her. Prince Charming transformed yet again. 'So, My
Lady,' he growled up at her. 'In this castle are ancestors,
but we're about to sell the castle and its contents. So we
don't know whose ancestors they will be. Mind, I shudder
to think that an unknown buyer could bring disgrace upon
what, I have no doubt, is an unstained escutcheon. Our escutcheon. We'll have to be very careful who we sell it to.'

'Escutcheon?' she said faintly and he grinned.

'Our unblemished pedigree, marred only by you not appearing to have a daddy, and me being raised surrounded
by pigs. But look at us now.' He waved down at the grand
entrance and the two astonishing suits of armour. 'Grand
as anything. Forget Major General Stanley. I'm dressed
as Lord Byron but I believe I aspire to the Pirate King.
All I need is some rigging to scale and some minions to
clap in irons.'

'I vote not to be a minion.'

'You can be my pirate wench if you like,' he said kindly.
'To scrub decks and the like.'

'In this dress?'

He grinned. 'You could pop into a bucket and then
swish across the decks with your wet dress. The decks
would come up shiny as anything.' And then he paused
and smiled at her, a smile that encompassed all of her. Her
beautiful dress with its neckline that was a bit too low and
accentuated her breasts. Her powdered curls. Her diamond
necklace and earrings and tiara.

But somehow his smile said he saw deeper. His smile
made her blush before he said anything more.

'Though I'd have better things to do with my wench
than have her scrubbing decks,' he said—and he leered.

How could she blush when there was a bubble of laughter inside? And how could she blush when he was as beautiful as she was?

And suddenly she wanted to play this whole game out to its natural conclusion. She wanted to play Lady to his Lord. She wanted Finn to sweep her up in her beautiful ballgown and carry her upstairs and…

And nothing! She had to be sensible. So somehow she lifted her skirts, brushed past him and hiked down the remaining stairs and across the hall. She removed her tiara and put it safely aside, lifted the helmet from one of the suits of armour and put it on her head. Then she grabbed a sword and pointed it.

'Want to try?' she demanded. 'This wench knows how to defend herself. Come one step closer…'

'Not fair. I don't have my cutlass.' He glanced ruefully at his side. 'I think there's a ceremonial sword to go with this but I left it off.'

'Excellent.' Her voice was sounding a bit muffled.

'Jo?'

'Yep.'

'Can you see in that thing?'

'Nope.'

'So if I were to come closer…'

'I might whirl and chop. Or…'

'Or?'

Or…uh oh… She bent—with difficulty—boned bodices weren't all that comfortable—and laid the sword carefully on the floor. She raised her hands to the helmet. 'Or you might help me off with this,' she said, a bit shakily. 'It sort of just slid on. Now…it seems to be heavy.'

'A Lady of the Castle pretending to be a pirate wench, in a suit of armour?' He stood back and chuckled. 'I think I like it.'

What was she doing, asking this man for help? What a wuss! She bent to retrieve her sword, an action only marred by having to grope around her swirling skirts. With it once more in her hand, she pointed it in what she hoped was his general direction. 'Help me or the giraffe gets it,' she muttered.

'Noddy?' he demanded, astounded. 'What's Noddy done to you?'

'Nothing, but we knights don't skewer lords. We hold them to ransom and skewer their minions instead.'

'So how will you find my...minion? Noddy's up in my bedroom.' He was smiling at her. It was a bit hard to see through the visor but she knew he was smiling.

'With difficulty,' she conceded. 'But I stand on my principles.' She tried again to tug her helmet off and wobbled in her tight slippers but she held onto her defiance. 'If you're the pirate king, I insist on equal status.'

'We can go back to being Lord and Lady of our real life castle.'

'I guess.' She sighed. Enough. She had to confess. 'Finn, this may look like a bike helmet but it seems the helmet manufacturers of days of yore had a lot to learn. Help me get this off!'

He chuckled. 'Only if you guarantee that Noddy's safe.'

'Noddy's safe.'

'And no ransom?'

'Not if I don't have to play wench.'

'Are you in a position to negotiate?'

'I believe,' she said, 'that I still have a sword and I stand between you and your dinner.'

'That's playing mean.'

'Help me off with the helmet or we'll both starve,' she said and he chuckled again and came forward and took the sword from her hands and gently raised her helmet.

She emerged, flushed and flustered, and it didn't help that he was only inches away from her face and he was smiling down at her. And he did look like the Lord of His

Castle. And her skirts were rustling around her and his dangerous eyes were laughing, and how they did that she didn't know but it was really unfair. And the look of him… The feel of his coat… The brush of his fingers…

The odds were so stacked in this man's favour.

He was Lord to her Lady.

Only, of course, he wasn't. He wasn't hers. He wasn't anyone's and she didn't want anyone anyway. In less than a week this fantasy would be over. She'd be on the road again, heading back to Australia, and she'd never see him again and that was what she wanted, wasn't it?

Goodbyes. She was really good at them.

Goodbyes were all she knew.

'Jo?'

She must have been looking up at him for too long. The laughter had faded, replaced by a troubled look.

'I…thank you.' She snatched the helmet from his hands and jammed it back on its matching body armour. Which should have meant she had her back to him, but he took the sword and came to stand beside her, putting the sword carefully back into a chain-meshed hand.

He was too close. She was too flustered. He was too…

'Dinner! And don't you both look beautiful!' Mrs O'Reilly's voice was like a boom behind them. How long had she been standing there? Had Finn known she was standing there? Okay, now it was time for her colour to rise. She felt like grabbing the sword again and…

'Knives and forks at noon?' Finn said and the laughter was back in his voice. He took her hand and swung her to face the housekeeper, for all the world like a naughty child holding his accomplice fast for support. 'Are we late, Mrs O'Reilly?'

'I'll have you know those clothes haven't been touched for hundreds of years. And, as for that armour, it's never been moved.'

'See,' Finn told Jo mournfully. 'I told you we're more interested in finance than war. Ours is not a noble heritage.'

'Just as well we're selling it then.'

'Indeed,' he said but his voice didn't quite sound right. She flashed him a questioning glance but he had himself together again fast. 'We're sorry, Mrs O'Reilly. It's to be hoped nothing's come to any grief.'

'It does suit you both,' the housekeeper admitted. 'Eh, you look lovely. And it's yours to do with what you want.'

'Just for a week,' Finn told her. 'Then it's every ancestor for himself. Off to the highest bidder. Meanwhile, Lady of the Castle Glenconaill, let's forget about war. Let's eat.'

'Yes, My Lord,' she said meekly, but things had changed again and she didn't know how.

After that they went back to their individual sorting but somehow the ridiculous banter and the formal dinner in the beautiful clothes had changed things. A night dressed up as Lord and Lady had made things seem different. Lighter? Yes, but also somehow full of possibilities. Finn didn't understand how but that was the way his head was working.

Through the next couple of days they reverted to practicalities. Jo still worked inside. He drafted the sheep into age and sex, trying to assess what he had. He brought the two cows up to the home field. One was heavy with calf and looked badly malnourished.

'They're not ours,' Mrs O'Reilly told him when he questioned her at breakfast. 'They were out on the road a couple of weeks back and a passing motorist herded them through the gate. Then he came here and harangued us for letting stock roam. I let them stay. I didn't know what else to do.'

'You've been making all the decisions since my grandfather became ill?' Jo demanded.

'I have.'

'Then I think we need to increase Mrs O'Reilly's share of the estate,' she declared.

'There's no need to do that,' the housekeeper said, embarrassed. 'There's nothing else I need.' She paused mid-clearing and looked around the massive dining room with fondness. Finn's suggestion that they eat in the kitchen had been met with horror so they'd decided for a week they could handle the splendour. 'Though I would like more time here. Do you think a new owner might hire me?'

'In a heartbeat,' Jo said soundly and the woman chuckled.

'Get on with you. But, if it happens, it'd be lovely.' She heaved a sigh and left and Finn turned impulsively to Jo.

'Come with me this morning.'

'What? Why?'

'Because I want you to?' There was little time left, he thought. Tomorrow the lawyer was due to return. They could sign the papers, and Jo could leave. He'd need to sort someone to take care of the livestock but Jo didn't need to stay for that. So the day after tomorrow—or even tomorrow night—Jo could be on her way back to Australia.

'I've found a bouncy bog,' he told her.

'A bouncy bog…?'

'Our south boundary borders the start of bog country. I checked it out yesterday. There's a patch that quakes like a champion.'

'You mean it sucks things down like it nearly sucked me?'

'I jumped,' he told her. 'And I lived to tell the tale. And Jo, I did it for you. The Lady of Castle Glenconaill would like this bog, I told myself, so here I am, my Lady, presenting an option. Sorting more paperwork or bog jumping.'

'There is…'

'More paperwork,' he finished for her. 'Indeed there is. I looked at what you've done last night and I'm thinking you've done a grand job. But surely the important stuff's sorted and maybe you could grant yourself one morning's holiday. No?'

She should say no.

Why?

Because she didn't trust him?

But she did trust him and that was the whole problem, she decided. He was so darned trustworthy. And his smile was so lovely. And he was so…

Tempting.

Go and jump on a bog with Finn Conaill?

Go with Finn Conaill?

This guy might look like a farmer but she had to keep reminding herself who he was.

He was Lord Conaill of Castle Glenconaill.

And worse. He'd become…her friend?

And he'd kissed her and maybe that was the crux of the problem. He'd kissed her very thoroughly indeed and, even though he'd drawn away when she wanted and there'd been no mention of the kiss ever since, it was still between them. It sort of hovered…

And he'd worn breeches. And he'd looked every inch the Lord of Glenconaill.

And she was going home tomorrow! Or the next day if the lawyer was late. What harm could a little bog jumping do?

With a friend.

With Finn.

There was no harm at all, she told herself, so why were alarm bells going off right, left and centre?

'I don't think…' she started and he grinned.

'Chicken.'

'I'd rather be a chicken than a dead hen.'

'Do they say that in Australian schoolyards as well?' He was still smiling. Teasing.

'For good reason.'

'Bogs don't swallow chickens. Or not unless they're very fat. I'll hold you up, Jo Conaill. Trust me.'

And what was it that said a man who looked totally trustworthy—who *felt* totally trustworthy, for her body was still remembering how solid, how warm, *how much a woman*, this man made her feel—what was it that made her fear such a man assuring her he could be trusted?

What made her think she should run?

But he was still smiling at her, and his smile was no longer teasing but gentle and questioning, and it was as if he understood how fearful she was.

It was stupid not to go with him, she thought. She had one day left. What harm could a day make?

'All right,' she said ungraciously, and the laughter flashed back.

'What, no curtsy and "Thank You, Your Lordship, your kind invitation is accepted"?'

'Go jump,' she said crossly and he held out his hand.

'I will,' he said. 'Both of us will. Come and jump with me.'

For the last couple of days the amount of sorting had meant every time they came together there was so much to discuss there was little time for the personal. But now suddenly there wasn't. Or maybe there was but suddenly it didn't seem important.

Jo was no longer sure what was important.

She'd never felt so at ease with anyone, she thought as they walked together over fields that grew increasingly rough the nearer they were to the estate boundaries. But right now that very ease was creating a tension all by itself.

She didn't understand it and it scared her.

She needed to watch her feet now. This was peat country and the ground was criss-crossed with scores of furrows where long lines of peat had been dug. That was what she needed to do before she went home, she thought. Light a peat fire. Tonight? Her last night?

The thought was enough to distract her. She slipped and Finn's hand was suddenly under her elbow, holding her steady.

She should pull away.

She didn't.

And then they were at a line of rough stone fencing. Finn stepped to the top stone and turned to help her.

As if she'd let him. She didn't need him.

She stepped up and he should have got out of the way, gone over the top, but instead he waited for her to join him.

There was only a tiny section of flat stone. She had no choice but to join him.

His arm came round and held her, whether she willed it or not, and he turned her to face the way they'd come.

'Look at the view from here.'

She did and it was awesome. The castle was built on a rise of undulating country, a vast monolith of stone. It seemed almost an extension of the country around it, rough hewn, rugged, truly impressive.

'For now, it's ours,' Finn said softly and Jo looked over the countryside, at the castle she'd heard about since childhood and never seen, and she felt…

Wrong.

Wrong that she should be signing a paper that said sell it to the highest bidder.

Wrong that she should be leaving.

But then she always left, she thought. Of course she did. What was new?

She tugged away from Finn, suddenly inexplicably angry. He let her go, but gently so she didn't wrench back but had time to find the footholds to descend to the other side.

To where the bog started.

'Beware,' Finn told her as she headed away from the wall, and she looked around her and thought, *Beware is right.*

It was the same sort of country she'd been caught in when Finn first found her. This wall wasn't just a property boundary then. It was the start of where the country turned treacherous.

For here were the lowlands. The grasses were brilliant green, dotted with tiny wildflowers. There were rivulets of clear water, like rivers in miniature. The ground swept away to the mountains beyond, interrupted only by the occasional wash of sleet-coloured water.

There were no birds. There seemed no life at all.

'I've been out on it,' Finn told her. 'It's safe. Come on; this is fun.'

And he took her hand.

Her first impulse was to tug away. Of course it was. Since when did she let anyone lead her anywhere? But this was Finn. This was Ireland. This was...right?

'I'm not hauling you anywhere you don't want to go,' Finn told her. 'This is pure pleasure.'

So somehow she relaxed, or sort of relaxed, as he led her across the stone-strewn ground to where the ground ceased being solid and the bog began. But his steps were sure. All she had to do was step where he stepped. And leave her hand in his.

Small ask.

'It doesn't hurt,' he said softly into the stillness.

'What doesn't hurt?'

'Trusting.'

She didn't reply. She couldn't. Her hand was in his, enveloped in his strength and surety.

Trust...

'That first day when I picked you up,' he said softly. 'I

pretty near gave you a heart attack. I pretty near gave *me* a heart attack. You want to tell me what that was about?'

'No.'

'Okay,' he said lightly and led her a bit further. She was concentrating on her feet. Or she should be concentrating on her feet.

She was pretty much aware of his hand.

She was still pretty much aware of his question.

'I couldn't handle it,' she told him. 'I had a temper.'

'I guessed that,' he said and smiled. But he wasn't looking at her. He was concentrating on the ground, making sure each step he took was steady, and small enough so she could follow in his footsteps. It was the strangest sensation… 'So what couldn't you handle?'

'Leaving.'

'Mmm.' The silence intensified. There were frogs, she thought. There'd been frogs in the last bit of bog but there were more here. So it wasn't silent.

Except it was.

'Will you tell me?' he asked conversationally, as if it didn't matter whether she did or not, and then he went back to leading her across the bog.

If he left her now, she thought… If he abandoned her out here…

He wouldn't. But, even if he did, it wasn't a drama. He was stepping from stone to stone and she understood it now. If he left she wouldn't be in trouble.

She could leave. She could just turn around and go.

Will you tell me?

'I got attached,' she said softly, as if she didn't want to disturb the frogs, which, come to think of it, she didn't. 'Everywhere I went. I think…because my mother was overseas, because she didn't want anything to do with me, because no one knew who my father was, it was assumed I'd eventually be up for adoption. So I was put with people who were encouraged to love me. To form ties. And of course I grew ties back.'

'That sucks.'

'It was only bad when it was time to leave.'

'But when it was…'

'It was always after a full-on emotional commitment,' she told him. 'I'd stay for a couple of years and we'd get close. My foster parents would apply for adoption, there'd be ages before an answer came but when it did it was always the same. My mother didn't want me adopted. She'd say she was currently negotiating taking me herself so she'd like me transferred close to Sydney, Melbourne, Brisbane—always the city that was furthest from my foster parents. She said it was so she could fly in quickly from Ireland to pick me up. I got stoic in the end but I remember when I was little, being picked up and carried to the car, and everyone I loved was behind me and my foster mum was crying… I'm sorry, but the day you first saw me I'd been stuck in the bog for an hour and I was tired and jet-lagged and frightened and you copped a flashback of epic proportions. I'm ashamed of myself.'

Silence.

He felt his free hand ball into a fist. Anger surged, an anger so great it threatened to overwhelm him.

'Let's revisit our bonfire idea,' he said. 'I'd kind of like to burn the whole castle.' He was struggling to make his voice light.

'We've been there. I couldn't even burn the horse.'

'Mrs O'Reilly said it made three hundred and fifty pounds for the local charity shop,' he told her. 'For kids with cancer.'

'As long as the kids with cancer don't have to look into its sneering face.'

'But that's what you're doing,' he said gently. 'Coming back to Ireland. You're looking at a nursery full of toys owned by kids who were wanted. You're looking into its sneering face.'

'I don't want to burn it, though,' she said. She turned and gazed back across the boundary, back to the distant castle. 'It's people who are cruel, not things. And things can be beautiful. This is beautiful and the people are gone.'

'And so's the horse,' he said encouragingly. 'And we can go put thistles on Fiona's grave if you want.'

'That'd be childish. I'm over her.'

'Really?'

'As long as you don't pick me up.'

'I won't pick you up. But, speaking of childish... You don't want childish?'

'I...'

'Because what I've found here is really, really childish.' He took her hand again and led her a little way further to the base of a small rise. The grassland here looked lush and rich, beautifully green, an untouched swathe.

'Try,' he said, and let go her hand and gave her a gentle push. 'Jump.'

'What—me? Are you kidding? I'll be down to my waist again.'

'You won't. I've tried it.'

She stared at it in suspicion. 'The grass isn't squashed.'

'And there's no great holes where I sank. There's a whole ribbon of this, land that quakes beautifully but doesn't give. Trust me, Jo. Jump.'

Trust him. A man who wore leggings and intricate neck-ties and looked so sexy a girl could swoon. The Lord of Glenconaill Castle.

A man in work trousers and rolled-up sleeves.

A man who smiled at her.

She stared back at him, and then looked at the grassy verge. It looked beautiful.

The sun was shining on her face. The sound of a thousand frogs was a gentle choir across the bog.

Trust me.

She took a tentative step forward and put her weight on the grass.

The ground under her sagged and she leaped back. 'I don't think…'

'You're not sinking into mud. This is a much thicker thatch of grass than where you got stuck. I've tried it out. Look.' And he jumped.

The ground sagged and rose again. Jo was standing two or three feet away from him. The grasses quivered all the way across to her and she rode a mini wave.

She squealed in surprise, then stared down in astonishment. 'Really?'

He jumped again, grinning. 'I found it just for you. Try it.'

She jumped, just a little.

'Higher.'

'It'll…'

'It won't do anything. I told you before; I've tried it. I was here yesterday, scouting a good bit of bog to show you.'

'You did that…for me?'

'I can't have you going back to Australia thinking all Irish bogs are out to eat Australians.' He reached out and caught her hands. 'Bounce.'

'I…'

'Trust me. Bounce.'

Trust him. She looked up at him and he was smiling, and he was holding her hands and the warmth of him… the strength of him…

He wouldn't let her down. How did she know it? She just knew it.

'Bounce,' he said again, encouragingly, and she met

his gaze and his smile said *Smile back* and somehow she felt herself relax.

She bounced and the lovely squishy grasses bounced with her and, to her amazement, she felt Finn do a smaller bounce as the quaking ground moved under him as well.

'It's like a water bed,' she breathed.

'I've never tried a water bed,' Finn admitted. 'I always thought they'd be weird.'

'But fun.'

'You've slept in one?'

'One of my foster mums had one. She had three foster kids and we all bounced. She was out one day and we bounced too much and she came home to floods. She wasn't best pleased.'

'I'd imagine,' Finn said, chuckling, and jumping himself so Jo bounced with him. 'Gruel and stale bread for a week?'

'Mops at twenty paces.' She bounced again, starting to enjoy herself. 'Foster parents are awesome.'

'Until you have to leave.'

'Let's not go there.' She bounced again, really high. The ground sagged but bounced back, so she and Finn were rocking with each other. The sun was on their faces. A couple of dozy sheep were staring over the stone wall with vague astonishment. A bird—a kestrel?—was cruising high in the thermals above them, maybe frog-hunting?

'I hope we're not squashing frogs,' she worried out loud and he grinned.

'Any self-respecting frog will be long gone. That was some squeal.'

'I don't squeal.'

'You did.'

'I might have,' she conceded, jumping again just because she could, just because it felt good, just because this man was holding her hands and for now it felt right. She felt right. She felt…as if this was her place. As if she had every right in the world to be here. As if this was her home? 'I had…provocation,' she managed. She was trying to haul her thoughts back to whether or not she'd squealed, but her thoughts were heading off on a tangent all of their own.

A tangent that was all about how this man was holding her and how good it felt and how wonderful that when she jumped he jumped, and when he jumped she jumped. And suddenly it had nothing to do with the bog they were jumping on but everything to do with how wonderful it was. With how wonderful *he* was.

'I should warn you, you're seeing the bog at its best,' Finn told her. 'Tomorrow it'll be raining. In fact this afternoon it may be raining. Or in half an hour. This is Ireland, after all.'

'I like Ireland.'

'You've seen approximately nought point one per cent of Ireland.'

'Then I like nought point one per cent. I like this part.'

'Me, too,' he said and jumped again and suddenly they were grinning at each other like idiots and jumping in sync and the world felt amazing. The world felt right.

'You want to explore a bit further?' he asked and her hands were in his and suddenly she thought no matter where he wanted to take her she'd follow. Which was a stupid thought. She didn't do trust. She didn't…love?

There was a blinding thought, a thought so out of left field that she tugged her hands back and stared at him in confusion. She'd known this guy for just over a week. You couldn't make decisions like that in a week.

Could you?

'What's wrong?' he asked gently and she stared at him and somehow the confusion settled.

He wasn't asking her to love him. He was asking her to explore the landscape.

With him.

'You know I won't let you sink,' he told her and she looked up at him and made a decision. A decision based on his smile. A decision based on the gentleness of his voice.

A decision not based one little bit on how good-looking he was, or how big, or how the sun glinted on his dark hair or how the strength of him seemed like an aura. He was a farmer born and bred. He was a farmer who was now the Lord of Glenconaill. Who could transform at will...

No. The decision wasn't based on that at all. It was simply that she wanted to see more of this amazing country before she left.

'Yes, please,' she said and then, because it was only sensible and Jo Conaill prided herself on being sensible, she slipped her hands back into his. After all, he was her guarantee...not to sink.

'Yes, please,' she said again. 'Show me all.'

He wished he knew more about this country.

If you drove quickly across bog country you could easily take it for a barren waste. But if you walked it, as he and Jo were walking it, taking care to stick to ground he knew was solid but venturing far from the roads, where the ground rose and fell, where the streams trickled above and below ground, where so many different plants eked out a fragile life in this tough terrain...if you did that then you realised the land had a beauty all its own. He knew the artist in Jo was seeing it as it should be seen.

And she was asking questions. She'd tighten her hold on his hand and then stoop, forcing him to stoop with her. 'What's this?' she'd ask, fingering some tiny, delicate flower, and he didn't know what it was and he could have kicked himself for not knowing.

He knew what grew on his farm. He didn't know this place.

But it was fascinating and Jo's enjoyment made it more so.

'I need to sketch,' she whispered, gazing around her with awe. 'I never knew...'

But she was going home, he thought, and more and more the thought was like grey fog.

They'd had their week at the castle. They'd had their fairy tale. After tomorrow they'd go back to their own lives. The castle would be nothing more than an eye-watering amount in their bank accounts.

And, as if on cue, the sun went under a cloud. He glanced up and saw the beginnings of storm clouds. You didn't expect anything else in this country. The land was so wet that as soon as it was warm, condensation formed clouds and rain followed.

It was kind of comforting. A man knew where he was with this weather—and if he had to feel grey then why not let it rain?

'We need to get back,' he told her. 'It'll be raining within the hour.'

'Really?'

'Really.'

She paused and gazed around her, as if drinking in the last view of this amazing landscape. Her hand was still in his.

Her hand felt okay. It felt good.

The feeling of grey intensified. Tomorrow it'd be over. He'd be back on his farm, looking towards the future.

He'd be rich enough to expand his farm to something enormous. He could do whatever he liked.

Why didn't that feel good?

'Okay,' Jo said and sighed. 'Time to go.'

And it was.

CHAPTER SEVEN

EXCEPT THERE WAS the cow.

They reached the home field behind the castle just as the first fat raindrops started to fall. Jo's hand was still in his—why let it go? Finn helped her climb the last stile and then paused.

He'd brought the two stray cows into the paddock nearest the stables so he could give them extra feed and watch the younger cow who he thought was close to calving. She was very young, he'd decided as he'd brought her to the top field, barely more than a calf herself. The cow she was with was probably her mother.

And now she was definitely calving, heaving with futile effort. The older cow was standing back, watching, backing off a little and then edging nearer, as if not knowing what was happening but frightened regardless.

She had reason to be frightened, Finn acknowledged as he got a clear look at what was going on. The ground around the little cow was flattened, as if she'd been down for a while. Her eyes were wild and rolling back.

Damn.

'Calving?' Jo asked and Finn nodded grimly. He approached with caution, not wanting to scare her more than she already was, but the little cow was too far gone to be scared of anything but what was happening to her body.

'Lord Conaill?'

Mrs O'Reilly was standing on the castle side of the field's stone wall underneath a vast umbrella. 'Thank heaven you've come. She's been down for two hours and nothing's happening. I didn't know where you were so I telephoned the veterinary. He's away. The lad who answers his calls says there's nothing he can do. If it's a stray cow, the kindest thing would be to shoot her, he said, so I took the liberty of unlocking your grandfather's gun cabinet. Which one would you be wanting to use?'

She was holding up guns. Three guns!

This was a stray cow, with no known lineage. It was a straggly, half starved animal and its mother looked little better. She'd fetch little at market, maybe a small amount for pet food.

He glanced back at Jo. Her face was expressionless.

'I've used the shotgun on the sheep when I had to,' Mrs O'Reilly said, sounding doubtful. 'But it made a dreadful mess. Would you be knowing more about them?'

Finn had been stooping over the cow. Now he straightened and stared at her. 'You shot…'

'Two sheep,' she told him. 'One got some sort of infection—horrid it was, and the old lord wouldn't let me get the veterinary—and then there was an old girl who just lay down and wouldn't get up. After two days I felt so sorry for her.'

'You've had no help at all?'

'He was very stubborn, the old lord. When my husband died he said it was no use spending money on the estate when it was just to be owned by…' She hesitated.

'By what?' Finn asked, still gentle.

'*Tuathánach*,' she muttered. 'I'm sorry but that's how he saw you. Which gun?'

'No gun,' Finn said grimly. 'We may be *tuathánach* but sometimes that's a good thing. Put the guns away, Mrs O'Reilly, and remind us to increase what we're giving you. You've been a hero but, *tuathánach* or not, we're in charge now. Jo, get yourself inside out of the rain. Mrs

O'Reilly, could you fetch me a bucket of hot soapy water, anything I might be able to use for lubricant and a couple of old sheets and scissors? I'll see what I can do.'

'I'm staying,' Jo said and he shrugged.

'As you like, but it won't be pretty.'

'Then isn't it good that pretty's not my style.'

'So what's *tuathánach*?'

Mrs O'Reilly had disappeared, off to replace gun with soap and water. Finn was gently moving his hands over the little cow's flank, speaking softly—in Gaelic? Did cows understand Gaelic? Jo wondered. Or maybe it was cow talk. This man was so big and so gentle...

Did she have a cow whisperer on her hands?

She didn't go near. When she'd gone near any of the livestock on the place they'd backed with alarm, but Finn seemed to be able to move among them with ease. When he'd approached the little cow she'd heaved and tried to rise but the effort had been too much. She'd slumped again but the moment he'd touched her, the moment the soft Gaelic words began, she seemed to have lost fear.

Maybe I would too, Jo thought, and then thought maybe she had. She thought back to Finn walking towards her over the bog, to Finn speaking in his soft Irish brogue, to Finn smiling at her, and she remembered how the terror of her situation had disappeared. She'd still been cold and humiliated and stuck but the moment he'd opened his mouth she'd stopped being afraid.

He was just plain lovely, she decided, wiping rain from her face. She was so wet now she was almost past noticing, or maybe it was that she was only noticing Finn. He was kind and he was funny and he was wise and he was strong—and it didn't hurt that he was so darned good-looking as well.

Did the little cow think he was good-looking?

'*Tuathánach* means peasant,' Finn told her. He'd taken a while to answer her question but she was forced to forgive him. You could forgive a lot of a dripping-wet man with his arm up a cow. 'That's what I am.'

'You're Lord of Glenconaill.'

'Who's just ruined a perfectly good shirt. Is that a lordly thing to do?'

'It's definitely a lordly thing to do,' she declared. 'Can I help?'

'If you must stay then you could rip sheets,' he told her. 'Do you faint at the sight of blood?'

'Excuse me?'

He grinned. 'Sorry. I forgot you're *tuathánach*, too. We peasants come from strong stock. But Jo, this'll get messy, I can't guarantee a happy ending and you must be wet and cold. You might want to go inside and wait.'

'Like a lady. Huh? What's the Irish for bastard?'

'Jo…'

'Tell me.'

'*Bastaird*,' he said reluctantly.

'Well, there you go,' she said, and hauled herself up on the stone fence, close enough to watch but not so close as to worry the little cow and the older cow still hovering close. 'A *tuathánach bastaird*. That's not the class who gets to block out the nasties of the world. You do what you have to do. I'm the support team. I might not be much help but I'm cheering from the sidelines.'

She hesitated and then looked at the little cow and the terror that was unmistakable in the creature's eyes. 'Do you really think you can help her?'

'If not, I do know how to use a gun,' Finn told her. 'I won't push past my limitations but I'll do my best.'

Jo sat on her fence in the rain and cut sheets into strips, as instructed, on the diagonal to give them more strength.

'I could use ropes but sheets will be cleaner and I don't have time to forage in the stables looking for the right type of rope,' Finn told her. So she sat and cut her sheets with care, as if it was very important that she get each line exactly straight. Mrs O'Reilly had brought an armload of linen. She tested each sheet and decided on the coarsest for strength and then worried that it might be too coarse.

She could go inside and do it but she didn't want to. This was a small job but she was focusing fiercely because it was the only thing she could do and she was desperate to help. She was hardly noticing that it was raining.

'Tell me what's happening,' she asked quietly, and she wouldn't have asked at all but Finn was speaking slow and steady to the little cow, as if to reassure her that he was no stranger but a man who knew his job, who was here to help her.

And it was surely working, Jo decided. The more she listened to his soft, reassuring brogue, the more she decided the calf would slip out to listen.

But of course the calf didn't.

'It's a big calf,' Finn told her, still softly, as if still talking to the little cow, though changing from Gaelic to English. Did cows understand Gaelic better?

Gaelic sounded…sexier.

'I'm thinking she's been got at by a bull that's not her breed.' Finn was lying flat in the mud. She couldn't see what he was doing from the angle where she sat but she could see enough to know it was hard. She could see the cow tense with contractions and she could tell by the way Finn's voice changed that the contractions were squeezing his arm.

'I'm suspecting the older cow's someone's house cow,' he said. 'She'll have got out with her nearly grown calf and wandered the roads. Somehow the younger one's been got at by a bull. I'm betting they'll belong to a hobby farmer, someone who spends weekends down here, doesn't care for the land. Doesn't search for missing stock. These two would have starved if Mrs O'Reilly hadn't agreed to take them. And now we get to pick up the pieces.'

'You love it,' she said slowly, hearing the anger in his voice.

'What, this?'

'No, farming.'

'I do.' He gave a grunt of pain. 'This calf has a big head and the legs are tucked back. I'm trying to haul the hooves forward between contractions but there's so little room.'

'Could I help?'

'You!'

' I have small hands. Plus you don't ride bikes like I do without gaining shoulder muscles. Try me.'

'Jo, you don't want…'

'Try me.'

So then it was Jo, lying in the mud, following Finn's directions.

'You need to wait until the contraction backs off to try and bring the hooves forward. But you're doing two things,' he told her. 'While the contraction hits, you need to hold the head back. Feel before the contraction hits, work out how you can cup the skull and push back. As soon as the contraction eases then try and hook the hooves forward. It's tight, and you only have until the next contraction. My hands just won't do it.'

'I'll try.'

'Of course you will,' he said. '*A mhuirnín*. I'm starting to think you can do anything.'

And what was there in that to make her feel warm despite any amount of mud? And determined to do this.

She concentrated. She held the head and rode out a contraction and then manoeuvred her fingers until she felt what she was sure was a leg. Or almost sure. She got a grip and tugged, and the leg slid forward. The hoof was suddenly in front of the little nose.

'I did it,' she breathed but then the next concentration hit and she went back to holding the head because she could still only feel one hoof in front. And the contraction hurt!

But Finn was holding her shoulders and it was okay.

It was okay as long as Finn was holding her.

'You're amazing,' Finn told her and because he said it she decided she was. 'You can do it,' he said and she took a deep breath and tackled the other side. And when the hoof slid up and she had two hooves facing forward she felt as if she were flying.

'I think we're ready,' she said unsteadily.

'Both hooves forward?'

'Yes.'

Finn lubricated his arm and she backed off. He checked, and his face broke into a grin that made her heart twist and the pain in her bruised arm fade to nothing.

'Now it's time for your sheets,' he said and she had to forget about his smile and hand him her strips of sheets and watch as he fashioned ties around the little hooves. Then she watched and waited as he pulled back at every contraction.

She watched as finally the little calf slipped out into the world, as Finn's face broke into the widest grin she'd ever seen.

She had to wait as he cleared the calf's nose and mouth. As he checked her and found her flawless. As he lifted her and carried her round so her exhausted mother could see her, smell her and then tentatively start the first lick of cleaning, of caring, of starting to be...family.

And then she had to hold her breath as Finn turned back to her. For a moment she thought he was getting on with the job of cleaning up.

Instead of which, he drew her gently to him.

And he kissed her.

'Jo Conaill, you are awesome.'

'So are you, Finn Conaill.'

'Yes, we are,' he said and kissed her again. 'You want a shower? It's stopped raining.'

So it had. She hadn't noticed.

Did she want a shower? She drew back and looked down at herself and laughed.

'Maybe.'

'Together?'

And that took her breath away.

She did, she thought. Of course she did. She could let herself sink into this man, into his body, into his smile, into his life.

She wanted to.

But at her feet the little cow mooed softly and struggled to shift so she could lick her calf more effectively and somehow a sliver of sense was gleaned from the pair of them.

Actions had consequences.

She was a loner for a reason.

'I think…separate showers,' she managed, and he hesitated and then nodded.

'That's probably wise.'

It was, but she was having a whole lot of trouble staying wise.

They had a very late lunch, interrupted by constant visits to the window to check how mother and baby were doing. The sun had come out again and they were looking fine.

Even Mrs O'Reilly detoured past the window every time she brought anything to and from the dining room, and she seemed to find a lot of excuses to come to and from the dining room.

'Eh, you've done well, the pair of you,' she said as she served them coffee. She beamed at them as if she was their grandma and all their useful attributes were due to inheritance from her side of the family. Then she whisked herself off and closed the door behind her.

'We did,' Jo said, suddenly just a little self-conscious. Actually, she always was self-conscious in this room. Mrs O'Reilly loved serving them here. She wouldn't hear of them eating in the kitchen but it was so ostentatious. If she had to stay here longer she'd insist on eating somewhere else, she thought. *Tuathánachs* should eat in the kitchen.

Tuathánach bastairds probably ate on the back step.

Which reminded her…

'*A mhuirnín*,' she said out loud and Finn stared.

'Sorry?'

'That's what you called me. What does it mean?'

He coloured, just a bit, which she liked. She liked it when he was disconcerted.

'My sweetheart,' he mumbled. 'Figure of speech.'

'I guess it's better than *tuathánach bastaird*.'

'I guess.' He was blushing, Jo thought with delight. Blushing! But, she reminded herself, she had refused the shower. She needed to get things back on an even keel.

'What will you do with them?' she asked, but he was still distracted.

'Who?'

'The cows.'

'I guess that's for both of us to decide.'

'I can't decide the fate of cows.'

'They won't sell. They're a motley collection of breeds. The calf's a heifer but she's a weird wee thing and they're all scrawny.'

'They could stay here until the farm sells.'

'I guess. I doubt Mrs O'Reilly will want the responsibility. We need to find an overseer until transition.'

'Because we're leaving,' she said flatly and he nodded. 'Because we're leaving.'

Silence.

What was happening? Jo thought. Things should be straightforward. This was an amazing inheritance. They'd sorted almost everything that had to be sorted. Tomorrow the lawyer would come, the papers would be signed and they'd be on their way, an enormous amount richer.

The doorbell pealed and they both started, then looked at each other and grinned. Two identical smiles.

'Are we expecting anyone—dear?' Finn asked, and Jo chuckled. They were sitting at an absurdly formal dining table, sipping coffee from heirloom china, waiting for their housekeeper to open the doors and announce whoever it was. It really was ridiculous.

'I can't think,' she murmured. 'But if it's a gentleman... dear...you'll need to take him into the study for port. The lady needs to retire to her needlework.'

His chuckle matched hers, but he rose and opened the dining room doors, to find Mrs O'Reilly welcoming a rotund little man, bald, beaming and sporting a clerical collar.

'Lord Conaill, this is Father...'

'Adrian,' the little man said, beaming and holding out his hand in welcome. 'No need to stand on ceremony, My Lord.'

'Then it's Finn,' Finn said, taking his hand. Jo watched as the little man pumped Finn's hand with pleasure and then beamed through to her.

'And this must be the castle's new lady. Fiona's daughter. You look like your mother, girl.'

'I'm Jo,' she said shortly.

'Lovely,' the priest said. 'Now, I know you're busy. So much to sort out. So sad about your...grandfather? I've let you be until now, knowing you need time to settle, but I thought I'd pop in now and let you know the whole village is eager to meet you. And when you're ready to join the community...' His beam faded a little. 'Well, your presence will be keenly felt. There's so much need. You know you're the biggest landholder here, and half the village pays you rent. But the land's bad. If you can possibly see your way to do something about the drainage...'

Whoa, Jo thought, but Finn was before her.

'The castle's for sale,' he said and the little man's face dropped.

'Really?'

'Really.'

And he slumped. The life seemed to drain out of him. He closed his eyes for a moment, then took a deep breath and tried to regroup. When he opened his eyes again, his shoulders went back as if bracing and he managed a weak smile to both of them.

'Well,' he said, 'I've heard rumours of the way the old lord treated you both so maybe I'm not surprised, but it's such a shame. I imagine the castle will be bought by foreigners. They almost all are, our stately homes. Corporates, mostly, where company executives can bring colleagues and clients for an Irish jaunt. They do the castles up, but the countryside...' He sighed. 'Well, if you're sure... It's no business of mine to be making you change your mind.'

Silence. Then...

'What's the story on the empty cottages on the road in?' Jo asked, and she said it even before she knew she was going to ask. Why was she asking? Mrs O'Reilly should usher the priest out, she thought, and then she and Finn should get on with sorting the last few things that needed to be done before the lawyer arrived tomorrow.

'The cottages...' the priest repeated and Mrs O'Reilly suddenly sprang to life, like a hunting spaniel at first sight of duck.

'I've just made coffee, Father,' she said. 'Would you be liking some?'

'Well, I would,' the priest told her, and Finn glanced at Jo, startled, and she shrugged because she didn't regret asking. Not really. She was walking away from this place. Surely she should understand what she was walking away from?

Once ensconced in a dining chair, in the midst of the absurd formality of the room, the priest seemed to relax. He took his time with his first couple of sips of coffee, seeming to consider what was best to say and then started. 'There used to be a village much closer to the castle,' he told them. 'That was before the clearing, though.'

'The clearing?' Jo asked, carefully not looking at Finn. She still wasn't sure why she was doing this.

'Nineteenth century,' the priest told her. 'The landlords found they could make a much greater profit if the land was rolled into one holding. The tenants were cleared, and of course the potato famine hit. These cottages seem to stand for ever, though. No lord's ever thought of pulling them down. There was a church here too, though that was pulled down to be used for the making of the church in Killblan. And a school, though that's rubble. I've often thought it would be grand to restore them, put in tenants, like an artists' community or somesuch. Something that could bring life to the district. Something...'

He searched for the right word and finally found it. 'Something fun,' he said at last. 'There's been little fun for a long, long time. No disrespect, but the old lord was a terrible landlord, as was his father and his father before him. I was so hoping...'

But then he stopped. He pushed back his cup as if he'd just realised he was speaking his own dream. The dream had already been dashed. He closed his eyes and then opened them and gave a brisk nod. Moving on to what was possible.

'But it's naught to do with you,' he said, gently now. 'You'll have your own lives to lead, and what's happening here is our business. I'm sorry to have bothered you. I'll let you get on. Bless you both, the pair of you, with what you decide to do with the proceeds of this place, though I'd be remiss if I didn't say a donation to the building fund of our church in Killblan would be very welcome. But if that's as far as you can manage...' He dredged a smile. 'Well, we're thankful for what we can get.'

And he was gone, with a warm word for Mrs O'Reilly, and not a backward glance at the pair of them. And Finn and Jo were left sitting at the dining table feeling...

Rotten, Jo thought. Really rotten.

Which was unfair. This had nothing to do with her. The family in this castle had rejected her out of hand. She'd been unwanted. The paintings, the tapestries on the walls, had no place for an illegitimate child of the daughter of the house. Neither had they a place for a man who was the descendant of an unwanted 'spare to an heir'.

But...

'What would you do if you stayed?' Finn asked.

CHAPTER EIGHT

WHAT WOULD YOU do if you stayed?

The question didn't make sense. Jo stared at Finn across the table and thought…actually the words did make sense. It was only everything else that didn't.

'What do you mean?' she managed.

'Just what I said.' But he wasn't looking at her. He was staring into the dregs of his coffee cup. 'Just for a moment, just for…fun. As the priest said. Think out of the box. If the lawyer wasn't coming tomorrow, what would you do?'

There was only one answer to that. 'I'd start a tapestry of you with the cows,' she flashed. 'You should be on these walls.'

He smiled, but his smile was strained. 'It'd need to be a portrait of both of us. You with your arm elbow-deep in cow. You could have a caption underneath: "I may need to clean my watch".'

'I'm right, though,' she muttered. 'You should be on the walls.'

'As should you. It's only an accident of birth that we're not. But we don't have a place here, Jo. It's not ours.'

'No.'

'But if it was…'

'What would *you* do?' she asked curiously, and was surprised by the look of passion that flooded his face.

'Drains,' he said. 'As Father Adrian said. I'd see to the drainage here on the castle land but, as he said, on the tenants' land as well. I haven't had time to even look at the tenanted farms but the land's a mess that could be fixed. If I had my way…' And then he stopped and the room was filled with silence.

'What would you do with the cows?' she asked at last.

'The cows?'

'There are three generations of cow looking in the window at us right now.' It wasn't true. They were half a field away but in her imagination Jo had them staring straight at them, knowing their fate was in their hands.

'The sensible thing…'

'You said we're not talking sensible,' she retorted. 'We're talking fun. What would you do…for fun?'

'Keep them to keep the grass down?' He grinned. 'No, okay, the sheep could do that. But we have a newly calved cow who'll produce more milk than her calf needs. It'd be fun to milk her once a day, to have fresh milk whenever we need it. And to watch the calf grow. Those little cows have had a pretty lean time of it. It'd be good to watch them fatten up.'

'But not for the knackery.'

'As you said, I'm talking fun, not sense.' He stared out of the window, across the fields. In the distance were the ruins of the old village settlement the priest had been talking of. 'You know…'

'They'd be great with people in them,' Jo finished for him because that was what she was thinking and maybe he was too? 'What did the priest say? An artists' colony, or somesuch? Wouldn't that be a fun project to bring people to the district? Maybe this castle could even be part bed and breakfast. An upmarket one. Maybe we could cash in on tourists wanting local colour.'

'It'd take a serious amount of money.'

'There is a serious amount of money,' she whispered. 'And we wouldn't have to do it all at once.'

They were staring at each other over the table. Jo could almost see their thoughts bouncing back and forth. There were things she was thinking that she didn't need to say— she could see the reflection of them in his eyes.

'We couldn't,' she said at last, but the frisson of thought kept flashing.

'Why not?' It was taking a while between sentences. They needed space between truly enormous thoughts.

'Your farm...'

'I could sell my farm if I had this one. It'd be a shift in loyalties but I could do it. But you... Jo, we couldn't do this apart. The castle needs the fortune that goes with it. It'd have to be a partnership. You'd have to stay here. You'd have to...settle.'

And there it was, out in all its enormity. Jo was gazing at Finn and he was gazing back. His look wasn't challenging, though. It was...

No. She didn't know what it was, but she did know that there was understanding behind his gaze. As if he knew how torn this whole thing could make her.

If they stopped talking of this as a fantasy... If they decided to make it real...

'You know,' he said thoughtfully when the silence seemed as if it might extend into the middle of next week— when the enormity of what was between them was starting to seem overwhelming— 'we don't need to decide right now.'

'What...what do you mean? The lawyer's coming tomorrow.'

'But I'm the Lord of Glenconaill,' he told her and his grin suddenly flashed out again. 'I'm a man with two suits of armour—okay, one if we share, but maybe one's enough. I believe the Lord of Castle Glenconaill, with or without armour, can decree when and if a lowly Dublin lawyer can and can't visit this castle.'

And Jo thought back to the smooth-speaking, supercilious Dublin lawyer who'd treated them both as if he knew what was best for them and she couldn't help it. She giggled.

'Would you phone him and say, "This is Lord Conaill speaking"?'

'I could do that.'

'Grandpa has a brocade dressing jacket in his room. One of those would be just the thing for such a phone call.'

'And I could say, "Myself and Lady Jo—" for if the priest is referring to you as the lady of the castle, who am I to argue and we're sharing, right? "—Our High and Mightinesses have mutually decided we wish for more time to decide on the fate of our heritage. So please delay your travel…"'

'"My good man",' Jo finished for him and giggled again and then she stopped giggling because what was happening was far bigger than a delay in a lawyer's visit.

Suddenly what was between them was huge.

'We've kissed,' she said, because the kisses were with her still, the way he'd touched her, the way her body had responded. 'It didn't…it doesn't…'

'It might,' Finn told her. He smiled across the table and his smile was enough to make her gasp. His smile was a caress all by itself. 'I guess this would give us a chance to see.'

And that took her breath away. *A chance to see…*

She didn't get attached. She couldn't get attached. She didn't have a home and she didn't want one.

So how had she ended up here, with a castle and a tattered teddy bear and three cows and… Finn?

The concept was terrifying. The concept was exhilarating.

'One day at a time,' Finn said very gently, and she thought, *He does understand. He won't be rushing me.*

But she almost wished he was. She almost wanted him to round the table and take her in his arms and say, *This is where you belong. You're staying here for ever. With me.*

Only that was the siren song. They were the words she'd been waiting a lifetime to hear, only when she had heard them they'd always turned into a lie.

'You want me to make the call?' Finn asked and she tried to think logically but his gentleness shook her logic.

His gentleness that made her want to stay.

'Only if you can do it without the dressing jacket,' she managed. 'Only if you can do it as you.'

'Then it should be a three-way call,' he told her. 'If I'm not doing it as the autocratic Lord of Glenconaill then it should be from you and me, from Finn and Jo, telling him we've decided to stay.'

'But only…'

'Only for a while,' he said, still gently. 'Only until we… see what might happen.'

'You wouldn't sell your farm straight away?'

'I have a manager and staff,' he told her. 'No one else needs me.'

Except someone did.

The call to his manager was tricky.

'I won't be home for a while,' he told Rob and there was a lengthy silence on the end of the phone while Rob thought about it. His manager was a friend of long-standing, and a man of few words. He wasn't a man to rush things. Maybe he'd buy the farm, Finn thought. He could make it easy for him. But that was for the future. Meanwhile…

'What about your Maeve?' Rob asked. 'Her father was here today.'

'Martin came? Did Maeve come with him?'

'She's back in Dublin. People are saying it's over between you, but her father talks like he's still expecting a wedding.'

'It is over,' he said heavily. 'But it's up to Maeve to tell him. I don't know why she won't.'

'Finn...'

'What would you have me do?' he demanded. 'Walk into Martin's living room and say, "I'm not marrying your daughter"? Maeve came over the day I left and asked me to give it a bit more time before she tells him. To be honest, I no longer know what Maeve wants, but it needs to be settled. It was only just okay to pretend before I met...'

And then there was silence.

'Before you met...?' Rob said at last and Finn tried to think of something to say and couldn't.

'This Jo,' Rob ventured. 'The woman you've inherited with. Your cousin?'

'We share the same great-great-grandfather. That's hardly a bar...'

'To what?' Finn could almost see his manager's eyebrows disappearing into his receding hairline. 'Marriage? Whoa.'

'Whoa's right. I hardly know her.'

'You've been in the same castle for a week.'

'It's a very big castle.'

'I'm sure it is.' And his manager was laughing. 'You seem to have yourself in the midst of a love triangle.'

Where was respect when you needed it? he thought. This was what happened when you employed friends. Surely the Lord of Glenconaill should be immune from ribbing. 'That's not the way it is,' he said bluntly. But he thought of Maeve, laying claim to him even now. And he thought of Jo, not laying claim to a thing.

Jo would never claim. She didn't think she had the right.

'There's nothing like that in it,' he said sharply. 'But Rob, the sheep here... I've not seen anything like the quality of their coats. Someone's put a huge amount into their breeding. I'll get you up to see them. I'd like your advice.'

'About breeding?' And Rob was still laughing. 'Of course,' he told him. 'Well, well. We live in interesting times but I think I need to avoid Maeve's father, don't you?'

'Raye?'

It was the first call Jo had made to Australia since she'd arrived; the only call she had to make. Raye was part owner of the last café she'd worked at. She had Jo's bike in the back of her shed.

'Jo!' Raye was brisk and practical and she sounded rushed. 'Good to hear from you, girl. When can we expect you back?'

'I've been delayed,' Jo told her. 'I'm sorry but I'm not sure when I'm arriving.'

'You know Caroline's heading back to the States next week. She's your fill-in, honey. If you're not back by then I'll have to employ someone else.'

'I know.'

'It's a pity. You're good. But it can't be helped,' Raye said. 'And I can't keep the bike much longer. My son and his mate are driving down from Brisbane next week. I told them they could use the shed for their car. What do you want me to do with it?'

'I'll find a storage place on the Internet and have them pick it up.'

'That'll cost you.'

'Yeah.' She said it flatly. It wasn't Raye's business what she did. It was no one's business but her own.

'It'll have to be collected between eight and ten, one morning before the kids arrive next week,' Raye said, moving on. 'That's the only time I'm here to hand over the keys. Let me know when.'

'I'll do that.'

'Right then. See you later,' Raye told her and disconnected and Jo stood still and thought Raye had been her boss for six months and hadn't asked why she was staying longer in Ireland or whether she was having a good time or…anything.

She had no personal connection.

That was what she wanted, Jo thought. Wasn't it? It was the background she'd carefully cultivated since the last disastrous foster home.

But still…

She was sitting on the bed in her Spartan little bedroom. The bald little teddy was sitting beside her. She picked him up and stared down into his lopsided eyes.

'I do like being alone,' she whispered, but she still held him and then Finn's voice shouted along the corridor.

'Jo, I'm heading out to check our calf before bedtime. You want to come?'

'Yes,' she called and then she smiled down at her scruffy, moth-eaten teddy. 'Yes, I do.'

The calf was fine.

The storm was well past and the night was warm and still, so Finn had decreed the threesome were best left in the field rather than ushered into the sheds. The little cow was placidly nosing her calf while her udder was being prodded and tugged, and the older cow was standing benignly beside them in the moonlight, to all appearances like a doting grandma.

'We've done well,' Finn said. They didn't go close, just stood back and watched. 'A couple of bruised arms for us and a happy ending all round.'

'It is a happy ending,' Jo said softly and then Finn caught her hand in his and held. Strong and warm and fast.

'It could be,' he said and there was all the meaning in the world in those three words.

She didn't pull away. She couldn't, even if she wanted to—which she didn't.

'It's too soon,' she murmured.

'Much too soon,' he agreed. 'But we're giving ourselves time. How long does it take to make the tapestry you're talking of?'

'Months.'

'There you go, then.' He sounded smug.

'Once I draw it I can finish it back in Australia.'

'I can't draft sheep anywhere but here.'

'You could always put in a farm manager and travel back and forth from your home to supervise.'

'So I could,' he said easily. 'If that's what I wanted.'

'Finn…'

'Mmm.'

'It is too fast.'

'It is and all,' he said and then he didn't say anything for a while. They simply stood, hand in hand, in the moonlight while thoughts, feelings, sensations zinged back and forth between them. Things changed. Things grew.

'I should…go to bed,' Jo said at last and the zinging increased a little.

A lot.

'So should I,' Finn told her. 'Noddy's waiting.'

'Your giraffe?'

'And your teddy's waiting for you,' he told her placidly, and she could hear the smile in his voice, even if she couldn't see it in the dark. 'So you'll be sleeping in your tiny bed with your teddy, and I'll be sleeping in my grand bed with my giraffe. Jo…'

'Mmm?' She was almost afraid to breathe.

'My bed's big enough for four.'

'It's…too soon.'

'Of course it is.' He was instantly contrite. 'Sorry I ever mentioned it. It's just that I thought Noddy and Loppy might sleep better with company.' His hand still held hers, and it felt…okay. 'Same with us,' he told her. 'I'm sure this castle has its share of ghosts. *Taibhse*. I thought I heard them last night, clanking round in the basements. I'm sure I'd sleep better with company.'

'Just to keep the *taibhse* at bay.'

'That's it,' he said cheerfully. 'I'm a 'fraidy cat.'

'I'm very sure you're not.'

'And you, Jo Conaill?' And suddenly his voice lost all trace of laughter. He turned and took her other hand so he had them both and he was gazing down at her in the moonlight. His grip was strong and sure, and yet she knew if she pulled back he'd let her go in an instant. 'Are you afraid, my Jo?'

'I'm not…your Jo.'

'You're not,' he told her. 'As you say, it's too soon. Too fast. Too…scary?'

And yet it wasn't. What was scary about leaving her hands between his? What was scary about taking this giant step into the unknown?

A step towards loving?

Why not? Why on earth not?

'I…it'd be only for Loppy and Noddy,' she ventured, and his smile played out again but it was a different smile, a smile full of tenderness, of promise. Of wonder.

'Only for the children,' he agreed. 'Jo…'

'Mmm?' She could hardly make her voice work.

'Will you let me carry you to our bedroom?'

Our bedroom. There it was, just like that. *Ours.*

She'd never had an *ours.*

And to be carried as she'd been carried before, heart-broken, kicking and screaming, being carried away…

But this time she'd not be carried away, she thought. She'd be carried to a bed with Loppy and Noddy. And Finn.

He was waiting for her answer. He'd wait, she thought,

this big, gentle man who was the Lord of Glenconaill and yet he wasn't. This man who was just… Finn.

Finn, the man who was holding her hands and smiling down at her and waiting for her to find the courage to step forward.

Only she didn't need to step forward. He was waiting to carry her. If she could just find the breath to speak.

'Yes, please,' she managed and his grip on her hands tightened. He knew how big this was for her. He knew her fear.

She felt exposed to him, she thought, in a way she'd never let herself be exposed before. This man held her heart in his hands. She'd laid herself open.

She trusted.

'You're sure, *a mhuirnín*?'

'Are you sure that means *my sweetheart*?'

'My sweetheart. My darling. My love. Take your pick.'

'I think,' she said, and her voice was so trembly she had trouble making it work at all, 'that I choose them all.'

And then there was no need for words for Finn's grip on her tightened. Before she knew what he was about he'd swung her up into his arms.

And she didn't fight him. Why would she? There was no need for fighting.

As three little cows basked peacefully under the moonlight, the Lord of Glenconaill carried his lady back into his castle, up the grand staircase and into his bed.

Into his heart.

CHAPTER NINE

THIS WAS A secret world. This couldn't possibly be real—and yet it was.

She was the Lady of the Castle. Castle Glenconaill was hers to wander at leisure, explore, to think about what could be done with all these treasures.

A week ago she'd been going from room to room deciding what was to be kept for some vague family archive—some family that wasn't hers.

Now she and Finn were hauling off dust covers, bouncing on sofas, saying, 'Let's keep this one...no, this one... how about both? How about all?'

She was a kid in a sweet shop, suddenly knowing every sweet could be hers. This world could belong to her and to Finn, and as the days went on it felt more and more wonderful.

It felt right.

Castle or not, it felt like home.

And it had nothing at all to do with the fact that this was a castle, part of an inheritance so large she could hardly take it in. It had everything to do with the way Finn smiled at her, laughed with her, teased her. With the way Finn took her to his bed and enfolded her body with a passion that brought tears to her eyes.

With the way Finn loved her...

And there was the heart of what was happening. Finn loved her.

It's hormones, she told herself in the moments when she was trying to be sensible. She'd read somewhere that no one should ever make a long-term relationship decision in the first few months of hormonal rush, and yet the decision seemed almost to have been made.

For Finn loved her and she was sure of it. In the closeness of the night he held her and he whispered words to her, sometimes in Gaelic, sometimes in words she knew, but, either way, the meaning was as obvious as the way he held her.

She was loved.

She was…home.

And surely that was the most seductive word of all. Jo Conaill had finally found a place she trusted, a place where she couldn't be turned out on the whim of her ditzy mother or the problems of a troubled foster parenting system. This was a place that was hers. Or, okay, it was half hers but it didn't matter that it was half hers because the other half was Finn's and Finn loved her.

And she loved him.

She loved everything about him. She loved that he was his own man. She loved that even on that first morning, after a night of lovemaking that made her feel as if her world had been transformed entirely, he'd pushed back the covers and smiled down at her and left.

'I need to check the cows.' He'd kissed her and went to check on the newborn calf, and she'd looked out of the window and seen him turn from the cows and gaze out over the land to the sheep grazing in the distance. She knew he cared about so much more than just her.

But then he'd come back to her and they'd showered together and made love again. Afterwards she'd taken more tapestries down to the stream. Life had started again, only rebooted with a different power source.

Rebooted with love and with trust.

It was almost dark now. She was sitting by the fire sorting threads she'd bought by mail from Dublin. She had enough to start her tapestry.

She could stay here until she finished it, she thought dreamily. She could walk the hills with Finn during the day. She could help him with the stock. They could put off contacting the lawyer until…until…

She didn't want to know until when. She just wanted to *be*.

'Hey.' He'd entered silently. She looked up and smiled, at her Lord of Castle Glenconaill in his stockinged feet, his worn trousers, his sleeves rolled to reveal his brawny arms. Her man of the land. Her lord and her lover.

'Sewing a fine seam, My Lady?'

'Help me sort the threads,' she said calmly. 'I want the blues sorted left to right, pale to dark.'

'Yes, ma'am,' he said and sat and sorted and she sat by the massive fireplace and thought she'd never been so at peace. She could never be any happier than she was right at this moment.

And then, when the blues were in a neat line, he looked up at her and his eyes gleamed in the firelight.

'Threads sorted, My Lady,' he told her. 'The work of the world is done. The castle's at peace and it's time for the lord of the castle to take his lady to bed. Are you up for it?'

And she grinned like an idiot, smiling into his laughing eyes, falling deeper and deeper.

And when he lifted her into his arms, as he did most nights now, there was no panic.

She was home.

Only of course she wasn't.

Paradise was for fools. How many times had she learned that as a child? Trust was what happened just before the end.

* * *

Finn was out with the sheep when he came. It was mid-morning. Jo had taken the farm truck into town to pick up feed supplement for the cows. They'd thought to go together but one of the sheep had caught itself on a fence and lacerated its hind quarters.

'I'm not good with blood,' Jo had said, looking at the sheep with dismay. 'I managed with the calf but that was because I could do it by feel, with my eyes closed. Yikes. Will you need to put it down?'

'I can stitch it.'

'You!'

'There's no end to my talents,' he'd told her, grinning. 'I wasn't always Lord Conaill, able to ring whoever and say, "Stitch it, my good man". Needs must.'

'Can you stop it hurting?' she said dubiously and he'd shown her the kit he always carried in the back of his truck and she'd shuddered and headed for the village so she didn't have to watch.

The sheep wasn't as badly injured as the amount of blood suggested. Finn cleaned, stitched, loaded her with antibiotic and set her free, then stood for a while looking out over the land, thinking of everything he could do with this place. Thinking of everything he and Jo could do with this place.

The prospect almost made him dizzy. This farm and Jo.

He'd never met anyone like her. His loyalties had somehow done a quantum shift. His castle, his lady. Jo made him feel…

'My Lord?' It was Mrs O'Reilly, calling from the top of the ha-ha. She refused to call him anything other than *My Lord* and lately she'd even started calling Jo *My Lady*. Much to Jo's discomfort.

He turned and saw the housekeeper and then he saw who was beside her.

Martin Bourke.

Maeve's father.

Mrs O'Reilly waved and Martin negotiated the ha-ha and came across the field towards him, a stocky, steady man, grizzled from sixty years of farm life, a man whose horizons were totally set on his farm and his daughter.

Finn's heart sank as he saw him. Now what?

'Martin,' he said, forcing his greeting to be easy-going. He held out his hand. 'Good to see you.'

'It's not good to see you,' Martin snapped and stood six feet back from him and glared. 'You're sitting pretty here all right. Lord of Glenconaill. Think you're better than us, do you?'

'You know me better than that, Martin.' He should. Martin Bourke had been his neighbour all his life. Finn and Maeve were the same age. They'd started school together, had been firm friends, had been in and out of each other's houses since childhood.

Maeve had been a friend and then, somehow, a girlfriend. There'd always been an assumption that they were destined to be a pair. But then things had changed...

'You'll come home and marry her,' Martin snapped and Finn thought, *Whoa, that's pushing things to a new level.*

'Martin...'

'I couldn't get any sense out of her. Nothing. That day you left... She came home weeping and went straight back to Dublin and have I got a word of sense out of her since? I have not. I thought there's been a tiff, nothing more, that it was more of this nonsense of giving her space, but yesterday I'd had enough. So I went to Dublin and I walked into this fine bookshop she's been working in and she was standing side on to the door. And I saw... She's pregnant. Pregnant and never a word to me. Her father. Did you know? Did you?'

'I knew,' he said heavily. 'She told me the morning I left.'

'So…'

'Martin, it's not…'

'Don't tell me,' he snapped. 'She says it's nothing to do with you and she'll come home at the weekend and we'll talk about it. Nothing to do with you? When she's been loving you for years? I know she's got cold feet. Women do, but if a child's on the way it's time to forget that nonsense. Look at you in your grand castle with your grand title. If you think you can walk away from your responsibilities… You'll come home and marry her or I'll bring her here, even if I have to pick her up and carry her. You'll make an honest woman of her, Finn Conaill, or I'll… I'll…'

'You'll what?' Finn said quite mildly. 'Martin, Maeve loves you. That's the only reason she'd marry me—to make you happy. I know that now. Will you push her into marrying a man she doesn't love because she loves you?'

The man stared at him in baffled fury. 'She wants to marry you. The farms… She wants that as much as I do.'

But she didn't. It was the curse of loving, Finn thought. Maeve's mother had died giving birth to the much wanted son who'd been stillborn, and Maeve had been trying to make it up to her father ever since. Until she'd fled to Dublin she'd never had the courage to stand up for what she wanted.

'I'm guessing this woman you have here is the reason,' Martin snapped. 'I saw her in the village when I asked for directions. "Where's the castle?" I asked, and they pointed to this trollop with piercings and hair cut like a boy and said she's the lady of the castle and would I be looking for her or for her man? And by her man they meant you. And your housekeeper says she's living here. Is that why Maeve's crying her eyes out? If you think you can leave her with a child…'

Finn raked his hair and tried to sort it in his head. He

thought of all the things he could say to this man. He thought of all the things he should say.

He could say nothing. It had to come from Maeve. She'd been his friend for ever. She was in trouble and he wasn't about to cut her loose.

'I'll go and see her,' he told him.

'You'll come with me to Dublin. Now.'

'No,' Finn snapped. 'What's between Maeve and me is between Maeve and me. You point a shotgun at the pair of us and it'll make no difference. Leave it, Martin. Go home.'

'You'll leave this trollop and fetch Maeve home?'

'If you ever refer to Jo as a trollop again you'll find your teeth somewhere around your ankles,' he said quite mildly. 'Go home and wait for Maeve.'

Martin left. Finn went inside and cleaned up and thought of what he should do.

Wait until tomorrow? Tell Jo what was happening? But it sounded sordid, he thought. *Jo, I'm going to Dublin to tell my ex-girlfriend to tell her father she's having a baby that's not mine.*

The words made him feel vaguely grubby. And angry. How was he in this mess? He should walk from the lot of them.

But his loyalty held him. Martin had helped him when his father died. Without Martin's help, the farm would have gone under.

And Maeve had been his friend for ever.

He could do this, he thought. He'd make a fast trip to Dublin, sort it out, bang their thick heads together if need be and be back late tonight.

Should he leave a note for Jo? How could he? How to explain the unexplainable?

He swore.

And then he lightened. This was the last obligation, he thought. The last link tying him to his old life.

He could do this and then come home to Jo. He could tell her what had happened face to face, and then they could move on with their life together. Here.

This was the start of a new loyalty, to this castle and to each other.

'He's had to go to Dublin on family business. He'll be back late tonight. He said don't worry and he'll explain things when he gets back.'

Jo stared at Mrs O'Reilly in bemusement. She wasn't so much worried about what the housekeeper was saying. There were any number of reasons why Finn could suddenly be called away. After all, he'd left his farm for longer than he'd intended. Things could go wrong. But it was the way the housekeeper was saying it, as if there was a well of titillating facts behind the words.

She wouldn't enquire, she decided. Finn's business was Finn's business.

She headed for the stairs. She needed to wash. One of the bags had split when she'd hauled it out of the truck. She'd scooped it back together but cow food supplement stank.

But Mrs O'Reilly didn't move and then she spoke again.

'He's got another woman and she's in the family way.' The housekeeper's words came out as a gasp. 'I shouldn't say, but girl, it's true. Her father came today, shouting, threatening, mad as fire. Five months gone, she is, and when's he going to marry her? That's what her dadda's demanding! And it seems she's in Dublin, all alone, and your man's saying it's naught to do with him. And I shouldn't have heard but sound carries across the fields and such anger... Two bulls at each other's throats. "You make an honest woman of her", her father said and loud enough to be heard from Dublin itself. So off they went, separate though, His Lordship looking grim as death and her father looking like he wanted his gun. And I don't like to break it to you, when you've been so good to me, but hiding things behind your back… Well, it's best you know. I'm sorry.'

Silence. Jo didn't say a word.

She couldn't.

What was there to say?

He's got another woman and she's in the family way.

This had been a fairy tale, she thought in the tiny part of her brain that wasn't filled with white noise. This inheritance, this castle, this…love story? This fantasy that she could possibly have found her home.

But fairy tales came to an end, and happy ever after… Well, that was just part of the fantasy. What happened to Cinderella after she married her prince? Did he go on being a prince while she went back to sitting by the fireside waiting for the snippets of time he was prepared to give her?

There was so much rushing through her head. Hammering at her were the times as a kid when she'd started feeling secure, feeling loved. *'Would you like to be our child? Would you like this to be your home?'*

She should never, ever have trusted.

'He'll be back for a late dinner,' Mrs O'Reilly said, sounding frightened. 'He said he just needed to sort things at home. He said not to worry. He'll be back before you know he's been gone.'

'You're…sure?' she managed. 'That there's another woman.'

'"My Maeve…"' Mrs O'Reilly told her, and she was quoting verbatim. 'That's what her dadda said. "You've been sweet on each other for ever," he said. "Look at you in your grand castle with your grand title and if you think you can walk away from your responsibilities… You'll come home and marry her or I'll bring her here, even if I have to pick her up and carry her."'

And there was that word again. Home.

It was such a little word, Jo thought bleakly. It was thrown around by those who had such things as if it didn't even matter.

You'll come home.

He'd said he'd had a long-term girlfriend, she thought dully, but she hadn't asked for details. It wasn't her business. But how could he make love to her, knowing what was in the background?

A woman called Maeve.

A baby.

'I'll make you some lunch,' Mrs O'Reilly said uneasily. 'Things always look better when you're fed.'

Right, Jo thought. *Right?*

She wanted, suddenly, desperately, to go home.

Home?

Home was her bike, she thought. Home was Australia—all of Australia. Home was wherever her wheels took her.

Home was certainly not in some great castle.

Home was not with Finn.

'I need to take some tapestries out of the stream,' she said and was inordinately pleased with the way her voice sounded. 'I'll set them out in the long room—the sun's warm in there. Would you mind turning them for me as they dry? Every couple of hours or so. I dry them flat but they need a wee shake every couple of hours just to get them ventilated underneath.'

'Why can't you do it?' the housekeeper asked, but by the look on her face she already knew.

'Because I don't belong here,' Jo told her. 'Because it's time I went…home.'

It was a long journey to Dublin, a fraught time, and then an even longer journey back to the castle.

Why couldn't they have sorted it between them? Still, at least it was done. Maeve's Steven was a wimp, Finn decided. He was even weaker than Maeve. No wonder they'd feared facing Maeve's father. He should have taken the two of them in hand a month ago and made them face the music. But at least it was now out in the open. Maeve's father was still blustering, but Finn was out of the equation.

'At least now I can organise a wedding,' Maeve had sobbed and he'd managed a smile. He knew Maeve. Now her father's distress had been faced, pregnant or not, she'd have a dozen bridesmaids and she'd have a glorious time choosing which shade of chiffon they'd all wear.

Jo wouldn't be into chiffon. The thought was a good one and he was smiling as he entered the castle, smiling at the thought of lack of chiffon but smiling mostly because Jo was here and he'd been away all day and she'd smile at him…

Only she wasn't.

'She's left,' Mrs O'Reilly said, and handed him an envelope before stalking off towards the kitchen. She slammed the door behind her so hard the castle seemed to vibrate.

He stood in the entrance hall staring down at the envelope, thinking, *What the…?*

Read it, he told himself but it took a surprising amount of resolution to slit the envelope.

It was brief.

I should have asked about your background. That's my dumb fault. You know all about me and I was so happy I didn't want to know that you had happy families playing in the background. But now Mrs O'Reilly says you have a woman called Maeve and she's five months pregnant. Happy families? I don't know what this is all about but you know what? I don't need to know. All I know is that nothing's solid. Nothing's true. I've known it for ever, so how dumb can I be for forgetting? For hoping things could change?

Finn, I know you want to farm the castle land and, thinking about it, I want you to have it. You're the Lord of Glenconaill and it seems right that your place is here. I know you can't maintain the castle without the fortune, but I don't need a fortune. I mean that, Finn. I'm no martyr, but I have a bike and I make good coffee. I'm free and that's the way I like it.

So I'll write to the lawyer from Australia. I won't be a total doormat—I'd like enough to buy myself a small apartment so if I ever fall off my bike I have security, and I'd like to upgrade my bike, but the rest is yours. It's the way it should be. For you're part of a family, Finn, in a way I never can be. In a way I don't want to be. Being a family is a promise I don't know how to keep.

So that's it. Don't feel guilt over what's happened. I'm over it already and I'm used to moving on. Keep the cows safe. Oh, and I'll do some research and send you details of someone who can be trusted to restore the tapestries.

Despite all this, I wish you all the best, now and for ever.
Jo

He stood in the entrance hall and stared blindly at the letter.

All the best, now and for ever.
Jo.

For ever.

Then he swore so loudly that Mrs O'Reilly came scuttling back from the kitchen.

'I need to go to Dublin,' he snapped.

'There's no use.'

'What do you mean, no use?'

'I heard her on the phone. She got one of the last tickets on tonight's flight to Sydney. That's why she had to rush.' She glanced at her watch. 'Her plane would be leaving now. Poor girl.'

The door crashed closed again and Finn stood where he was, letting his emotions jangle until he felt as if his head was imploding. Then he walked out to the field where the little cows stood. The calf was suckling. The light was fading and the mountains in the background were misty blue.

This place was heaven. This place called him as nothing ever had before.

Except Jo.

He should have told her. He should have talked of his problems. Even though what was between him and Maeve was essentially private, essentially over, even, he conceded, essentially humiliating, he should have shared.

He could phone her, he thought. As soon as she reached Sydney...

Did he have a number? No.

Email then? No.

Follow her? Catch the next flight? Pick her up and bring her home?

Home. The word was a sudden jolt, tumbling through his jumbled thoughts. Where was home?

Home could be here, he thought, gazing out at the land of the Conaills, of the land of his forebears. He could make this wonderful. This place should be where his loyalty lay.

But Jo...

Being a family is a promise I don't know how to keep.

How could Jo fit into his vision of home? Into his vision of loyalty?

He couldn't pick her up and carry her anywhere.

Did he want to?

He was suddenly thinking back over twenty years, to

the night of his father's funeral, sitting in the flower-filled living room trying to stem his mother's inconsolable weeping. He was the oldest and he'd been thought of as the bright one of the family. There'd even been talk of him going to university. But never after that night.

'Please don't leave us,' his mother had sobbed. 'If you leave the farm I'll never be able to support the young ones. Finn, I need you to be loyal to this farm. It's our home.'

So he'd built it up until he could survey it with pride. He'd thought he loved it but now...

He stood in the stillness and wondered whether it was the farm he'd loved or was it the people who lived there? He'd thought of selling it to move to the castle. Love, then, wasn't so deep.

And Maeve? Had he loved Maeve or was it home and place that she represented? She'd been his friend and that friendship had morphed into something more. But caught up in his relationship was his love for the land and Maeve's loyalty to her father. And overriding everything was her father's unswerving loyalty to his farm.

Maeve's father had encouraged their courtship since they were teenagers, aching for the farms to be joined. He'd almost lost his daughter because of it.

The night wore on. His thoughts were jumbled, confusing jolts of consciousness he was having trouble sorting, but he was getting there.

He was moving on from Maeve...sorting the mess that loyalty to place had caused...

He was focusing on this castle and Jo.

He'd fallen for the two of them. From the time he'd first seen the castle he'd felt a deep, almost primeval urge to work on this land, to restore this estate to what it could be. But part of that urge was the fact that Jo was in the deal. He knew it now because Jo wasn't here and the place felt empty. Desolate.

His thoughts moved back, to Maeve and her father and the not too subtle blackmail.

'If you love me you'll never leave,' Martin had told his daughter. 'This is our farm. Our place. Marry Finn and we'll join the boundaries. It's our home.'

He'd thought this castle could be home. He'd thought this place could hold his loyalty.

He thought of Jo, heading back to Australia. With no home.

Her home should be here.

And then he thought, *Why?* Why should it be here? What cost loyalty?

He stood and stared at the distant mountains and he felt his world shift and shift again.

Jo.

Home?

CHAPTER TEN

THREE WEEKS LATER saw Jo running a beach café on the south coast of New South Wales.

She hadn't returned to work in Sydney—why would she? She didn't want work colleagues asking how her trip went. Instead she'd ridden south, to a small holiday resort gearing down for the Australian winter. The owners had a new baby, the baby was colicky and when Jo answered the advertisement she was offered as much work as she wanted. She took a vacant room above the shop and got on with her life.

Except she missed things. Things she wasn't allowed to miss?

She worked long hours, from breakfast to dinner. At night she'd pull out her partly done tapestry, of Finn beside cow and calf, with the castle in the background. She wanted it done but she couldn't work on it for long.

It was because she was tired, she told herself, but she knew it was more than that. She could hardly bear to look at it.

Sleep was elusive and her dreams were always the same.

Now, three weeks after she'd arrived back in Australia, she woke at dawn feeling as if she hadn't slept. But work was calling. Even this early, she knew she'd have locals waiting for the café to open. By now she knew them all and they treated her as a friend.

But she wasn't a friend.

'Don't get too attached,' she muttered to herself as she headed downstairs and saw them waiting through the glass doors. 'I'm itinerant. I should have a sign round my neck that says Born To Move On.'

And then she paused because it wasn't just her usual locals waiting. There was someone behind them. Someone with deep brown hair with hints of copper. A big man, half a head taller than anyone else. A man with green eyes that twinkled in the early morning light. Strikingly good-looking. Gorgeous!

A man called Finn.

Her heart did some sort of crazy backflip and when it landed it didn't feel as if it was in the right position. She stopped on the stairway, trying to breathe.

She should head back upstairs, grab her things and run. For a dizzy moment she considered the logistics of hurling her bag from the window, shimmying down the drainpipe and leaving.

But Finn had come and her locals were looking up at her in concern.

'Jo?' Eric-the-retired-librarian called through the glass door, no doubt worried that she'd stopped dead on the stairway and wasn't rushing to cook his porridge. 'Are you okay? Should we wake Tom and Susy?'

Tom and Susy were the owners and she'd seen their light on through the night. She knew they'd been up with their baby daughter. She couldn't do that to them.

So no shimmying down drainpipes.

Which meant facing Finn.

'You can do this,' she muttered to herself and somehow she put on a cheery smile and headed down and tugged the doors open.

It was brisk outside, with the wind blowing cold off the ocean. Her locals beetled to their normal tables clustered round the embers of last night's fire. Eric started poking the embers and piling on kindling.

None of them seemed to notice that Finn Conaill had walked in after them.

'Good morning,' he said, grave as a judge, and she almost choked.

'What are you doing here?'

'I'm here for coffee,' he told her. 'And a chat but maybe it should wait until we're fed. Eric tells me you make excellent porridge and great coffee. Could I help you in the kitchen?'

'No!' she said, revolted, and then she looked closer and realised he was wearing leathers. Bike leathers?

He looked...cold.

'Where have you come from?' she managed and he smiled at her then, a tentative smile but it was the smile she remembered. It was the smile that told her her world could never be the same now this man had entered it.

'From Ireland three days ago,' he told her. 'But it's taken me all that time to organise a bike. I wanted the biggest one but hiring one's impossible, so I had to buy. I picked it up from a Sydney dealer last night.'

'You rode from Sydney this morning?'

'I did.' He even looked smug.

'On a bike.'

'Yes.'

'I didn't know you rode.'

'There's lots of things we don't know about each other yet,' he told her and smiled again, and oh, that smile...

He was tugging his gloves off. She reached forward and touched his fingers, a feather-touch, just to see. His fingers were icy.

'Wh...why?' How hard was it to get that one word out? And of course she knew the answer. He wouldn't come from Ireland to Australia without a reason. He'd come to see her.

Maybe this was the Lord of Glenconaill being noble, she thought wildly. Maybe he was objecting to the letter she'd sent to the lawyer. She'd listed what she could use from the estate and she'd stated that the rest was Finn's. He could do what he wanted with it, with or without a woman called Maeve.

'I've come home,' he told her, and the jumble of thoughts came to a jarring halt.

Home?

The word hung. Behind them the locals had abandoned tending the fire. They weren't bothering to peruse the menu they always perused even though they must have known it off by heart for years, but instead they were looking at them with bright curiosity.

They lived here, Jo thought wildly. She didn't.

Home was nowhere.

'What do you mean, you've come home?' she demanded and if she sounded snappish she couldn't help it. Of all the stupid things to say…

'It seems a good place,' Finn said, looking around the cosy café with approval. 'Nice fire, or it will be. Warm. Good view. And porridge, I'm told. What's not to like? This'll do us until we move on.'

'Finn!'

'Jo.' He reached forward and took her hands. His really were freezing. She should tug him forward to the fire, she thought. She should…

What she should do was irrelevant. She couldn't move. She was standing like a deer caught in headlights, waiting to hear what this man would say.

'I should have told you about Maeve,' he said. 'It was dumb not to tell you. When I first came to the castle, when I first met you, I had a worry about Maeve in the background. In retrospect, I should have shared that worry with you.'

'You should have shared that worry with her,' she managed and it really was a snap now. 'You're having a baby and you don't even talk about it? You don't mention it? Like it's no big deal. That's like my mother…'

'It's not like your mother.' She copped a flash of anger from him then. 'I know your mother thought a baby was no big deal.' The grip on her hands tightened and she could hear his anger in his voice. 'Have a baby, head back to Ireland, refuse to sign adoption papers? Your mother used the fate of her child to try and shame her father, and that seems a very big deal to me. I wish she was alive so I could tell her.'

'But you and Maeve…'

'Jo, it's not my baby.' He paused and his anger faded. His voice became gentle. 'Maeve and I have been best of friends since we were five years old. We always assumed we'd marry. Why not? We loved each other. We always have and we still do. But Maeve's dad is the worst kind of emotional blackmailer. Her mum died when she was seven, and she spent her childhood trying to make him happy. But making her father happy was always a huge ask. He dreamed that we'd marry, that I'd be the son he lost when his wife died in childbirth. We'd join our two farms together, make the empire he'd always dreamed of. It made me uneasy, but I loved Maeve and there was no point in fighting it.'

'You loved Maeve…' She was struggling. They should find somewhere private to talk, she thought. Somewhere like the kitchen. But her onlookers seemed fascinated. Keep the punters happy, she decided, and then she decided she was pretty close to hysteria.

'When you grow up with someone, you do love them,'

Finn told her. 'They become…family. I know you don't get that, Jo. I'm hoping I can teach you.'

'But Maeve…'

'Maeve and I loved as best friends,' he told her, smiling down at her with a smile that did her head in. 'And Maeve's father used her loyalty to him and to his farm to coerce her. I never guessed the pressure. More fool me, but then…' He shrugged. 'I was one-eyed about my farm as well so maybe I was part of the problem. Marrying Maeve was just an extension of that loyalty. But over a year ago she found the strength to run. She told her father—and me—that she needed time out before marrying and she took a job in a bookshop in Dublin. And promptly met the owner and fell in love. Really, truly in love. She was so much in love that for the first time in our lives she didn't want to talk to me about it. But her father's emotional blackmail continued. He's had one heart attack and terrified her with the thought of another. She kept telling both of us that she just wanted space.'

'Which broke your heart?' she ventured. She was finding it hard to breathe here. He was so close. He was here. *Finn.*

He grinned at that. 'Um…no,' he conceded. 'Sure, I was puzzled, and yes, my pride was hurt, but we've been apart for over twelve months now. And in truth I wasn't all that upset. Maybe a part of me was even relieved. But then she told me she was pregnant and she wanted me to face her father with her. She thought it might make things better if I was there when she told him, but I thought it'd make things worse. I thought she should face him with Steven, the father of her baby, and I told her so.'

'Oh…' She'd forgotten her audience. She'd forgotten everything. 'Oh, Finn…'

'So that's where it was when I came to the castle,' Finn told her. 'Maeve and I were over. That's when I met you and that's when I knew for certain that Maeve was right. What she and I had was nothing compared to how I felt about you.'

And what was a girl to say about that? Nothing, Jo decided. Nothing seemed to be working. Certainly not her voice. She seemed to be frozen.

'She still didn't have the gumption to face her father,' Finn told her. 'But he finally discovered she was pregnant. Instead of confronting her, he came to find me.'

'And you went…'

'To knock some sense into the three of them,' he told her. 'Yes, Maeve was still terrified but I collected the family doctor on the way back to her father's farm. It was insurance, and her father turned purple with rage and distress, but there wasn't a twinge of heart trouble. They survived and it's sorted. They're about to live happily ever after; that's assuming they have enough gumption to find their way out of a paper bag. But enough of Maeve. Jo, I came here to talk about you. About us. And even about marriage?'

There was a concerted gasp behind them. Jo tried to speak. She couldn't.

And then her locals took over.

'You've come all the way from Ireland to propose?' It was a snap out of left field. Eric had abandoned his fire lighting and now he stalked up to Finn like a small, indignant cockerel. 'So who are you to be asking?' He poked him in the chest. 'You can't just sweep in here and carry her off.'

'Ooh, maybe he can,' one of the ladies behind him twittered. 'He's beautiful.'

'He's a biker. A biker!'

'So's she.'

'Yes, but…'

But she was no longer listening to her locals. She was only listening to Finn.

'Jo, I'm not here to carry you anywhere,' he said softly, smiling at her now, his lovely, gentle smile that kick-started her heart and had it doing handsprings. 'I wasn't so much thinking of me carrying you off but us riding into the sunset together. But there's no rush.' His grip on her hands was infinitely gentle. They were warming, she thought. She was feeding him warmth.

It was a two-way street. The zing between the two of them…

'I'm not here to take you back to the castle,' Finn told her. 'Jo, I'm not here to take you anywhere. I'm here because I'm home.'

'What…?' It was so hard to make her voice work. 'I don't understand.' When her voice finally did work it came out as almost a wail.

'Because where you are is my home,' he said softly and he drew her a little closer so his lips could brush her hair. 'That's what I figured. And I also figured how I'd loved you back in Ireland was dumb. I just assumed you'd be part of the package. Castle and Jo. We'd marry, I hoped, and live in our castle for ever. But then you were gone and I looked around the castle and thought: I don't love the castle. It's just a thing. It's just a place. How can I love a thing or a place when the only way I can truly love is to love you?'

Then, as she said nothing—for how could she think of a single thing to say?—his grip on her hands became more urgent. 'Jo, you said you don't know how to do family. You said you don't do home. But, the way I see it, home is us. Family is us. As long as you and I are together we don't have to strive for anything else. No castles. No farms. Nothing. Not even our bikes if we don't want them.'

Bikes. It was a solid word, the one tangible thing she

was able to get her head around. She looked out through the door and saw a great, gleaming Harley parked to the side.

'I don't… I don't have a Harley yet,' she managed which, in the circumstances, made no sense at all.

'We can fix that. We don't have to but we can if we want. Jo, if you'll let me stay we can do anything we want.'

'You want the castle,' Jo whispered.

'Not as much as I want you.'

'Your farm…'

'I'm selling the farm. Where you go, that's where I belong.'

'So you'd follow me round like a stalker…' She was fighting to keep things light but she was failing. Miserably.

And Finn got serious.

'I wouldn't do that to you, Jo,' he said softly. 'If you say the word I'll go back to Ireland. Or I'll get on my bike and ride around Australia to give you more time to think about it. The decision's yours, love. I won't carry you anywhere and I won't follow unless you want. All I ask is that I love you but that love's dependent on nothing but your own beautiful self. Not on location, loyalty, history. Simply on you.'

'So…' She was starting to feel almost hysterical. How could she believe this? It was a dream. How could she make her thoughts work? 'You'll just abandon the castle? The sheep?'

'That's why it's taken me three weeks to be here. That and the fact that you weren't kind enough to leave a forwarding address. I had to take our slimy lawyer out to dinner and ply him with strong drink before he'd give me your mail address and it took sheer force of personality to make your last employer tell me who'd checked recently on your references. And then I had to find someone to take care of the livestock because I don't like Mrs O'Reilly's cure by gun method. Luckily she has a nephew who's worked the land with his dad and he seems sensible. So our castle's secure in case we ever wish to come back, but if we decide we don't want to come back then we can put it on the market tomorrow. The world's our oyster. So love... As your astute customer suggested, I'm here to propose, but there's no rush. While you're thinking about it...maybe you could teach me to make porridge?'

'Excellent,' Eric said darkly but he was punched by the lady beside him.

'Eric'll make the porridge,' she said. 'You two go outside and have your talk out. Though can I suggest you head to the side of the shed because the wind's a killer.'

'He can't go down on one knee behind the shed,' Eric retorted. 'It's gravel. And I don't know how to make porridge.'

'That's what the instructions on the packet are for,' the woman retorted. 'And it's only you eating it.' She turned to face Finn. They were all facing Finn. 'So, young man, do you want to pick her up and carry her somewhere you can propose in privacy?'

'I'll carry her nowhere she doesn't wish,' Finn said and his smile was gone and the look he gave Jo was enough to make her gasp. 'Do you wish me to take you outside and propose?'

And there was only one response to that. Jo looked up at Finn and she smiled through unshed tears. She loved this man so much.

He'd given up his castle for her.

He loved her.

'I do,' she whispered and then, because it wasn't loud enough, because it wasn't sure enough, she said it again, three times for luck.

'I do, I do, I do.'

* * *

They stayed until the owners' baby had outgrown her colic. They stayed until Jo had not a single doubt.

She woke each morning in the arms of her beloved and she knew that finally, blessedly, she'd found her home.

The two bikes sat outside waiting, but there was little chance—or desire—to use them. Finn refused wages. 'I'm a barista in training,' he told the owners when they demurred. 'Jo's teaching me to make the world's best coffee.' But they worked side by side and they had fun.

Fun was almost a new word in Jo's vocabulary and she liked it more and more.

She loved the way Finn watched her and copied her and then got fancy and tried new ways with the menu and new ways of attracting punters. She loved the way he made the customers laugh. She loved the way he failed dismally to make decent porridge. She loved the way the locals loved him.

She loved him.

And each night she loved him more, and finally she woke and knew that a line had been crossed. That she could never go back. That she truly trusted.

She was ready for home.

'Surely a man's home is his castle,' she told him. 'Let's go.'

'Are you sure?' He was worried. 'Jo, I'm happy to be a nomad with you for the rest of my life.'

'Just as I'm starting to love not being a nomad,' she chuckled and then got serious. 'Finn, I've been thinking… We could do amazing things with our castle. We could run it as an upmarket bed and breakfast. We could ask Mrs O'Reilly to help us if she wants to stay on. We could make the farm fantastic and set up the little cottages for rent by artists. We could work on the tapestries…'

'*We?*'

'If you want.'

'I'm bad with a needle,' he told her. They were lying in bed, sated with loving, and their conversation seemed only partly vocal. What was between them was so deep and so real that it felt as if words hardly needed to be said out loud.

'You're dreadful at porridge too,' she said lovingly. 'What made you try a porridge pancake? Eric'll never get over it.'

'It was a new art form,' he said defensively. 'It stuck on the bottom. I'd made a crust so I thought I'd use it.'

She chuckled and turned in the circle of his arms. 'Finn Conaill, I love you but I've always known you're not a maker of porridge. You're a farmer and a landowner. You're also the Lord of Glenconaill, and it's time the castle had its people. It's time for us to make the castle our home.'

'It's up to you, love. Home's where you are,' he said, holding her close, deeply contented. And she kissed him again and the thing was settled.

They went back to Ireland. They returned to Castle Glenconaill. Lord and Lady ready to claim their rightful place.

And three months later they were married in the village church, with half the district there for a look at this new lord and his lady.

And they decided to do it in style.

In the storeroom were wedding dresses, the most amazing, lavish wedding gowns Jo had ever seen. Soon they'd give them to a museum, they'd decided, but not until they'd had one last use from them.

She chose a gown made by Coco Chanel, worn by her grandmother, a woman she'd never met but whose measurements were almost exactly hers. It was simplicity itself, a wedding gown straight out of the twenties, with a breast-line that clung, tiny slips of silk at the shoulders and layered flares of creamy silk with embroidery that shimmered and sparkled and showed her figure to perfection.

Its nineteen-twenties look seemed as if it was her natural style. With her cropped curls, a dusting of natural make-up and a posy of wild flowers, she was stunning. All the villagers thought so.

So did Finn.

But Jo wasn't the only one who'd dressed up. Finn had dressed up too, but the twenties were a bit too modern, they'd decided, for a true Lord of Glenconaill. 'Breeches,' Jo had decreed and he'd groaned and laughed and given in. They'd chosen a suit that was exactly what Jo imagined her hero should wear. Crisp white shirt and silk necktie. A magnificently tailored evening jacket in rich black that reached mid-thigh. Deep black breeches that moulded to his legs and made Mrs O'Reilly gasp and fan herself.

A top hat.

It should have looked foppish. It should have looked ridiculous. It didn't. Bride and groom stood together as they became man and wife and there was hardly a dry eye in the congregation.

'Don't they look lovely,' their housekeeper whispered to the woman beside her in the pew. 'They're perfect. They're the best Lord and Lady Glenconaill we've ever had.'

'That's not saying much.' The woman she was talking to was dubious. 'There's been some cold souls living in that castle before them. Kicking out younger sons, disowning daughters, treating their staff like dirt.'

'Yeah.' Mrs O'Reilly's nephew was standing beside them, looking uncomfortable in a stiff new suit. He'd spent the last three months working side by side with Finn and if he had his way he'd be there for ever. 'But that's what toffs do and Finn and Jo aren't toffs. They might be lord and lady but they're… I dunno…okay.'

'Okay' in Niall's view was a compliment indeed, Mrs

O'Reilly conceded, but really, there were limits to what she thought was okay. And something wasn't.

For the bride and groom, newly married, glowing with love and pride, were at the church gate. Jo was tossing her bouquet and laughing and smiling and they were edging out of the gate and then the rest of the gathering realised what Mrs O'Reilly had realised and there was a collective scandalised gasp.

For they'd grabbed their helmets and headed for Finn's bike, a great beast of a thing, a machine that roared into life and drowned out everything else.

And Jo was hiking up her wedding dress and climbing onto the back of the bike and Finn was climbing on before her.

'Ready?' he yelled back at her, while the crowd backed away and gave them room. Roaring motorbikes did that to people.

'I'm ready,' she told him. 'Ready for the road. Ready for anything. Ready for you.'

And he couldn't resist. He hauled off his helmet and turned and he kissed her. And she kissed him back, long and lovingly, while the crowd roared their approval.

'Ready for the rest of our lives?' Finn asked when finally they could speak.

'Ready.'

'Ready for home?'

'I know I am,' Jo told him and kissed him again. 'Because I'm already there.'

* * * * *

AN OFFICER AND
HER GENTLEMAN

AMY WOODS

For Mason Dixon, US Navy, with love and respect.

And to Renee Senn, LCSW, for her generous help
with research. Any errors are mine.

Chapter One

A blast rang out in the still night air, rattling windows and setting off the bark alarm of every canine within a mile radius.

In a small guest room of her younger brother's ranch-style home, Avery Abbott's eyes shot open as she was ripped suddenly from what had passed as sleep for the past few months—a shallow, daydream-like consciousness that really didn't qualify as true rest.

Pulse thumping against her temples, Avery kicked her legs free from tangled sheets and fumbled in the darkness for the baseball bat she kept nearby, cursing when her fingers didn't grasp it immediately. Her nerves had always been her biggest weakness during army basic training. Even the tiniest spark of fear or anxiety could transform her otherwise capable hands into jelly. The slightest hesitation or worry over a possible imperfection had the potential to eradicate months of training in an instant, leaving Avery, who was at the top of her class, one of only a handful of females in a company dominated by males, frozen and utterly useless. It hadn't happened often during her service, but the occasion it did stood out in her memory, far above her many accomplishments.

Seconds, Abbott—her sergeant's voice boomed through her brain as Avery finally gripped solid material and held it poised—*seconds mean the difference between the life and death of your comrades.*

As she made her way from her room into the hallway, through the house and out the front door into a thick darkness punctuated by only a thin sliver of light from the waning crescent moon, her nightmare blended seamlessly with reality.

Her brother's small farmhouse and the old red barn disappeared as Avery stalked the grounds, weapon firm and steady against her side, its material solid and reliable in her grip, searching for the source of the noise that had awoken her and threatened the safety of her fellow soldiers.

When the flashback gripped Avery, it was no longer cool, wheat-colored, late-autumn grass her bare feet plodded through, but the warm desert sand of a country in which she'd served three tours.

She wasn't safe at home in Peach Leaf, Texas, anymore, but a stranger in a foreign land, her vulnerability evident in every accented word she spoke, in her uniform, in the caution she knew flickered behind her eyes each time she faced a potential enemy.

She would be okay, she thought, pacing the too-quiet darkness, so long as she didn't run into any kids.

The women and children were the worst part of combat. You never knew whose thumb they were under, who controlled their futures…who'd robbed them of their innocence, threatened their families if met with anything but obedience, and turned them into soldiers to be sacrificed without a choice.

Regardless of where their loyalties were planted, they were children… It didn't make sense to hold them responsible for their misguided actions.

Avery wanted to bring the many homeless ones back with her when she returned to the US. She had something in common with them. She knew what it was like to be an orphan, to feel alone in the world, unprotected.

Once, before she'd been adopted by a loving couple, the birth parents of her brother, Tommy, Avery, too, had known firsthand what it was to be without a family.

But that was a long time ago, and now she needed to focus on the threat at hand. Still holding her weapon, she used her forearm to brush a strand of long blond hair out of her eyes. When she'd tumbled from bed, she hadn't time to twist her hair into its customary bun. There was only room in her brain for one objective: locate and—if necessary—eradicate the cause of the blast.

She paced silently through the muggy night air, the blanket of darkness hiding any detail so that all she could see were the shapes of unfamiliar objects.

In her mind, it was her first week in Afghanistan, and she was afraid.

Despite extensive predeployment training, nothing could have prepared her for what it would feel like to be hunted. She knew she shouldn't be outside of her bunker alone, but evidently no one else had heard the explosion, and for all she knew her team could be in danger at that very moment.

So First Lieutenant Avery Abbott pressed on through the black night, searching, searching, searching.

Isaac Meyer was humming along to the local country music station when a rear tire blew out just a quarter mile away from home, causing his truck to skid into a ditch on the side of the road.

Only seconds passed before he got it under control and pulled to a stop, but they felt like hours.

"You okay, girl?" he asked his backseat passenger, still trying to deep breathe his way back to a normal heart rate. His palms were shaking and slick with sweat despite feeling like ice, and his brain was still too rattled to discern whether or not he was okay. But he needed to know if his best friend was all right before he made a single move.

He turned and still couldn't see her. Then Jane gave an uncharacteristically high-pitched *woof* from the seat directly behind him, letting Isaac know she was startled, but the absence of any cries of pain settled his stomach a little, and a second later her sandpaper tongue swept along his elbow.

Isaac heaved a sigh of relief and unbuckled his seat

belt before getting out of the truck to check on his companion.

As soon as he moved up his seat to let her out, Jane bounded straight into his arms and both dog and human crashed to the ground in a heap.

"I'm so sorry, sweetheart," Isaac said, stroking Janie's coat and feeling her limbs and ribs for any injuries. "I sure am glad you're not hurt."

His statement was conservative. They were *damn lucky* to be okay. After all, it was pitch dark on the gravel country road to his ranch house; even with his bright headlights on, they could have hit just about anything swerving into that ditch. Not to mention they'd have to walk home now, and Isaac was bone tired after a long day on his feet at work. All he wanted was a cold beer and his bed. He could only imagine that Jane, who'd worked just as hard as he had training a new puppy for a recently returned veteran, felt the same.

"All right, girl," Isaac said, attaching Jane's leash to her collar. "Let me just grab my stuff from the truck and we'll head home the old-fashioned way."

He'd only gotten as far as reaching into the cab before Jane erupted into a low growl, followed by loud, staccato warning barks.

A tingle of apprehension fluttered up Isaac's spine and the tiny hairs on the back of his neck stood at attention.

Jane wasn't the sort to cry wolf; she wouldn't give a warning unless she'd seen, heard or smelled something beyond the range of Isaac's senses.

"What is it, girl?" he whispered, turning to peer into

the curtain of trees on the other side of the ditch while reaching under the driver's seat of his truck for the hunting knife he kept there. Jane would have to be his eyes and ears. He couldn't see squat with everything obscured by the thick darkness.

The dog let out another growl and raised her hackles.

Finally, Isaac caught sight of something moving in the blackness. He squinted, trying to see a little better, as a shadowy form emerged from along the tree line. His instinct was to simply shout out a greeting. This was Peach Leaf, after all. The idea of a prowler out on the lonely ranch road leading to his home was almost laughable. But until he got a better look at whatever or whoever was traipsing through the night, he'd be wise to assume the worst.

Suddenly, the figure—almost certainly human, he could now tell—crouched down low and crawled quickly toward the ditch. Jane barked furiously at this new development and tugged at her leash to be set free so she could investigate. But a threat to Isaac was a threat to her, so he called her to his side and patted the truck seat. Jane gave a whimper of protest but obeyed, jumping up into the cab. Isaac quickly rolled down the window an inch and locked the door, pocketing his keys and knife.

He expected more movement from the ditch, but all remained still. Part of him knew it wasn't too bright to follow up on whatever or whomever lay there in the dirt, but he didn't have much of a choice. If he and Jane headed off down the road toward home, whatever it was might follow, and he'd rather deal with it now than have to look over his shoulder on his way back to the house or potentially deal with a break-in later in the night. On the other hand, it could be some runaway kid, lost or potentially hurt, and he wouldn't be able to sleep wondering if he might have been able to help one of his community members.

He realized he'd been standing still while he thought this through, but that settled it, so he grabbed his cell phone from his back pocket and turned on the flashlight app. The low-battery warning flashed across the screen a second later and Isaac cursed under his breath.

He told Jane he'd be right back and climbed up out of their place in the ditch so he could walk along the edge. That way, he'd have the upper hand once he made it to wherever *it* was, and if Jane started barking again, he could run right back to the truck.

He stepped slowly, holding the light out in front of him until he spotted a dark lump, stopping abruptly to get a better look.

"What the—" he murmured, powerless to make sense of what he saw until it moved, which didn't help at all as things only became less clear.

The *thing* was a woman, Isaac realized.

For a full minute, he simply stood there, unable to pick up his suddenly leaden feet. His heart might have kicked up its pace again at the sight of her, if it hadn't already tumbled down into his stomach.

Being the youngest child, and still single, despite the town's many ill-advised attempts to remedy that situation, Isaac had never had anyone to protect. He had Jane, of course, but the spitfire dog who'd landed on his doorstep a few years back, demanding a home, had always done a damn good job of looking out for herself—and now she lived in the lap of luxury, spoiled beyond belief by her human.

But he'd never really experienced that protective instinct, had never known the feeling that another person relied on him for safety.

Until now.

For some reason—as he stared down into that ditch at the pathetically thin, shaking woman curled into a ball there—a fierce burning sensation flooded his insides.

He didn't know who she was, or what in the hell she was doing there, but somehow something outside of him pulled Isaac toward her.

Somehow, he knew she needed him.

When the flashback subsided and Avery finally came to, she had no earthly idea where she was.

This wasn't the first time it had happened.

It wouldn't be the last.

She closed her eyes and pulled in a deep breath, but, as usual, the terrible shaking wouldn't cease. The air around her was humid, and a warm spring breeze rustled through some nearby trees every now and then, but inside Avery was freezing, even as sweat rolled down her arms.

Too-skinny arms, Tommy would say. She was thankful every day that he'd let her live in his house when things had become…too much…but sometimes his constant concern for her—the endless checking up to see if she was okay—was another kind of too much.

"Ma'am?"

The male voice came from somewhere above her head and, within seconds, Avery had uncurled from her position and bolted upright to face its owner.

The last time she'd had an episode, her sister-in-law, Macy, had found Avery in Sylvia's room. That was plenty awkward, especially when the two women had to work out how to explain to Avery's five-year-old niece why her aunt was crouched, armed, in the child's bedroom closet.

That was when her brother insisted they clear the house of anything "dangerous" she might end up wielding in self-defense when one of the flashbacks hit. He didn't know about the baseball bat she kept hidden under her bed in case she needed to protect her family.

"It's not that we don't trust you," Tommy had said in the same sotto voce he used with his children, while refusing to meet her eyes. "We just can't risk anything happening. It's for the best."

Avery's stomach churned at the memory. The worst part was, her brother was absolutely correct. If she'd had anywhere else to go after that, she would have. But she did not. And, worse, she was completely dependent on the few remaining people in her life—the few that hadn't given up on her—for everything.

But that was the last time.

This time, from what little she could deduce in a quick survey of her surroundings, might just turn out to be downright humiliating.

He spoke again. "Is there anything I can do to help you?" he asked. "Are you lost?"

Avery almost grinned at that last part, because yes, indeed, she was very, very lost.

The only thing that stopped her was the tone of the man's voice. Glancing around, she could see that she was completely alone in some dirt hole on the side of a gravel country road, in—she looked down at her body—a thin white tank and army-issue workout shorts. Clearly she was at the mercy of this guy, who'd evidently stopped to check on her. Under other circumstances, her training would have kicked in and she'd have flipped him onto his back in mere seconds.

But something told her he wasn't a threat.

His voice.

It was deep and smooth, his words bathed in the local accent, and full of genuine concern. On top of that, he stood above the ditch staring down at her, hands at his sides, and hadn't made a single move to come closer. The man seemed...*safe.*

Having lost her bat somewhere along the way, she braced herself for an attack when he bent his knees, but instead of jumping into the ditch with her like she thought he might, the man simply knelt down.

The movement brought attention to long, muscled thighs beneath faded denim jeans, and when he leaned an elbow on his upright knee, Avery noticed the stretch of tendons in his sinewy forearms.

How ridiculous it was, she thought, for her to notice such a stupid thing when her life could be in danger for all she knew. Seeing as how the guy hadn't mauled her by now, it probably wasn't, but still—it could be.

Avery crossed her arms over her thinly clad chest. Not that there was much to see there. Not anymore.

"I'm fine, actually. Just…taking a walk. Enjoying the stars and all." She waved a hand above her, indicating the spread of twinkling lights above them. It was plausible.

But when she looked up into his eyes, she could tell he didn't agree. The man looked to be somewhere near her own age, maybe slightly older, and Avery was surprised she'd never seen him before. She'd grown up in Peach Leaf and knew just about everybody, so it was strange that she hadn't met this person.

Sure as hell would remember if she had.

Not only did he have the toned body of someone who either worked at it or had a very active job—he had a face to do it justice. Clear, dark chocolate eyes—eyes that had a certain glint in them, as though they saw more than most—a strong jaw and hair the color of a panther's coat.

Right now those brown eyes narrowed with what appeared to be strong suspicion, but after a few seconds, they filled with a certain kind of warmth Avery wasn't used to seeing anymore.

Pity—she was used to that—but not warmth.

"It is a beautiful night, isn't it?" he said, seeming to relax a little.

There was something easy about him that made Avery want to let her guard down a smidge. It was almost as if his mere presence lowered her blood pressure.

"That it is," she agreed, wanting the strange exchange to be over so she could figure out how far she'd gotten and how, for the love of all things holy, she was supposed to get back home.

"Name's Isaac," the man said, stretching out a large hand.

Even in the dark, Avery could see calluses and healed-over scratches. Must be some kind of laborer.

She just stared at him, not offering her name, willing him to take his leave. It would be futile to try to explain the complexities of her *condition*, as she'd come to think of it, to this handsome stranger. She didn't even completely understand it herself, even after almost a year of therapy. Besides, her knees were beginning to feel a little wobbly and a spot just above her left temple had started to ache…

"Well, if you're all set here—" he looked like he believed her to be anything but "—I've got a walk ahead of me."

Isaac hesitated for a long moment, then nodded and turned to leave.

Avery was about to do the same when everything went blacker than the night sky.

Isaac had just started back toward his truck—every nerve in his body telling him to stay behind—when he heard a thud.

He whipped back around and broke into a run when he saw that the woman had collapsed in a heap, dust billowing around her.

Crap.

He knew he should have stayed put and tried to talk her into letting him help. It didn't take a genius to see she was in some kind of trouble.

Walking even a few yards away from her had gone against his every instinct, but he hadn't planned to actually leave her alone in the middle of the night, not for a single moment. He just needed a second to regroup.

His legs made quick work of the distance that separated them and seconds later he plunged into the ditch and reached her side, lifting the woman's negligible weight into his arms and propping her up so she might draw in deeper breaths. Her skin was clammy and she seemed to flutter on the verge of consciousness as she pulled in shallow doses of air.

Isaac had no idea what steps to take from there; as a certified dog trainer, he was generally better prepared for canine emergencies than those of his own species. His heart beat frantically for several long minutes as he held her, waiting for her to come back so he could better help her. As slow seconds beat past, he studied the woman in his grasp, seeing for the first time how lovely she was.

Her long blond hair seemed to shimmer in the moonlight, its corn-silk strands tickling his arms where it fell. Creamy skin, just a shade or two lighter than her hair, lay like soft linen over sculpted cheekbones, creating a perfect canvas for full lips and large eyes, the color of which he suddenly longed to know.

She wore a white T-shirt and athletic shorts, and Isaac grimaced when he caught sight of the sharp ridge of collarbone peeking out the top of the threadbare cotton. She was so very thin. No wonder lifting her had felt no more difficult than picking up Jane. A glint of metal got his attention and he reached up to search for a pendant attached to a silver chain around her neck, adjusting her so he could remain supporting her with one arm.

Running his finger along the tiny links, Isaac finally touched an ID tag of some sort and pulled it closer to his face.

It was an army-issue dog tag; he'd recognize it anywhere because of his brother, Stephen, and working with so many veterans and their companions at his dog training facility. This one was engraved *A. Abbott*.

Somehow seeing her name made him even more impatient to wake her up. He knew nothing about the pretty woman, except that she looked like she could stand to eat a quarter pounder or two, but something about her pulled him in and wouldn't let go.

His buddies would've teased him relentlessly if they could have seen him then. *Meyer can't resist a damsel in distress*, he could almost hear them say, joshing at his tendency to offer assistance to every granny who chanced to cross a street in Peach Leaf or any single mom who needed the use of his truck for a move.

But this one was different.

Before she'd tumbled to the ground, Isaac had seen enough to know that Abbott was no damsel in distress. Her voice had been tough—commanding, almost—and, despite her smallness, she'd stood tall and carried herself with authority and confidence. It was her body that had finally lost its resolve—no doubt, from the look of things, due to not eating enough—not her mind or her survival instinct.

Now that he'd seen the tag, he understood why.

Now that he'd seen the tag, he'd also begun to form an idea of what might have happened to her and, more important, how he might be able to help.

Chapter Two

Avery woke for the second time that night about an hour later.

For a moment, forgetting the strange dreamlike events of the night, she thought she might be back at home safe in her bed while Tommy and Macy cooked breakfast for her niece and nephew.

But when Avery sat up and opened her eyes, a rush of panic hit her like a bucket of ice water and she shot up from an unfamiliar couch, gasping for breath as she fully realized that she had no idea where she was.

Again.

A hand-knit afghan in alternating tones of light and dark blues tumbled to the floor, covering her feet, and as her eyes adjusted to the golden light coming from a nearby table lamp, Avery glanced briefly around the room. It was minimally decorated but cozy, and she wondered at the comfort it provided despite its newness to her.

"Easy there," a low voice came from behind the sofa and she nearly jumped out of her skin.

Avery put up her fists and turned around in one quick motion, ready to face whatever situation her unpredictable, unreliable mind had gotten her into now.

"Who are you, and where the hell am I?" she spat out, willing her voice to mask the fear that was quickly weaving its way from her gut to her chest.

The nightmares were bad enough, but the flashbacks, rarer though they were, absolutely terrified her. This wasn't the first time she'd found herself in a place from which she couldn't retrace her steps. If it happened on too many more occasions, she didn't even want to think about the action her family and therapist might agree on against her will. She'd already lost her job and her own place. The thought of being locked up somewhere…

The man in front of her gently placed the cell phone he'd been holding on a small end table, immediately holding up both of his hands. She vaguely recalled his handsome face as a tiny slice of memory slipped from the recesses of her mind, but it vanished before she could catch it, leaving her with nothing helpful.

"My name's Isaac. Isaac Meyer. I'm not gonna hurt you. And obviously you don't remember—you were pretty out of it—but we did meet earlier." A Southern accent similar to her own slid over the man's words like hot gravy, identifying him as a local.

"Avery," she murmured.

He stood completely still as Avery looked him up and down, her soldier's instincts and peripheral vision checking every inch of his person, even as her eyes remained steadily locked on to his. They were a rich brown, she noticed, instantly chastising herself for wasting time on such a silly thought when she faced a potential enemy.

When Avery didn't speak for a long moment, he continued.

"Look, I know this has been a strange night, at least for me, but—" He hesitated and seemed to be working through his thoughts before speaking. "I found you on the side of the road. In a ditch. Jane and I didn't know what to do and there wasn't a damn thing could be done to help you out there in the dark, so we brought you back here."

He lowered one hand, slowly and cautiously as if trying not to unsettle a rabid animal, and pointed toward the phone before putting his hand back up. "I was just about to call 9-1-1 and see about getting someone out here to check on you. Then you woke up and, well, here we are."

Avery had no recollection of meeting him earlier, only his word to go on and the vague, déjà vu–like inkling that she'd seen him before. The past few hours were as blank as a fresh sheet of paper. In all he'd said, only one insignificant thing stuck out to her. That seemed the way of it lately. If she couldn't focus on everything, she picked out the smallest bit and used that to ground her in reality. It was one of the few things her therapist had taught her that she'd actually practiced.

"Jane? Who's Jane?" she asked, wondering, of all things, why that particular piece of information mattered.

At the mention of the name, Isaac's features noticeably softened and Avery let her body do likewise, relaxing a little as she checked off facts in her head. One—if he'd a mind to, he could have murdered her already. Two—the man had placed a homemade blanket on her, for goodness' sake. What murderer did such a thing? And three—if he was to be believed, and there was no clear indication why he shouldn't at this point, as she was standing there unharmed in his comfortable home, he'd been about to call for help, something she absolutely did *not* want him to do. Thank goodness she'd woken up in time to prevent that from happening. The very last thing she needed right now was for Tommy or her parents to have another reason to worry about her. Of all the things she hated about her PTSD, perhaps the worst was the way it had turned a grown, successful woman into a child, or at least that's how her family saw her.

She had to get back home as soon as possible, but first, she needed to find out exactly how far her deceitful mind had dragged her this time.

She waited for an answer to her question but instead of providing one, Isaac gave a sharp whistle and a large dog of an unidentifiable breed, with an unruly coat consisting of about a hundred varying shades of brown, strolled into the room to sit beside him, looking up at its human with what could only be described as pure adoration. Man looked down at dog with open pride.

"Avery, meet Jane," he said, then gave the canine some sort of hand signal.

Before she could protest, the dog was standing in front of her. She watched, unmoving, as Jane reached out a large, fuzzy paw and stared expectantly up at her with huge brown eyes. The whole thing was so absurdly cute that Avery couldn't keep a smile from curving at the edge of her lips. Noticing for the first time that she still held her fists defensively in front of her, Avery lowered both hands and reached one out to grasp the offered paw. The warm, soft fur was instantly soothing, but when Jane took back her paw and pressed her large, heavy head against Avery's thighs, her tail breaking into a slow wag as she waited for her doggie hug to be reciprocated, Avery's heart caught in her throat.

A wave of emotion swept over her like an evening tide and her knees nearly buckled beneath her. She was suddenly, desperately sad. And oh-so-tired. Tired of being dependent on others to keep her safe when she'd once been so self-reliant. Tired of being locked inside her own head. Tired of being afraid to go to sleep, knowing the nightmares would meet her there like a mugger waiting in the shade of night for his next victim, and tired of feeling crazy when she knew—even if everyone else believed otherwise—that she was not.

She gently pushed the dog away and sat down on the sofa. Jane jumped up, too, but sat a few feet away, as if giving Avery her space. Isaac moved across the room to sit in a chair on the other side of a mahogany coffee table. He folded his hands in his lap and looked at the floor. Avery knew she should keep an eye on him until she could get out of there but her lids felt weighted and she let them slip closed for just a second as she gathered her thoughts.

"How long was I out?" she asked, swallowing, not really wanting to know the answer. Her flashbacks, blackouts, whatever the hell they were, sometimes lasted for hours before she came back around. She hated the loss of control and the resulting feeling of irresponsibility, as though she'd had too much to drink and passed out at the wheel.

She looked up at Isaac, meeting his eyes. In them, she found none of the things she'd expected: pity, irritation, confusion. Instead, they were like deep woods in the middle of the night—quiet, dark, mysterious—but for some reason, she felt safe there. She knew enough to sense menace when it lurked, and so she knew then as sure as she knew her own name and rank that this man was not dangerous.

"About an hour," he said, his voice smooth like strong coffee. "Took me half of that to get you here. My truck broke down just up the road and my cell had almost no charge left. You were pretty cold when Jane and I got you inside the house, so I covered you with a blanket and plugged in the phone for ten minutes or so. You didn't seem wounded or anything, but it's not every day I find people prowling around in the dark, so I figured best thing to do was call the authorities and let them make sure you're okay and sort you out."

Isaac paused, brow furrowed, and it seemed he might say more, but then he closed his mouth and looked at her expectantly.

She sifted through his comments, appreciating his effort and the fact that, other than to carry her, he hadn't handled her any more than necessary; in fact, he seemed wary of being anywhere near her—a thought that touched her heart with the gentlemanliness it bespoke. His simple, strong kindness reminded her of some of the men she'd served alongside, and for a fleeting moment, she missed her comrades.

There had been a time, not that long after returning home, when she would have done anything to forget her tours overseas if it would have helped her blend back in to civilian society. But after being back in Peach Leaf for a few months, newly burdened with the knowledge that such a wish might never come true, she'd begun to long for another deployment, if only for the fact that she didn't know how to be "normal" anymore, whatever that meant. She didn't belong in her own world, and she hadn't truly belonged in that barren, violence-riddled land, so the question was, as always: Where, if anywhere, did she belong?

"You could have left me there, you know," Avery said. "I didn't need any help." The words sounded hollow and impractical even as she spoke them.

"We both know that's not true," he answered, his tone thankfully free of judgment.

She didn't want to have to explain herself to a complete stranger. Even a kind, gentle, admittedly handsome stranger.

"All the same, though," he continued, "I don't think it's safe for you to walk home on your own and, as I said, my truck's out of commission for the night. Is there anyone you can call to—"

"No!" she shouted as her body simultaneously lurched forward a few feet, startling them both. She covered her mouth with her hand, the skin icy against her warm lips.

"Look, if you're in some kind of dicey situation, it ain't any of my business, but I can't let you stay out here alone in the dark, either.

She shook her head and lowered her hand, clasping it between her knees. "No, no, it's not like that. I'm not… I mean… I just have these episodes sometimes, and occasionally I lose track of where I am." She stopped abruptly, not really knowing what else to say but thankfully, he didn't seem to expect much more. Trying to put her problems into words was always a fragile balancing act of saying too little or too much. Even though they appreciated her service, she'd quickly discovered that most people would rather not think or talk about the things that Avery had experienced, and it was hard to describe something she herself didn't fully understand.

Isaac swallowed and held out his hands, palms up. His face was difficult to read but not hardened, and his expression gave her the idea that he was genuinely waiting to hear what she had to say, who she was, before making his mind up about her. It was refreshing. In her small town, Avery was used to people thinking they knew everything about each other just because they'd racked up some years together in the same place. They made the frequent mistake of assuming that you'd always be who you once were.

"Speaking of," she went on, struggling to hide her sudden embarrassment at having to ask, "would you mind telling me where we are?"

Isaac's lids lowered and his mouth relaxed into an easy grin, as if he'd been waiting for her to ask so he could have something helpful to offer. "Sure thing. We're about two miles outside of Peach Leaf proper, and my house is about half a mile from Ranch Road 64. Closest landmark is Dewberry Farms, my neighbor."

His neighbor. Her brother.

Avery released an audible sigh of relief that she hadn't wandered too far from home in her—she looked down, suddenly aware of the goose bumps that had formed a tiny mountain range along her arms—*very* thin pajamas. Thank goodness she'd been unable to shed the habit of sleeping in her sports bra or she'd have been sitting in a stranger's living room without a shred of modesty.

"Dewberry is my home, at least for now," she said, and Isaac nodded, seeming unsurprised. He probably knew her recent history as well as any of the other locals. It said a lot about his character that he wasn't acting as though that meant he knew *her*.

"Well, as you know, it's not far from here. I think I feel well enough to walk back now. If I don't make it home before everyone wakes up, they'll be worried, so—" she pointed a thumb in the general direction of the front door "—I should probably get going."

Isaac held out a hand as she stood. "I don't think that's such a good idea."

"Why not?" She rolled her eyes almost immediately,

sitting back down as the inside of her head did another dizzy spin. "I mean, I know why not, but how is it any of your business? I appreciate you helping me, but I'm okay now."

Isaac shook his head. "For one thing, you're pale as a ghost, and let's not forget you were passed out for a solid hour. Plus, pardon my saying so, but you look like you could use some energy if you're going to walk a half mile, which, for the record, I'd recommend putting off until the sun comes up."

Avery bit her lip, considering. Everything he said was absolutely right, but she couldn't risk letting Tommy or Macy find her bed empty again. She wouldn't put them through that worry another time.

Her brother and sister-in-law had already given her a place to stay and a hell of a lot of support through the lowest point in her life so far, for which she'd never be able to repay them. They said they were glad to do it and they meant well, but Avery wasn't naive, and she wasn't blind; she could see the way they looked at her when they insisted she was no imposition, as if they weren't sure what she might do next, or worse, how her involuntary actions might affect their kids. She could see the way they walked on eggshells around her. The familiar guilt made her empty stomach clench in pain.

She sat back down on the sofa and Jane thumped her tail against the worn fabric. Avery reached over to pet the dog's soft fur, surprised once again at how comforting it was just to stroke Jane's broad back. When she gave Jane a few scratches behind her enormous, fuzzy ears and the scruffy mutt closed her eyes in bliss, Avery was pretty sure she'd made a friend for life.

"It makes me feel so calm, petting her." Avery was surprised to hear herself state the thought out loud, but the combination of the kind stranger's presence and the silky sensation of the dog's warm coat made her feel more at ease than she had since she'd been home.

"She tends to have that effect on people. Lots of dogs do," he said.

Avery looked up to find Isaac beaming with pride, and she noticed again how good-looking he was, in such a different way than the men she'd been attracted to before. His features were less sharp than the square-jawed, light-featured military types she usually preferred. His hair was collar length, wavy and dark, almost black, in the soft glow of lamplight flooding the living room, and his eyes were nearly the same shade of brown. He reminded her of a rakish lord from one of the historical romances she devoured at an incredible pace, one of the few pastimes that allowed her to completely escape the bleak hollows of her own thoughts.

It wouldn't be inaccurate to describe him as *devilishly handsome*, she thought, a smile blossoming over her lips before she caught herself and bit the bottom one.

He caught her smiling and she pretended to study Jane's fur, the heat of a blush rushing to her cheeks. She couldn't remember the last time she'd felt drawn to someone that way, much less *blushed* over a man, for goodness' sake. She'd had a few boyfriends before her first deployment, but it always seemed sort of futile to get into something serious when she'd been on active duty, never knowing when she might have to pack up and leave at last-minute notice. Sure, lots of people made it work, as her mother constantly reminded her, probably with visions of more grandbabies dancing through her head, but Avery had seen enough hurt in that area to last a lifetime.

She swallowed against the dull ache that rose in her heart every time the memory of her best friend crossed her mind, at least a thousand times per day—her punishment for being alive when Sophie was not. Sophie, who'd left behind a husband and child who blamed Avery for Sophie's absence in their lives. It didn't matter whether it had been Avery's fault or not—the center of their world was gone, and Avery had been the last one to see her.

It was Avery who'd promised them she'd watch over their wife and mother, and it was Avery who failed to keep that promise.

She felt Isaac's eyes on her and looked up to meet them.

"You're right about it not being a good idea to walk back in the dark," she admitted. "If it's not too much trouble, I'd like to stick around until the sun comes up, then I'll head back that way."

If Isaac's house was as close to Tommy's as he'd said, it would take her less than ten minutes to jog back at daybreak, and she could slip in the back door and make it into her bed before anyone tried to wake her. Tommy would be making coffee and Macy would be busy with the kids.

He nodded. "Not a problem. If you passed Jane's

character test, then you're welcome to stick around as long as you need to," he said, his tone lighter now. "On one condition."

Avery stopped petting Jane and raised an eyebrow in question.

"Let me cook something for you."

Chapter Three

As he waited for her answer, Isaac glanced at the grandfather clock near the hallway, one of the many things he'd been unable to part with when Nana had willed the old ranch-style home to him a couple of years ago. Its iron hands indicated the hour was near two o'clock in the morning.

They had plenty of time for a bite before daylight when Avery would leave and go back to Dewberry—a thought that, had he more time to entertain, he might have admitted he didn't much care for. He liked the quiet comfort and surrounding memories of the house he'd spent so many happy summers in as a child, and most of the time he was okay with the fact that he lived in the country and didn't entertain a lot of visitors, but there were times when he got lonely. Even though Jane was one hell of a listener, she didn't do much in the way of talking.

It was nice to have a woman in his home. He liked the way Avery's presence added a certain softness to the atmosphere, and he found himself caring whether or not she liked the place.

"I'm not really very hungry," she answered, earning a pointed look from him.

"Come on, now. I'm a very good cook. I'm famous for my barbecue, but I can make a mean sandwich in a pinch. Seriously, call your brother and ask him," Isaac joked, regretting the words when he saw they'd caused her to wince. Tommy had mentioned, of course, that he had a sister who'd recently come home after a few tours in Afghanistan, but since they'd never been introduced or run into each other anywhere in town—which was odd in itself—Isaac hadn't given much thought to the mysterious female Abbott. He and Tommy crossed paths frequently, as the farm always provided food for the events Isaac hosted on behalf of his dog training center, Friends with Fur, but he'd never once seen Avery.

He wouldn't have forgotten her if he had.

The locals talked about her enough; they all had theories about how she might be doing now that she was back, what kind of girl she'd been growing up and—these comments were always in hushed tones accented with the sympathetic clicking of tongues—how she wasn't quite *right* anymore, *bless her heart*. But in Isaac's line of work, he'd learned to withhold judgment until he got to know someone.

And he knew that when broken people kept to themselves, holed up behind walls built to keep out hurt, eventually their family and friends, even the closest ones, stopped asking the hard questions and accepted the new, hollow versions, forgetting that at one time those wounded people were whole.

He got up from his chair and moved toward the couch to scratch Janie's pink tummy, which she'd shamelessly turned over and exposed so that Avery could have the esteemed privilege of rubbing it.

He raised his eyes and watched as Avery pet Jane, admiring the way the dog's gentle serenity seemed to seep into the woman's weary bones.

"Tell you what—I had a long day and I'm hungry, so I'm going to start up a grilled cheese sandwich." He watched Avery for any change in her expression, but her features remained still. "You're welcome to join me if you want to, and I'd be happy to make two."

She raised her eyes then and he was reminded of how blue they were, like shadowy mountaintops at dusk.

"I wasn't always like this, you know," Avery said, her voice so quiet he wasn't sure the words were meant for him to hear.

Even though her gaze was on his, Isaac could tell her thoughts were far off somewhere he couldn't reach. He'd seen the same look on many of the veterans he worked with at the training facility, and he'd learned not to push too hard. Sometimes it was best to stay silent and let the person decide how much he or she wanted to say or not say.

"I used to be strong. Independent." She glanced away. "I can't tell you how humiliating it is to be sitting here in your house, having to trust your word on how I got here."

Isaac's insides ached at her admission and he had the sudden urge to reach out and hold her hand. He wouldn't, but he wanted to.

He'd always had an easier time relating to canines than to his own kind, a product of being homeschooled by a widowed young mom who'd been overwhelmed by the world outside their door, with only his older brother and a series of family pets to keep him company. He would never complain about his childhood. After all, it had been safer and saner than many of his friends' and colleagues', but it had also been lonely.

Ever since he'd moved away briefly for college and then come home to start a business, Isaac had longed for a family of his own. He wanted life to be much different from the way he'd been raised; he wanted kiddos running around shouting happily, dogs barking joyfully and, above all, lots and lots of laughter.

Most people wanted quiet when they came home at the end of a long workday, he thought with a chuckle, but Isaac craved noise.

He wasn't sure what he could say, but he gave it a try anyway. "I know I don't know you, so my saying so doesn't mean much, but you have nothing to be embarrassed by."

He looked up in time to see Avery shaking her head, but he went on, sharing things he rarely got a chance to. "You served your country with honor, and I can bet you dealt with a lot of things no one should ever have to, but that doesn't mean you're different than any other human being. People aren't meant to be around the things I'm sure you were, and come out the same on the other side. War is bound to do some damage to a person's soul. I don't think anyone expects you to come back and pick up where you left off without a few hurdles to jump."

Avery closed her eyes and then opened them slowly, regarding him with an expression he couldn't read.

"Sometimes it feels like that's exactly what they expect."

"Well, they shouldn't," he responded. "And I think that's just a product of not really being able to understand what you went through over there."

Not wanting to say anything that would make Avery uncomfortable, that would make her retreat back into her shell, Isaac gave Jane one final pat and then headed off to the kitchen.

He'd pulled cheese and butter out of the fridge and was opening a wooden bread box when he heard her soft footsteps behind him. He tossed a welcome grin over his shoulder, pleased when he noticed that she wasn't alone. Jane, his big, goofy sweetheart, had followed Avery and was glued to her side. It was one of the characteristics he loved most about dogs. They were quick to make friends.

"How are you so wise about this stuff?" Avery asked, giving him a sad little smile. "Did you serve, as well?"

He shook his head. "No, but in my work, I meet a lot of people who did, and I've learned a few things along the way." He bit back the urge to mention the brother he'd lost; talking about what happened to Stephen would likely be unhelpful at that particular moment.

Her eyes, huge and dark blue in a small, lovely, heart-shaped face, were full of questions and she seemed almost eager, for the first time that evening, to talk with him.

"What kind of work do you do?" she asked, not meeting his eyes as she ran a finger along the glossy edge of the oak table in the adjoining breakfast nook.

"I own a dog-training facility. I opened it a couple of years ago and I have a few assistants now, other trainers. We do all kinds of work—basic obedience, scent, search and rescue—but my most recent project is working with veterans."

"Do you mind if I ask, I mean, how well does that usually work? The vet-and-dog combination?"

Out of the corner of his eye, he watched her sit down at the table and he began cutting squares of cheese off a block of cheddar.

Isaac gave a rough little laugh. "You're not the only one who wants to know that," he said. A lot of people—influential people—wondered the same thing, and soon Isaac hoped to have a way of answering that with his own research, so that he could raise the necessary funding to expand his project. A project that, thanks to great dogs and veterans willing to work hard to overcome their pain, had already changed several lives for the better. He enjoyed all kinds of training, but this particular sort had become his passion over the past couple of years.

"Quite well, actually."

Avery's forehead wrinkled in curiosity, which he took as an invitation to keep talking. Normally, he was a pretty quiet guy, even a little on the shy side, one might say, but when it came to his career, he could go on all day.

"Service animals make some of the best companions to soldiers who've returned from war carrying more than physical baggage. With the right training, they can be a huge asset to people dealing with past trauma or symptoms of PTSD, and they can be even better than medication at calming soldiers in the midst of panic attacks, or…even flashbacks."

He wasn't going to put a label on what had happened with Avery that night. He wasn't a doctor and he didn't have all the details, but his gut told him that's what had occurred to her prior to him stumbling upon her in that ditch.

"Sorry if I sound like a public service announcement. I just care a lot about this stuff. It's affected a lot of people I care about."

Her shoulders let go of some of their tension as he spoke, and there was even a hint of hope in her eyes as he explained the process of rescuing dogs from the local shelter and giving them homes, purpose and new, full lives.

"So basically you're saving two people at once," she said, her eyes brighter than they had been since he'd met her. "Or, well, one person and one dog—you know what I meant," she said, her cheeks turning a pretty, soft pink.

He bent to pull a skillet from a low cabinet, partly so he could warm up a pat of butter and start the sandwich, and partly so she wouldn't see the way her sweet expression had affected him.

He didn't mind helping her out—any decent guy

would have done the same—and he was glad to let her stay awhile until the sun came up. He was even happy to make her a much-needed meal. He told himself it was harmless to feel attracted to a too-thin but still gorgeous woman he'd happened upon by some stroke of fate, but what he could not allow was for that attraction to go any further.

From the looks of things, Avery Abbott needed a lot of help, some of which he might even be able to offer, but it was highly unlikely she was looking for a relationship. Not with what she was obviously going through right now.

And Isaac, truth be told, very much wanted one.

He lit the stove and waited for it to heat, finally placing the butter in to melt.

"I haven't saved anyone," he said. "They save each other."

While the butter changed from solid to a sizzling little pool, he put cheese between bread slices and arranged two plates to hold the finished food. Once he'd set the first sandwich in the pan, he chanced another look at her, surprised to see unshed tears shimmering in Avery's eyes. She rubbed at her lids and he looked away, kicking himself for saying something that might have added any more pain to her already awful night. He wanted to apologize, but wasn't sure what to say; words had never been his strong suit. He much preferred movement and action, but those weren't always what was required.

Five minutes later, he plated the sandwiches and brought them, along with two glasses of water, over to the table to join Avery, who smiled up at him as he sat, all traces of moisture gone from those sapphire eyes.

"Thank you for this," she said softly, "and for everything. I owe you one."

"You don't owe me anything," he said. "What was I supposed to do, leave you out there alone on the side of the road? What kind of man would that make me?" He winked and picked up his sandwich.

That coaxed a little grin out of her, which gave him more satisfaction than it should have.

"I have to say, Mr. Meyer, you do seem like a stand-up guy. Do you make a habit of rescuing lost women in the middle of the night?" she asked, and he had the distinct feeling she was flirting with him a little.

Something fluttered in his belly, and he didn't think it was hunger.

"I haven't before," he answered, "but after tonight, who knows? Maybe I will."

Avery laughed so hard at that cheesiness that the sip of water she'd just taken almost came out of her nose. Within minutes, they were both laughing like idiots, at what he really couldn't say.

But it felt good.

After the weirdest night of his life, and after the too-strong sense of relief he now felt seeing that this woman, this soldier, could still laugh despite the things life had thrown her way, it felt good to join her in a moment of ridiculousness. It was almost as if something in his heart had come unknotted.

Even though he knew it was completely irrational, he realized suddenly, with as much certainty and force as one might realize it's raining as drops hit the ground, that he would do absolutely everything he could to help her get better.

Chapter Four

Avery's heart hammered out a quick rhythm as she opened the back door slowly and with measured care—then winced as it squeaked loudly in protest, as if its intention was to inform the entire house of her... adventures.

She resented feeling like a teenager, sneaking into her brother's home. Just another reminder that her life as of late was anything but normal. And, oh, how she craved normal.

"Morning, sweetheart."

Despite its softness, Macy's greeting caused Avery to gasp and turn around so fast that whiplash wouldn't have been an implausible outcome.

"Holy goodness, Mace. You scared the living daylights out of me," Avery said, shoving a hand against her heart. As she leaned back and let her spine rest against the closed door, fighting to catch her breath, she studied her sister-in-law. Macy was, as always, as pretty at the crack of dawn—with her golden hair all messy and the imprint of a pillow seam etched into her cheek—as she had been on her and Tommy's wedding day. Avery indulged in the memory—a time when everything was simpler, purer—before she'd brought home a personal hell that had begun to seep into all their lives.

"Speaking of daylights," Macy said quietly, tugging her frayed, pink terry-cloth robe tighter around her waist, "the sun hasn't even risen and here you are looking like you've had quite a night."

Avery's lips formed a thin line, but she held Macy's gaze, despite the temptation to look away from what she saw in the sweet, open face.

"What do you want me to say?"

Macy closed her eyes and then opened them again, sympathy etched into her features. "I just want you to be okay, honey, that's all. We all do." She looked as though she might want to touch or hold Avery, but knew better from experience.

Even though the conversation wasn't anything new, something tugged at Avery's heartstrings and for a second she longed to just collapse and let it all out—to tell someone how desperately scared she was, how the nightmares kept getting worse, and how she couldn't always tell the difference between those and the flashbacks. How sometimes she wasn't sure whether she was awake or asleep.

But something else, something strange and new, told

her this wasn't the time or place…but that maybe she was getting close to being able to do just that…and that maybe Isaac was that place. As Macy waited for an answer to the questions she hadn't voiced out loud but were always there, Avery thought back to the man she'd met that morning.

Even under the strange circumstances that brought them together last night, he had been so calm, so sturdy and safe, like a lighthouse in a raging storm. He'd taken care of her without hesitation, and for some reason she knew he would have done the same for any wayward creature.

He was the embodiment of that most rare and beautiful thing, something Avery had seen precious little of over the past few years: basic human kindness.

"Well, now, there's something you don't see every day," Macy said, a giggle bubbling up around her words. "You want to tell me what has you smiling like that, or is it a secret?"

Avery, disbelieving, reached up and touched a finger to her lips, realizing only upon feeling their upward curve to what her sister-in-law referred. Before she could form a response, Macy's eyes lit up and her mouth opened wide.

"Oh, my gosh, Avery," she blurted. "Were you—" she crossed her arms over her chest and leaned forward "—were you…with a guy?"

"No!" Avery spat, but she wasn't fooling anyone. She winced. "Well, technically, yes, but it's not what it seems." She held her palms out, hoping for emphasis.

Macy eyed her with blatant skepticism. "Yeah," she

said, grinning, "usually when people say that, it's exactly what it seems."

A little unexpected laugh escaped from Avery's throat. She peered at her sister, her friend, with narrow eyes. "You've been watching too many romantic comedies," she said, hoping to divert attention away from herself, blushing a little at the mere thought that Macy's suggestion put into her head.

She had a feeling it wouldn't go away as easily or as quickly as it had arrived. Isaac's dark, unruly hair twisted around her fingers, those deep brown eyes gazing at her with...with what, exactly? Lust? Over *her*?

Not likely, at least not in her current state of skin and bones. She'd need to put on a good ten pounds before anything like that happened, or someone might get hurt. Before she could stop them, more thoughts tumbled in, unbidden. Suddenly, she remembered being carried in those arms—strong arms, brandished a deep gold by the Texas sun—and, for once, the thought of being held didn't seem quite so scary. It was nice to feel attraction to a man, a welcome distraction from her usual preoccupations.

"Something tells me I'm not too far off," Macy said, interrupting Avery's ridiculous reverie.

It would be great if her dreams were more like that than the terrifying things they actually were. She met her sister-in-law's curious gaze. "No," she answered truthfully. "I did run into your neighbor Isaac Meyer, but it's not like what you're thinking."

Macy's shoulders sagged and Avery's heart bruised.

How desperately she longed to bring smiles to her loved ones' faces—not pain or disappointment.

Macy reached out a hand, tentatively, and after a second's hesitation, Avery grabbed it, anxiety and a desire for comfort raging a familiar battle at the sensation of human contact. Macy's expression registered the wound, but there wasn't much to say on the subject that hadn't already been rehashed a hundred times.

Her family knew she'd suffered plenty of emotional trauma during her last tour; she spared them the details of what happened in that place. She knew that these people who loved her were not the enemy. She knew they meant her no harm, but her body, and parts of her mind, still struggled with the difference between a friendly touch and a hostile one.

"I'd be lying if I said it wouldn't be nice to see you spending some time with a sweet fella," Macy answered. "Isaac Meyer definitely fits the bill, and that boy has been single for way too long." She gently squeezed Avery's hand before tugging her in the direction of the kitchen. "Come on. Let's get some caffeine in you and you can tell me what exactly did happen."

She winked and Avery rolled her eyes, but allowed herself to be led toward the energizing scent of fresh coffee.

Maybe it wouldn't hurt for her to talk to Macy about the strange past few hours. Maybe it would be nice to share breakfast and silly, carefree chatter about a man, like the old days.

Or at least she could pretend to, for her family's sake.

* * *

"All set?" Macy asked later that morning as Avery stepped into the lobby following her weekly appointment with Dr. Santiago, her therapist.

Avery nodded and Macy smiled warmly as she put down a magazine she'd been reading, grabbed her purse and stood to leave. They walked quietly to the elevator, Avery reviewing her session with Dr. Santiago. Though she saw the doctor regularly, most of her previous appointments ran together, characterized only by the strong feeling that nothing ever really changed; some days were better than others, but overall, she felt she'd made no true progress over the past several months, a thought that only served to decrease her confidence that she would someday get past it all.

But today—something felt different. Something felt...better. She couldn't quite put her finger on it. Was it that she had tried harder to talk about her struggles? Had she simply opened up more? Yes, and no. She shook her head as she reached out to punch the down button on the panel between two elevators. Perhaps she'd made a little more effort than usual to speak frankly with the doctor, but it wasn't just that. She always did her best during her sessions, always pushed as far as she could go, working to excavate that deep abyss of painful war memories. No. This time, it was something else. Something to do with her night with Isaac.

"So, I was thinking," Macy said, her words tentative, almost as though she knew before she spoke them that whatever idea she had would be shot down. Avery winced, fully aware that she had a large part in making her sister-in-law feel that way around her.

Avery looked over to see Macy fiddling with her purse strap, her forehead creased. "What is it?"

"Well, you know that new nail salon they just opened up the street from here?"

"Uh-huh," Avery answered, her thoughts still partly focused on her session with Dr. Santiago. She heard Macy swallow.

"I was thinking we could stop on the way to the grocery and maybe get pedicures or something." She looked over at Avery, cautious hope in her eyes. "My treat."

A sharp *ding* sound rang out and the elevator doors slid open. Once they'd stepped inside and chosen the ground floor as their destination, Avery glanced over at Macy, who was biting her lower lip now, her features giving away her trepidation.

Avery's heart sank. How many times had she said no to such a simple request, to things that Macy offered as a way to reach out to her, in constant effort to help her through her tough times? How many times had she denied those offers, yet they kept coming? She smiled softly at Macy, realizing for the first time how lucky she was to have this persistent, positive woman in her life. How many others had she hurt and pushed away because she was too afraid they wouldn't be able to handle the new, dark parts of her soul?

"I'd like that," she said, and Macy's face lit up. Macy squeezed her palms and raised her forearms, then lowered them quickly so as not to appear too excited.

"It's okay," Avery said, giggling. "You can be happy about it."

"Yay!" Macy cried out as she did a little bounce, causing them both to laugh.

The elevator stopped and both women stepped out into the parking garage.

"Look, Macy, I know it must be hard for you to keep...trying...with me, and—" Avery swallowed over the lump developing in her throat, startled by the sudden onslaught of emotion "—I want you to know I notice how hard you've been trying to make me feel better." She closed her eyes, working to organize her thoughts around the most important thing she needed to get across. "I mean to say that I'm thankful for you. For all that you and Tommy do for me, really. But especially you."

Macy stopped and turned toward Avery, her eyes filling as she reached out and wrapped her sister-in-law in a hug, squeezing hard.

When she let go, they walked to the car in silence, both smiling. It felt good to say yes to something, even something as small as a pedicure with a special family member—and friend—who'd remained close, no matter how hard Avery unintentionally pushed her away. She thought of that night with Isaac, how she'd allowed him to feed and care for her, despite feeling afraid of what conclusions he might draw about the state of her mental health. It was almost as though that choice—the choice to let someone new in, despite the difficulty it took to do so—was an opening for other opportunities that she'd been missing out on for so long.

Besides, she thought, grinning to herself, she could use some color on her toes. She decided then that she would pick something bright, something that would make her feel uplifted when she looked down at her feet. Something that maybe Isaac might notice and like.

As Macy pulled her car out into the sunshine, a small spark of life lit up somewhere deep inside the darkest place in Avery's heart.

Chapter Five

What had seemed like a good idea earlier that morning was really just a sack of zucchini in the light of day.

Isaac could have kicked his own ass for not coming up with a better ruse for stopping by to check on Avery Abbott after the night they'd spent in each other's company. A week had passed since that strange night—the slowest week of his life. He'd only been able to go through the motions during that time, each task permeated with thoughts of a woman unlike any other he'd ever met.

But still…zucchini? Anyone would be able to see through his excuse. The vegetable was insanely easy to grow, even in a dry-as-a-bone Texas summer like the one they were having—they were so good at growing that anyone within a hundred miles of Peach Leaf who wanted the vegetables already had enough to feed an army. People could only stand so many salads and breads and desserts with the stuff snuck in. But, for some knuckleheaded reason, Isaac had decided that bringing a bag of the green things would pass as a decent excuse to visit his neighbor's farm.

Yes, that's correct, he thought. *I'm bringing a crap ton of zucchini...to a farm.* He shook his head. Hell, it might have *come* from that very farm, he noted with a sinking sensation in his belly.

With so many well-meaning locals—overwhelmingly widows and grannies...and widowed grannies—dropping off food at his place on a regular basis, he lost track of its origins. He didn't hold it against all the sweet gals, but once in a while, it was enough to make him consider moving to Austin, where a thirtysomething bachelor wasn't likely to turn so many heads.

He pulled his four-wheeler into Tommy and Macy's drive, careful to watch out for free-range chickens and goats. He got out and Jane jumped down from her perch on the seat in front of him, hightailing it up the porch steps. As the front door swung open, the scent of something sweet cooking wafted out into the already warm air.

"Hey, Janie girl," Tommy said, scratching the dog between her ears before she invited herself into the house. "Hey, bud," he said, turning to Isaac and heading down the steps, cup of coffee in hand.

"Mornin', Tom," Isaac said, returning the greeting as he reached into the seat compartment to pull out the embarrassing sack of vegetables.

Tommy's eyebrows rose up so far they almost met

the brim of his straw Stetson. When Isaac just stood there, holding the offending sack away from him like a baby with a dirty diaper, realization crossed Tommy's features and he started to slowly back away, holding up a hand. "Aw, no way, man. Macy's got so many of those damn things. If she strung all the little bastards together, they'd reach the moon and back."

Isaac cursed and swung the bag over his shoulder, feeling more and more like a complete idiot.

"What in the world were you thinking bringing those things here?" Tommy continued, keeping his distance. "You lost your ever-lovin' mind, my friend?" He took a long sip of his coffee, clearly waiting for a response.

The two men had been good friends ever since Isaac inherited his grandma's property and moved in to the old ranch house. They were living proof that opposites really do attract. Isaac, who wasn't usually keen on too much chatter, had taken an instant liking to his neighbor, despite the fact that the man never shut his mouth and could carry on a conversation with just about anybody or anything. His easygoing habit of yakking made Isaac comfortable, mostly because he didn't have to say much for them to get along just fine, and, well, Tommy was just so damn nice. Also, it was obvious that the man doted on his family, as if Macy had hung the moon, and their two little ones, all the stars in the sky.

It was exactly the kind of family Isaac had always pictured having himself one day. If only he could find the right girl. Someone who wouldn't mind his quiet nature and his shyness around new people. Someone, maybe, kind of like Avery Abbott—his true reason for dropping by.

"Oh, just forget about those things and come on in. Macy's got breakfast on. But, if you think it's just flour, milk and sugar in those waffles, guess again. It's like I said before, that girl has stuffed those green devils into everything we've eaten in the past month because she hates to waste them, and, I'm telling you, at least fifty more popped up in her garden overnight."

Isaac smiled at his friend's happy chatter.

"Don't be surprised if next time you stop by, I've turned into one of 'em." Tommy stopped suddenly at the top of the steps. "What'd you say you dropped by for, again?" He lifted up his white hat and scratched his forehead. "Not that you need a reason. Just want to make sure you don't leave here empty-handed if you were needing something—"

"Tom?" Isaac said quietly, seeking a brief break in his friend's out-loud thinking.

"—Macy would never let me hear the end of it if—"

"Tom!"

He finally turned around, a sleepy smile on his face. Isaac had never known his friend to wear any other expression.

"What's on your mind, bud?"

Now that he had Tom's attention, Isaac hesitated, unsure what can of worms he might risk opening if he answered the question truthfully.

He knew Tom was protective of Avery beyond what would be expected of a brother, and he could understand why. From what he'd seen the other night, what folks said about her time in service, and from the way she seemed to socialize far less than other locals, he could guess that she'd come back from war bearing a few scars—the kind you couldn't see with a good pair of eyes.

The jumpiness he'd witnessed in her that night and her disorientation in an area she was familiar with were textbook post-trauma symptoms. He recognized them from the vets he trained service dogs for, and from— the memory still ached in a part of Isaac's heart that he knew would never heal—from his brother. Which was why he'd avoided visiting the farm and his friends the past few months since he'd heard that Avery moved in. Working with PTSD victims in his job was one thing— watching his friend's sister struggle through it was entirely another.

She needed help. More help than whatever Veteran Affairs currently provided, more help than her family would know how to give her, regardless of how much they loved and supported her.

Isaac knew, better than most, that love wasn't always enough.

Love couldn't always save someone.

So, as much as it might cost him in the long run, Isaac decided it was best to be open with Tom, for Avery's sake. He'd just have to make sure Macy didn't read too much into his visit, or she'd be on his case, and he'd find himself being set up again, only to turn up disappointed if it didn't work out.

The other night, despite her condition, he could feel the electric hint of possibility between them, and he couldn't deny that she was the prettiest woman he'd ever laid eyes on—but for now, all he wanted to do was help.

He set his shoulders back and held up a hand to shade his brow against the first rays of the rising sun. The day was already plenty warm, and he could tell it would be a hot one.

"Actually, yeah. There is something on my mind. Two things, actually. I'm so sorry I haven't stopped by to see you guys lately, and, well, I'm not here to see you now, to be honest."

Isaac ignored the goofy grin on Tommy's face, not really caring that he wasn't making any sense.

"I'm here to check on Avery."

Avery accepted the mug Macy handed her and took a long sip of the rich, strong coffee it contained, closing her eyes as the taste of good beans, a little sugar and a splash of fresh cream washed over her taste buds.

Macy was grinning from across the table when she opened her eyes.

"Good?"

"The best. I've always loved your coffee. Not like the coffee-flavored water Tommy always made before you came along," Avery said, laughing.

Macy beamed with pride. "Well, I'm glad you like it, and it's here every morning, but it's not enough to put meat on your bones, girl. You can't keep going on caffeine and the occasional bowl of cereal. You need to eat. You've barely had a real meal since you moved in here."

Avery took another sip and nodded in agreement. "I know I do."

"So, tell me what it is. Is there something I can make that you'd wolf down? When I first met Tommy, you were a nachos-and-beer kind of girl. Maybe we just need to get you to a Tex-Mex place, stat." Macy's voice was light, but Avery didn't miss the hint of seriousness in the woman's words.

"It's hard to explain, Mace. It's almost like…like everything tastes stale or cardboard-y. I couldn't tell you why. Ever since… I just can't seem to eat like I used to. But I'll try harder. Really, I will. And last week, I did eat a pretty mean sandwich at Isaac's—"

At the sound of the front door swinging open, both women exchanged glances and then turned their heads to the kitchen entryway.

"Honey, is that you?" Macy called out.

"Me and company," Tommy bellowed from the hallway.

A racket started at the front door and thundered down the hall, and suddenly Isaac's dog, Jane, was rushing through the kitchen entrance, headed straight toward the table. Macy's eyes widened in surprise but Avery's heart swelled at the sight of the dog.

"Janie!" Avery said as the giant mutt bounded over to her chair. She stopped short and sat in front of Avery, her behind wiggling with the effort of not jumping into Avery's lap. She reached up a paw and Avery touched it, laughing. "High-five!"

"Goodness," Macy said. "Someone's in love."

"Who's in love?" Tommy asked, entering the kitchen and heading over to kiss the top of his wife's head, then on to the coffeepot. "Mornin', sweetie. Mornin', Ave," he said as Isaac sidled up behind him to prop a shoulder against the doorway, arms crossed over his broad chest.

Avery's breath caught at the sight of him. Good Lord, he was even better looking in the morning light: shoulder-length hair still unruly but obviously moist and gleaming from a shower, dark eyes glittering as they met hers. He was dressed in faded jeans and a cobalt-blue T-shirt that brought out the olive tones in his sun-kissed skin.

"Avery," he said, his voice velvety-soft. He nodded at her, his lips offering just a hint of a grin, and, if she hadn't been sitting in a chair, she was fairly certain she'd have melted into a puddle right there on the kitchen floor.

Thankfully, he turned from her to say good morning to his hostess, who jumped up from the table to give him a big hug. "Isaac," Macy said, squeezing his midsection before turning to get him a cup of coffee. "It's so good to see you. You've been such a stranger lately." She held him at arm's length so she could get a good look at him. "I've told Tom to head on over and check on you and Jane, but he insisted you've been fine, just busy."

"And he's right," Isaac reassured her. "But I do appreciate you thinking of me."

Macy let go of him and picked up the carafe to pour him a mug, and, without asking how he took it, left it black and set it at the place next to Avery on the round, antique oak table. She winked and Avery felt her cheeks warm.

They'd been talking about him just before.

He walked in. As he drew near and pulled out the

chair only inches away from hers, Avery had to remind herself that he wasn't aware of that fact.

It was true that her family had spent a lot of energy worrying about her lately. She'd been back home for almost six months and dutifully kept her appointments with her therapist at the VA clinic in downtown Peach Leaf, but her symptoms weren't going away; in fact, they hadn't even gotten better. Sometimes, she thought, they seemed to be getting worse.

And with each flashback, each nightmare, each— her favorite—panic attack, Avery lost more and more of her self-esteem.

Where was the strong woman who'd enlisted after nursing school, hoping to see the world and serve her country as a medical professional? Where was the girl who'd always been drawn to the needs of others, to healing broken bodies?

She couldn't help anyone in her current state—least of all, herself—and it killed her a little more each day.

Avery hadn't realized it, as lost as she'd been in her own thoughts, but when she looked up, she met Jane's brown eyes, and noticed that her hand was buried in the dog's fur, stroking it. The repetitive movement and the feel of the satiny coat soothed her. If she focused on that motion instead of the turbulence inside her mind, things began to settle down.

She turned to Isaac and he met her eyes. There was a gentle smile in them that made her think maybe it wouldn't be so hard to try, just a little.

"I've always liked dogs so much," she said, still petting Jane, who promptly rolled over to expose her pink belly.

Avery and Isaac both laughed.

"She's a big, spoiled-rotten ham," he said. "A very good girl, don't get me wrong. But spoiled nonetheless."

"No way," Avery said, defending her new best friend from Isaac's good-humored chiding. "She's a sweetheart."

"Ha! She's got you wrapped around her paw there, I see," Isaac answered, shaking his head.

Macy informed him he'd be staying on for breakfast and it didn't take too long for him to give up his protest that he had work to do and didn't want to be in their hair all morning. Finally, he agreed to stay for waffles. Avery's niece and nephew joined the adults, rubbing their eyes from sleep. She snuck kisses on their matching strawberry-smelling, soft, flyaway blond hair before they saw Jane and ran over excitedly to pet the dog, completely ignoring everyone else in the room until Macy gently scolded them to say hello to Mr. Isaac. They did, before promptly returning their attention to Jane.

Avery chuckled. The dog *was* indeed spoiled, but she deserved it.

Tommy headed off to wash up from the morning's milking, which he always did alongside his six hired hands, and Macy busied herself with the waffle batter.

"You're a natural with Jane," Isaac said as she set places with plates and utensils, then sat back down at the table, having been shooed away from her offers to help Macy prepare breakfast. "Mind if I ask why you don't have one of your own?"

Avery fingered the yellow stars that decorated her favorite black coffee mug. "Well, I haven't really given it much thought," she answered, noticing that Isaac's eyes traveled over her face with intensity that made her both extremely flattered and disconcerted. As one of just a couple of females among the majority of males that had made up her team, she wasn't used to such attention. She was used to being just one of the guys. Part of her thoroughly enjoyed the way those brown eyes studied her features with obvious interest; another part warned her to turn and run. She wasn't relationship material—now or possibly ever. Too much baggage. Too much damage.

"Before I went into the army, I was a nurse, and my shifts didn't allow time for me to be a good pet owner." Nervous, she tucked a strand of hair behind her ear, wondering, for the first time in a long time, how it looked and when was the last time she'd brushed it or had a proper trim. It occurred to her that it wouldn't hurt to ask her stylist friend Jessica if she could squeeze in an appointment during the upcoming week.

A little change might make her feel better.

Isaac nodded, so she continued. "Then, when I joined, well…that's no mystery." She offered a soft smile. "I wouldn't have wanted to leave a pet behind for my family to care for in my absence, and I'm enough of a burden on them as it is for me to bring someone else into their home."

Wow. Her mother would turn over in her grave if

she'd heard Avery sharing something so private with a relative stranger. The thing was, though, he didn't feel much like a stranger.

She turned quickly away and stared into her coffee mug. But before her eyes had left his, she'd seen the flash of sadness on Isaac's features and chided herself to be more careful; she didn't want him feeling sorry for her. Him or anyone else.

"Sounds to me like you'd make a wonderful pet owner," he said, surprising her. "You've obviously thought through these things, which is more than I can say for a lot of people."

"What do you mean?" she asked, unable to keep her eyes from him. Something about the man drew her in, and the more time she spent around him, the more she realized his company was like a balm to her frayed nerves. He was like a dip in cool spring water on a hot summer day, and she'd have to be very, very cautious to avoid getting pulled under.

"Just that a lot of people get pets, especially dogs, thinking that the animals will just be happy to have a home and food, but they need so much more than that. They need love and attention and medical care and training. They're incredibly wonderful, but a big responsibility. Most people don't think about all of those things, but it's obvious that you have, and I just think you'd be a wonderful dog mom if you ever decided that you wanted to be."

He gave her another one of those sweet but sexy grins—the kind that made her forget she was in a room full of other people, full of her family and full of the morning chaos of another busy day. Though she was apparently the only Abbott born with a black thumb, Avery did her best to help out around the farm— watching the kids so Macy could bake or have some time to herself, riding one of the horses out to check fences and crops with one or two of the hands, or helping Tommy with the milking.

Six months ago, when she'd come to live with her brother and his family, she'd thought that kind of work would save her from the persistent, dark memories she'd brought home from war. But now, after living through several months of hard, manual labor–filled days, she knew it wasn't enough. It was just another kind of running. She could cover a thousand miles, and those same memories would always be one step ahead of her, ready to knock her back down into the pit.

But something about Isaac's compliment, about the idea of a dog, sparked her interest. Something about the thought of having a living thing to take care of—one that was all her own—offered an inkling of hope. But with hope came the risk of opening up, of putting her heart out there, and she wasn't quite sure she could do it just yet. Still, maybe if she took the tiniest of steps in that direction…

She cleared her throat and looked back to Isaac, who was draining the last of his coffee. "Tommy tells me you've helped a lot of vets with your training," she said, her voice sounding uncertain even to her own ears. "I'd love to hear more about it."

"Well, I'm certified in general canine training, and I do all kinds of basic and advanced behavioral training, plus some search and rescue and drug-finding stuff for the local sheriff's department, and I do work with vets sometimes, mostly pairing them with companion animals that we all feel are a good fit. Then I tailor the training to whatever a client's particular needs are. I've taken several courses in training therapy dogs, but I'm always learning more, especially from working directly with veterans."

He stopped there and she could tell he was trying not to bore or overwhelm her, which shouldn't surprise her after the other night. Most people would have labeled her crazy and gone on about their business. Isaac was different. He was testing the waters and giving her room to go at her own pace, to seek information rather than being force-fed facts. It was a relief after all of the VA appointments and therapy sessions.

"What happens then?"

Isaac's brow furrowed. "Well, as you've seen with Jane, dogs can be very calming. They can relax us when we're getting to that breaking point where nothing's helping and we just need a lifeline—someone to pull us back from the edge. All dogs, all breeds, have the potential to be amazing with humans, given a chance. But they're just like people in that they don't all get along. Not every dog likes every other dog, and not every dog is right for every person. It's a matter of finding the right dog for the right vet. When that happens, it's incredible what they can do for each other."

Okay, now she was really interested.

As a waffle-filled plate appeared in front of her, Avery looked up to find Macy smiling. She rolled her eyes but the truth was, she was glad to have someone to talk to who didn't seem to judge her. Someone who had seen one of her worst episodes and hadn't overreacted or, well, freaked out the way most people did. She was lucky Isaac was the one who'd found her wandering around in the darkness. It could have been anyone— but it was him. He'd taken care of her as though she belonged to him, as though she was his to keep safe and protect. And, because of his work, which she'd grilled Macy about the week before—something she'd made her sister-in-law swear to secrecy—he had the knowledge and experience to maybe help her, or to at least be her friend.

After what they'd been through in just a short amount of time, Avery knew he wouldn't scare easy the way most people did. She didn't blame them, really. It usually was just a matter of not knowing what to say, not knowing how to talk to her about her experiences in a combat zone most had only seen on edited television. Still, it hurt that her old friends seemed almost…afraid of her, as though she might break at any moment. And, to be fair, she could.

But Isaac wasn't like that. He was gentle and careful with her, but at the same time, he didn't treat her with kid gloves. He'd gotten her to talk more about her problems last week than her therapist had in months of trying different approaches. Plus, the idea that he could somehow even help her to get better—could maybe even work with a dog to help her—brought her more optimism than she'd felt since coming home, and she was smart enough not to resist a good thing when she saw it.

Also, it didn't hurt the situation that he was the most ruggedly beautiful man she'd ever seen.

"I want to know more," she said, pushing her shoulders back and meeting his eyes, a dose of bravery coursing through her veins. "How do I do that?"

Isaac's eyes flashed with interest and pride as he swallowed the bite of waffles he'd taken and set down his fork. Avery noticed that he'd finished over half of the food on his plate while she hadn't eaten a single morsel. "First, you eat."

"Oh," she said, looking down at her food. It did look good, but she knew that when she put a forkful into her mouth, it would taste like nothing. "I'm not really hungry."

He pulled a face that told her he wasn't buying the excuse. "All right, Abbott. Let's make a deal."

The twinkle in his eyes sent an arrow through that surge of bravery she'd felt only a moment before, but she wouldn't let him see. Over three tours, she'd had plenty of practice pretending to possess courage when in fact she did not. "Fine."

"Good," Isaac said, folding his hands in his lap. "Eat at least half of those waffles, and instead of telling you more about my training, I'll do you one better."

"How's that?" she asked, eyeing her food, deciding if she was really up for the challenge.

"You can come in to the office with me tomorrow."

"You've got work tomorrow?" she asked, and he nodded. "It's Saturday. I thought only us farm folks and emergency professionals had to report for duty so early on the weekend."

Isaac smiled and his eyes crinkled at the corners, lending sweetness to his sharp features.

"Yes, well, running a small business means there's always work to be done, and even when I do take a day off, it's hard not to think about all the things I could be doing."

"Sounds like a lot to handle," said Avery.

He nodded but his eyes held only satisfied joy, and she found she wanted to learn more about something that brought such contentment to his life.

"It is that, but I absolutely love the work. I opened the training center a couple of years back when my grandmother left me her house and land here. And, after having worked a corporate desk job since college, I'll never go back. Being my own boss and setting my own schedule is the best thing in the world."

"Even when you have to work weekends?" Avery asked, grinning.

"Even then," he said, returning her grin.

Isaac's eyes lit up when he talked about his work, and his enthusiasm got her excited about the opportunity to see where he spent his days. But, behind all of that, a little bit of sadness stung inside her chest. She missed her own work. She missed her patients at the hospital, her daily rounds and having the chance to give back to her community by caring for people. For Avery, being a nurse was more than just a job—it was a calling, something that filled her soul. And, even more simply, she felt lost without the daily routine of getting up and driving into town.

She'd tried to build a new life for herself on the farm

after the incident she'd had at work. It still made her face burn to remember her boss finding her huddled up in the corner of a patient's room, having mistaken the sound of a dropped food tray for an explosion. The resulting mandatory vacation leave her boss had ordered was justified, but it wasn't easy adjusting to time away from work. Despite pushing herself for long hours in the Texas sun to help her brother, she felt useless there. It would never be enough to replace nursing.

"Did I say something wrong?" Isaac asked, worry lines etching the dark skin of his forehead.

"No, no," she answered, surprising them both when she reached out and gently lay a hand across one of his. Even more startling was the absence of need to pull it away.

Isaac looked at their hands, then back at Avery, before winding his fingers through hers. The motion pulled all of the air from her lungs for just a second, but she didn't flinch.

Be brave, she told herself. *It's just a friendly gesture. It's just ordinary human contact.*

And, much to her pleased relief, it worked. As she allowed him to hold her hand, ignoring everything else in the room, her fear trickled away drop by drop. It was, after all, just a hand—but it belonged to Isaac, which made it okay somehow. Safe, steady Isaac.

She thought suddenly of the towering stack of historical romance paperbacks on her night table, of all the ways the authors described the heroes therein. In those books that she loved so much, the rakes and Vikings were always full of adventure and the promise of pulse-pounding, high-stakes danger, and though Avery could lose herself in those stories for hours, she'd always had difficulty relating to heroines who would want all of those things, when she herself craved just the opposite.

To Avery, the most romantic thing in the world was also the simplest: a partner who provided a safe home, gentle hands, stability and unconditional love.

She'd had enough adventure to last a lifetime, and all she really wanted now was a soft place to land.

She hadn't spent much time before, considering what that might look like in her own life, but seeing Isaac's hand wrapped around her own and the warm affection swimming in his dark eyes, she was starting to get a pretty good idea.

Avery cleared her throat and shook her head. "No, you didn't say anything wrong." She gave his hand a little squeeze. "I was just thinking about my own job, hearing you talk about how much you enjoy yours."

He was silent for a moment, just looking at her, no judgment discernible in his expression. When he spoke, his voice was kind but determined. "Listen, Abbott," he said, "whatever happened to you over there, whatever made you stop doing something you love, you can't let that make you quit for good. If you want to go back to nursing, or even train for a different career, you absolutely can. And I think I can help."

No hesitation, no "Let's take things slow," no "Maybe someday in the future"—none of the platitudes she was so used to hearing—just pure confidence in her ability to help herself get better.

It must have been exactly what she needed to hear,

because in just a short time with Isaac Meyer, she felt better than she had in months. And to think he'd been there all along, just a short walk up the road.

She was tired of taking baby steps and getting no-where, tired of carefully stepping on stones across a deep abyss only to fall over and over again, then to face the challenge of climbing back out over slippery walls. Her therapists at the VA were wonderful, and she knew she needed their help to find balance again. But it wasn't enough to commit to doing the mental work; she needed some actionable steps to take in order to feel more than passive in her own journey.

She'd read about service dogs for vets with PTSD, and most of the research was positive. Besides, she had nothing to lose. Everything she'd known before—the life she'd left with when she joined the military—was gone, and she knew it would probably never return. So, if Isaac wanted to help her with this new one, and if the way to do so was by working with a dog, it was worth one hell of a try. She wanted to be whole again, whatever that meant, and she was willing to try some-thing innovative to get there, even if being whole now wouldn't look the same as it had before she'd left.

In fact, she was beginning to hope it didn't, because before, Isaac hadn't been a part of her world, and she'd decided this morning that she very much liked him in it.

Chapter Six

Friends with Fur had started out as just a business for Isaac—a way to earn a living and to get out from behind the desk that he'd sworn at the time would eventually kill him—but in the years since its opening, it had become so much more.

Even looking back on those *before* days from a safe distance made him cringe, and caused a trapped feeling to rise up like a scream from his chest to his throat. He'd been thirty when Nana passed and surprised the hell out of Isaac by leaving him her farm and savings. Inheriting Nana's property shouldn't have come as a shock because his mom hadn't survived her last heart failure, and of course his brother, Stephen, was gone long before that, but it had nonetheless. Suddenly, he'd been given a chance at a new life, and he didn't take that lightly.

After years of working his way up from mail clerk to a corner office at an investment firm in Austin—a relatively reliable job with a steady, respectable paycheck—Isaac had begun to feel the claws of suffocation wrapping around him, longing for days that didn't all look exactly the same as the ones that came before and after. He'd gone to college mostly to please his mother and to get a taste of city life, but everything that followed seemed to rush in as smoothly as though he'd been on autopilot, just following a predetermined set of steps. Internships, job offers and a ladder to climb.

He'd gotten very near the top, but it wasn't enough. When he'd confided in his friends about his increasing longing to do something else, most had responded in the same way his mom had: they'd told him he was lucky to have a high-paying job, and he could do what he pleased as soon as he retired. He knew there was an element of truth in their statements, but there was also fear. Something inside him burned for change, and he didn't want to wait thirty more years to feel that his days had real purpose. Surely, he'd begun to dream, there had to be some way to earn a living doing something he loved. And just when he'd worked up the courage to take a leave of absence to try and figure out what to do about his future, Nana had gotten sick.

He'd come back to Peach Leaf to take care of her and to make certain she lived her final days in peaceful comfort. When she breathed her last, she gave him a new beginning. The farmhouse where he'd spent his summers was old, but in decent shape, and with Nana's life savings, he'd fixed it up and studied to become a certified animal trainer. Then, along the way, he'd bought the building that now housed his facility.

Often, he thought of the irony. Animals—dogs in particular—were his greatest love as a little boy. Had he listened to and followed his passion earlier in life, well… It didn't do much good to dwell on the past. He was happy in his job now and absolutely loved getting up for work every morning. He had what so many people wished for but never obtained: a beloved career that brought satisfaction and joy, and that also made it possible to pay the bills.

Isaac had started small, with just a website and cheap business cards, training pets in clients' homes, and eventually word of mouth spread and he'd hired on Hannah and Mike. Now they offered training at all levels from basic to specialized service, along with pet sitting and customized curricula for owners with individual needs.

At first he'd been reluctant to train dogs as companions for veterans with psychological struggles. The pain of Stephen's death was still too raw. But when a friend of his had returned home from war and requested Isaac's help to keep from drowning at the bottom of a bottle, he couldn't say no, and that aspect of his training programs had grown. Now, vets from all over Texas came to Friends with Fur to meet and train with dogs to take home and make their lives infinitely better.

Isaac's heart lifted each morning when he drove into

the parking lot, but it rose a little higher as he did that Saturday with the beautiful Avery Abbott by his side.

He hadn't specifically planned on convincing her to spend the day with him when he'd visited her home the morning before. But when he'd walked into Macy Abbott's kitchen, he was a goner. Avery's blond hair was wet from a shower and her skin glowed dewy fresh. He loved that she didn't need to fuss or put on a bunch of makeup; she was naturally beautiful, dressed in a fitted blue T-shirt, faded jeans and bright green flip-flops. When he'd sat down next to her at the table, the scent of apple shampoo from her freshly washed hair had filled his nostrils and made it damn hard not to draw closer to her as he'd focused on getting her to eat her breakfast.

He wasn't one to fall quick. Hell, he wasn't one to fall at all if the past was any indication. Aside from a couple of short-term college girlfriends and the nice-but-not-for-him dates the women in town set him up with, Isaac didn't have much of a romantic past to speak of. It wasn't that he didn't want love, no, it was more that he wasn't sure it was even possible to find what he wanted.

His mom and dad had been the perfect bad example of the kind of relationship he was looking for. He had to thank them for that. They'd taught him exactly what he did not want. What he did want was something simple, but right. Someone he could trust with every fiber of his being, someone who wasn't intimidated by the fact that he loved his work and that it was more than just a job and he'd have to put in long hours sometimes to make sure he got things done well. Someone who wanted to be a mom to his kids, and to help him raise them with good old-fashioned manners and sense.

Yet again, he thought, Avery brought all of this to the surface when he usually just ignored it and plugged along, happy to be single, but wishing for more. But what did he know about her, really? How could he even think of her that way when clearly all she wanted or needed was his help? It would be wrong to hope for more from her, wrong to show interest at a time when she was at her most vulnerable...wouldn't it?

"I've been by this place so many times," she said softly as he stopped the truck they'd borrowed from Tommy for the day, "but I always thought it was just a doggy day care or something. I didn't realize you were doing such important work in there."

Isaac smiled at the sound of her voice. As she unbuckled her seat belt, he snuck another good look at Avery over Jane's furry head between them. She looked refreshed after eating the blueberry muffin Macy had pushed on her as she'd left the house that morning, which he'd then insisted she finish, but he knew she'd probably done so more to prove that she could meet his challenge than to add weight to her thin figure. Oh well, he would take it, and if he had to spend every meal by her side that day to get her to eat, then so be it. She was his to take care of, at least for the day, and he meant to do just that.

He let Jane out and then opened Avery's door for her. She took his offered hand and he found great pleasure in the pink clouds that floated across her cheeks when their palms touched. Her beauty was quiet, like a landscape painting of a bright summer day. Makeup-free, it didn't demand attention, but once he'd laid eyes on her, he'd known he would miss her face if a day passed when he couldn't see it.

Isaac didn't want to think about what that meant.

For now, all he wanted was to spend time getting to know her better, helping her if he could.

"Oh, wow," Avery said as he unlocked the back door and led her into the building, Jane trotting happily along at their feet. "It's like doggy heaven."

She faced him with sparkling eyes and he laughed.

"Well, I'm glad you think so," he said. "That's exactly what it's supposed to be."

Showing the training facility to Avery gave Isaac the opportunity to view it with new eyes. He led her down a long hallway, showing her inside each of the different classrooms, stocked with supplies for all sorts of training exercises. There was a puppy room featuring long leads for recall training, toys and, of course, paper pads in case tiny bladders needed sudden relief, a large arena floored in Astroturf for agility training, and—Avery's favorite—the search-and-rescue classroom with its boxes labeled for different scents that would be filled and closed for dogs to identify. Finally, he took her past his office and up to the storefront, where his staff sold good pet supplies at discount prices, so clients could pick up what they needed on their way out after classes.

Seeing Avery's enjoyment of her personal tour gave him a burst of pride in the business he'd started.

"I love it," she said. "Very cool." She reached down to pet Jane who, Isaac noticed with a grin, had helped herself to a tennis ball from one of the classroom bins along the way.

"She has a mild rebellious streak in her, doesn't she?" Avery asked, teasing.

"Doesn't get it from me," Isaac said, thrilled when Avery let go a small rush of musical laughter. "But it's one of the things I love about Janie. She's loyal and reliable and obedient about ninety-nine percent of the time, so it just adds to her charm."

Avery stroked Jane while she listened to him talk.

"But damn, was she ever a mess when she found me. I suppose it was mutual, though," he said, his tone more serious than he'd planned. "I wasn't a very happy man at the time, and she'd just come from being a homeless puppy, so we both had some fixing to do before we were on good terms."

"And are you now?" Avery asked, her light blond eyebrows furrowed.

"Am I what?"

"You know," she said, as if he held the key to some mystery she didn't quite dare talk about. "Happy."

He stopped walking and turned to face her, thinking in silence for a moment, lost in the blue-gray storm clouds in her eyes.

"That's a complicated question, isn't it?"

"Not particularly," she challenged, a twinge of sorrow in her voice.

"Well, then, perhaps it's the answer that's complicated."

"Yes, maybe so, but I still want to know—are you happy, Isaac Meyer?"

In her question, Isaac sensed she was really asking something else—something along the lines of *Is it possible that I will ever be happy again?*—and he wanted, badly, for her to believe that, yes, she could be. Yes, despite everything that had happened to her, despite all the evil he could assume she'd witnessed, she could indeed find happiness again.

And, more important, she deserved to.

So he thought very carefully before responding, "Yes, most of the time, I am."

"And the others?"

He nodded. "Other times, I cling to the times that I am, and trust that if I'm patient, I'll find my way back to that place."

He looked down at Jane's happy dog face, remembering the days just after Stephen's death when he could barely breathe, let alone find the strength to drag his body out of bed to help his mother with her own grief.

"Sometimes happiness takes work," he said, ignoring the tension that came over Avery's body at his words. "Hear me out," he said, his voice firm. "We don't always want to do the work, the hard stuff, to put ourselves back together after something awful knocks us to pieces. But that's when it's most important to try, to keep doing the things we love and being with the people we love, until it meets us halfway. Some days, Avery, showing up and doing the work is enough."

He hadn't meant to say so much about how he'd handled his own pain after he lost his brother, and the liquid shimmering in her eyes hit him like a punch to the gut, but if his own experience could make hers even a fraction easier to bear, then it was worth pulling the stitches out of those wounds.

For her.

There was a great deal he would do to see this woman smile—this new, complex, damaged-but-not-destroyed woman who'd quite literally walked into his life.

He reached out and took her hand, glad when she only twitched a tiny bit at his touch before letting their palms fold together.

"There's someone I want you to meet."

Avery's shoulders rose a little and tension tightened her fingers around his; she didn't seem to realize how hard she was gripping him until he asked what was bothering her.

"I'm not… I don't really…"

"It's okay," Isaac said, running his thumb softly over the tips of Avery's fingers. Her eyes were huge, and even as he focused on how to calm her, he couldn't help but notice how their clear blue shade resembled the beautiful cloudless Texas sky above as they'd driven into town earlier. "It's just one of my trainers, Hannah, and a puppy we've been working with."

A smile spread across his lips involuntarily. "I think you'll really like him. He's a little fireball, but he's got all the makings of a great service dog, if we can match him to the right person."

She swallowed and some of the tension eased out of her grip.

"I think that person might be you, Avery."

"I'm just not sure if I'm up for meeting someone right now. It's been a few weeks since I've even—"

unmistakable embarrassment crossed her features "—well, since I've even left the farm, aside from wandering onto your land, of course. I'm just not sure if I can handle meeting a new person yet."

Though Avery's jaw was set with stubborn resolve, Isaac wanted to wrap his arms around her and tell her she had absolutely nothing to be ashamed of. He could see the scared girl behind the strong woman's facade, and his instinct was to protect her from any harm or pain, but he also knew from experience that she wouldn't get better by isolating herself from other people.

"Listen, Hannah works with combat veterans all the time, and she is one of the kindest, gentlest people I know. And I'll be right here, right by your side," he offered. "But if you want me to take you home, say the word and it's done. You don't have to do anything you're not comfortable with, Avery."

As he continued to hold her hand, Avery bit her lip, considering. Isaac gave her all the time in the world to decide if she was up for it and eventually, she pulled her hand from his and shook out her shoulders. "All right," she said, tossing him a confident grin as she rubbed her palms together. "Let's do this."

"Okay, then. That's my girl."

The words were out of his mouth before he could even think, and, slightly overwhelmed with what they implied, Isaac simply turned to lead the way back to Hannah's office near his own at the rear of the building.

But when he glanced over at Avery, he caught the

smile in her eyes and the way her lips curved slightly at their corners.

Just one of those smiles, he knew, could keep him going for a week.

Avery was out of practice.

It had been over a month since she'd met someone new, before she'd stumbled into Isaac, of course.

In her job as a nurse, she'd encountered new patients every single day, and for a time after returning from war, she'd managed not to let that intimidate her. But, as she had come to realize over the past few weeks, there were some things she didn't yet understand about her PTSD diagnosis, some things that reared their ugly heads when she least expected. Somehow, difficulty being around people she didn't know—and, more important, didn't know if she could trust—was one of those things. It didn't matter that logic wasn't involved; most citizens of sleepy, friendly Peach Leaf weren't out to ambush her in broad daylight. It was easy to rationalize, far more difficult to put into practice.

But, like Macy always said, she could fake it till she made it.

For some reason, she wanted Isaac to be proud of her, to feel comfortable introducing her to his staff and friends, so she would put on a brave face and try to keep her trepidation from reaching the surface.

He'd looked so happy when she agreed to meet Hannah and the puppy. It was adorable, really. How long had it been since someone had been so interested in her reaction to a new situation? How long had it been since someone had dared take her out in public and have her meet new people without worrying how she might behave? She couldn't tell if he just wasn't aware of how big a deal it was for her, or if he was doing this intentionally, to give her a chance to feel like a real person again, a person who could be okay in normal social situations. Either way, his thoughtfulness touched a place deep within her heart and somehow lent her courage.

Plus, if she were honest, she was absolutely dying to see the pup Isaac was so excited about. It was adorable the way his face lit up over a little furry guy. As far as Avery was concerned, a guy who loved animals already had a lot going for him. Maybe that was one of the reasons she found she could trust him so easily, even though they'd known each other for less time than it took her to binge-read a new historical romance series.

And goodness, how she loved the way her hand felt in his, and the way he'd grabbed it without making a big deal out of anything. He seemed to have an intuition for what would push her just beyond her comfort zone without making her feel pressure.

He was...wonderful.

They reached a door at the end of the hallway and Isaac knocked gently before slowly pushing it open. Jane rushed forward into what Avery assumed was Hannah's cozy office, stopping only when she reached a red-and-blue-plaid dog bed tucked into a corner. Avery yearned to see the little guy immediately, but she knew she needed to focus first on being polite to the woman who stood up from a desk and came forward to greet them, reaching out a hand.

"Hi, I'm Hannah. You must be Avery."

Avery shook Hannah's warm hand and, even though her heart raced a little, she was able to force herself to relax, knowing that Isaac was nearby and had her back.

"I am. It's nice to meet you, Hannah."

Hannah was petite with short brown hair, wide, lovely green eyes and an open smile that filled her heart-shaped face. If she was half as sweet as she looked, Avery could see why she'd be good at working with war-scarred veterans and dogs, and she could even imagine making a new friend.

"When Isaac texted to let me know you two were coming in this morning, I got so excited." Hannah squeezed her hands into fists at her sides and her enthusiasm for her work was palpable. "We've been working with Foggy for a few months now, and we know he'll be wonderful, but we just haven't found the right person to take him home yet."

Hannah and Isaac exchanged looks, but Avery was too interested in meeting the puppy to pay much attention.

"Can I meet him?" Avery asked.

"Of course!"

Hannah led the way over to where Jane had high-tailed it upon entering the room. She stopped a few feet away from the doggie bed and called, "Foggy, come."

Seconds later, the cutest little thing Avery had ever seen came trotting out from behind Jane and plopped his bottom down right in front of Hannah, and Avery fell instantly in love.

Chapter Seven

When she thought of service dogs, a very specific picture came to mind for Avery, and that image was about as far-flung from the little furry bundle that trotted forward at Hannah's command as it could be. This was no regal Labrador retriever or German shepherd dog; no, this fuzzy creature looked more like he belonged on a greeting card or a bag of dog food than in a serious working situation. Granted, he wore a little blue vest that said SERVICE DOG in bold white lettering, but other than that, he could have passed as anyone's beloved family pet.

Avery's hand flew to her mouth to hold off the baby talk and cooing noises that threatened to escape against her will. She was an army medic, trained to keep a clear mind and to control her emotions even under the most extreme duress. So how could one little dog turn her insides to complete mush?

Unbelievable.

She had to touch him. The urge was fierce, automatic and impossible to resist.

Avery began to reach out her arms, but Hannah gently held up a hand to prevent her from doing so. The young dog halted immediately. Hannah turned up her palm, lifted it a few inches, and the dog sat quickly and quietly in front of the two women, waiting for his next move.

Avery's face must have registered her confusion because Hannah turned and gave her a reassuring smile. "We're just reinforcing how to politely greet humans. Foggy's doing wonderfully with all of the basics, and we've recently moved on to some more advanced commands. He'll make someone an excellent companion and helper."

Hannah beamed with pride at her little charge, whose tail slowly began to swish back and forth.

"Foggy?" Avery asked, and Hannah nodded.

"Because of his coloring."

"It suits him."

And it did. He was the cutest, scruffiest little mess she'd ever seen, with a coat of wiry fur in all possible shades of gray. Avery hadn't known there could be so many. His paws and forearms were snowy white, resulting in what looked for all the world like four little boots, and his tail appeared to have been pinned on as an afterthought, for it was long, thick and black as coal, mismatched from the rest of his little body. And his face—oh, that face—a large black nose surrounded by smoky whiskers, mustache and beard, dark-rimmed, huge brown eyes with long midnight lashes, and triangle-shaped ears that bent forward at their tips like little question marks. And her favorite part of all—bushy gray eyebrows that curved over and down into his eyes. It was a wonder he could see at all, but they were too cute to trim.

That face could thaw the iciest of hearts, Avery mused. This little bundle of innocent happiness was in stark contrast to all of the dark things she'd seen; it didn't make sense to her, in that moment, that humans could be so evil in a world that was home to creatures such as Foggy the dog. Her chest swelled and tightened and moisture poised behind her eyes.

"Yeah," Hannah whispered at her side. "I know, right?"

Avery couldn't speak without blubbering cutesy nonsense, so she simply nodded and stood staring for another long moment. When Hannah's tentative touch grazed her forearm, she jumped a little, then apologized.

"No, no—don't you do that," Hannah said, her voice laden with tenderness.

"Can I pet him?"

"Of course, darling. Go right ahead. Just hold your hand out like this—" Hannah squatted down and held out her hand, low, palm up, demonstrating "—so he can meet you."

Avery followed Hannah's lead and Foggy sniffed at her hand, his cold wet nose tickling her skin. Satisfied that they were now friends, he looked up at her with his giant eyes and wagged his tail at top speed. He spun in two quick circles and then showed her his good-boy sit again, offering up a paw.

Avery shook it and then laughed, covering her heart with a hand, feeling lighter than she had in ages. This happy little dog made joy surge inside her like a wave, and the foreignness of all that raw emotion—the sort she'd come in contact with so frequently since meeting Isaac—was almost too much to bear. She reached down and stroked Foggy's ears, slowly calming as she ran her fingers over their velvety fur. It was the same effect she'd experienced when she had pet Jane for the first time the week before, except, it seemed, even more special.

It occurred to her that this little guy could be her dog, and she could be his person, if he liked her as much as she already liked him, and if Isaac and Hannah agreed it was a good match. She might actually get the honor of being his dog mom, and, if Isaac was right, Foggy could help her with some of her PTSD symptoms; he could help her take care of herself a bit better.

They could take care of each other.

On top of that, she would have someone to look after, someone to love—someone who saw only Avery, not the bad stuff that had happened to her, not the mistakes she'd made or her bad calls, or the fact that it was her fault she had lost her best friend. Foggy wouldn't judge her the way people did, and he wasn't scared to be near her.

As she looked into his eyes and ran her hands along his sweet muzzle, she felt an instant bond that surpassed all logic, reason and science. It was like she knew they belonged together.

She ruffled the fur on Foggy's head and it stuck out in a thousand directions, making Avery and Hannah laugh. Then she tilted back on her heels and stood up, catching Isaac's gaze from a few feet away. What she found there nearly overwhelmed her. He looked so self-lessly pleased to see Avery getting along with the dog, it was as if his happiness and hopes for her were even bigger than her own.

He cared for her—it was written all over his face—and that scared the living daylights out of her.

The last non-family member Avery had cared for, had loved, was laid to rest in the Peach Leaf Cemetery.

She tore her eyes from Isaac and pushed aside So-phie's memory. Nothing she did could bring back her best friend; Avery would have to live with that for the rest of her days, but what she could do, what was in her power now, was to make sure something like that never happened again. And the best way to prevent someone she cared about from getting hurt was to keep her distance.

She decided then and there that she would let Isaac help her, and she would let herself spend time with him so that she could get better, so that she could be trusted again by her own family, so that she could get her life back together. And she would even allow herself to love this little dog. It was healthy to love, her therapist said, it was good for Avery to have reasons to get out of bed every day, but she would exercise extreme cau-tion when it came to Isaac Meyer. She couldn't let him get too close. She'd already proven that she was dangerous, that for someone to risk loving her was potentially lethal, and she wouldn't let it happen again if she could help it.

What Isaac felt when he watched Avery meet Foggy was unlike anything he'd ever experienced before. In all of his years matching veterans with dogs, he'd seen plenty of compatibility and plenty of love grow from just a tiny mutual need for someone to care for. But this...this was something special. He could tell instantly that dog and woman were perfect for each other. Inside he breathed a sigh of relief, and when he exchanged glances with Hannah, he knew she was doing the same thing.

They had taken a chance on Foggy. Instead of the usual routine where they chose a puppy from a reputable breeder with a line of dogs of appropriate temperament, Foggy was an experiment, one that Isaac hoped with every ounce of his being would work out.

He caught Avery watching him out of the corner of his eye.

"Where did you find this little dude?" she asked, almost as if she'd picked up on his line of thought.

Isaac cleared his throat. "Foggy's from the local shelter."

"Oh," Avery said, not sounding surprised.

"Up until now, we've only worked with dogs raised specifically for therapy and service, but Hannah and I happened to visit the veterinarian a few months back to check on an injured cat she had found and taken in—she adopted him when he was free to go after surgery—and we met Foggy."

Isaac watched Avery, trying to decide how much to tell her. Working with animals wasn't always easy; heartbreaks happened now and then, and he didn't want to cause her undue pain. At the same time, though, Avery was tough, and if she was going to adopt Foggy, she deserved to know as much about him as she could.

"He was unwanted and abused by his owner, whose dog apparently wasn't spayed and had puppies with a stray. The doctor found Foggy on his clinic doorstep one morning along with his brothers and sisters, and he fixed them all up. Luckily they all found good homes, but Fogs was the last one and he was on his way to the shelter that morning when Hannah and I showed up."

Avery listened intently, her beautiful face full of emotion as she hung on to his every word, hungry for knowledge about the dog, just like a new parent learning to take care of a baby. She would make an amazing dog mom, Isaac thought again.

"It took him a little while to warm up to us, and then we had to get him to trust us, which took even longer, but from day one, he's been calm and easy, and, miracle of miracles, he doesn't overreact to stimuli. He's got all the makings of an awesome service companion. He's just special, I guess, despite what's happened to him, and we just couldn't bring ourselves to pass him up."

If Isaac could, he would take every animal home with him from the shelter. They all deserved far better than the cards life had dealt them. And now that he'd realized how much he could help them, he knew it would be the very hardest part of his job to visit that place and have to select which ones to take with him.

Avery nodded.

"After we found him, Hannah and I decided that we only want to work with shelter dogs from now on. It'll take some extra legwork to make sure that we find dogs with the characteristics needed to do this job."

"What kinds of things do you look for?" she asked, bending back down to rub Foggy's back as the dog reveled in her undivided attention.

"Friendliness, confidence in lots of different situations and with different types of people, predictable, steady behavior, and—most important—temperament. Dogs, even ones who have been severely mistreated, can almost always be rehabilitated if people spend the time and effort necessary to do so, but they're not always good candidates to be service animals. For that, we need to make sure that we're choosing dogs who have never, and aren't likely to, display any kind of aggression."

"Makes sense," Avery said, standing up. "I think it's awesome that you're choosing to work with rescue dogs."

Isaac smiled, warmed by her encouragement. "It's not been easy to convince new clients that this is the right thing to do, but we're working on it. Every dog that we pull from the shelter that ends up being a good fit is more proof that this can work. We loved doing this before, but if we can save homeless dogs instead of creating a demand for new puppies, then it's better for everyone. We save them, and they save people. Everyone wins."

"And they do deserve a chance, don't they," Avery said. It wasn't a question, and she was so right.

"They absolutely do. Dogs don't ask too much of us. They want to be fed, sheltered, healthy and loved. It's not a lot. And so many of them love having a job to do. I'm not sure they understand it, but it gives them purpose, and if they're anything like me, that means the world."

Color drained from Avery's face and Isaac caught his mistake too late.

"Oh, Avery. I'm sorry. I didn't mean—"

"I know you didn't. It's okay. I don't want you walking on eggshells around me, Isaac. I need for you to tell me the truth and to speak openly and plainly to me always, even if no one else in my life will." She walked over and set her hand on his arm. "I'll find my purpose again, even if it's different than my nursing job."

"Yes," he agreed. "I have no doubt that you will, and Foggy and I will do everything we can to make sure that happens sooner rather than later."

A flush of color returned to her cheeks and Isaac felt a thousand times better. He clapped his hands against his thighs. "Ready to get to work?"

"Definitely. Where do we start?"

Hannah shoved closed a file-cabinet door and joined them, a manila folder in her hand with Foggy's name scrawled along the tab in thick blue marker. She looked back and forth at both of them, grinning, and for the very first time since he'd hired her, Isaac wished she wasn't so damn observant. Hannah was a very intelligent woman, but she also had a gift for reading people

down to their very depths. It was a little eerie sometimes. And right now she had that look on her face—
the one that told Isaac she knew exactly what he was
thinking about Avery Abbott.

He was in trouble.

A little involuntary cough escaped and he purpose-
fully averted his eyes from his very astute assistant,
which only made her chuckle.

"I've got all of Foggy's records here," she said, coming shoulder to shoulder with Avery so she could share
the papers. "I've been keeping a journal of our training sessions, and since he's been bunking with me at
night, I've also got all of his basic care info, down to
the last poop."

A totally ungraceful and absolutely adorable laugh
burst out of Avery.

"You keep a…a *poop* schedule for him?"

Hannah, so accustomed to working with new pups,
didn't get the humor. "Well, yeah, why wouldn't I?"

Avery giggled and Isaac couldn't help but join her.

"Hannah's very thorough," he said. "It's one of the
many reasons I need her around here."

Understanding crossed her features. "Oh, yes. I
keep meticulous records whenever we get someone
new. Dogs need structure to be productive, just like
folks do, so as soon as a little one arrives, I get him or
her all set up on a food schedule and, well, you know,
so we can make sure potty training goes…ahem…as
smoothly as possible."

"Ha!" Isaac and Avery both chimed, and even Hannah had to laugh at that one.

"All right, all right." She poked Avery playfully. "You'll get used to it soon enough if you decide to join forces with this little ball of love."

She reached down and gave Foggy a treat from her pocket, which he gobbled up immediately.

Hannah caught Isaac's attention and got down to business, going over each task she and Foggy had practiced enough that the dog performed them consistently. The two had mastered *sit*, *down*, *come*, *stay*, dropping and leaving items alone, waiting patiently at doorways, walking on a leash, exits and entrances into vehicles and buildings, settling down on mats and crates, and—as Foggy had so awesomely demonstrated with Avery— greeting people with excellent canine manners.

Isaac could see that Hannah was as proud of the dog as she would be of her own child. He couldn't wait to get to work with Avery and Foggy.

Once he and Hannah had finished going over Foggy's training log, Hannah reminded Isaac that she had other things to do.

"I'll leave you to it," she said aloud, then, leaning in to Isaac's ear, she whispered, "Alone."

She winked at Isaac and it took all his resolve not to roll his eyes. Of course Hannah would know he didn't mean it and that her intuition about his budding feelings for Avery was spot-on, which would only make things worse. She knew him well and obviously loathed the fact that she herself had been happily wed to her high school sweetheart since graduation, yet couldn't inflict her own marital bliss on everyone around her.

He knew. She'd been trying for years.

"All right, Hannah Banana. That's enough from you now. I won't be requiring any further assistance."

He'd used his most serious voice, but Hannah only laughed and hit him in the arm with Foggy's file before holding it out so he could take it. She glared at him playfully before pulling her giant sunglasses down from their nest in her poofy curls and over her eyes.

"I'm off to check on the play area fence out back. Let me know if you guys need anything, you hear?"

"Will do," Avery called from where she'd been practicing high fives with a delighted Foggy.

Isaac waved to Hannah and went over to join them. He was a pretty content man before he'd met this woman, but seeing Avery having so much fun with her new friend pushed him right over the edge into full-blown happy.

She was beautiful when she let go of her shield and put on that radiant smile that brought light into her entire face. For a moment, all of the shadows were gone, and there was only sun. What made him even happier was that she looked at him that way, too. It was often easier, of course, for someone with her past to befriend an animal than a human. Humans weren't as simple or as pure. They came with baggage and history and a thousand secrets upon that first meeting.

Nevertheless, she'd let him come near her, physically and emotionally, the other night and that morning. He was so lucky, he knew, to have the privilege of getting to know her. He got the distinct feeling that she didn't let many people get even that close, so it made him feel special that she'd chosen him; he wouldn't take that lightly.

He looked forward to every second of their time together that day and dared to hope that there would be countless more to come.

Avery practically bounced back over to join him, Foggy at her heels.

"So, where do we start?" she asked, optimism lilting in her voice.

"At the top, of course," Isaac said, tucking a finger under her chin. He was rewarded with a sweet smile that reached all the way into those blue eyes he'd begun to like so much that his need for them bordered on becoming a craving. It struck him instantly and with great force that what he wanted to do in that moment was kiss her nose.

Chapter Eight

How ridiculous that his impulse was so sweet, so innocent, almost childlike in its purity and simplicity.

Most of his relationships with women—if they could be called that—up until that point had been casual dates that occasionally culminated in physical intimacy. Nothing serious, nothing complicated. He just hadn't met the right woman yet, to want more. He'd never felt a strong pull to get inside a woman's head, to know what made her heart set fire, what made her happy.

With Avery, already it was different. He wanted, no, needed, to know everything about her. He wanted to hear all the silly small stuff, like what her favorite movies were and what she liked to read. Was there something she loved to eat or drink? What were her thoughts on current events? What had she been like as a child? What did she want more than anything else in the world?

It was strange that he'd been so physically close to women before and yet had felt nothing like what he did when Avery was simply standing in the same room as he, breathing the same air. It scared him a little, yes, but he'd wanted to feel that way for so long that the fear did nothing to deter him from moving forward. It was too soon, he knew, to figure out whether or not this was what love felt like, but that didn't stop him from wondering.

It was certainly possible, wasn't it? It didn't matter that they'd only known each other for little more than a week, did it?

Isaac didn't think so. Life was short, and if something awesome came along and bit a man in the ass, it would be stupid to ignore it, to waste it. He had no intention of making that mistake.

"Everything okay?" Avery asked, and Isaac realized he'd been staring at her without blinking or breathing or doing any other normal thing to make him seem not kooky.

"Everything's great," he said, pulling in a breath.

Surely she couldn't read all the thoughts he'd just been having about her, about him, about the two of them. Surely she couldn't tell that he wanted to pull her close and bury his face in her golden hair, and much, much more. He studied her eyes, but they gave nothing away except obvious amusement.

"You sure?" she asked, tilting her head to the side, looking insanely cute.

"Absolutely." He cleared his throat.

Best get to work so his mind would have something to concentrate on other than Avery's lovely face.

"So, just a little info first. For dogs, trust is as important as it is for humans, although they're a lot quicker to give it away. For them, at least if they're raised from puppies, it's not so much that it has to be earned— although it did with Foggy at first, on account of his unfortunate past—as that you don't want to break it. If you show him that you'll reward good behavior, he'll give it to you consistently."

Avery nodded, her features registering discomfort at the subject of trust. Isaac knew it was something difficult for her, as it was for many people with PTSD. He knew it would always be something he'd have to work hard to show her if they were to build a relationship. That would bother a lot of men, he knew, but it didn't bother him. He was willing to work to earn Avery's trust. He would never break it if she offered it to him.

"And all dogs have something that motivates them."

"Like what?"

"Like toys, or affection, or food. You'll want to give all three of those things, but it's helpful to figure out what drives each specific pup. Foggy, for example—" the little guy's ears perked up at his name and he tilted his head to the left "—happens to love treats, so he's pretty easily motivated by food. Don't you, boy?"

Isaac dug a piece of dried chicken jerky out of his pocket and said, "Sit."

Foggy obeyed instantly, earning the bite.

"Very good boy," Isaac praised. He pulled more food

from his pocket and gestured for Avery to open her palm, then dropped it in. "Now you try."

Avery set her shoulders back and stood stiffly, almost as if she were at attention. Isaac smiled at her seriousness, but regarded her with great respect. She understood how important her relationship with Foggy could be, and he loved that about her.

"Sit," she said, then laughed immediately as Foggy just grinned at her. "Oh, geez," she said, turning pink. "He's already doing that, isn't he?"

Isaac burst out laughing. "I'm sorry, Ave. My fault. Let's get him to stand up first." Isaac winked at Avery before asking Foggy to stand. "Up," he said, satisfied when the dog promptly stood to face them, earning another treat.

Avery watched Isaac carefully as he showed her one more time how to request that Foggy sit down, holding out his palm the way Hannah had earlier, then lifting it slightly.

"You can either just say the word *sit* to get him to do so, or you can give him the hand signal. That way, you've got both a verbal command in case you're too far away for him to see, like in another room, for example, or, if you're in a place where you need to be quiet, you can give him the visual cue."

Avery smiled, obviously enjoying the lessons as much as Foggy clearly did. Isaac hadn't spent as much time around him as Hannah had, but he could tell already that the dog was alert, responsive and extremely calm. It didn't even seem to faze him at all that Jane was amusing herself by tossing a tennis ball up in the air and chasing it around the room as they worked. He would be an excellent companion for Avery, Isaac was certain.

"So, I can take him with me…anywhere?" Avery asked, obviously pleased at the idea.

"Oh, yeah, that's the whole point," Isaac reassured her. "He's got his practice vest now, which should let store owners and restaurants and such know that he's allowed to be there, and then he'll get his official vest when he takes his exam."

"Awesome," Avery said, her face lighting up. "I can't wait to see what my niece and nephew think of him."

For the next few hours, they practiced through several basic commands until Avery was completely at ease asking Foggy to do all sorts of things he'd need to know in order to move around comfortably in public. Isaac showed Avery how to let Foggy know that he was off duty by removing his vest, and he and Jane chased each other around the room, stopping at intervals to show their play bows and wrestle, while Isaac and Avery laughed themselves to tears.

Foggy and Avery were a natural fit, Isaac could plainly see, and they were already becoming fast friends. Plus, he couldn't help but notice how well Foggy and Jane got along, which was wonderful on the chance that, someday in the future…

He couldn't let that thought stretch too far. Avery was already warming up, even after only a couple of hours with her new bud, but he had to remind himself that he didn't know what she wanted. There was something between them that couldn't be denied, something palpable and solid, but he wouldn't push her.

Even if she was beginning to have feelings for him the way he most definitely was for her, she would need time to come to terms with what that meant. She'd been on her own for a long time now. She was a trained servicewoman and she hadn't depended on anyone except her fellow soldiers throughout her time in the military, and it was probably difficult for her to depend on her family now, so Isaac couldn't ask her to lean into him.

And yet…

What he could do was give her a safe place to be herself, to open up and start letting those deep, invisible wounds begin to heal.

The office door opened and Hannah poked her head through the door as Isaac turned.

"Hey, guys!" she called, pushing the door and walking into the room. "How's it going?"

"Going great," Avery answered, giving Hannah an easy smile. "Foggy is just…"

Avery looked up at the ceiling as if it might offer a word big enough to describe her feelings for her new sidekick, but then just shook her head and raised her hands in surrender.

"He's wonderful, isn't he?" Hannah offered.

"I can't get enough of him."

Hannah put her hands on her hips. "Has he been doing okay with all the basics?"

"Better than okay," Isaac said. "He's one hundred percent on everything. You did good, Hannah Banana."

Hannah shrugged. "It's my job."

"He's probably ready to take his test, but it'll be a

couple of weeks before I can get our usual guy out here to run the exam. I have no doubt he'll do great. And, if Avery's ready then, too, she can take it with him as his handler."

Avery bit her lip—a sign that she was a little nervous, Isaac had learned by making a study of her pretty face.

"We've got plenty of time," he said. "And there's absolutely no pressure on you at all."

Hannah sent him a look but he shook his head. He would bring up the subject of the local animal shelter's upcoming 5K walk/run fund-raiser when the time was right and ask her if she'd like to attend.

There were a couple of sponsors coming that word of mouth told him were interested in Isaac's new veterans program, and he'd hoped to run into, and if possible speak to, one in particular at the end of the walk that day. Having the owner of Palmer Motors offer to fund the program would be a dream come true—the money would make it possible to pull more dogs from the shelter to match up with veterans who couldn't afford to go through the training out of their own pockets.

Plus, it would be an excellent place for Avery to test things out with Foggy—all kinds of distractions would be present. But for now, she had had a long morning and was probably getting tired.

What they both needed was lunch. He wouldn't even pretend it wasn't an excuse for him to spend more time with her, to get to know her better, and he knew just the place.

"Well, guys," Hannah said, looking at her watch. "I've got to run." She pointed over her shoulder to the back of the building. "Isaac, the fence out back is fine. One of our new clients and his puppy are coming in later today to practice commands outside—" she raised her eyebrows at Avery "—and this little dude has a bit of a squirrel-chasing fetish. Had to make sure he won't get out of the play area and into the street. I'm determined to get him to focus, even with the little furry things jumping through the trees to tease him."

She winked and grabbed her purse from the file cabinet by her desk, then called to Foggy. "Are you coming, Fogs?"

Foggy stopped pawing at Jane and looked from Hannah to Isaac, then to Avery. He came to a decision and trotted confidently over to Avery's side, where he apparently intended to stay indefinitely.

"All right, then," Hannah said, feigning a bruised ego. "Point taken. Avery?" she asked. "Would it be okay if this little guy spent the night with you?"

Avery looked surprised, but then childlike pleasure took over. "Um, yeah, that would definitely be okay." She clasped her hands together in front of her chest, elated.

"Okay, it's settled," Hannah said, grinning at Isaac. "Let me grab his supplies. Next time you come in to train, I'll pull all of his veterinary records from the computer and print them out for you. He's been neutered and is up to date on all of his shots, of course, and he's had regular treatment for fleas and parasites. We use organic stuff as much as we can, and I'll be sure to give you a supply, you know—if things work out." She winked, obviously confident that they would.

Hannah set about piling up Foggy's leash, food and toys, then wished them both a good day and headed out.

Immediately, Avery rushed over and wrapped her arms around Isaac's waist, taking the breath straight from his body.

"Thank you," she said. "Thank you, thank you, thank you."

For a second, all he could do was stand there, speechless and unable to move. But then, when the woman didn't let go, he decided he would. Isaac put his hands on Avery's back slowly, tentatively, in case she decided she didn't want to be touched in return, but she didn't even flinch.

Finally, he wrapped her small form in his embrace and tucked his chin into her hair, feeling, for the first time, that he'd found his perfect fit.

"Well, hey there, stranger! I haven't seen you in years, honey, how have you been?" Barb's voice carried all the way across her popular diner as Avery, Isaac and Foggy—looking adorable in his service dog vest—stepped inside. Avery's stomach did a little nervous flip, but she took a deep breath and grasped Foggy's leash tighter as she steadied herself for what she knew would be a big hug and lots of chatter.

"Come here right now and give me a big hug, honey," Barb said, coming out from behind the front counter. Avery did her best to smile as Isaac tossed her a concerned look. On the way to grab lunch, they'd had a chance to talk about some of the things that Avery felt she struggled with the most, and she'd shared how her heart beat faster and her palms became sweaty whenever someone came too close to her. It wasn't so bad with people she knew well, but strangers were another thing altogether. She'd had plenty of panic attacks by now to know the signs, and he'd promised to spend the rest of the afternoon teaching Foggy how to block people from getting too near.

As Barb hurried over, Avery concentrated on the red vinyl bar stools and the black-and-white-checkered tiles that she'd seen so often when she'd waitressed for Barb part-time in high school. Focusing on the familiar setting soothed her, and as Barb wrapped her in a mama bear hug, Avery's pulse finally slowed back to normal.

"I'm so glad to see you, Avery," Barb said before turning to Isaac. "She was my best waitress of all time."

"You say that about all your waitresses," Avery teased, making both Barb and Isaac laugh. "You look fabulous, by the way—haven't aged a day." She meant every word. Her former boss's curly hair had a little more salt to balance out the pepper beautifully, and her blue eyes were as bright as they always had been.

Barb's cheeks took on a rosy hue even as she playfully swatted Avery with a kitchen towel.

"I'll let you girls catch up," Isaac said, squeezing Avery's shoulder before heading off to put in their order.

Barb and Avery sat at a table and caught up while Isaac waited for their food, and Barb gave Foggy plenty of compliments on his excellent behavior. When their order was up, Barb disappeared into the kitchen and returned with a baggie full of chicken scraps. "For Foggy," she said. "Don't worry, it's nothing fatty."

"Why don't you take a break and join us for lunch?" Avery suggested, thrilled at how pleased Barb seemed with the suggestion. "Macy and Tommy and the kids are coming by, too." She glanced at her watch. "They should be here to meet us any minute now."

Barb's eyes sparkled. "I'd love to."

Warmth spread through Avery's veins. Normally she wouldn't have asked anyone to join her for a meal, preferring the company of her family, the only people who wouldn't judge her, who were accustomed to her edginess. Then again, nothing about that day was normal, was it? She had a dog now, she thought, smiling as she looked down at Foggy, whose paws spread across her feet where he lay, and she had a new friend.

Perhaps more.

There had been a moment back at the training center with Isaac... She was certain he'd almost kissed her, or at least had wanted to, and the thought surprisingly didn't scare her. She would have let him. She would have loved it.

"There they are!"

Her niece's high-pitched squeal at the sight of Foggy pulled her from her thoughts and Avery looked up to see Macy, Tommy and the kids crowding through the front door, bringing happy noise with them to the table. She and Barb stood for hugs all around, and Tommy went to help Isaac carry over several trays of food. After Avery introduced everyone to Foggy, whom the kids adored, of course, it was quiet for a bit while they dug into Barb's amazing fried chicken, the only sound a moan of happiness here and there. And it didn't take long for the hungry kiddos to finish up and run off to the playscape out back.

"Hang on, wait for Mommy," Macy called after them. "I better follow those guys," she said, getting up from the table, but Barb put a hand on her shoulder and gently pushed her back into her chair.

"You stay here and spend time with your family. My staff's got everything taken care of, the lunch rush is winding down, and I need more time with those little ones. It's been a while since I got my kid fix." She smiled around the table before hurrying off behind Sylvia and Ben.

"What'd you two work on this morning?" Tommy asked before taking a sip of his iced tea. Only moments before, his plate had been piled so high Avery could barely see around it, yet Tommy was as thin and solid as a post from all the farm work. It was a tender reminder that he'd taken a rare afternoon off to spend time with her.

"Mostly basic commands," Avery said, smiling at Isaac.

"These two get along like peanut butter and jelly," Isaac chimed in. "I think they're going to be perfect for each other."

"Anything we can do to help?" Macy asked, setting down her fork to wipe her hands.

Isaac nodded to Avery so she could answer. "Actually, maybe so," she said, looking back to him for reassurance.

"We do need a third person for an exercise we talked about earlier," he said. "The idea is to teach Foggy how to act as a sort of barrier between Avery and anyone that might get too close for comfort, like a stranger in a store aisle or out in public, that sort of thing."

Macy and Tommy nodded, eager to help. Isaac stood and they all followed to an open space near their table. "You remember the sit and stay commands from earlier?" he asked.

"Sure do."

He smiled at her, his expression proud.

"It's just a step beyond that. So what you'll want to do is tell Foggy to sit and stay in front of you, but facing away from you. It's a little tricky at first, but you'll get it."

He showed Avery how to circle a treat around in her hand until Foggy was facing out from her front. It took a few tries, but Foggy was a great sport, and eventually they got it down and practiced several times to reinforce the move.

"All right, so now what we need to do is have one of you—" he waved at her brother "—Tommy, you'd be good since you're larger. Come up to Avery and stand a bit too close like you're in a crowded spot."

Tommy moved in, holding his arms out like a zombie, and they all burst into laughter when Foggy began barking at him.

"Thank you, Foggy, but that's enough," Isaac said, and Foggy quieted down, keeping a side eye on her oh-so-threatening, goofy brother. "See, he's already got the right idea," Isaac said, chuckling, "but we need to redirect it a little."

They spent the next several minutes practicing having Foggy stand in front of her to prevent Tommy from getting too near, applying the "block" command when he performed the move correctly, so the dog would have a clear indicator of what to do if a similar situation arose, like in a grocery store line or on a bus or plane. Isaac also showed her that she could just have her pup sit in front of her, facing her, so that she could focus on him as a barrier between her and anybody else while she did some grounding and breathing exercises to calm down. It wasn't long before they had it down pat, and Tommy and Macy had fallen in love with her new furry friend.

As they chatted happily, Avery took a moment to enjoy the sweet little family surrounding her, as well as Isaac and Foggy, and her heart swelled.

She'd missed so much, had spent so long in darkness that she hadn't been sure she would ever again see light. But this…this was a glimmer. It was like waking up from a long, fitful sleep.

She knew she still had such a long, long way to go. But she had to start somewhere, and, as she let herself soak in the enormity of the blessings surrounding her, she realized a simple afternoon spending time with the people she cared about the most was as good a place as any.

Chapter Nine

When they visited the park a week later, Avery had the strong sense that if Isaac and Foggy were not at her sides like two guards, she couldn't be sure that she wouldn't have just run away. The noises, colors, smells and all the chaotic stuff of life surrounded her as if she'd walked into a theme park on spring break opening day.

Gripping Isaac's large, steady hand in one of hers and Foggy's leash in the other, she closed her eyes and then opened them again, this time forcing herself to focus on one thing at a time.

There, beneath her feet, was the vibrant, soft Bermuda grass, a hardy green carpet formed from millions of thin, silky blades. She lifted her eyes and, straight ahead, they landed on the long, oval duck pond in the center of the park, gravel paths surrounding it like wagon wheel spokes. Above, the sky was the cobalt color of a robin's feathers, accented here and there with cottony clouds and glints of golden sunbeams. Several yards to her right, on the crest of a small hill, a young family enjoyed a picnic lunch consisting of what looked like chicken-salad sandwiches, dill-potato salad and spongy slices of pink strawberry cake adorning plates strewn across a red-and-white-gingham blanket.

The woman fed grapes to the small boy, who released peals of magic laughter each time she circled a plump purple orb round and round before popping it into his little round mouth, and a handsome man sat behind them, one hand at the small of the woman's back, the other capturing mother and child with his cell phone camera.

Down the path, an elderly couple strolled hand in hand, their papery fine skin linking them together as their matching silver hair reflected light from the sun's rays. College-aged men and women played a loud and happy game down at the tennis courts.

When she could pause and grant herself the patience required to take things in, one at a time, the barrage of anxiety that resulted from overstimulation subsided and the park was just a park, not a combat zone loaded with hidden dangers.

It was home.

This wasn't the place that had damaged her and turned her into a hypervigilant, fearful version of her former self. Instead, it was the one she'd fought for—imperfect, but full of hope and beauty—and freedom.

And, if she could only relearn to embrace it as her

own, retrain herself to know that it belonged to her, she could keep going.

She understood now, after months of therapy, that her PTSD would never go away; there was no cure for it. It would always be her silent enemy, lurking in the corners of her life like a predator, waiting for a weak moment to pounce and bring her down again. It would simply be a part of her forever. But hope wasn't lost, and she refused to focus on it, to give it strength. And she could develop the skills necessary for coping with the symptoms; she would survive. If she were lucky, she could even prevail.

Isaac's hand was on her shoulder then, its warmth reaching the skin through her T-shirt like a rich balm. "Okay there, sweetheart?" he asked, squeezing slightly.

Her lips curved upward at the buttery-smoothness of his voice and the term of endearment he'd used so casually.

"Yes, I am," she answered simply, not needing to say more.

Since they'd met, she and he had exchanged plenty of words, and talking and listening to him was, she found, a surprisingly welcome pleasure. But even more than that, she enjoyed their silences, those quiet moments of peaceful company, of just being together, that stretched out between them and required no dressing.

Now, though, she wanted to talk.

There was an itch in her chest and throat that she needed to scratch with words, with truth about the pain she'd suffered and had not, until now, had the courage to share with anyone—not even, if she were honest, herself.

It was time to open up.

She didn't care that the person she felt most comfortable with was someone she'd met only recently. If war had taught her anything good, it was that time was not the most valuable or the most important factor in a bond forged between two people. Rather, Avery thought, it was trust, which sometimes took years to build, yes, but could also be earned in mere moments, in small or large actions that communicated: *I am here for you; I will not abandon you.*

Isaac had given her that when he'd taken her into his home, fed her and offered sanctuary from her living nightmare. He'd done it by introducing her to Foggy, by intuiting that the dog would be a good companion for her and a protective layer between her and the world.

She could open her heart to this man, and if it bled, he would not startle at the droplets; he wouldn't run from her darkness. She didn't need months to know that much was true. She'd been given a gift in his kindness, in his generosity, and she was thankful.

Avery turned to face him and as she did, he cupped her face in the hand that had been resting on her shoulder. She closed her eyes, letting the heat of his skin seep into her cool cheek.

Wanting him to kiss her, to have him pull her near and cover her lips with his own, but knowing it wasn't yet time for that, Avery smiled and took his hand in her own, then led him across the grass to the duck pond. They sat together on the limestone wall that surrounded the pool of water. Foggy and Jane sat, too, at their feet, but their little doggie bottoms wriggled impatiently as they suppressed their urge to bark and chase the blue and green birds floating along the liquid surface.

"I never killed anyone over there," Avery said, her voice gravelly and so low she thought perhaps Isaac hadn't heard her.

He was silent for a full minute before responding, "You didn't have to tell me that."

Avery shook her head. "I did. I did have to tell you that." She turned and met his eyes. "It's what everyone wants to know, what everyone's thinking when they see me in town or talk about me behind my back, trying to figure out what happened to me over there. Sometimes, I wish they would just ask."

Isaac nodded. "Well, if it helps you to tell me, then I'm so glad you did. I'm glad you can trust me enough for that, though we haven't known each other long enough for me to expect it of you, and you never have to tell me any more than you feel comfortable with."

"I know that," she said. "It was my choice to tell you, and yes, it does help me to get that off my chest."

She looked out at the water and ran a finger over a long crack in the stone underneath her thigh. "I think people might believe I'm still human if they knew that about me. They might be less afraid to speak to me and say hello when they pass me on the street the way they used to, before I left and became someone else."

Avery could feel his gaze on her as she kept her eyes down, not sure if she wanted to look into his just then.

"You don't owe anyone any explanation, Avery. You

have the right to say or not say what you choose. And you did not become someone else. You may have added some terrible experiences to your résumé, but you are still Avery Abbott, and the people who love you know that."

"I'm not so sure sometimes, but I don't blame them, either."

"What makes you say that?"

"Just certain things have changed. At my job—my old job, I guess—for example. I was a great employee for years before I left, and I was thrilled when they wanted me back at the hospital after I came home. I was always at my best, always one hundred percent accurate in my diagnoses and medication calculations, often even more than the doctors I worked under. I never missed a day, I won awards and patients seemed to like me. Then, one day, something—I still have no idea what—triggered a flashback, and, well, you know how that looks. Anyway, after all of that time, I made one mistake and I lost everything. And I know that I scared the patient who was there when it happened. I can understand why they thought it best to put me on leave, but it still hurt."

She closed her eyes, remembering that tense, painful conversation with her boss. Avery couldn't help but feel betrayed.

"And with Tommy. The last time I had an episode like I did recently, he made it clear that if I couldn't get better, I couldn't stay in his home." The words caught in her throat and she struggled with the effort it took to say more.

"And the thing is, I don't blame him one bit—him or Macy. They have little ones to take care of, and if one of them had been awake, had come across my path when I was lost to reality, well—"

"Hey, hey," Isaac soothed, putting a hand over hers. Her fingers ceased their repetitive motion over the rock. "It's no good talking about what might have happened. The important thing is that your niece and nephew are fine, and what Tommy did was to protect them, yes, but it was also to protect you. Besides that, you are doing the work you have to do to get better. You're going to your therapy appointments, and now you've got Foggy and me to help."

She smiled at his sweetness, at his unfailing optimism. How wonderful it would be to have Isaac with her always, to lift her spirits each time they fell. But no matter how great he was, he couldn't fix her heart. She would have to do that herself.

"If Tommy really wanted to protect them, he should have tossed me out a long time ago."

"I disagree, and he and Macy would, too. They love you. They wanted you to realize how much pain you were truly in, and to help you find a way out. I just think they may not know the best way to do that. By giving you an ultimatum—a wake-up call, so to speak—they forced you to look for other options besides therapy. My brother was in therapy for a few years, and he still couldn't handle the symptoms. There is only so much doctors and medicine can do in certain cases. Sometimes you need a little something more, a little something off the beaten path."

It was Avery's turn to comfort Isaac. Lines creased his usually smooth forehead and his eyes were suddenly full of darkness she hadn't seen before.

"I didn't know you had a brother," she said carefully, not missing the past tense Isaac had used. "What was his name?"

Her statement seemed to pull him out of the depths of thought he'd been falling into, but the storminess remained in his face.

"His name was Stephen. He died when I was just out of college."

"Oh, Isaac," she said, resting her head on his shoulder. The gesture was meant to calm him, but it was possible that she'd benefitted the most from it. "I'm so very sorry for your loss."

"It was a very long time ago," he said.

"I'm not sure that matters, though, does it?"

"No, you're right. It doesn't. It still feels like he's going to walk back into the house and ask what's for dinner. And expect me to cook, of course. Stephen always was great at eating, terrible at preparing food."

He chuckled at the memory and Avery's heart picked up speed at the sound, glad he hadn't been pulled completely down into his sorrow.

"Do you mind my asking what happened to him?"

Isaac swallowed and tilted his head to the side, and for a second, Avery thought he might say that yes, he did mind.

"No, not at all. He took his own life when he was about the age I am now."

There was nothing she could say or do to express

how acutely she felt his pain, and she wished for all the world that she could take it away, that she could bring his brother back for him.

Isaac was the closest person she had to a friend since she'd returned from war, battered and bruised in invisible ways, and if she were honest with herself, she wanted more from him than just friendship. So it hurt that she had nothing to offer in the way of consolation. The only thing she could do was to be there, and be open, the way he was for her.

Isaac spoke, softly. "He was very sick, and I can't say that I was…surprised…but that didn't make it any easier on me, or on Mom. I did the best I could for her, afterward, but she was never the same. I think she lost a lot of herself when her first child passed, and even though I knew, always, that she loved me just as much, I couldn't replace him."

Isaac's jaw set hard and Avery could see the extent of his hurt, despite his attempt to rein it in.

"He fought hard, he really did, but it wasn't enough. His death is what spurred me on when I left my old job and started to look for something more important to do with my life. I wanted out of the office, big-time, but a lot of my motivation to do something more was my need to live life to its fullest—for Stephen. It was almost like I had a duty to live enough for both of us, since he didn't have the chance.

"He's what led me into working with service dogs. I knew there had to be something different for people who weren't making it with the usual medication and psychiatric help. It wasn't until Stephen that I came across research that supported what I always felt to be true about animals—that they can feel strong emotion and can even help us when we are overwhelmed with our own. They love us without judgment, even when we can't love ourselves and when we think no one around us can, either. They don't care where we've been or what we've done. They care only about the present, about living in the moment the best way possible. It's a beautiful thing and humans could certainly stand to take a cue from our animal friends sometimes."

"Was he—" Avery chose her words carefully, not wanting to press on any nerve endings or cause any more hurt than he already felt, but wanting to know more, because she cared deeply about the man next to her. "Did he serve in the military? In combat?"

"Yes, he did." Isaac looked up at her, and even though his eyes held sadness, they were also full of optimism, and she wondered how someone who'd been through something so difficult could maintain his humble generosity, his pure but somehow not naive, outlook on life.

"Is that why you help people like me?"

Isaac grinned and Avery's heart lifted, relieved to see that wonderful sight again.

"To answer your question—yes, Stephen is the big reason why I got into training dogs for vets. I don't want to see anyone in my community go through the same stuff that he did and believe that there is no way out, that there can't be life on the other side—full life."

After a long moment, he raised both palms to her face and stared straight into her eyes with more intensity than she'd seen up to that point. Flecks of gold danced around his irises as he gave her a crooked, perfect smile, and Avery noticed for the first time that he had adorable dimples in both cheeks.

Sparks of electric joy shot through her entire body.

"But I have to correct you," he said, suddenly quite serious.

She knew that this…this was the moment she'd wanted so badly only minutes before. Instinctively, she could feel that this was one of those times she would look back on someday with great happiness.

The moment she started to think she might be able to find it again, to find love.

Take a chance, a little voice inside her prodded.

"Why's that?" She bit her lip, nervous and elated, sad and hopeful, vulnerable and brave, all at once.

He smiled, his brown eyes glittering in the sunshine. "Because, Avery, you asked if I help people *like you* because of Stephen, when, in fact—there is no one like you."

He caught her smile in his lips as he gently pressed them into hers, kissing her with a delicious combination of tenderness and passion. She closed her eyes and let herself drop over the edge into something new, losing herself in the moment, enjoying the sensation of falling, falling, falling, with the knowledge that she was safer than ever before in Isaac Meyer's strong hands.

It was incredibly liberating to forget everything that had happened to her before that moment, every cut, every scar, every bruise that had pulled her further and further away from her true self, from the strong woman she knew was still inside somewhere, waiting to be set free. And she knew he couldn't do that for her. Only *she* could fight her demons, only she could push until she reached the other side of the horrors that she feared would always return in her nightmares.

She knew all of those things as she kissed him back, wrapping her arms around his firm torso. But she had to admit, it was mighty damn nice to have someone at her side while she did the hard work.

Kissing Avery was far more than everything Isaac thought it would be. He supposed they were still there in the park near the pond, with the dogs at their feet and sunshine soaking through their shirts, but at the moment, he wouldn't have been able to tell if his life depended on it.

Wrapped up in the sweet, honey taste of her lips, the ones that were definitely, incredibly, kissing him back, he lost all sense of reality, all sense of time, all sense of anything except *her*.

He didn't care that this was probably too soon, that it would mean things might change for them more quickly than either was prepared to handle.

It didn't matter.

This wasn't an ordinary girl, and this wasn't an ordinary relationship.

But there would be time for all of that later. Right now, all he wanted was to memorize the summery scent of her hair as its strands danced around her face in the gentle breeze, and the way her soft cheeks warmed under the touch of his fingers as they trailed along her jawline.

The way, when he'd finished kissing her, for now—he'd already decided that there would be so much more—Avery's blue eyes fluttered open as if coming out of a dream. A very good dream.

As she covered his hands with her own and pulled them gently away from her face, Isaac remained still, mesmerized by her beauty.

"Kisses look so good on you," he said, not caring that the words might be cheesy. Hadn't she told him that she always wanted the truth from him, no matter what? And it was the absolute truth. Her cheeks were rosy, which only made her blue eyes shine a shade brighter, and her lips were the color of strawberry jam, plump from their collision with his.

She smiled and gazed down at their joined hands. It didn't bother him that she didn't say anything. There was no need to. Everything they needed to say had already been stated in that kiss. The air buzzed between them with excitement and possibility, but they had plenty of time to figure things out.

A loud growl interrupted the quiet and for a second, Isaac thought it had come from one of the dogs.

"Someone's hungry," Avery said, laughing. She reached over and poked Isaac in his abs. Not a vain man, he was nonetheless glad he kept in shape, and her touch so near his groin set his mind off on a path that would be hard to come back from.

"Starved," he said, glad for the distraction.

He'd brought her to the park after their training session to relax and let the dogs out into the fresh air, but the park also happened to be the home of a food truck that served excellent burritos. The thought of lunch set Isaac's stomach to grumbling again.

"Let's do something about that, shall we?" Avery suggested, grabbing Foggy's leash and standing up.

Isaac did the same with Jane, but his girl wasn't a service dog, so it took a bit more work than just the "let's go" command to get Jane's mind off the ducks.

He'd kept an eye on Jane as they'd sat admiring the water. She had some hound in her, he was pretty sure, along with a thousand other things, and whenever she came across small animals her ears perked up and she fancied herself a hunting dog. Not that she was any threat. Whenever Jane got anywhere near a cat or a squirrel after a chase, she simply stood staring down her opponent, waiting to see if it would run off and start up their game again. She was completely harmless and a big doofus, but still, he always tried to make sure she was on her best behavior in public places.

"Come on, Jane," he said. "I promise I'll share some of my lunch with you if you'll promise me you won't run off after those ducks," he said, joking, but gripping her leash a little tighter all the same. At the mention of lunch, Jane's thoughts switched over to food and she finally decided that it was okay to leave the pond.

Isaac grabbed Avery's hand and they walked the hundred yards to where the food trucks parked. A row of shiny Airstream trailers, promising every variety of Texas cuisine, beckoned as they arrived at the gravel parking lot. Picnic benches painted in primary colors were scattered about, and kids ate rapidly melting ice-cream cones while their moms and dads munched on burgers and quesadillas.

"Wow," Avery said, her eyes wide at the sight. "I hadn't realized how much I missed this place until now."

Isaac shielded his eyes from the sun and smiled at her, glad that he'd picked a good place for their first date. Jane sniffed the ground, searching for dropped crumbs, and Foggy's nose twitched at the savory scents filling the air.

"We used to come here in high school," she said, her expression gone soft at the memories.

"Yeah, you were lucky to have it," he said.

"What? It wasn't here when you were at Peach Leaf High?"

"Nope. I'm a couple years ahead of you, according to Tommy. They built this right after I graduated."

She squinted, thinking about the timeline. "Oh yeah, you're right. It was my junior year when this all went up." She grinned. "I just remember sneaking over here on lunch break to grab hot dogs. We weren't supposed to go off campus until senior year," she said, giggling. "But you know, teenagers always follow the rules."

Isaac chuckled with her.

"So...you've asked Tommy about me, huh?"

Her voice was lighter than it had been before, and Isaac was almost certain it was more playful. His grin stretched from ear to ear when he realized suddenly that she was flirting with him.

"I have," he said, meeting her tone. Then he switched his voice to sound gruffer. "But, you know, I'm a professional and you're technically my client now."

He stopped walking and turned to face Avery, slipping a strand of hair behind her ear, enjoying the fact that he could touch her now without causing her to jump. "I make it a practice to know what I need to know about the people I'm working for."

"I see," she said, tucking a finger under her chin. "And what is it that you need to know about me, Mr. Meyer?"

There was genuine curiosity in her voice alongside the flirtatiousness. She wanted him to ask about her. This was the invitation he'd been waiting for.

"Everything," he said truthfully.

Chapter Ten

"I want to know everything about you, Avery Abbott," he said, staring into her eyes in the hope that she could fully recognize his sincerity.

She swallowed, appearing suddenly nervous.

Had he been too honest? Said too much? He retraced his steps, wishing he could put that carefree look back on her face.

"But first—lunch."

She relaxed, giving him a smile, and he reminded himself to take things slow. He hated the thought of going anything but full speed ahead now that he'd been around this woman enough to know he wanted more, more, more, but if he pushed too hard, he could lose her altogether, and that simply was not an option.

"Anything you want, sweetheart. Take your pick."

Avery crossed her arms over her chest and surveyed the selection. Isaac's favorite were the massive, over-stuffed delicacies from Freddy's Fajitas, but if pressed he'd have to admit that anything from any of the food trucks was guaranteed to be fantastic.

"I'm actually pretty darn hungry," Avery said, sounding surprised at herself.

"That's great news, and something we can definitely fix."

They must have been on the same wavelength be-cause Avery's eyes wandered over to Freddy's and she headed in that direction. They ordered and walked away carrying giant tortillas stuffed to the gills with chicken, avocado, onion, sour cream and enough jalapeños to light the town on fire.

"A girl after my own heart," Isaac said, nodding at the spicy fillings spilling out of Avery's meal.

"Oh, don't get me started. I can't get enough. Macy is the only one who can make salsa that's hot enough for me, and I could beat the guys right out of my unit in pepper-eating contests. Every time."

She winked at him, proud, and he was thrilled to hear her sharing fun memories of her time in service.

"Man, I missed Tex-Mex while I was gone," she said, reminiscing and pulling her food a little closer to her as they walked over to a butter-yellow table and set down their cardboard boats of food, their drinks and a few paper napkins. Isaac excused himself and headed to the food truck to grab a plastic bowl, then took it over to a water fountain and brought it back to the table, placing it underneath for Jane and Foggy to share.

"How long were you over there? Afghanistan, right?" Isaac asked, watching her closely.

"Yep, that's right. Three tours, six months each."

"Wow. That's…a lot."

"It was," she said, nodding as she sat across from him and spread a napkin over her lap. "The time went by fast, in a way, but there were nights when I really, really wanted to be back in my bed, when I just wanted to be home again."

"I can only imagine."

"A lot of bad things happened, but…there were good times, too. At first it's hard, especially in Basic, because you don't know anyone and you miss home and everything is physically demanding and weird and it makes you all emotional."

She took a sip of her iced tea and peered into the distance, a trace of a smile crossing her lips as she watched a mom feeding a toddler little cut-up bites of pizza.

"And then, of course, you don't want to show everyone that you're emotional, so you try to hold it in and it just sort of comes out of you at random times."

Avery laughed at a memory. "Once, my friend Sophie and I were just chilling out after a drill, listening to the radio, and an old stupid song from the eighties came on. You know, one of those ridiculous, drama-queen hair band ballads, and I just completely lost it. I'm pretty sure Sophie thought I'd lost my marbles."

Isaac's chest tightened at the bittersweet picture she'd painted.

"Thank God I had Sophie with me over there. I don't know what I would have done without her." Avery's words came out a little squeaky and she hurried to tuck into her food.

They ate quietly for a while and Isaac relaxed into the silence. Jane and Foggy were lying under the table next to each other, their tongues hanging out.

They both took big bites of their fajitas and giggled as juice inevitably escaped to roll down their chins. Isaac pulled out a piece of chicken, wiped off the sauce and pretended to drop it under the table so that Jane could pick it up.

"Can you feed them people food?" Avery asked.

"Yeah, you can give them plain meat, particular veggies and fruit, eggs, stuff like that. Remind me later and I'll print you out a list of doggie no-nos. Certain things, like grapes and chocolate, are dangerous and potentially deadly to their systems, but there are quite a few things they can share with us."

He shook his head and gave Jane a look.

"I would not recommend feeding them from the table most of the time, though," he said. "It's hard to get them out of the habit of asking for scraps once you start. I've already ruined Jane for that. Foggy's so well-trained that you might be able to get away with it on occasion."

He pointed as Jane put on her very best sad face and rested her furry chin on his knee. "See what I mean?"

"Oh, goodness," Avery said, cooing. "She's too cute. How can you possibly resist her?"

"That's just it," he said, shrugging his shoulders. "I can't."

"I miss Sophie so much, sometimes," Avery said, so softly Isaac wasn't sure he'd heard her correctly.

"You were close, huh?" he asked.

Avery nodded, her lips forming a thin line.

"We grew up together and hung out all the time, but we weren't that close until we decided to join the army. I'd finished getting my RN at community college and was ready for a change, and, well, Sophie was tired of working low-paying jobs to get by. You know how Peach Leaf is," she said, glancing up at him. "Not a lot of work to go around."

He nodded in agreement. It was true. Lots of folks who were raised in their small town couldn't find well-paying jobs. The options were simple: go off and get a degree or other vocational training, or work for peanuts. Most people who left didn't come back, finding that they'd outgrown their hometown. Isaac could totally understand and had grown up telling himself he'd never come back except to visit Mom and Nana, but after he'd been gone a few years, he'd begun to miss something about this place. Even if it wasn't perfect, and hell, nowhere was, at least there were people in Peach Leaf who knew his past, who knew who he was down to his bones and knew what he'd come from and where he'd been. There was something solid, something important about a person's home. You might not always love it, and you sure as hell might not always like it, but home was home. He imagined Avery knew that very sentiment well.

"I do know," he said, giving her a soft smile.

"So Sophie and I decided to go big or...well...stay home." Avery grinned. "So that's what we picked. She didn't meet her husband until later, on one of our visits home, and then they had Connor a ways down the road."

"It must have been hard, being so young and leaving your family."

Avery shook her head. "Well, I don't know if Tommy's ever told you, but our parents were killed in a car crash when I was twenty-two and Tom was a bit older."

"God, I'm so sorry," Isaac said, putting down his fajita. He touched Avery's hand and she closed her eyes, evidently enjoying the touch he'd offered to soothe her. "You've been through so much for someone your age."

"That might be true, but you know, things could always be worse. I'm lucky to have Tommy and Macy and the kiddos, and this town, and I was lucky to have Sophie and to make it home in one piece. Or, you know, mostly."

Avery choked up a little.

"I just wish, sometimes—" she looked up at him under hooded eyes, as if choosing her words with caution "—sometimes I wish that Sophie had been the lucky one. That it had been she who made it home alive."

Isaac winced at her words and at the similarity they held to some of Stephen's later statements. He put down his food, suddenly not hungry anymore.

"Avery, please don't say things like that."

"I'm sorry, Isaac. I don't mean to be morbid, and I don't mean to sound like I'm not thankful to be here, but there are times when I think… I mean, I can't understand why it was me and not her."

She poked at her fajita with a fork, pushing around the contents that had escaped the flour tortilla.

"It's my fault, you know," she said. "It's my fault she's gone."

Avery's eyes glistened with moisture and Isaac reached over to stop her anxious fidgeting, covering her hands with his own.

"How can you think something like that?" he asked.

She looked up at him, her eyes huge and shiny and full of sorrow.

"Because it's true."

"Look, Avery. Whatever happened, whatever you think was your fault, please believe me that it wasn't. I know you."

Her brow furrowed and he could sense her skepticism.

"I know, we've only known each other for less than a month, but don't tell me that I can't feel your heart after that amount of time. You know there's something... something going on between us. Something special. And I don't need much time to be a good judge of character. And your character, Avery, it's the best."

She smiled sadly and he wondered if she didn't believe him. It would take more than words to convince her that what he felt was real and true.

"You wouldn't say that if you knew the whole story," she said, pulling her hands away from his to rub at her eyes.

"Then tell me. Tell me the whole story."

She closed her eyes and Isaac gave her the time she needed, taking a moment to check on Foggy and Jane under the table. The two dogs were snoozing side by side, their limbs and tails curled up, as though they knew they were meant to be together.

If only it were that simple with people.

If only he could convince Avery that he would be here for her, that he would support her as long as she would let him. That he wouldn't let what happened to Stephen, happen to her. He'd dedicated his life's work to ensuring that for as many men and women as he could help, but he hadn't known until Avery how much it really mattered that his program worked. It really could mean life or death for certain veterans. And those lives—lives that had been offered up in the most dangerous situations imaginable in an attempt to stand for the freedom of humanity—mattered. So much.

He looked up from under the table to check on Avery and noticed instantly that her expression was one of terror.

"Avery, what's wrong?" he asked.

The color had drained from her face and her skin was white as a ghost despite the afternoon heat, and her eyes were huge as she focused on something in the distance. Isaac followed her line of vision, but all he could see at the end was a man about his age, and a cute little boy who looked to be three or four years old.

Avery got up from the table as if in a trance, heading toward what he assumed were the dad and son.

"Avery. Avery?" he called after her, but she either ignored him or couldn't hear.

Isaac checked on the dogs again to make sure they were still asleep and hurried after her.

* * *

As soon as she'd seen them in the distance, Avery was pulled in their direction as if an invisible fishing line had begun to reel her in.

Nathan and Connor Harris.

Sophie's Nathan and Connor.

Her best friend's husband and son were sitting at a table enjoying a meal of their own, not too far from where she and Isaac had sat down to eat. Even from a distance, Avery could see lines on Nathan's young face that shouldn't have been there yet. He looked way too old for a man in his midthirties.

And it was Avery's fault.

She didn't know what she would say when she arrived at their table, which now seemed miles away as she trudged forward as if through mud. She just knew she had to see them, had to get close. She needed to make sure that they were okay.

Nathan had refused to speak to Avery at Sophie's funeral, and she couldn't blame him. She had decided that he agreed with her that it was her fault his wife, her best friend, was gone.

Nothing could convince her otherwise. It was her idea to trade shifts that day. It didn't matter why. It was her decision that had cost them all an amazing woman. How could Nathan—and even Connor, one day, when he became old enough to learn what happened to his beautiful mother—ever forgive her?

How could she ever forgive herself?

She neared the table and Nathan looked up, the smile that had covered his face as he watched Connor play with a fire truck evaporating when he saw who approached. He wiped his hands on his jeans and stood, covering the distance between them to meet Avery before she made it to where they sat.

"Avery," he greeted awkwardly, placing nervous hands in his pockets. She couldn't read his tone; it was absent of any emotion that might give her some clue as to how he felt upon seeing her.

Suddenly, she regretted coming over, wishing she'd opted to grab Isaac and run instead.

What had she been thinking?

They weren't exactly on decent terms. She had no right to just waltz up to Nathan like this and remind him of something he probably tried every minute of every day to forget. Just glimpsing her face probably brought back a million painful memories.

Suddenly, Isaac was at her side. She could feel him there as if he were a part of her own body, but for some reason she wasn't able to pull her attention from Nathan.

"It's been so long. I haven't seen you around town," Nathan said, his words shaky but not unkind. What had she thought he would do? Yell at her in a public place? It would be what she deserved.

"It's…good to see you, Nathan. How are you holding up?" The words burned her throat as they came out.

"I'm actually doing okay," he said. "Despite… everything." He tried to smile but it wouldn't quite take. "How about you, Avery?"

"The same," she said.

"How's your family? Tommy and Macy and the kids?"

Images flashed before her eyes of all of them gathered together, the Thanksgiving before her and Sophie's last tour. It was the last time she'd seen Sophie with her boys, and her heart ached at the memory; she was suddenly quite certain that her chest was going to explode.

"Nathan, I'm so sorry."

He held out his hands. "Don't say that, Avery. You know it won't help."

"But I am," she said, taking a step toward him.

Warmth spread through her lower back. Isaac's hand was there, holding her steady, but she couldn't look at him, afraid that she might cry if she did.

And she couldn't cry. Soldiers didn't cry. Tears were for release, to make people feel better. Avery wouldn't allow them.

She remembered when she and Sophie had first gone into that home to speak with a few of the local women who had gathered for tea. Avery's job was to check on them, to see if they needed any medical care or advice, to build trust so that they could later ask questions, draw information. Sophie, a fellow medic, was her partner.

They'd been surprised that day at how much they enjoyed spending time with those women—sweet, shy ladies who were apprehensive at first, but opened up over several weeks, eventually inviting Sophie and Avery to come by weekly. She and her best friend, using what little they'd learned of the local language and a lot of smiles, had established a repertoire with them, had almost come to trust them, though they both knew that was a very dangerous place to tread.

Avery felt the desert heat again, the dry, sandy air

surrounding her as she cared for an injured patient that morning, a soldier who had lost a leg to a daisy-chain IED only an hour before. She'd stayed late to prep him for emergency surgery and, when Sophie showed up to relieve her, had offered to extend her own shift so she could check on the progress of her patient.

Avery found out later that Sophie had decided to use the extra time to meet with the women, eager to get back early enough to take a Skype call from Nathan and Connor before picking up Avery's later shift. Sophie had taken another soldier with her, and they had both lost their lives when a bomb exploded inside the house where they met.

If Avery hadn't been so invested in working on that soldier that morning, if she'd just checked out and let Sophie work her regular shift, her best friend would be there now, sitting in the park with her husband and son, just as she should have been.

"Nathan, please. You have to know how sorry I am," she said, careful not to let her voice break.

"I can't do this, Avery. Not here, not with Connor."

She looked over Nathan's shoulder at the little boy. With his auburn hair, bright emerald eyes and a sprinkling of freckles like cinnamon across his button nose, he was the spitting image of his mother. Nathan must have seen her every day in their child.

"Can…can I see him? Can I talk to him?" she asked, folding her hands together at her waist.

Nathan's eyes narrowed and he averted his gaze from hers, his jaw clenched.

"I don't think that's a good idea, Avery. I'm sorry. I just don't think I can handle it right now."

She closed her eyes, willing the tears to stay put behind her eyes.

Isaac's voice came, low and soft. "Is everything all right, Avery?" He didn't bother introducing himself to Nathan. As it had been for the past couple of weeks, all of his attention and concern was focused on her. He was an amazing man, better than she deserved.

How could she let herself be so happy in his presence when her best friend was dead and it was all her fault? How could she allow herself joy when Sophie would never breathe again, would never again hold her little boy or see him graduate, get married?

Her stomach clenched. She couldn't.

Everything went blurry and she had to get out of there before she got lost again in the past.

"I'm so sorry, Nathan," she said, then turned and began to run.

She ran until she got to the duck pond and stopped, her breath coming in fits and starts as the panic threatened to return. She would never outrun it, could never escape it. It would always be there, lurking in the corners, ready to attack her at any second. She would never be safe again.

Her knees buckled beneath her at the reminder and she sat on the ground with a thud, curling her arms over her head as the tears broke free and spilled forth, dropping like rain into the dirt beneath her.

"Avery, sweetheart, it's okay. It's okay."

Isaac's arms were around her and he was rocking

her back and forth like a child. He sat next to her and pulled her into his lap, wrapping her up and soothing her, stroking and kissing her hair.

Safe in his embrace, she let the tears come again.

Foggy forced himself into her lap and curled into a ball, raising his head to lick away the moisture from her face and all of a sudden, Avery started laughing. And then she couldn't stop.

We must look ridiculous, she thought, *like a crazy, mismatched set of Russian nesting dolls.*

She laughed and laughed until her stomach hurt, knowing it was her body's weird way of reacting to all the pain that had surfaced when she'd seen Nathan. She wished he'd let her near Connor. All she wanted was to look into his little face and see Sophie again, just one more time.

But she understood. She didn't have the right to ask such a thing. Nathan had already suffered enough at Avery's hands.

Isaac's arms loosened and she felt his chin nestled between her shoulder and neck. She leaned back into his chest, savoring the feel of his strength against her back for just a moment. He didn't speak for a long time, just held her and let her cry softly.

"I'm a hot mess," she said finally, earning a little laugh from him.

"Everyone is, Avery. Everyone's a hot mess at some point in life. I don't think there are too many who make it out of here without some crap happening that breaks them apart for a while."

"Yes, but I'm the worst."

"No," he said, "you're not."

"How do you know?" she asked, turning so she could see his face just above her shoulder. She scratched behind Foggy's ears.

"I just do," he said. "But, Avery, you scared me back there."

"I'm sorry. That was Nathan. He's…"

"I know, I guessed. It's okay. You don't need to apologize. I just got worried. I thought he might be upsetting you and I didn't want you to be afraid."

She shook her head. "It's not that. I just misjudged the situation. I thought maybe enough time had passed that he would let me see Connor again. We all used to be so close and I miss that kid. He doesn't understand that his mom is gone, and to tell you the truth, I don't really, either, sometimes. I just thought if I could see him… I know it's crazy, but I thought… I thought for some reason that it might make me miss Sophie less. He looks so much like her."

Isaac nodded, his stubbly chin tickling her cheek.

"But Nathan's right not to let me near him. I've already done enough damage as it is."

"I don't think that's the case, Avery, but we don't have to talk about that right now if you don't want to."

She rested her head under his chin.

"What is it that you'd like to do? Right now?"

"I think I'd like to go home, if that's okay with you."

"Absolutely," Isaac said, standing up slowly and offering his hands to help her up. Foggy stood as well, waiting for one of the crazy humans to tell him what to do, while Jane bounced on the end of her leash, eyeing the duck pond in vain once again.

How strange, how incredible it was that she was now part of this little crew. How odd that she'd somehow taken up with a gorgeous, sweet man and two fuzzy mutts in a matter of less than a month.

And how beautiful, too.

Chapter Eleven

The sun was sinking lower into the western sky as Isaac pulled into his driveway in Tommy's old spare truck; his own had been towed to the shop and would be fixed within the next couple of days. Tommy had offered to accompany Isaac to pick it up when it was ready, but he'd already decided that, if it was safe for her to drive the short distance into town with him, he would rather have Avery's company.

She was asleep on the seat next to him and didn't wake even when he pulled to a stop. He let the dogs out but left Foggy's things in the truck so they wouldn't forget them whenever he dropped Avery off at her brother's house. When she'd said she wanted to go home, Isaac had assumed she meant Tommy's, but when he'd started to drive away from the park, she'd shyly asked if it was okay if they go to his house for a few hours instead. He hadn't asked why, glad that she'd wanted to spend more time with him, but he could guess that maybe she needed some time away from family, some peace and quiet to put herself back together after what had amounted to a long, tough day.

He'd texted Tommy and let him know he'd bring Avery by when she was ready, and to confirm that Foggy would have a permanent home with their family, something he and Avery had forgotten to discuss thus far. The kids would be thrilled to have him stay, Tommy had texted back, and he was happy that Avery would have a companion. She'd been lonely, he had said, and he was glad she and Isaac had happened upon each other.

Isaac didn't need Tommy's permission to hang around Avery; she was a grown woman and could make her own decisions, but it was great to have all the same. The two men were neighbors, and Isaac valued Tommy's friendship and opinion. Plus, he'd really enjoyed their fried chicken lunch the other day and liked the idea of becoming closer with the whole Abbott clan.

After unloading the truck, when the dogs were safe inside the house, Isaac headed back outside to gather Avery. When he opened the door, she was still sound asleep, her blond hair strewn across her shoulder like a scarf, eyes fluttering with dreams he hoped were happy ones. He pulled her arm over his shoulder and placed his hands beneath her back and knees, lifting her out of the passenger seat with minimal effort. Her head tilted in against his shoulder and her soft breath brushed against his chin as he carried her into the house and laid her on the couch.

The similarity to that first night didn't escape him, and he realized with a jolt how different things were now, how much more he knew about this woman who'd stumbled into his life.

How, even in such a short time, he couldn't imagine a day without her.

Nor did he want to.

He wanted her to be his—his to protect, his to take care of, his to…

Well, maybe it was too soon for that. It was crazy to be thinking about that already—or was it?

Of course it was. Avery was different from anyone he'd been with before. She needed more from him. Isaac didn't want to push things so far, too fast.

But then again, what if?

She was a powerfully sexy woman, after all, whether she knew it or not, and he wanted her more than he could stand to think about without sending his body into overdrive. With all of his strength, he pushed the thought aside, for now.

While Avery snoozed, Isaac took the dogs out back to do their business before setting up Foggy's bowl next to Jane's in the kitchen and filling them both with food. He checked that there was fresh water in the large bowl and, when the dogs were crunching away at their kibble, he grabbed a beer on his way out of the kitchen.

He'd expected to find Avery still sleeping, but when he got back to the living room, she was on the far side, staring at a collection of photos on the wall.

She turned to face him, hair falling onto the afghan she'd wrapped around her shoulders. "Is this your family?"

He nodded, holding the beer bottle out to Avery. She took a sip and handed it back to him. "Would you like one?" he asked.

"No, thanks. I'm careful with alcohol…with my meds and all. And I've seen too many of my friends spiral down with it, trying to medicate themselves." She shook the thought away. "I love a good brew now and then, but I don't want to take chances."

Isaac admired her. Like Avery, he knew many veterans—many people, really—who tried to find peace at the bottom of a bottle, but the end result was the same as if they'd been searching for a pot of gold at the end of a rainbow, and it would kill him to see something like that happen to Avery.

"That's just another thing that makes you strong, Avery," he said, reaching up to touch her hair. She closed her eyes as he ran his hand over her back and he pulled away, very much aware of the impulses coursing through his veins.

She was vulnerable, and he would not let anything happen that she might regret, just because her wounds were open and she'd had a trying day. If she wanted him as much as he wanted her—and God, he hoped she did—there would be plenty of time for that when she was ready.

"So," she said, opening her eyes and tilting her chin toward him. "Introduce me."

Isaac smiled and set his beer down on an end table.

"All right, but most of these are my nana's photos, so I take no responsibility for any stupid ones of me."

She laughed, the sound like a balm to his soul.

"So, this is Nana herself, as you might have guessed. She was an amazing woman—strong, smart, kind— like you." He touched Avery's cheek briefly, the gesture softening her blue eyes. "And this is me when I was a teenager."

"Very, very handsome," she said, winking at him over her shoulder. "Too bad we never had a chance to meet back then. I would have definitely been interested."

The breath disappeared from his lungs and Isaac sucked it back in, willing himself to calm down, to focus on something other than the beautiful woman standing right beside him, telling him she would have dated him if only they'd met years before, hoping that what he read between the lines was accurate.

He went on, desperate for a distraction from the sweet scent of her skin, from those berry lips he'd gotten to taste only hours ago, an action that had only served to make him want so, so much more. She was in his system now, he realized, and he needed another dose of her to keep him going.

"This is Mom," he said, pulling his eyes away to point at a faded snapshot of his mother holding a baby version of himself in her arms, three-year-old Stephen by her side, just after his father had left the three of them alone, choosing to start over and make another family instead.

Those had been hard times, with little money for a

woman with two growing boys to feed. It wasn't until
high school that Stephen had been able to get a part-time
summer job and help out; Mom hadn't allowed him to
work during the school year, concerned that his stud-
ies would be neglected. He had then gone on to train as
an electrician—work that seemed to make him happy.

Then 9/11 happened; Stephen was twenty-five, older
than many of the people in his basic training, but Mom
had been so proud.

Their lives would never be the same after that. If only
it were possible to jump into that picture and warn them.
Then his brother would still be alive, and he wouldn't
feel so alone in the world, so rudderless without family.

Avery pointed to another photo, one of Stephen in
his dress uniform, the red, white and blue of their country's flag forming a backdrop. "This is Stephen?" she
asked, touching the photo gently through its glass cover.

"Yes," Isaac said, his voice breaking a little before
he coughed and set it right. "My big brother."

Avery turned then and buried herself in Isaac's chest,
wrapping her thin arms around his waist. He let her
hold him for what seemed like hours. The world slipped
away when she was that close to his body, and it took a
herculean effort not to react to her touch.

He pulled back, not wanting to overwhelm her.

"It's okay, Isaac. I'm a big girl," she said, looking up
at him with a hint of amusement.

"Avery, I... I don't want to push you into anything
you aren't ready for. It's been a rough day and you're
probably a little shaken up right now."

A tiny hint of annoyance flickered across her features and he hated even the idea that she might think he didn't want her.

"Trust me...if things weren't so volatile, if...if we'd known each other for longer and been on a couple of real dates at least, then this would be different."

She looked away and, though she still had her arms around his torso, tension had tightened her limbs.

"Hey," he said, urging her to face him by gently pulling her chin back until she met his eyes. "I want this. I definitely, definitely want this. But now isn't a good time."

She nodded. "You're right, Isaac. I don't want to go too fast, either." She said the words, but he detected a hint of doubt or disappointment in them—maybe both.

"We really haven't known each other all that long," he said.

Avery giggled, but then her face became serious. "The best weeks of my life."

Isaac started to speak but she put a finger to his lips. "I mean that," she said, and he believed her. "In spite of everything, and it has been a weird whirlwind, I mean it. Before the night we met, I didn't have Foggy, and I didn't have you, and I wouldn't change that for anything."

She rose up on her tiptoes and kissed him. This kiss was different from before—deeper and more intense. Avery opened her mouth and Isaac slipped his tongue gently inside, letting his arms slip farther down her back as he relished the honey flavor of her mouth, stroking along her teeth and the inside of her lips.

In seconds he was back on the edge, wanting her

with every cell in his body, lost in the wet heat of her mouth, all the while struggling to maintain some semblance of control.

He lifted her in his arms and carried her to the couch where they continued, hungry for more, but happy all the same just to be able to share kiss after kiss. He was careful with his hands, but couldn't keep himself from sliding them under her shirt, pressing his palms into the warm skin of her back. When she did the same to him, and just before he was certain all bets were off, he pulled away gently, settling her shirt back down as he placed a few more kisses on the tender skin beneath her ear.

Every inch of her body was on fire as Isaac's fingers danced over her flesh, and Avery cursed them both for agreeing not to go any further. At least not yet.

Now that she'd had a tiny sample of what Isaac Meyer could do to her, Avery's appetite was sparked.

He was right, of course, wasn't he? Maybe it was too soon for things to escalate any more, but that didn't mean it was easy to hold back. In fact, it was the hardest damn thing she'd ever done.

How long had it been since she'd been touched like this? How long since she'd last been with a man whose skin felt like lightning when it came in contact with hers?

Never, she thought. This was a first.

No one else had ever made her this desperate for more…of everything. More kisses, more touching, more time together. No one else could set her pulse racing with one look and send it into dangerous territory with a single kiss.

This was all new. This was something *more*.

As Isaac placed a few last kisses on her neck, sending tingles all the way down to her toes, Avery closed her eyes. He pulled away slowly, but immediately she wanted him back against her form, his heated skin soaking through her shirt the way it had been before.

"Ugh, you're torturing me on purpose," she said, her voice husky and full of thinly veiled desire.

"Trust me, I know the feeling," he said, and the gravelly, sexy sound of his words did nothing to calm her nerves.

"Would you like some tea?" he asked, changing the subject for both their sakes.

"I would, yes. Actually, if you don't mind, what I'd really like is to get cleaned up first."

"Anything you want." He gave her a sweet smile before getting up from the couch.

He headed down the hallway and a moment later, Avery heard him fiddling in the bathroom, followed by the sound of bathwater running. She hadn't even thought of that and assumed he'd just grab her some fresh towels and she'd shower. But a bath sounded much better.

Foggy and Jane bounded in from the kitchen.

"Hey, guys," Avery said, glad to see their sweet faces.

Isaac had fed them and they must have been playing together after they'd eaten. She patted the couch next to her and they both jumped up, happy when she covered them in pets, Avery laughing as they licked her face. When they settled down on either side of her, Foggy rested his muzzle in her lap and she scratched behind his ears, smiling when his eyelids lowered in pleasure.

Isaac padded back into the living room and handed her a steaming mug before sitting in the easy chair across from Avery and their dogs.

"I realized something earlier today. One thing we can do to help you out is teach Foggy how to get my attention if I'm near and you feel the symptoms of a panic attack coming on."

She nodded.

"I noticed that when you got too close to Nathan, you started to shake. And even if it wasn't him, even if it was just memories coming on too fast, I think it might help if Foggy had the ability to get me if I happen to be nearby."

"Yeah," she said, rehashing the incident in her mind. "That would be good."

She was quiet for a moment, looking down into her tea, thinking about all that had happened.

Isaac's brows knit. "I'm sorry I didn't get to you sooner. I wasn't completely sure what was going on until it was too late. I should have been there faster for you."

She took a sip of her tea, letting the smooth liquid warm her as she considered the apology she hadn't needed him to offer.

"It's not your fault at all, Isaac, and you know that. I just lost myself when I saw Connor's little face. He looks so much like his mother, it was like seeing her ghost."

"I can't even imagine, Avery. I'm so sorry you had to go through that."

She released a long sigh, pushing the air out slowly, trying to relieve some of the pressure that had built up inside of her over the course of the day. Isaac was correct; it had been a long one. And it was only the beginning—there would be so many more to go as she walked the road of recovery, able to see only a few feet in front of her, having to trust that the path wouldn't lead her back to where she'd started.

"Can I tell you something that I've never told anyone before? Something I would never say out loud to most people." She had to get this off of her chest for some reason. Maybe, maybe, she hoped, it would help. She knew she didn't deserve to let go of the guilt, but she wanted to see what someone else thought about something that had always puzzled her.

"Of course you can."

She twined her fingers together, making a little steeple as she'd done as a child, thinking about how best to share what had hidden so deep inside her mind for so long.

"I never… I never understood how she could leave him," she said, the words raw inside her throat. "How Sophie could leave Connor to go off to war, to a place she knew she might not come back from."

Isaac was silent, his expression void of even the slightest hint of judgment. She appreciated that he didn't try to find a solution to the situation, didn't try to make her feel better about it. He just let her say what she needed to say. Few men were like that. Few people were like that. And perhaps the world would be a friendlier place if more could find the patience and the discernment to know when to listen, when to let others release built-up toxins from their hearts without trying to ease the discomfort that resulted.

"I don't think I could have," she said. "And sometimes I can't decide if it was brave or…" She couldn't say the rest, but she knew he understood.

"When I left, I didn't leave anything behind except my brother, and he didn't need me to survive. I had no strings, and I wanted to serve my country, but I also wanted adventure. I wanted to get out of Peach Leaf and see something different than what I had every day of my life up to that point. But Sophie… Sophie had so much here at home."

Isaac let her words settle before speaking. "You were her very best friend, Avery. The two of you had so much history together. Do you think that maybe she did it for you? So you wouldn't have to go alone?"

Tears pooled behind her eyes. She hadn't ever heard anyone put it into such stark terms, in black and white, but maybe he was right.

A sob escaped. "That makes it so awful, doesn't it?"

Isaac got up from the chair and was at her side in an instant, his arms around her shoulders.

"It was her choice to make, Avery. She was a grown woman, and she made an impossible choice. It doesn't make her bad, and it doesn't make her good. It just is. It was her life and her decision to make, not yours."

He drew her into his arms.

"Don't you think she knew what she was doing,

sweetheart? Don't you think she weighed everything out? Just because she was a mother did not mean she had any less ambition than you, any less of a need to serve her country. It's possible she had more of a reason to go. What greater sacrifice could she have given her son than to fight to make his world a better place? To attempt to secure the freedom so many of us take for granted every day? And she obviously trusted that her husband and son would survive if something happened to her."

Everything he said was true, and somehow he was both completely honest, yet gentle at the same time, careful of her tender heart.

"You cannot blame her, and you cannot blame yourself. Neither of you knew what would happen that day when you traded shifts. And, someday, when her son is old enough, he will understand how brave his mother was, and how much she cared about his future, and when he does, you will need to be there for him. You will need to tell him how much you loved Sophie and how much he meant to her."

Avery nodded, wiping tears from her eyes with the palms of her hands. "I would if Nathan would let me. I don't understand why he won't."

Isaac rested his chin against her head. "Give him time," he said. "Give him time to understand that you just want to be there for them. He's mourning her, too, and everyone's grief takes on a different form.

"Okay?"

She closed her eyes, nodding. "Okay."

Sharing that with Isaac had lifted a ton from her

shoulders, and she felt like she could breathe again. His presence was healing her, a little at a time, in a way medicine and therapy had not been able to. She knew they were valuable, but being with someone who supported her unconditionally was worth just as much on her journey to recovery. She could see now that isolating herself from community hadn't been the best for her.

Now that she knew it was possible to find light at the other side of all that darkness, she began to hope that she might be able to repair other areas of her life, and maybe even get her job back someday.

Though, now that she considered it, she wasn't sure she wanted to go back to the same job. There was a time when it had felt like the only thing she ever wanted to do, but now that she'd been exposed to something new, she was beginning to think she might want to work with animals. She was a skilled health professional and had given much of herself to making other people better, but being in the company of Foggy and Jane had opened her up to something different, and she had the idea that she might enjoy caring for animals instead. Their presence was so soothing and full of so much joy. They didn't ask for much, just wanted to be treated with respect. It was something she could get used to.

"Now," Isaac said, getting up from the couch. He had to push a few dog limbs out of the way to disentangle himself from the wad. "Your bath is ready, my dear."

He reached out a palm and gave a little bow, making Avery laugh. When she offered him her hand, he helped her up and led her down the hall to the bathroom, making sure she had plenty of fresh towels and anything else she needed before he shut the door, leaving her alone with a tub full of fluffy, inviting suds. On the counter, she noticed, he had set out a T-shirt and sweatpants of his own for her to change into.

Cared for, calm and one hundred percent comfortable in this kind, generous man's home, Avery undressed and slid down into the perfectly warm water, her heart more at ease than it had been since she could remember.

But only a few moments passed before she wanted him back by her side.

She was ready now, to have everything.

"Isaac?" she called.

She heard his footsteps coming closer down the hall and then they stopped just outside the door.

"What is it?"

"I need one more thing," she said, gripping the sides of the tub to lift herself from the warm water.

"Anything. Just say the word." His voice, so near, yet so distant, on the other side of the door, vibrated up her spine.

She bit her lower lip to keep from grinning like a madwoman, to quell the raging desire growing swiftly in the most neglected parts of her body. Drawing in a deep breath, she headed for the door, slowly opening it until she stood completely bare before him. His dark eyes said far more than any words might have as they took in the whole of her form. She'd already given him her heart; now she wanted him to have all of her.

"I need you."

She didn't have to say another word. He gave her the sultriest smile she'd ever witnessed and, within seconds, he'd wrapped his arms around her naked body and carried her, dripping wet, down the hallway to his bedroom, closing the door behind them.

The only light in the room came from the last soft rays of evening sun that slipped in through Isaac's window, but his eyes seemed to be on fire as he laid her gently on the bed, taking a moment to drink in the sight of her once more.

She felt no shyness under his gaze, only raw need as he tugged off his shirt and came closer to the side of the bed, to her. She lifted her torso and wrapped her arms around his waist, hugging him tightly before she let go and slid her fingers up to the waistband of his jeans.

But then he pulled her hands away and lowered himself until he was eye level with her. "Avery, are you sure this is what you want?" he asked, his breath halting over the words, forehead knit with concern. Her insides ached at the knowledge of what she was doing to him, and at how much he respected her boundaries. But that was just it—she wanted no more boundaries between them.

"Absolutely," she said, drawing his mouth to hers as she threaded her fingers through that thick, unruly, dark hair she loved so much. Then his palms were against her cheeks, his thumbs tracing over her face as the kiss deepened, further and further until both of them needed something far more intense.

Isaac rose again and, this time, made no move to stop her undoing his jeans. When they fell to the floor in a heap, leaving only the stark outline of his desire for her against the taut material of his boxer briefs, it was her turn to study him unbridled.

And study him, she did.

He was incredible in every way possible, this man who loved her, and she wanted him more than anything else in the world.

Resting her hands on his waist, she pulled him down to join her on the bed.

"We can go slow. There's no rush, you know." She heard the words, but they didn't sound too convincing.

"Actually," she said, giggling as she admired the view of him hovering above her, "I am in a rush." His brows rose in confusion, but she went on. "It's taken my whole life to find the perfect guy for me, and now that I have you, I'm totally ready to dive in."

His head leaned back and he laughed, the warm sound affecting her almost as much as the hands that soon covered her breasts. With her, all their clothes and inhibitions now gone, he was wilder and more sensual than any of the rogues and rakes that populated her favorite novels. And it occurred to her suddenly, she was the lucky heroine who got to belong to him, to be the one he placed above all others, the one he fought for and rode off with into the sunset.

"Well, in that case…"

He leaned down to kiss her flesh, moving one hand to stroke the heated center of her, eliciting a moan so primal she wasn't even sure it was she who'd uttered it.

As he drove her to the edge of sanity, she reached out to hold him, drawing his aroused body closer to her own until neither of them could stand to wait any longer, and Isaac paused briefly to get a condom from his bedside table. Their breath came in heavy waves, skin burning with hunger for each other as their mouths met again. And when he finally crashed into her, filling every empty space inside, Avery let go completely and gave him everything she had.

Hours later, Avery stirred in a fitful sleep, tossing her arms and legs as she struggled against another horrifying nightmare.

In the dream, she and Sophie were together again. Instead of trading shifts, they had gone to visit some of the Afghan women at their normal time. The sun was high in the desert sky as they made their way down the dirt street to the home, and their hearts were lighter than usual. The rays beat down but their skin was protected from the worst of it by the burkas they wore with their uniforms.

The house was quiet as the two women were invited in, welcomed warmly and given tea as usual, but something was different. There was a new woman amidst them, one they hadn't met before who seemed to stare at them with apprehension, and something more. Something like thinly veiled hatred.

Tension buzzed and the air was thick with electricity, as just before a storm. Avery sensed that they shouldn't linger, and she finished her refreshments quickly before suggesting to Sophie that they ask if any of the women needed any medical help and then return quickly to their turf, where they would be relatively safe.

Even as she slept, Avery knew how the dream would

end. She knew there would be nothing she could do to stop the bomb from going off while she and Sophie remained in the house. She didn't know why she was with her friend in the dream when she had not been in real life; perhaps on some level it was what she wanted subconsciously, what she wished had happened so that they would both be gone and she wouldn't be home, alone, living with too-heavy guilt in a place where no one understood what she did.

But this time, as she braced herself for the blast, something changed.

When she reached up to touch her face, instead of sand there was moisture, and…something warm. Confusion set in as her eyes fluttered open, and there he was. There was Foggy, his paws near her shoulders as he licked her cheeks with vigor, willing her to wake up and see that she was okay. She wasn't in that desert like she'd been the last time she'd had that nightmare.

Though this time, it didn't take long for her to remember that she was in Isaac's home—that in fact she lay next to him in his own bed. After several hours together the evening before, they'd opened the door and let the dogs pile up at the foot of the king-size bed. Sensing her distress even as she dreamed, Foggy must have crawled to her side.

Coming to, she buried her fingers in the fur just behind Foggy's shoulders and pulled his head close, hugging him for dear life, realizing with elation that he'd woken her up on purpose. He'd saved her from the worst part of the dream. He reminded her what was real.

She put her hands on the sides of his face and planted

a giant kiss on his cold, wet nose. "You wonderful little dog," she said, sitting up in bed and reaching around to hug him some more. "You amazing little creature."

Tears began to spill down her cheeks as she understood fully what Foggy had done for her. She held him close for a long time, starting only when she felt Isaac's hand on her shoulder.

"Hey there, handsome," she said, wiping at her eyes with the palms of her hands, as laughter welled up inside.

Isaac sat up and scooted closer to her side of the bed. As she turned to him, her eyes slid over the hard planes of his chest and abs, then back up to his gorgeously stubbled face. His dark hair stuck out all over the place and she wanted to run her fingers through it and mess it up even more.

"Come here," she said again, and Isaac scooted even closer, snuggling her against his chest and burying his sleepy face into her hair.

"Is everything okay? I think I heard you crying but it took me a minute to fully wake up."

"Yes, it's okay," she said, giggling now between little happy sobs. Images filled her mind of him kissing her good-night a few hours before, just after they'd made love for the countless time, bringing a glass of water to place at her bedside table. He'd made sure she had everything she needed to be comfortable in his home before he crawled under the sheets by her side, both of them happily exhausted.

"What happened? Did you have another nightmare?"

She nodded and Isaac's hand landed on her thigh,

warm even through the sheets. "But it's all right this time."

Isaac looked confused and she pointed at the dog in her arms.

"It's all right, because this time, Foggy saved me."

Chapter Twelve

"Avery, I'm so very glad to see you," Dr. Santiago greeted as Avery opened her office door at the Veterans Affairs outpatient clinic the next Thursday, right on time for her one o'clock appointment.

The doctor stood and shook Avery's hand, welcoming her with a broad, sincere smile. "I always look forward to our appointments. Would you like something to drink today? I have the usual Coke and water."

Avery tilted her head and chewed her lip. "I'll have a Coke today, if you don't mind."

Dr. Santiago paused in front of the minifridge in the corner behind her long, oak desk. "Special occasion?" she joked, and Avery smiled.

"No. Just feeling adventurous, I guess."

"Well, by all means. Coke it is." She pulled out a

can and handed it across her workspace before sitting down. Avery gripped the ice-cold drink and flipped open the tab to take a sip. It had been ages since she'd had a Coke and she'd forgotten how much she enjoyed the sugary, caramely soda.

"My goodness, this is good," she accidentally said out loud.

Dr. Santiago grinned as Avery took the seat across from her. "I'm so glad you like it. It's good to see you indulging a little."

They had spoken before about Avery's diminished appetite and low body weight, but the doctor had always been kind and gentle, urging her patient to speak about why it was difficult for her to eat, sometimes even having Avery list the things she used to enjoy eating in the hopes of encouraging her hunger to perk back up, so she wasn't surprised at the comment.

"It feels good to enjoy something like this again, even something so insignificant."

"Or maybe not so insignificant," Dr. Santiago suggested. "Sometimes it's the littlest things that give us something to cling to, almost like a breadcrumb to help you find your way back."

Dr. Santiago was tall, with silky black hair and matching eyes, and a deep but soft, soothing voice infused with a native Puerto Rican Spanish accent. She was Avery's favorite therapist, the only one she had been able to commit to seeing on a regular basis. Some of the others had cold, overly bright offices and demeanors that Avery's body actively resisted, making it impossible for her to relax or trust them, but Dr. Santiago had decorated her space in peaceful deep purples and soft greens. The velvety indigo couch Avery now sat on was overstuffed and comfortable, situated directly across from a gorgeous print of the Sangre de Cristo Mountains.

The picture reminded Avery of their first consultation. She'd asked Dr. Santiago if she had ever been to those mountains, and, unlike most of the doctors Avery had visited, this one did not try to avoid the question and redirect her back to the horrors of her own mind. Instead, Dr. Santiago had offered Avery a warm smile and answered, telling of her annual trips there, of the solace she found hiking those foothills with the little terrier that was her constant companion.

Avery considered what the doctor had said about breadcrumbs and trails. "I think I may have found another breadcrumb."

"Oh?"

Avery's lips turned up involuntarily and she hoped she wasn't blushing like a little girl. "I met someone recently...someone very interesting, very different and incredibly sweet. Isaac."

Dr. Santiago leaned forward, and for a moment Avery recalled what it was like to share something exciting with a close girlfriend. She hadn't realized until that moment how much she missed female companionship. Macy was wonderful, but it wasn't often that the two of them were alone without the kids. She should remedy that, Avery thought, and suggest that Macy join her for a drink sometime, out of the house, away from all the everyday stuff. There was a time when going out like that had been a weekly Friday thing, something she looked forward to.

Why had they stopped?

Because of me, Avery thought. Her friends and sister-in-law probably didn't know what to say to get those girls' nights out started up again. Her impulse was to blame them, but Avery knew it was just as much on her end. Maybe they could reach out to her a little more, but she hadn't exactly been outgoing lately. She could stand to make more of an effort, and maybe they would meet her in the middle. Her friends loved her, she knew. They had come by in droves after she'd come home, bringing flowers and magazines and the romance novels she loved, treating her like she might be sick.

And she was. But there was no medicine that could make her wholly better. And she'd thanked them, but eventually pushed them all away, as much afraid of them as they were of her. She realized that now, the same as she realized she needed them.

Maybe they *were* the medicine. Her friends, and Foggy, and Isaac, and her family. She could hold on to them if she wanted to, if she could let herself be that vulnerable, and they would be her borrowed strength until she built enough of her own to stand up again.

"Avery?"

"Hmm?"

"If you want to share, I'd love to hear more about Isaac."

"Oh, yes, Isaac." She let his name linger on her lips, enjoying the soft symmetry of its syllables. "Isaac."

Dr. Santiago smiled.

"He's a certified dog trainer, actually, who also happens to be my brother's neighbor. Oddly enough, even though he lives literally just up the road, I only met him a few weeks ago, and I've been spending almost all of my time with him since." She paused at the memory, thinking of how a bad situation turned so quickly, so unexpectedly, into something good.

"I was having one of my flashback episodes," she said, looking up to meet Dr. Santiago's eyes. They were concerned but nonjudgmental, full of kindness and understanding, much like those of the man she was describing.

"He found me, or I found him, and he took me home, fed me and took care of me. I was terrified when I realized what had happened, but he was so wonderful with me, so patient and compassionate when I told him what was going on. Then, when I found out that he works with service dogs for veterans with PTSD, it was almost like…like it was meant to be, even though I don't really believe in that nonsense. I can't explain the way I feel around him—it's something completely new to me."

Dr. Santiago nodded, urging Avery to go on.

"He took me to his training facility the next week and introduced me to a dog that he'd been working with. They hadn't found a person for him yet, so Isaac asked if I might be interested in training with the dog— Foggy—and of course I was. I've always loved dogs. We've been working together a little bit every day, and Isaac and I have been on a couple of wonderful dates. This weekend, we're going to the 5K walk/run for the local animal shelter. It'll be a good place for Foggy and

I to practice being around a bunch of people and dogs at the same time, plus a lot of other stimulation, though I have no doubt we'll do wonderfully."

"That sounds marvelous, Avery. I'm so very happy for you."

"It is. It is marvelous. I feel so lucky, you know. Sometimes it takes ages for people who need them to get service dogs, yet this one just sort of fell into my lap and I have no idea why."

"Who knows why? But this is a good thing for you, Avery. I'm giving you full permission to enjoy it. In fact, that's my medical advice for you in this situation. Enjoy it to the fullest."

Avery laughed, but she did let the doctor's words sink in. "I'm just not sure I deserve something so amazing."

"Oh, but you do. I cannot convince you of that—it's something we've talked about previously and it's something you know you'll have to come to embrace on your own—but you very much do deserve good things in life."

Avery nodded, trying hard not to argue with what, on some level she hadn't yet acknowledged, she knew to be the truth.

"Another thing—I've seen this many times—your insurance may or may not have covered a service animal if you had sought one on your own and put in a claim, and in my experience, they can cost twenty-thousand dollars or more. In this field, we are just beginning to understand how valuable these interspecies relationships can be, and we know almost without a doubt that dogs, horses and even other animals can serve as excellent helpers with victims of psychological trauma, but we've only scratched the surface of compiling enough solid research to convince the insurance companies of the numerous benefits."

Avery's eyes widened at the amount. She had never even thought about getting a dog to help with her PTSD. Not until she'd met Isaac. But now, now that she'd met Foggy and spent time with him, she could see his incredible value, and she knew firsthand that it took a long time and a lot of funding to train a service dog. More important, she missed him every second he was away from her, almost as much as she did Isaac. Even then, as the two guys waited for her in the lobby, she had a hard time fathoming her life without either. She needed them. It was a huge sign of weakness, of vulnerability, to need them, she knew. But it was also completely normal. It was human.

"So, in my opinion, based on what you've told me, it sounds like you've stumbled upon a very favorable situation."

Avery beamed. She hadn't known she'd wanted Dr. Santiago's advice, but now that she had it, she felt even better. She knew, and her doctor knew, that she wasn't one to jump headfirst into things that she wasn't 100 percent confident about. It was a leap of faith to choose to trust Isaac, and even though she was still skeptical that any person could be trusted, she knew he was worthy.

"Thank you, Dr. Santiago. That means a lot to me."

"You like him very much, don't you?"

"Yes, very much. In fact, I think I might even be falling in love with him."

"I haven't seen you looking this well or thinking this positively since we met, you know."

"I know."

Sensing that their session was drawing close to the end of its allotted hour, Avery pulled her cell phone out of the pocket of her jeans and slipped her finger across the screen to wake it up. Sure enough, it was almost time for her to go. She usually hated leaving these appointments, knowing that her world would be unsteady until the next one, that she'd miss Dr. Santiago's sanctuary of an office and the woman herself more than was possibly healthy. But today was different. Today, she had time with Isaac and Foggy to look forward to. They were waiting outside the door. For her. And she couldn't wait to see them again and to find out what Isaac had in store for their afternoon.

Their dates were always so much better than just going out to dinner, though they had done plenty of that, as well. So far, Isaac had taken her to pick fresh peaches at the orchards of their town's namesake, which they'd taken home and baked into an incredible cobbler. They'd been boating at the lake, window-shopping downtown, to the dog park and to a movie at the local outdoor drive-in. Each day and night with him was like a new adventure, and even when they just stayed in and hung out together, she was happier than she'd ever been in her life.

She checked the time and put her phone away.

"Okay, for homework—which I already know you

don't like—I want you to write down five things that make you happy."

It took concentrated effort for Avery to restrain her reaction to this week's assignment, but she had to laugh at how well the psychiatrist knew her patient.

It wouldn't hurt to be more open. After all, look how much good had happened once she'd chosen to open her heart to Isaac.

"All right, and then what do I do with the list?"

Dr. Santiago took a sip of the peppermint tea she favored. Avery liked the way its subtle, calming scent filled the office. Together, many times, they'd explored Avery's tendency to rush ahead, to try to reach for solutions before she'd really begun to understand a problem—a characteristic that well served her military career, but wasn't always an asset in civilian life.

"For now, just the list, okay?" Dr. Santiago smiled, her eyes filled with warm humor. "Then, we go from there."

Avery nodded, agreeing to another exercise with what small portion of faith she could muster. She had a journal full of these little tasks, half-completed, and would try this one as well, but she'd done enough of them not to get her hopes up. She was fairly certain by now that writing in a journal like a teenage girl, pouring her feelings onto the page, wasn't going to fix her problems. Still, sometimes it helped to get things out of her head and down on paper, and even when it didn't, at least seeing her thoughts in black and white on a physical page often made them clearer.

"I come from a family of Southern farmers, doctor.

We don't have time for pain. If you break your arm, you still have to milk the cows."

"I know this well," Dr. Santiago replied, pointing a finger across her desk even as she jotted a few quick notes with the other hand. Avery appreciated that she never took notes during their sessions and each time only spent a few minutes doing so afterwards. Her focused attention when they spoke made an immense impact on how well Avery was able to connect with Dr. Santiago, to open up during their meetings for the sake of her own well-being.

"But you'll recall I've met your brother, Avery, on a day when he had to milk the cows—" she smiled, reaching across the desk to pat Avery's hand "—and I could see instantly that he loves you and wants to help you get to feeling better. Sometimes we have to teach the people around us how to care for us. They don't always know best." She set down her enameled pen and looked up, folding her hands on top of the notepad.

"Isaac is different," Avery said softly, without intending to. But when the doctor nodded, she continued. "He seems to know what I need, when I need it, without me having to tell him. He is kind and emotionally mature. And—"

She didn't think Dr. Santiago needed to know that just the sight of him made her heart run wild like an off-leash greyhound.

"He sounds wise and supportive, Avery." She paused, blinking. "I think this is a good thing, spending more time with him. Do you agree?"

"I think so," Avery said, hearing the waver in her own words.

Very little ever got past Dr. Santiago.

"But?"

"But—" Avery shifted, suddenly restless despite the couch's soft, inviting cushions "—even though he's wonderful, for some reason, I'm almost as afraid of him as I was of going off to a combat zone, and then of coming home," she admitted. Just saying the words out loud brought a little relief, but not enough.

When Avery stopped speaking, Dr. Santiago was silent for a few seconds. Avery liked that about her. The doctor didn't try to fill quiet with questions, but she also didn't hesitate to ask the often-difficult things that helped Avery get to the bottom of her fears. They had covered much ground together, but the thought of how much more there was to go made Avery feel suddenly fatigued even after the progress she'd made in their hour together.

"Well, let's talk this through, then," Dr. Santiago proposed, apparently ignoring or not overly concerned that their time was up. "What is it that you're afraid might happen?"

Avery considered the gently prodding question. If she'd learned anything about psychotherapy, it was that mining a heart was exhausting, painful, frustrating work that didn't yield overnight results. In the time that she'd been home, she'd only just scratched the surface of what she knew to be a vast iceberg, the largest portion of which remained hidden underwater. She'd come home thinking everything would be okay, but she quickly realized that although her military training covered extensive wartime coping mechanisms, she didn't know much of anything about returning to normal life.

Medication helped with her anxiety symptoms, at first, but it didn't help her forget the things she'd seen—the darkest corners of human behavior—and there were days she'd do just about anything to empty her mind of all she'd been exposed to. She wanted to believe that people were good, that they did the best they could with what they were given, but she wasn't so sure she bought that theory anymore.

"I guess I'm—"

The words to articulate her emotions wouldn't come, and a knot of frustration began to rise in her throat. Oh, how she hated to cry, especially in front of other people. She'd managed to get through years of providing medical care for battered soldiers without more than a few tears, but once she'd returned, it was as if all of those experiences joined to form a deluge, and there were days she couldn't keep her eyes dry.

"I think I'm afraid that it might be harder to let him all the way into my heart than it would be to shut him out."

Dr. Santiago took another sip of her tea, closing her eyes for a moment, thinking things over the way a friend would.

"What might happen if you show him the darkest parts of you, the places that scare you the most?" she asked, replacing her blue-and-white teacup in its saucer.

"I might—" Avery pulled in a breath as memories

slipped past floodgates "—I might love him someday. Maybe I already do. And then I might lose him."

Images of her best friend's face the last time she saw her, of the casual way, on the day Sophie died, that they'd traded shifts so Avery could care for her injured patient. Avery couldn't have predicted or stopped the downward spiral that resulted from a single wrong decision. On some level, she knew that. But it didn't change the fact that Sophie's son would grow up without his mother. It didn't change the fact that every time she ran into Sophie's husband—a circumstance she avoided more and more as much as she could—he would look at Avery and wonder why it was she who'd survived, and not his lovely, sweet wife.

Dr. Santiago must have understood the path Avery's thoughts had taken from the expression on her patient's face. She removed her hands from the teacup and folded them again across the notepad on her desk. Finally, she spoke quietly.

"That's very true," she said. "When we allow others to love us, and when we love them, there is always a price to pay, and paying that price is part of being human. We do it because none of us can be our best selves without others. None of us truly wants to be always alone."

It was Avery's turn to nod.

"But think of it this way, Avery." Dr. Santiago turned her hands, palms up. "If you really enjoy Isaac's company, if he brings you happiness and support, and all of the other wonderful things you've described—don't you think that you deserve those things?"

"No," Avery said, quickly. She didn't need to think about the answer to that question.

"I disagree," Dr. Santiago posed. "I'm sure Isaac has a choice in whom he spends time with. Why would he be spending so much time with you if you weren't also bringing him joy? Do you not deserve to take what he's offered in return?"

Avery didn't respond. Her heart was too full of aches and she was getting tired. They'd gotten to a place they couldn't surpass that day, or maybe ever, and suddenly, she just wanted to go home.

"Let's meet again next week, Avery. You've done so well today, and I know it's very hard on you." Dr. Santiago leaned over on her elbows, her forearms covering the large calendar that covered her desktop. "Listen. I want you to know how brave you are for coming in to see me, for keeping your appointments. The work you're doing here is difficult, but it's important, and you are doing an excellent job."

Avery felt that she was anything but brave. Bravery was what the soldiers she'd cared for had; it was in the sacrifices they'd made to serve their country in an effort to make the world a safer place. It wasn't sitting in a psychiatrist's office, talking about why she couldn't risk spending so much time with Isaac Meyer.

She picked up her shoulder bag and headed for the door.

Chapter Thirteen

The day of the 5K, Isaac stopped by Tommy's house to pick up Avery, pulling another box out of the back of his truck. But this time, it wasn't zucchini.

It was going to be a warm day. Already the sun was hot against his back as he headed toward the porch, Jane at his heels, but he didn't care. All he could see were hours and hours of time with Avery, hours he would fill doing his new favorite thing—making her as happy as humanly possible.

He rang the doorbell and Macy opened it with a big smile for him, getting flour all over his clothes as he stepped into her arms for a hug. "Oops," she said, attempting to wipe it off as Isaac laughed and batted her hands away so she couldn't just make things worse.

"Avery's in her room," she said, "I'll go get her for

you. Just head on into the kitchen and help yourself to a muffin."

Isaac stopped midstep. "There aren't any zucchini in them, are there?"

Macy winked at him over her shoulder. "Wouldn't you like to know?"

Armed with what he took to be a warning, he obeyed her anyway and found Tommy munching away on breakfast at the table.

"Isaac!" Tommy said, getting up to shake his hand. "Glad to see you, man." He offered Isaac a cup of coffee and brought one back, black, handing it across the table as he took his seat.

"It's good to see you, too."

"Sounds like you and Avery have become mighty close over the past few weeks," Tommy said, grinning over his World's Okayest Dad mug, which was made even funnier by the fact that Tommy was an inarguably excellent father.

"We have. And I'm glad you mentioned it because I want to talk to you about her."

Concern knitted Tommy's brows and Isaac waved his hand in the air to indicate that everything was okay.

"Nothing's wrong. Nothing at all. I just wanted to let you know that…that I'm in love with her. And that I have every intention of one day asking her to marry me."

Tommy beamed. "That's just wonderful! I'm so happy for both of you, and you absolutely have my blessing."

He looked over Isaac's shoulder and then lowered his voice.

"Just don't tell Macy. She'll go nuts and start planning things left and right before you even have a chance to pop the question. Trust me on that one."

Isaac laughed, happy to have told Avery's brother, his friend, and relieved that he'd reacted the way he had. "Oh, don't worry. I won't. And I'm not going to ask anytime soon."

He took a sip of his coffee, strong enough to add hair to his chest, just the way he liked it.

"Avery needs time. I want to make sure she's ready when I get to it and, anyway, people would think we were crazy if I asked her after less than a month."

Tommy narrowed his eyes. "Since when do you care what people think of you?"

Isaac grinned. "I don't. But Avery might. We're taking things slow, doing things right, building a solid foundation. We have all the time in the world."

Tommy nodded. "Have you told her how you feel, at least?"

Isaac shook his head. "I'm going to. Just haven't found the right moment yet."

"Well, when you do, I have no doubt you'll be pleased with the outcome." Tommy reached over and punched his friend in the shoulder. "That girl is head over heels, man. Head over heels. And I couldn't be happier that it's with my best friend."

"Morning, boys."

Isaac looked up at the sound of Avery's voice in the doorway, warm as butter. He practically jumped up from the table, eager to be near her, to touch her and to breathe in the sweet scent he'd missed overnight in her absence. They had agreed not to spend every night together, and he couldn't wait for the day when all he'd have to do was roll over in bed each morning and she'd be there, hair golden across her pillow in the morning light. He knew that he wanted to spend the rest of his life with her, and he hoped to God she felt the same.

He'd start to tell her that this morning.

Avery wrapped her arms around him, snuggling in close as he hugged her tight. "Good morning, sweetheart," he said into her hair. "How'd you sleep?"

"Like a baby." She looked up at him and her eyes were clear in the morning light peeking through the kitchen window. "Foggy's been good to me."

Her affection for the dog was evident in her voice, and Isaac thanked the stars that the two had made as good a fit as Hannah had thought they would. He made a note to do something special for Hannah as a thank-you.

"Where is the guy?"

"Oh, he's with the kids. They adore him."

Tommy chimed in. "It was a little tough getting them to understand what it means when his vest is on, but once we got that down, everybody's happy."

"Although they like him best off duty," Avery said, a grin brightening her already lovely face.

She wore a blue tank top that matched her eyes over another white one, and Isaac noted with pleasure that she'd already gained a couple of pounds. Skinny jeans hugged her perfectly curved bottom and he resisted the urge to put his hands all over her.

He always made sure their dates involved food, and even though Avery had called him out on it, she'd started to enjoy eating a little bit more, and they had a blast rediscovering her favorite meals.

"I've got something for you," Isaac said, taking Avery's hand to lead her out of the kitchen.

"See you kids later," Tommy called after them.

"What is it?" she asked, and Isaac laughed. Impatient—just like a kid at Christmas.

"You'll have to wait and see, now, won't you?"

He tugged her down the hallway and sat her down on the couch in the front sitting room, pulling the box he'd brought over to place at her feet. He'd taken a leap of faith on this one, and he hoped she'd like it.

"Open it," he said, and her eyes widened, pretty little crinkles at their corners as she smiled.

She picked up the box and pulled off the giant yellow bow, then made quick work of the soft green paper he'd chosen. Isaac couldn't remember when he'd last been so nervous. It wasn't like he was proposing now, yet the world seemed to hold its breath as he waited to see what she thought.

She pulled out each item, touching them softly, and as she realized what he'd done, her eyes filled with moisture.

"Oh, Isaac."

"I hope this is okay," he said, apprehensive.

On Thursday, after he'd picked her up from her therapy appointment, when Avery was busy with Foggy, he'd noticed a piece of paper on the ground in the room they'd been using at the training facility. Not wanting any of the dogs to get hold of it, he'd picked it up, intending to toss it into the recycling bin out back. But when he picked it up, the paper unfolded, and Isaac had seen what was written on it. It was a list, and he had everything on it memorized by now:

Things That Make Me Happy

Regency romance novels
The Beatles
Blue nail polish
80s movies
Homemade chocolate-chip cookies
Isaac Meyer
Foggy

He watched as she laid each object out on the floor—five of her very favorite Regency romances, he'd double-checked with Macy; every John Hughes film ever made; a few Beatles box-set albums; every shade of blue nail polish he could find; and a dozen chocolate-chip cookies, freshly baked in his kitchen that morning, using Nana's famous recipe—forming a circle around her.

When she was finished, she covered her mouth with a fist, and tears began to slide down her cheeks.

"I didn't mean to invade your privacy, Ave. I found the list on the ground at the training center, and, well… I couldn't help myself. I hope it's okay."

"Shut up, Isaac," she said, crawling out of her circle

of happiness and into his lap, covering his face with kisses as he laughed, thankful he hadn't screwed up.

Finally she stilled, looking into his eyes. "You know, I don't have any of this stuff. When I left for the military, I pretty much got rid of everything, and when I got back, I never got around to buying any of the things I enjoy. I guess I wasn't sure if I would stay."

He brushed hair back from her eyes and kissed her, long and slow, on her sweet mouth.

"Please do," he said. "Please stay."

"I plan to," she said. "Now that I have you."

He smiled, leaning his forehead against hers.

"Thank you, Isaac," she whispered. "Thank you. For everything."

Later that morning, they all piled into two trucks and drove to Peach Leaf Park, where the local animal shelter's 5K fund-raiser was scheduled to take place.

Avery and Isaac unloaded Foggy and Jane, snapping on their harnesses and leashes and Foggy's vest, ready to practice being in public in a place chock-full of every kind of distraction available.

A banner welcomed them as they entered the park, Tommy, Macy and the kids trailing along behind. The air was thick with the smell of delicious food: hot dogs, funnel cake and popcorn, all ready to reward the serious racers after a day's run, Isaac joked.

Avery definitely planned to sample everything, glad that her favorite jeans were close to fitting again, proud of the feminine curves that had begun to make their reappearance. Most women would be horrified to gain five pounds in a few weeks, she mused, but she needed the weight, and Dr. Santiago would be thrilled at her progress. Avery definitely was.

Isaac made everything better, even food.

She made no effort to hide the fact that she was checking him out as they walked. He looked great in a soft, dark green T-shirt that hugged the muscles underneath, and khaki cargo shorts. His unruly hair—hair she'd had plenty of chances to bury her fingers in—just touched his collar under an ancient Peach Leaf Panthers baseball cap.

Her hand felt right at home in his as they walked, a dog on either side, and for the moment, Avery couldn't imagine how her life could be any more perfect, or any different from what it had been a few weeks ago.

She hadn't even known what she wanted until it landed right in front of her. Now she would do anything to keep it, to keep him.

Isaac. *Her* Isaac.

They strolled around the park for a while, checking out all the booths and making sure Foggy and Jane had plenty of water before they set off to walk the three-plus miles. Isaac told Avery that the race organizers, being animal folks, of course, had opted to start the race by shouting into a megaphone, rather than using the customary air horn or gunshot.

Finally, they gathered at the starting line, waving at Tommy, Macy and the kids, who were going to cheer them on from the sidelines. When the announcer gave the go, Isaac and Avery set off at a quick pace, Foggy and Jane trotting just ahead.

They'd spent a couple of hours that week working with Foggy on Isaac's idea of keeping people at a safe distance from her with the block command, and he showed off his training with honor that day, making sure to keep in front of Avery so that she didn't get too close to anyone, and the crowd, overwhelming at first, lessened its effect on her after a time. She relaxed into her footsteps, keeping a steady pace, enjoying the late spring sunshine on her face, the gentle breeze in her hair and the cool, dewy morning air.

Occasionally, as they walked, Isaac looked over to check on her, and they stopped every once in a while to give the dogs water in a little travel bowl.

The four of them together felt…like family, and Avery let every minute of it soak into her soul, replacing bad memories with good ones. If she spent enough time with Isaac, she knew, the happy would begin to outweigh the sad. It was only a matter of time.

At the finish line, Sylvia and Ben greeted them with fresh water bottles, and they accepted the paw-shaped medals the race officials draped over their necks for completing the distance.

They were headed toward the food booths when Avery thought she heard someone calling her name. Isaac turned as she did and she saw Nathan coming toward them, Connor hurrying to keep pace, his little hand in his father's.

"Avery," Nathan said, breathing hard. He stopped a few feet away and lifted Connor into his arms. "If you've got a minute, I'd love to talk to you. That is—"

he glanced from her to Isaac and back again "—if that's okay with you."

She swallowed, her throat tight, and Foggy must have picked up on her nervousness because he stepped forward and sat down between her and Nathan, calmly but with obvious confidence. He didn't even need the block command; he would protect his girl if he needed to without being asked. He would make sure nothing got to her that might cause her to be afraid or upset.

Her heartbeat slowed to normal, knowing her furry companion was there. She lowered a hand and placed it on his neck, letting Foggy know she was okay, and that she appreciated his gesture.

"Yes, that would be all right with me," she said, her voice sounding stronger than she'd anticipated. She looked to Isaac, whose hand had come to rest on her shoulder, reassuring her that he was there for her, as well. Her two guys, there to keep her safe. "I'll be right back, Isaac."

"We'll be right here," he said, taking Foggy's leash as she handed it over. The dog wasn't too happy about having her leave him behind, but he calmly cooperated and followed Isaac and Jane to a nearby drink stand.

She and Nathan walked over to a picnic table and sat down across from each other. Nathan put Connor down next to him and handed his son a fire truck from his backpack.

It must be his favorite toy, Avery thought, as she recalled seeing it the other day.

"Avery," Nathan said, his voice full of emotion. He looked down at the table and she could see that whatever he was about to say was taking a lot of his courage to get out.

"I'm surprised you want to talk to me after the other day," she said.

"I know, and, Avery, I'm so sorry about what happened then. I didn't mean to act like that. I was a real jerk and I wish I could take it back."

"No, Nathan. I'm the one that's sorry. I shouldn't have pushed myself on you like that. It wasn't fair after all you've been through. I was being selfish as hell and I want you to know I didn't mean to bring all that back for you."

He was quiet for a long moment and Avery sensed that he was getting his bearings, that he was trying to hold on to his emotion so it didn't break free and embarrass them both. She wanted to tell him that he would feel better if he just let it go, that it only hurt to keep it inside, as she'd only recently begun to learn, thanks to Isaac's presence and support in her life.

If everyone had their own equivalent of an Isaac and a Foggy, she thought, *the world would be a better place*.

"I miss her so damn much, Avery. Sometimes I can't stand it. Sometimes I think I can't go on because of how much it hurts to do all this without her." He put his face in his hands and glanced over at Connor as if worried that his son might hear, but the child continued to play happily with his truck, lost in his own safe, peaceful world.

"But you have to, don't you, Nathan?" she said firmly, giving Nathan some of the courage she'd gained from Isaac. "You have to keep going for Connor. He needs you. Sophie trusted you to take care of him if something happened to her, and she would want you to be strong." She offered him a weak smile as he swiped his hands over his face and met her eyes.

"Yeah, she would, wouldn't she?" he said, his eyes softening at her memory.

"She was so strong," Avery said. "She was the bravest, best woman I've ever known, and I wish I had her back. I miss my best friend, and I know you miss your wife, but she wouldn't have been too happy if she'd seen the hot messes we've turned out to be."

Nathan laughed, a tight, sharp sound that hinted at the extent of his sorrow.

"I lost a friend," she said, her voice quiet, "but you lost your wife, and I can't even begin to imagine how hard that must be for you."

He closed his eyes.

"But that doesn't give me the right to shut you out, or to keep you from seeing Connor. Sophie would have hated that I've done that for so long."

Shame filled his face, and Avery wanted to tell him that he'd done nothing wrong, that grief was almost impossible to bear sometimes, and other times, it could only barely be tolerated.

He looked over at Connor. "The only reason I've done so is because it was too hard for me, but seeing you the other day...it brought back too many memories of all the good times the three of us had when she was alive, before you both left. I realized how much I've been shielding him from because of my own pain.

And that's not fair. I owe it to my son to be the best father I can be, and I know now that I wasn't doing that."

He looked up at the sky as if deciding whether or not to say more.

"Did you know I don't even have photographs of her in our home? I put them all away when she died." His voice wavered. "I just couldn't bear to look at her, you know?"

His eyes were rimmed with red as he reached over and took Avery's hand.

"That's in the past now. I took them all out the day we saw you in the park, and I've been showing them to Connor every day, so that I can teach him how wonderful his mama was."

Avery felt tears prickle at the back of her eyes.

"And I'm sorry, Avery. I want you to know that I don't blame you for what happened to my wife. She was stubborn, and what she wanted, she got. And she was an amazing woman who wanted to serve her country almost as much as she wanted to be a mom. It was important to her to do her duty, and it was important to her to go with you. She loved you so much, you know. I think she would have followed you anywhere."

They both laughed at the truth of his statement and Avery choked up, wiping away a few drops that had fallen from her eyes.

"I want you to know that you can see Connor anytime you want. You are always welcome in our home, as are Isaac and your dogs." Nathan smiled at Connor. "I'm sure this little guy would love to have them over for a playdate sometime. In the near future, Avery, you hear?"

"Of course." She squeezed his hand. "Thank you, Nathan. I didn't know how much I needed to hear those things until now. I promise I won't be a stranger."

He nodded, and they were both quiet, realizing they had broken frozen ground and could now sow seeds that would become their futures. They could make choices for themselves now, rather than holding on to the grief that had rendered them immobile for so long.

"You know," Avery said, speaking almost as much to herself as she was to Nathan, "when I joined the military, I knew the risks and the danger, and even though there was always a little fear, I felt prepared."

Nathan nodded as his eyes filled, and she continued.

"I knew exactly what I was getting into—" she swallowed "—but I had no idea how to get out. They don't tell you how hard it's going to be to get back to a normal life, if that's ever even possible."

Nathan squeezed her hand. They didn't need to say any more about it.

When Connor grew bored with his fire truck, Nathan reminded him who Avery was, and the two of them chatted for a long time about preschool and when would she please come over and bring her puppies to see him.

Avery's heart was loads lighter when they parted ways and she returned to Isaac's side. He handed her a fresh-squeezed lemonade from a nearby stand and gave her back Foggy's leash.

"Everything okay with Nathan?" Isaac asked, his

brown eyes full of worry as he studied her face for clues about how their visit had gone.

"Better than ever," she said. "We're okay now." She took a sip of the drink, sweetness and tartness teasing her taste buds at the same time.

"So glad to hear it, sweetie."

"We'll have to bring Jane and Foggy by to meet Connor sometime. He's super excited about being around dogs. Nathan works full-time and Connor goes to preschool, so they can't have one of their own right now. It would mean a lot to them if he could play with ours."

"Consider it done," Isaac said, smiling. "He seems like a sweet kid."

"He is, just like his mom was."

"Do you want one someday?" Isaac asked. "Kids, I mean."

Avery looked up at him, surprised. "Isaac Meyer," she teased. "Are you asking me if I'll have your children someday?"

He gave her his sexiest grin, tilting his head so that his dark hair grazed his shoulder, looking for all the world like a rake from one of her favorite books.

"Would that be a problem?" he asked.

"Actually, no," she said, pushing her chin forward to show him she wasn't intimidated by his suggestion of commitment. "And yes, I do want kids. Someday."

Isaac's expression showed her he wasn't satisfied with her answer.

She took another sip of lemonade, drawing it out to bug him.

"My kids?" he asked.

"Yes, idiot," she said, reaching across the table to poke his chest. "Your kids."

They were both being silly, mostly, but now they were dead serious as they caught each other's eye.

It was in that second that Avery knew precisely how she felt about Isaac Meyer—there was no longer any question—and exactly how to articulate it.

The words were on the tip of her tongue when she heard the first blast. Lemonade spilled across the table as she knocked it over in her hurry to get cover. She flew under the picnic table and huddled there, her arms wrapped over her knees, head down as a few more explosions erupted and, once again, the world went black around her.

Chapter Fourteen

Isaac rushed to Avery's side where she crouched under the table, but Foggy made it to her first. He was licking her face between sharp barks, doing his best to get his body as close to hers as possible, but it wasn't helping.

She shook violently, her skin pale and cold like marble, and her hands whipped at him when he tried to touch her. Finally, he was able to get her into his arms, where he held her for several minutes until the rapid heaving of her chest began to subside. He lifted her up and lay her down in the grass underneath the picnic table. Foggy draped himself over her torso, waiting patiently for her to get back to normal.

Isaac knew she kept antianxiety medication at home, but she'd told him she didn't need to bring it with her, that she was okay without it almost all of the time.

Now he cursed himself for not insisting that she bring it along, just in case; he wouldn't make that mistake again.

But as he watched, Foggy began to lick her face again, and eventually her eyes lost their glaze, their iciness returning to their calm, ocean-water appearance. She noticed the dog and wrapped her arms around him, pulling him close as he continued to wash her with kisses.

Foggy worked almost as fast as medication, without the unpleasant side effects that sometimes accompanied drugs.

Isaac's heart nearly burst as he watched the dog take care of his person, and a thought hit him like a bullet to the chest.

If only Stephen had waited. If only he'd stuck around for just a few more years until Isaac started this business. If only he hadn't left before Isaac got a chance to save him.

As Avery looked into his eyes, he felt anger flood through him like hot blood, misplaced rage at his inability to keep Stephen from taking his own life, and instead of doing what he should have, instead of comforting her and making sure that she was okay after what she'd perceived as trauma, he took that out on her.

He grasped her forearms and forced her to look at him. Her eyes were full of fear, *of him*. He hated himself for that, but couldn't stop once he'd started. All the things he'd never been able to say, all that he'd never been able to express to his brother, who'd selfishly left him here to take care of their mom, to fend for himself without a father.

"You can't do this to me, Avery. You can't leave me like that. It scares the crud out of me to think I've lost you when you disappear on me that way."

She stared at him, confusion etched into her features now, her eyes huge. "It's okay, Isaac. I'm fine. I just heard the fireworks and got startled, but look, I'm okay." She held out her arms for him to see. "Foggy helped me and my episode lasted only a few minutes. Everything's fine. Really."

"No, Avery. It's not fine," he shouted. He didn't know what was happening to him but he couldn't keep his voice down. "They should know better than to allow fireworks at something like this, where there are animals everywhere anyway, but you can't do that to me— you can't scare me like that. I thought I'd lost you."

His head spun as he fought desperately to make sense of the confusing flood of emotions darting through his brain and heart.

"What's the matter with you, Isaac?" she asked, and he caught the hurt in her voice. He knew he should apologize, but somehow he couldn't form the words.

What *was* the matter with him? This wasn't Stephen. He knew that. At least part of him did, but another part…another part wasn't able to separate the two. He'd loved his brother, yet he'd been unable to save him. No matter how much he'd wanted to, he'd never been able to heal that dark space inside of Stephen. And now… now he wondered if he would ever be able to do that for Avery.

If he cared for her as much as he knew he did, would he always wonder about the possibility of danger, of her

PTSD taking over, of the darkness winning? Would he live his life afraid of losing her?

A small voice inside said *yes*. Yes, he would. And as much as it had hurt to lose his brother—losing Avery would somehow be worse. Losing Avery, he knew suddenly, would destroy him.

"I see," she said, her features resigned. She looked… shattered. "Look, Isaac. I laid everything out on the table when we met. You know that I have some pretty big problems—they were never a secret. Because of the way we met, I never even got a chance to decide if I wanted them to be, not that I would have been able to hide them for long. But if you can't handle being around me, if you're going to freak out like this whenever something happens to me, well…I can't. I just can't do this."

She crawled out from under the table as he watched, frozen in place, powerless to stop her. It was too late when he came to his senses, when he finally understood that the reason he'd lashed out was the very reason he absolutely needed her to stay.

"Avery," he called after her as she grabbed Foggy's leash and started jogging away without looking back, leaving him and Jane there in the dirt. "Avery, wait!"

But it wasn't enough. She was gone, and it was his fault.

Avery had no idea where she was headed. She just ran and ran, poor Foggy jogging along beside her.

She finally stopped when she reached the duck pond. She sat on the rock bench to catch her breath and pulled Foggy's portable dish out of her pocket, pouring water from her bottle into the little bowl and setting it down. Foggy lapped it up quickly and she gave him more until he was no longer thirsty.

Tears came, fast and hot, but no matter how many times she went over the scene in her head, she couldn't figure out what had happened to Isaac back there. What on earth had made him so blistering mad at her? He'd been so out of character, yelling at her like that, and it scared her. She hadn't understood him when he'd tried to explain why he was so upset; none of what he'd said had made sense. What was that he'd said about losing her? He wasn't going to lose her. She was right freaking *there*. And she'd given him more of herself than she'd shared with anyone in as long as she could remember.

She shook her head and pulled in deep breaths, going over the previous moments until her temples began to throb. She had no idea how long she sat there like that, staring into the water, right at the same spot that Isaac had first kissed her.

Everything had been so perfect.

What had she done to make it so wrong?

"Avery."

His voice behind her back caused the hair on her neck to stand. She was mad at him, but still her body reacted viscerally to his nearness as he came into view, sitting beside her on the rock as Jane wandered over to stare at the ducks.

A long silence passed before he spoke.

"Avery, please forgive me. I don't know what got into me back there."

"Well, that makes two of us, then," she said, her voice sad and bitter.

They sat in silence until he cleared his throat.

"Just tell me this."

She turned to look at him.

"Are you okay?"

His eyes were full of agony, and she wanted to touch him. But she wasn't sure if that was the right thing to do. He'd been so angry at her for no real reason, and it had challenged her trust in him.

"Yes, I'm okay. Are you?"

"I think so," he said, his voice pleading. "Avery, I'm so very sorry."

"What was that, Isaac? What happened? Why did you blow up like that on me? I hate that you shouted at me that way."

He shut his eyes tight at her words.

"I was taking something out on you that had nothing to do with you."

"I don't think I understand."

"I was the one who found Stephen," he said, barely able to hear his own words. "I was the one who found him after he died, and it nearly killed me. I think a part of me sees you as being fragile, like he was. And if you don't get better, the same thing might happen to you."

She put her hand on his forearm and her touch warmed his skin.

"Oh, Isaac," she said. "I'm not Stephen. I'm not going to hurt myself. I've got so much to stick around for. I've got you and Foggy and my family. I'm not going anywhere. Not if I can help it."

"I'm so sorry I lashed out at you like that, but I can't lose you. I just can't."

"I do worry, though, sometimes. It's just that…well… I worry that I might not ever get completely better. What if I always have these involuntary responses to things, and I'm never all the way back to normal? What if I can't ever hold down a job again? What if I'm a danger to you, or—" she swallowed "—to…to a child?"

"You'll lean on me," he said. "Whatever happens, you and I will handle it together. You won't have to be alone anymore, not if you don't want to."

She thought about what he'd said, wanting desperately to tell him that everything was okay, that they should just forget about it. But she knew that wasn't entirely true. Everything wasn't okay, and if she was going to start a relationship with this man, to maybe start on a path to building a life with him, then she needed everything to be out in the open. She wanted everything this time—no secrets, no holding back. She knew there would always be things to be afraid of. Just like him, she was afraid of losing something precious to her, but somehow she knew they were both ready to take that risk.

If the past few weeks had taught her anything, it was that some things were worth being afraid for. And he was worth it.

"Look, Isaac, I want to forgive you, and I want us to get past this, but if we're going to do that, we have to be honest with one another."

His eyes met hers and the threat of fresh tears choked her next words.

"I need you to know that I'm not your brother. I'm not going to end my life." She offered him a sad smile. "I have too much good to even think about taking that path out. But at the same time, I can't have you treating me like I'm another project. I know you love working with people with PTSD, but somehow you have to find a way to separate me from your work. I refuse to live my life wondering if you're just using me to atone for what you *think* of as your failure to save your brother."

He nodded, slowly, and stayed silent for a long moment.

"You're right about that, Avery. I didn't see it before, but I think I may have thought of you that way at first."

He reached over to grasp her hands, threading their fingers together, sending sparks through her.

"But I don't any longer. I understand that now. In just a short time, you've become everything to me, and I think I worried that I might lose you just as fast. I placed the weight of Stephen's choice on you, and that wasn't fair. I see now that you're your own woman, with your own life to live, and I know now that you're far stronger than Stephen ever was."

She swallowed, working to hold back an onslaught of relieved tears.

"I don't see you as a project—I see you as a partner. Someone I want to share my world with. I think it took this situation for me to truly understand that, and I'm so very sorry that I lashed out at you. I didn't know what to do with this new knowledge, with the realization of how much I care for you, but I do now. I want to continue helping you to train Foggy, but I also want much, much more. I will make you my world, if you let me."

As she looked into his eyes, she knew he meant every single word he said. In just the past few weeks, her life had changed completely, for the better, and Isaac was at the center of those changes.

She knew he couldn't *fix* her, and she didn't need him to. She would do the work herself, and she would be the victor over her own struggles. But he was right—they could be partners. They could share their pain and joy; they could encourage each other through the worst of it and laugh together through the best. She wanted that as much as he did.

"I'm in. But only if I can convince you that you're not going to lose me, Isaac. I promise you that. I'm here for good." She tickled his chin with her fingers, then pulled it so that he would look into her eyes. "Whether you want me or not."

Now was the time they'd both been waiting for. Now was the time to tell him how she felt.

"I do. I do want you." He swallowed, putting his hands on her face. "I love you, Avery Abbott. And I always will."

Her blue eyes filled, spilling over when she closed them. When they opened again, they were overflowing with joy, with peace.

"I love you, too, Isaac Meyer."

As they made their way back to the chaos of booths and families and food, hand in hand, a man dressed in a navy blue polo shirt and slacks—a bit formal for a

5K on a warm spring day—approached and stopped in front of them, holding out a hand.

"Are you Mr. Isaac Meyer?" he asked.

"I am," Isaac said, shaking the man's offered hand. "What can I do for you, sir?"

"Quite a bit, I hope," the man said, giving a little laugh.

Isaac smiled tentatively, uncertain what was so darn funny.

"Mr. Meyer, I'm Fred Palmer," the man said, continuing when Isaac stared back at him with a blank expression. "Fred Palmer," he said again, "of Palmer Motors."

"Oh, yes," Isaac said, the pieces clicking into place. "I didn't recognize you, sir. You look a little different from your TV commercials.

Mr. Palmer laughed again and Isaac decided he liked this guy.

"As well you shouldn't. The wife's had me on a diet the past few months and I've lost about thirty pounds, but they needed to go."

"Well, then, congratulations are in order," Avery chimed in.

Isaac apologized for not introducing them and was quick to remedy that.

"Mr. Palmer," he said, "This is Avery Abbott." He turned to Avery, who stood near his side, holding Foggy's and Jane's leashes, and his heart nearly burst through his chest at the sight of her beautiful face. "My girlfriend."

She beamed at him before he turned back to Mr. Palmer.

"Pleased to meet you, Ms. Abbott," the older gentleman said. "I knew your father—we went to school together at Peach Leaf High, ages ago. And, may I say, thank you for your service."

Avery lowered her chin a little, nodding in gratitude.

He turned back to Isaac.

"Mr. Meyer, let's get right down to business. I have a proposal I'd like to make."

"Of course, sir, I'd love to hear it. What's on your mind?"

A broad smile spread across the man's face, lifting his plump cheeks.

"Well, son, if I do say so myself, my company's doing pretty good, and when that's the case, I like to show my thanks to the community in some way. I wouldn't have the business that I do if it wasn't for the great folks in this town."

"That's very generous of you, Mr. Palmer. I know Peach Leaf owes a lot to you."

The older man waved a hand. "It owes me nothing, son. I was born and raised here and I run a solid company. It's in my power to give back and it's something I enjoy doing, but that's beside the point."

Isaac was beginning to realize where this was going and he couldn't help the excited energy that sprinted up his spine. Mr. Palmer was known for his donations to local causes, and if what he'd heard about the man was even half-true, he could help a lot of people in the near future.

"The point is, son, I've been watching you for a long time, and you're doing some amazing work with vets and rescue dogs, and, well, I've got a soft spot for them—" he glanced in Avery's direction "—for you."

Isaac nodded, his palms sweaty.

"So, here it is. If it's all right with you, I'd like to make a donation, Mr. Meyer."

Isaac stifled a laugh. "Of course it's all right with me."

Avery squeezed his hand.

"In the amount of half a million dollars."

"Holy cow!" Avery bounced up and down with the energy of a happy child and Isaac couldn't help but do the same right along with her before smothering their generous donor with a thousand thank-yous.

"No need to thank me, son," Mr. Palmer said gruffly before moving on, but Isaac caught the shimmer at the corner of the old man's eye.

"I'd like you to use it to sponsor as many veterans as you can, as long as you keep taking and training dogs from the local shelter. You've got a gift for it, Meyer, and I've seen how much you've helped the ones who serve our country—especially my own boy."

Isaac recalled training with Gary Palmer and his Lab, Tex, a few months back. Gary had lost his legs to a mine and was wheelchair bound. Tex had given Gary his smile back, not to mention helping him perform daily tasks with a lot more ease.

"Thank you, again, Mr. Palmer, but Gary and Tex did all the work."

Mr. Palmer chuckled and Isaac nearly choked, overwhelmed at the amount of money the man had just given his organization.

"Truly. I can't thank you enough. You're helping a lot of folks, Mr. Palmer."

"You are, Isaac. You are," Mr. Palmer corrected.

The old man shook Isaac's hand again and bid them good day, promising to be in touch with the details of the donation the following Monday.

As soon as he walked away, Avery threw herself into Isaac's arms and peppered his face with kisses. He twirled her around and around, causing Foggy and Jane to bark at their outburst of glee.

"Oh. My. Goodness," Avery screamed. "Can you believe it? Half a million dollars? Half a million bucks, Isaac. Can you imagine how many people that will help?"

Isaac burst out laughing. "I can, actually," he said. "I'm doing the math in my head right now, and it's… epic."

He stopped spinning and set Avery's feet back on the ground, kissing her nose. She was absolutely beautiful in the afternoon light, sunshine glinting off her golden hair, her blue eyes sparkling with delight. Her happiness, new and precious and hard-earned, was contagious. This joyful Avery was the most magnificent thing he'd ever seen.

He pulled her close so she could see his face.

"But with that much financial backing, I'll need more help, you know?"

"Of course. You'll have to hire more trainers and have people to help you find dogs at the shelter, and—"

"And, I want you," he said.

"Me? What do you mean?"

"I mean, I want you to join me. I'm going to pro-
mote Hannah to manager, and I want you to be my
new assistant."

Avery's face lit up when she got what he was saying.

"Are you serious?"

"As a heart attack."

"But I have no training. I'm a nurse, not a dog
trainer."

"But you have what it takes to make a great one.
You're a natural with Fogs and you'll be amazing once
you're certified. Besides," Isaac said, grabbing her hand
to lead her back to Tommy and Macy, "we have plenty
to fund your classes now, don't we?"

"I would say so," she answered, giggling.

"I've had you with me for almost a month now, and
it has been, without contest, the best almost-month of
my life. I'm not about to let you go now, Avery."

He stopped to kiss her long and hard, right there in
the middle of the park. When they caught their breaths,
Avery gave him a big smile, her face flushed from sunshine and the sensation of his lips on hers.

"Well, that's good news," she said, "Because I wasn't
lying when I told you I'm not planning on going anywhere. And pretty soon, I'm going to need a new job."

"You've got one," Isaac said, pulling her close. "As
long as you want."

"How about forever?" she asked, the question holding far more weight than what her words had indicated.

"Forever isn't long enough," he answered.

"Are you happy, Isaac Meyer?"

"The happiest," he said. "Because of you."

Epilogue

July Fourth, one year later

Morning light slipped in through the blinds of Isaac and Avery's bedroom window, spreading golden rays across her blond hair.

He watched her sleep, humbled by the simple rise and fall of her chest as she inhaled and exhaled in perfect rhythm, wondering again where he'd gone so right—how he'd become the lucky man who got to wake up next to such a beautiful, amazing woman each morning.

Isaac leaned over to kiss her forehead, glad when her lips curved to smile at him. Slipping out of bed, he tucked the sheets around her shoulders and roused the dogs from where they slept, tangled together on the window seat.

The three of them went downstairs and Isaac opened the back door to let Foggy and Jane out, turning on the coffeepot. As it sputtered to life, starting up the strong brew he preferred, he walked into the dining room where he kept a small desk for business when he wasn't at the training facility. Grinning, he pulled out the office chair and sat, reaching into the bottom drawer, all the way to the very back.

He stopped when his fingers touched cool velvet, and pulled out a small box, lifting the lid. It still took his breath away every time he looked at this symbol of his love for her.

The past year of his life had been wonderful beyond words. Avery had passed her dog training certification exam with flying colors, and she and Foggy were an incredible team. Watching the two of them work together to help other veterans and dogs form partnerships brought him more happiness, more fulfillment, than anything he'd ever witnessed before in all the years he'd owned the facility. And to him, she was a greater partner than he ever could have hoped for.

Of course they had their tough days; of course things weren't perfect, but that didn't matter. What mattered, he had come to understand, was that they were together through the ups and downs. She was there for him, truly understood him when the ache of missing Stephen was too much to bear. And he did his very best to be a source of strength for her when she had nightmares and the—thankfully rare, now—panic attacks that still scared her so badly.

Each time he glimpsed the simple, elegant ring, he

grew more and more excited about this day—a day he'd anticipated for so long now.

And today—the big day—was no different. He couldn't wait any longer; it was time.

Grabbing a piece of string and snapping shut the lid, Isaac headed back to the kitchen and poured a cup of coffee for himself, leaving it black, then one for Avery, stirring in the ample amount of cream and sugar that his girl liked so much.

He set the cups on the kitchen counter and opened the back door, letting the dogs back in.

"All right, Foggy. You ready for your big job?"

The dog sat and raised his paw, giving Isaac a high five.

"Okay, then," he said. "Good deal. Let's get you all set."

He knelt down, pulled the ring out of his pocket and made a loop through its band with the piece of string, then tied it to Foggy's collar.

"This is it, boy," he said. "Have you got my back?"

Foggy barked.

"Shhh! We don't want to wake Mom just yet, okay?"

Back in the kitchen, he picked up the coffees, padding back upstairs as quietly as he could with two rambunctious dogs in tow.

When he reached the landing, Isaac took a deep breath, not because he had doubts, but because he could hardly contain the joy that threatened to burst out from under his skin.

That is, if she said yes.

He had to remind himself that there were two possible outcomes, though only one was worth dwelling on.

Avery woke to kisses, lots and lots of wet kisses.

"Foggy!" she chided. "I wasn't having a nightmare, boy."

She laughed and opened her eyes.

"What has gotten into you?" She tried to push the dog away, but he wasn't having it. Foggy jumped up onto the bed and lay down, paws on her chest.

"Morning," Isaac said, coming into the room, holding two cups of coffee. He kissed her forehead and put Avery's cup on her nightstand, then walked back to his side of the bed and slid under the covers.

"I think Foggy's trying to tell you something."

Isaac had a funny look on his face—overwhelmed, but happy—as if he anticipated something good, like a little boy on Christmas.

Avery didn't give it a second thought. He always looked like that since she'd moved in, a fact that made her smile every time she thought of it.

She rubbed her eyes and looked at the clock on her bedside table, groaning when she saw the hour.

"You guys are up way too early."

Isaac just grinned and took a sip of his coffee. He set the cup down and snuggled in closer.

"Foggy," he said, "roll over."

"What are you goofs up to?"

Foggy obeyed and flipped over to show off his tummy, making Avery laugh.

"I see you've learned a new trick, boy. Is that what you guys have been doing so early this morning?"

She gave his tummy an obligatory scratch, then rubbed under his chin. Something cold and metallic tapped against her fingers.

"What's this, Foggy?" she asked, tugging it out from the folds of his fur, gasping when it finally dawned on her what she held in her hand. Her pulse drummed at her temples, blocking out all sound.

"Oh, my gosh," she cried, a hand flying to her mouth as tears brimmed at the edges of her lids. "Isaac. It's just beautiful."

She gripped the ring and, with shaking hands, untied the string that attached it to Foggy's collar. Pulling in a breath, her eyes surveyed her surroundings, soaking in everything so she could remember it every day for the rest of her life.

A life she would spend with Isaac, a man she'd grown to love more than she ever thought possible.

He lifted the ring from her palm and got out of the bed, moving to kneel at her side.

"Avery Abbott. Will you marry me?"

She nodded, unable to say anything for a moment as tears rolled down her cheeks. Then, finally, it came—the word that would seal them together forever.

A word she'd said many times over the past year.

To new friends, to a job as a trainer that she absolutely adored, to events and places and things she'd never dreamed she would be able to experience.

And now to the man she loved more than anything else in the world.

"Yes," she said. "Yes, Isaac. I absolutely will marry you."

He slid the ring on her finger, then jumped up from the floor and right into the bed, covering her in kisses, wrapping his arms around her as she laughed, and cried, and laughed some more.

* * * * *

THE MILLIONAIRE'S
REDEMPTION

THERESE BEHARRIE

For my husband,
who was the official consultant for this book (and the
unofficial consultant for every other). Thank you for
making me see that I am more than enough.

For my mother, who taught me that the best way to
deal with bullies is to believe in myself and work
even harder. Thank you for helping me through it.

And Lunelle, who's always willing to defend me
(even when it isn't necessary).
Thank you for your love and support.

I love you all.

CHAPTER ONE

'AND THE SOLUTION you've come up with is *marriage*?'

Lily Newman's steps faltered at the words. Not because she was at an engagement party—her best friend Caitlyn's—where marriage was supposed to be celebrated, but because of the anger that stiffened every word she'd overheard.

There was something familiar about the voice, though not because she knew the person speaking. It was just something in the tone… But that was ridiculous, so she focused on the fact that since she didn't recognise the voice entirely she couldn't be overhearing either of the individuals she was celebrating that evening.

She looked around to check whether she might be caught eavesdropping. Not that she *wanted* to be doing that. She had come upstairs to have some time alone. Yes, maybe it *did* have something to do with seeing her ex-fiancé Kyle arrive with the woman he'd cheated on Lily with. Okay, maybe it had *everything* to do with that.

Because she hadn't wanted to face it, she'd escaped the lavish party Caitlyn's wealthy fiancé Nathan was hosting at his newly purchased home, thinking she might as well explore considering the time she would spend there once her friend was married. But her exploration had ended fairly quickly when she'd heard those angry words from the room she was now standing outside.

'Mr Brookes, we think—'

Brookes was Nathan's surname, she thought, and realised why the man's voice had sounded so familiar. He was one of Nathan's family. Perhaps the brother Caitlyn had told her Nathan had a tenuous relationship with. The one she'd never met and knew not to bring up in front of Nathan after Caitlyn had told her not to. She knew she should give him his privacy, and was about to leave when the man spoke again.

'It doesn't really sound like you were thinking at all, Jade.'

The voice hadn't risen in volume, but Lily felt a chill go through her.

Poor Jade.

'We…we actually *did* put a lot of thought into this, Mr Brookes.' A male voice took over from Jade, though his words were no more confident.

'Then take me through your thought process.'

Careful, Lily thought.

She looked around again, saw that she was still alone, and leaned against the wall.

'We did the research.' Jade was speaking again. 'The file we mailed you has all the results from various avenues—test groups, opinion polls, social media. Yes, you're a successful businessman *now*, but you've done that largely outside of the public eye. People still remember you as the man who lost the Shadows Rugby Club their chance to compete internationally. They remember you as the man who would do anything to win a game, but took it too far in the end.'

There was a pause, and then Jade continued hesitantly. 'And then all the attention was on your suspension, and the partying you did during the year after your last game for the Shadows…'

'You're not telling me anything new.' The words were flat. 'I hired you because I knew that it would be difficult to…restore my image. But I'm doubting my decision now, since you're telling me marriage is the only way I can do that.'

'It's not the *only* way,' the other man Lily had yet to identify said quickly. 'But it's the fastest way. And considering that the buy-out is time-sensitive…' He trailed off.

There was silence for a while, and Lily pushed away from the wall. Guilt spread through her when she realised she shouldn't be listening to a private conversation. Sure, she wanted to know more about Nathan's mysterious brother—if that was who he was—but it was purely out of curiosity. There really wasn't a *reason* for her to listen to Nathan's family's business.

She turned away, forcing herself to act like the confident woman she was trying to be and face Kyle, but she paused when she heard the voices in the room again.

'I shouldn't have asked you to come to my brother's engagement party.'

So he *was* Nathan's brother.

'We can discuss this tomorrow, after the TV interview.'

Her thoughts froze when she realised the man was now walking towards the door, and her legs moved just in time to avoid being caught. She hurried down the passage and turned the corner that led to the stairs…

And then stilled when she saw the man she was trying to avoid walking *up* them.

Kyle.

His date—the other descriptions in her mind weren't

quite as polite—was giggling as he whispered something into her ear. Lily had never bothered to learn the woman's name—why would she need to know the name of the woman she'd caught naked in her fiancé's arms?—but she *did* remember the red hair and petite frame.

It made her pull at the dress Caitlyn had begged her to wear a few days ago. It was too tight, Lily thought desperately. She wished with all her might that it wasn't in a shocking red colour that did nothing to hide the curves Lily had plenty of—too many, in fact.

Her pretend confidence was already dwindling, she realised. And although there was a part of her that told her it was to be expected when she was about to face the man who had broken her down throughout their relationship—who had cheated on her—she had expected more of herself.

It also did her no good to notice how much *smaller* than Lily Kyle's date was. She watched the man she had once thought she loved slide a hand around the woman's tiny waist, pulling her close enough that there was no space between them. They were sneaking away to fool around, she realised, nausea fierce in her belly. How many times had she thwarted Kyle's attempts to do just that with *her* when they were at parties? He hadn't only found a woman smaller than her, Lily thought. She was also the risk-taker Kyle had always wanted and Lily would never be.

In the split second before Kyle saw her Lily decided to take a risk. She wanted Kyle to think that she had been making out with someone upstairs. That the thing she had refused to do with him—the thing he had found someone else for—she was now doing with someone *other* than him.

She would probably think that it was a terrible decision later, but as she fluffed her coiled curls and rubbed her lips together to smudge her lipstick she only hoped one thing—that Nathan's brother had a sense of humour.

'Lily?'

Kyle's voice immediately sent her skin crawling and her heart galloping. She couldn't believe that she'd once found that voice attractive. Now she heard the slime curl around every word.

She lifted her eyebrows. 'Kyle? I didn't see you there. How are you?'

The *of-course-you-saw-me* glint in Kyle's eyes set her teeth on edge and had a small part of herself recoiling.

'I'm well. How are you? I heard you managed to get that bookstore up and running eventually.'

'It's doing really well, actually. My initial investment was quite substantial, as you know.'

Kyle's eyes hardened, and satisfaction pumped through her. But then it gave way to the usual feelings of disgust at the thought of how their relationship had ended. At how she'd compromised her integrity, her dignity.

She ignored the fact that her self-confidence was deteriorating with every moment she spent in his presence.

'You've never met Michelle before, have you? At least not officially.' Kyle pushed the woman forward. 'We're getting married in a few months.'

'Congratulations,' she answered, and though ice stiffened her spine at the woman's cold look she felt nothing else at the news that Kyle was getting married.

That didn't mean relief didn't wash over her when she heard steps behind her.

Not even considering that it might be someone else, she spoke again. 'I didn't think you needed that much time to recover, honey…'

She turned around, and the words tailed off when she

saw her supposed 'boyfriend' for the first time. His skin was the colour of coffee with cream, complemented by dark hair tousled in a style that made her fingers wish they'd been the ones to style it. His dark eyes were stormy, and she realised she had taken a massive gamble with the man—he was clearly still upset about the conversation he had just had.

But the storm cleared immediately after that thought, and was replaced by a look of calm that made her feel even more uneasy. His eyes flickered over her, and then looked at Kyle before resting on her again. The calm then transformed into interest—amusement, too, she thought—with the faintest hint of some secret knowledge that made her skin heat.

He looked nothing like his traditionally handsome brother. His face was made of rugged planes that suggested he had a thousand stories to tell, and just above his mouth was a scar that she could imagine feeling during a kiss.

When the sides of the lips she was admiring curved upwards, she flushed. He might not be traditionally handsome, but he sure as hell was sexy.

'"Honey"? You and Jacques…you're dating?'

Kyle interrupted her perusal, and Lily felt her tongue stick in her mouth when she realised that Kyle *knew* Nathan's brother—Jacques.

You should have thought of that, Lily admonished herself.

She knew that Kyle was here because Nathan worked in Kyle's family's law firm. Nathan loved his job, and hadn't wanted to upset the prestigious Van der Rosses by not inviting the man who would one day become his boss. Caitlyn had assured her it was the *only* reason Lily's ex-fiancé had been invited.

'Yes, we're dating.'

The smooth baritone of Jacques's voice sent shivers down Lily's spine, and she struggled to shake the feeling.

'For how long?' Kyle said, and she turned back to see the smugness disappear.

It bothered him, she thought, her heart accelerating in an instinctual response to Kyle's anger. But then she paused, and told herself she didn't have to be worried about him lashing out.

She didn't have to worry about him at all any more.

'Almost six months now,' she said as Jacques moved down a step to stand beside her. He was a full head taller than she was, and she tried to ignore the awareness that realisation brought.

'Six months?' Kyle repeated, and she saw his eyes flash.

They'd broken up a year ago, and clearly he thought six months was too short a time for her to mourn for him.

'It doesn't feel like six months, though,' Jacques said, and she shifted her gaze to him. 'I barely feel like I've scratched the surface with you.'

So he *did* have a sense of humour, she thought, and smiled. When he responded with a smile of his own her breath caught and she thought something crackled between them. Her heart thudded when Jacques wrapped an arm around her waist, and for a moment she forgot that it was all a game and lifted her hand to brush at a piece of his hair.

'How did you two meet?'

Kyle's voice punctured the tension in the air and she looked at him with a foggy mind. It took her a minute, but when she came out of her Jacques-induced haze she noted the grim set of Kyle's lips. He *really* didn't like this, she thought, and waited for the panic. For that quick rush of trepidation that anticipated that she was about to be put in her place.

But nothing came. And somehow she knew it was because of the easy strength exuded by the man at her side.

'I'd love to tell you all about it, Kyle, but we were up there for far too long.'

Lily shot a flirtatious glance at Jacques, and briefly wondered how deep a hole she was digging when she saw a flash of heat in Jacques's eyes.

'We should probably spend some time with the happy couple. Enjoy the rest of your evening.'

Taking Jacques's hand, she hurried down the stairs, weaving her way through the guests. She only stopped once they were outside on the balcony, and then she immediately let go.

'I'm so sorry about that,' she said hurriedly, her chest suddenly tight.

Just breathe, Lily, it's over now.

'Care to explain?'

There was a slight breeze in the air and Lily walked to the edge of the balcony, turning her face towards the wind. It helped steady her, and when she opened her eyes—when she saw the view in front of her—that did, too.

Nathan's new house stood at the top of the Tygerberg hills in Cape Town, and she could see Table Mountain and most of the city from where she was. It reminded her of how small her problems were.

Even the after-effects of a bad relationship.

'How about we start with an introduction?'

Her words were said a little breathlessly, and she cleared her throat. Nerves had replaced panic, and she glanced around. No one was paying attention to them. That helped.

'Lily Newman—best friend to the bride-to-be.' She offered a hand.

'Jacques Brookes—brother of the groom-to-be.'

He took her hand and it was like touching the coals of a fire. It made her want to break the contact immediately, but he held on, shaking her hand slowly. The heat went up her arm, through her chest...

Before it could move any further she pulled her hand away. 'Nice to meet you,' she said, and folded her arms, constraining the hands that suddenly wanted more of the fire. 'It probably would have been better if that had happened before the whole debacle inside.'

'I don't know,' he answered with a sly smile. 'It was much more interesting than the way I usually meet girls.'

'I'm sure you must mean *women*, because clearly...' She gestured to herself, and then flushed when she saw appreciation in his eyes.

But he only said, 'Touché,' and made her wonder why she'd said those words.

They'd made her sound sassier than she was. As if she was in his league. As if she was used to playing the cat-and-mouse game of flirtation. She almost laughed aloud at the prospect of being in *any* league.

No, she thought as she took in how effortlessly Jacques's muscular body wore his suit. He was *way* too attractive to be interested in her. Someone who looked like him spent time with models and actresses—definitely not with women who had more than twenty-five per cent body fat.

She distracted herself by offering the explanation he'd asked for earlier. 'Kyle's my ex-fiancé—'

She broke off when he lifted a hand, and she saw that his ring finger was a little crooked.

'The one who dumped him a month before the wedding?'

'Yes.'

'I always thought the woman who did that had some balls.'

She smiled. 'Thanks.'

'It doesn't explain why you dated him in the first place.'

It was the same thing she'd asked herself when she'd realised how poorly he'd treated her. But that realisation had only come at the end—when she'd been *forced* to see the truth. She'd been blinded by how charming, how handsome he was at first. And at all the times when he'd switched it on again sporadically throughout their relationship.

But the simple truth was that the blinkers had been kept in place because he'd been *interested* in her. It had been intoxicating—until it hadn't been. And then she'd found him with a naked woman and regained the gift of sight. It had grown clearer with each hour that had passed after she'd ended it. With each phone call Kyle had made. With each threat…

She was ashamed that she'd dated a bully—that she would have *married* him—just because she didn't think enough of herself. She'd dealt with bullies her entire life—she should have known better. And then there was the guilt, the *indignity* of her actions after the break-up…

'Some things you only realise with time,' she finally answered Jacques.

'Touché,' he said again.

She watched him shift his weight from one leg to the other and frowned. The movement was so out of place for a man who clearly had an abundance of confidence. She thought of the conversation she'd overheard, wondered if what she saw was vulnerability, and felt it hit straight at her heart.

No! she commanded herself. She had her hands full with her own problems. Like the store she'd wanted all her life—had sold a piece of herself to start—which was failing. She needed to focus on fixing *that*—on fixing *herself*—before she could even *think* of getting involved with someone else's problems.

And yet when she looked at the sexy man in front of her the resolutions that she'd thought were firmly in place seemed hazy.

'Kyle didn't seem to like you,' Lily said to distract herself. 'Why is that?'

Jacques moved closer, and the breeze brought his fresh-from-the-shower scent to her nose. Her insides wobbled as attraction flowed through her, but she chose to ignore it.

Or tried to.

'We have history.'

Lily waited for him to continue. When he didn't, she said, 'That's all you're going to tell me?'

He chuckled. 'Apparently not.'

He leaned against the balcony's railing.

'Our families run in the same circles, so I'd met him a few times before Nathan started to work for him. Because I knew he was a—' He looked at her, as though checking what her reaction would be, and then continued with a grin. 'Because I knew he wasn't a very nice person, I used to make a game out of stealing his dates.'

Her heart raced. 'But you stopped?'

Something sparked in his eyes. 'A while before you, yes. Unfortunately.'

Her face heated and she leaned against the railing as well, looking away from the view he was facing towards.

She didn't want him to see how uncomfortable he made her. And heaven only knew why she was staying there with him so that he *could* make her uncomfortable.

'Why?'

'Why did I stop?'

She nodded, and he sighed.

'Because Nathan started working for Kyle's firm. Because I stopped going to events he would be at.'

Jacques fell silent, and Lily wondered if he was remembering why he'd stopped going to those events. Had it been because he'd started playing rugby? Because he'd stopped? Had it been during the year *after* he'd stopped?

She folded her arms again when guilt nudged her at the way she'd got the information to wonder those things at all.

'And,' Jacques said after a while, 'because I didn't have time to deal with the punches he tried to throw at me.'

Surprise almost had her gasping. 'Kyle tried to *hit* you?'

His lips curved and her pulse spiked.

'*Tried* being the operative word. It was entertaining for me...painful for him, I imagine.'

'You hit him back?'

'Don't sound so surprised. I was defending myself.'

It took her a moment to process that, and then she laughed. 'I would have *paid* to see that.'

He smiled. 'You could still see it.'

She gave him a look. 'I'm not *actually* going to pay you to hit my ex.'

Jacques laughed. 'It wouldn't cost you much if you wanted me to, but I wasn't talking about that. I saw the way he looked at us when he heard we were together. He *hated* it. So I bet if you and I go into that party right now and pretend to be a couple for a while longer his reaction would pretty much be the same as a punch in the gut.'

She'd barely had enough time to consider his proposal before he'd pushed up from where he was leaning and moved closer to her, sliding an arm around her waist. Her eyes widened and her mouth opened as she drew a quick breath. She watched his eyes lower to it. He only needed to dip his head—it was barely five centimetres away—and she would know if she could *really* feel that scar during a kiss…

He moved his mouth until it was next to her ear and whispered, 'Kyle's watching, so you might want to make that decision quickly.'

CHAPTER TWO

JACQUES COULDN'T DENY enjoying the way the woman he'd only just met shivered in his arms. Or the look her ex—a man he had a *very* low opinion of—was aiming at him. But those things were irrelevant to him at that moment. What *was* relevant was an opportunity to do just as his PR firm had advised. An opportunity that had just fallen into his lap, and would get him exactly what he wanted if he used it properly.

Lily shifted, reminding him that the opportunity wasn't an *it* but a *who*.

'If I say yes, will you let go of me?'

She asked it in a shaky tone, and he looked down into uncertain eyes. They became guarded a moment later, and he frowned, wondering where the spirit he'd admired earlier had gone.

'I'll let go of you regardless, Lily.'

He spoke softly, but forced his heart to harden. He couldn't feel anything for her—including empathy. It would make using her a lot more difficult.

It sounded harsh, even to him, but he knew he would do it if it meant he could redeem himself from the mistakes he'd made in the past. He'd been trying to do that since he'd realised he was only proving people right—

specifically his father—by acting the way he had during the year after his suspension.

The realisation had had him channelling the 'I'll do whatever it takes' motto he'd been known for during his rugby days into building a sporting goods company. Into making it a success.

Now it was. And yet people *still* thought of him as the bad boy who'd beaten up his opponent seven years ago, and it grated him. So when he'd heard that his old rugby club was being sold, he'd known it was an opportunity. He could go back to the root of it all—to where his problems had started.

The irony was that he needed a better reputation to get the club he believed would change his poor reputation. And Lily was the key to that.

'Let's do it.'

The words were said firmly, surprising him after the brief moment of vulnerability he'd just seen, but he simply asked, 'Are you sure?'

'Yes.'

She gave a quick nod, and then moved her mouth so that it was next to his ear, just as he had done to her earlier. It made it seem as if she was responding to his question—something her action made seem suggestive—and he would have appreciated the strategy if a thrill hadn't gone through his body, distracting him.

'We'll have to tell Caitlyn about this. If she sees us and thinks we're together she's going to freak out.'

She pulled back and laid a hand on his chest—an intimate gesture that had his heart beating too hard for his liking.

'That would probably be best,' he answered stiffly.

It took him a moment to figure out whether his tone

came because of the effect she had on him or the prospect of speaking to his brother.

A fist clenched at a piece of his heart as it always did when he thought of Nathan, but he tried to focus on his task. He took Lily's hand and led her through the crowd of people he no longer cared enough about to know to where his brother and Caitlyn were standing.

Holding Lily's hand sent awareness up and down his arm, but he ignored it. Attraction wasn't something new to him. *There's more with her,* a voice taunted, and again he tried to think of something else. But his options seemed limited to things he *didn't* want to think about, and he sighed, realising he would have to face at least one of them.

His brother won, Jacques thought as they reached the circle of people Nathan and Caitlyn were surrounded by. The easy air that Nathan carried around him—the way it translated into ease around people—had always been something Jacques had admired. Sometimes envied. Until he'd realised that people were overrated. One day they saw you as a hero, doing things they admired—the next those very things were criticised and *that* was how they defined you.

But Jacques knew it was also the easy way Nathan approached their less than stellar parents. How he was still in touch with them when Jacques hadn't seen them in years. How he could still want to be a part of their family after all they'd had to deal with growing up…

He stopped that train of thought when he saw they'd attracted Nathan's attention, and with a slight nod of his head Jacques indicated they go to a quieter corner of the room.

'I'm glad you came,' were the first words from his brother's mouth.

'You knew I would.'

Nathan sent Jacques a look that had a lance of guilt piercing his chest. It made him think about how he hadn't seen either of his parents there that evening—*Surprise, surprise,* he thought, despite the relief coursing through him—and he realised it was disappointment, not accusation, that had Nathan doubting Jacques. And that it wasn't exactly *Jacques,* but their whole family.

While Jacques sympathised with his brother, that feeling was capped by the memory of the thousands of times Jacques had warned Nathan to stop *hoping* with their parents. Jacques had learnt a long time ago that it would get him nowhere. His anger about it had ended his career, after all. Had taught him to stop trying. And, since he hadn't seen them in seven years, he figured he'd succeeded in that.

'Congratulations,' Jacques said, remembering that this was the first time he'd seen his brother and his fiancée since they'd got engaged.

He brushed a kiss on Caitlyn's cheek, enjoying the smile that spread over her pretty face, and then went in for the obligatory handshake and pat on the back with his brother.

'While that was both amusing *and* touching,' Lily interrupted with a small smile, 'I know you both have to do the rounds, so we just wanted to tell you we're going to pretend to be dating so that I can make Kyle feel a fraction of what I felt when I walked in on him and her—' she nodded a head in the woman's direction '—naked.'

By the time she was done Jacques could tell that she was out of breath. Which didn't surprise him, since with each word the pace with which she'd spoken had increased. What *did* surprise him was what she had said— that Kyle had cheated on her. While he'd been amused at being roped in to being a pretend boyfriend earlier, he understood why she'd done it now. And he no longer felt amusement over the situation.

There was a stunned silence, and then Caitlyn said, 'Honey, are you okay?'

'I'm fine.' Lily brushed one of her delightful curls from her face. 'We just wanted to warn you in case you wondered. Or got asked about it. And, while we're speaking about that, we've been dating six months. You and Nate introduced us.'

Jacques's lips twitched at the way their story had evolved, but the amusement faded when he wondered how Kyle could have cheated on someone like Lily.

Someone like Lily? a voice questioned, and he realised it sounded crazy. He barely knew her—she might have cheated on Kyle first. But given what he knew about Kyle and the few moments he'd spent with Lily he highly doubted that *she'd* been in the wrong.

His opinion of Kyle dropped another notch, and the temptation to relive the night he had knocked the man out boiled in Jacques's blood. He frowned, wondering where the intensity of his feelings—a mixture of anger and protectiveness—came from. And then he felt his brother's gaze on him, and looked up into a flash of warning.

Since he'd experienced a surge of protection for Lily himself, he understood it. But it singed him to know Nathan was thinking about Jacques's past with women. And it burned to know his brother's warning was on point, considering what he planned to use Lily for.

'You don't have to worry, Cait,' he said, distracting himself.

He knew Caitlyn was the one to win over if he wanted his plan to work. Caitlyn gave him a quick nod, then turned her attention to Lily.

'You know I never liked him—especially after everything...' She trailed off, glancing at Jacques. Then she quickly said, 'I give my blessing for this fake relationship in the name of payback.'

Caitlyn had sparked his curiosity, but it was forgotten when Lily smiled and his chest constricted.

Simple attraction.

He willed himself to believe that when his skin prickled as she took his hand again. And when she looked back with those beautiful eyes of hers to check whether he was okay with it and his heart raced.

He gave her a quick nod, and she started towards the doors that led to the side of the balcony that held the pool. Before he could take more than a few steps with her, someone touched his arm and he looked back.

'Please...be careful with her,' Caitlyn said, looking at him with eyes that reflected her plea.

'I... I will,' he answered, before he could think to say anything else, and the gratitude that shone from her face had his stomach dropping.

He glanced at his brother, saw the frown that suggested Nathan didn't believe him, and his stomach dropped even further. He turned back to Lily, following her until she stopped next to the pool, and tried not to think about the interaction he'd just had. It made him wonder what it was about Lily that inspired the protectiveness he'd seen in the two people he'd just spoken to—the protectiveness that he'd felt himself.

He cleared his throat. 'Are we going for a swim? I didn't bring my swimming trunks...although I have nothing against stripping down to my birthday suit.'

'What?' she gasped, and a smile spread across his face.

'I'm kidding, Lily. Unless...?' he teased, and enjoyed the way red tinted her olive skin.

The colour made him think of the other women he'd dated—he used that term loosely—who spent hours in the sun trying to get that tone. Something told him that Lily would never spend so much time on such a vain endeavour. Not when he was sure the messy auburn curls surrounding her face hadn't been tampered with. When he was sure her beautiful face bore almost no make-up. Her hazel eyes weren't highlighted by mascara or liner. The blush on her high cheekbones wasn't artificial, nor was the pomegranate hue of her full lips.

As attracted as he was to the outside—he took a moment to enjoy the way her body filled out the dress she wore, just as he had when he'd been coming down the stairs—he found himself more intrigued by what the outside *told* him. How many women did he know who would come to an upper-class party *without* plastering their faces with make-up? How many would leave their hair in its natural state when every other woman had hers sleeked up in some complicated style?

Certainly none of the women *he* knew, he thought.

And her reactions to his teasing were so refreshing. Endearing. It made her feel more authentic. And it made her perfect for his plan.

It also made him realise how little innocence the women he'd spent his time with in the past had had. But then innocence wasn't exactly something he'd been looking for in the past. No, he'd been looking to forget the way he'd screwed up his life. And then the public had turned on him—had destroyed him in the media—and he'd begun to wonder what the point of trying was. If they wanted a bad boy, that was what they would get. And they had—for an entire year. The worst time of his life...

'I don't know why I let you fluster me.' Lily's words tore him from his thoughts. 'I know you're teasing.'

'And if I wasn't?'

She sent a look at him that had him smiling.

'Nice try, but it isn't going to work again.'

'It was worth a shot. How else would I be able to see the wonderful colour your cheeks turn when you're flustered?'

She shook her head, and with her bottom lip between her teeth looked away.

Because he saw the very colour he'd been talking about again, he grinned. 'This is fun.'

'For you, maybe,' Lily answered, but she didn't seem upset. 'What did Caitlyn say to you when she called you back?'

'You saw that?'

She nodded, and it took him a few seconds to decide what to say to her.

'She told me to be careful with you.'

Lily nodded again, her face pensive, and then her eyes shifted to something behind him. She moved closer and gave him a whiff of citrus and summer. It was a heady combination, he thought as his body tightened, and he assured himself that that was the only reason for his reaction.

'Our plan seems to be working.' Her curls shook as she lifted her head to look at him. 'Kyle barely seems to be paying attention to his—'

Her eyes widened and she bit her lip again. The prickle in his body became an ache.

'Date?' he offered, to distract himself, but couldn't help the hand that lifted to tuck a curl around her ear.

'Sure—let's go with that,' she murmured, and fluttered those dark lashes up at him.

The ache was replaced by a punch to the gut.

'Why do I need to be careful with you?'

It suddenly seemed imperative for him to know.

'You don't…' she breathed, and electricity snapped between them.

'Are you sure?'

'No.' She shook her head. 'I'm tired of being treated like I'm going to break. My fiancé cheated on me. I was—' She stopped, and there was a flash of vulnerability on her face before it was replaced with a fierce expression. 'You don't have to be careful with me. Treat me as you would any other woman.'

CHAPTER THREE

JACQUES'S EYES FLICKERED down to her lips, and Lily realised how her request sounded. Under any other circumstance she would have been mortified at the implication of her words. Now, though, she *wanted* Jacques to take advantage of the ambiguity. She wanted to be taken advantage of...

'I wouldn't be pretending to be your boyfriend if you were any other woman.'

His voice broke into her thoughts and she blushed at the direction of them, wondering where they'd come from.

'Why are you doing this for *me*, then?'

The heat she'd thought she'd seen earlier in his eyes cooled into an enigmatic expression.

'Besides the fact that you basically forced me to on the stairs?'

She nodded, feeling her blush deepen.

'At first because I couldn't imagine anything better than making Kyle Van der Ross uncomfortable. Now it's because I want to make him jealous.'

He looked at her, and she realised they were having this conversation in an awfully intimate position. She took a slight step back, to give herself some air—and to prevent herself from being distracted by his scent—

but stopped when he placed a hand gently on the small of her back.

It sent her next question stammering from her mouth. 'Wh…wh…why?'

He smiled at her—a soft smile that was in stark contrast to his intimidating masculine presence—and she wondered what she was missing. A man like Jacques wouldn't be interested in *her*. And even if he was the last thing *she* wanted was to get involved with someone who could shatter the self-esteem she had fought so hard for.

The self-esteem she was *still* fighting for.

'He cheated on you, Lily. And only the most despicable of men hurt the women they claim to love in that way.' His face no longer held an easy expression. 'Besides, I *like* helping you. And before you ask me why, it's because I like *you*.'

'You barely know me,' she retorted. It was easier than acknowledging the truth of his words.

'I know that you had the guts to leave someone who cheated on you. I know that you're loyal enough to come to your best friend's engagement party even though you knew your ex would be here. You're innovative—I don't think I know many other people who would come up with the idea of a stranger pretending to be their boyfriend—and you're thoughtful enough to let your friends know about the charade so that they don't get upset. What more is there?'

He grinned, but she couldn't bring herself to respond. Hearing him describe her like that sent a gush of warmth through her body. But it didn't seem right. Not when she was used to harsh words. Not when she was used to people telling her how she should look. How she should be. And from her parents—from Kyle, too, she'd realised too late—how much *better* she could be.

'Fine—you know things about me,' she said, when the silence had extended a tad too long. 'How about you share something about yourself, then?'

'Sure,' he replied easily, and touched her waist to shift her to the left. 'It's easier for Kyle to see you like this.'

Her skin felt seared at his touch, and her thoughts went haywire for a second. And in that second she saw herself pressed against Jacques, kissing him until she no longer knew who she was.

She shook her head, thinking that she didn't know who she was *now*. This woman having inappropriate thoughts about a man she barely knew was definitely not her. She'd never gone that far—even in her most lonesome of days.

When she'd been overweight it had been easier to avoid attention. And even when she'd lost some of her weight she had still been too afraid to put herself in a situation where men might hit on her.

It had been on the one night Caitlyn had convinced her to go out—in their final year at university—that she'd met Kyle. He'd been the first person to treat her like a woman, and not like 'the girl who lost weight'. His attention had been flattering, overwhelming. She'd fallen hard, and had been swept into his world like a commoner into a castle.

His offhand comments about her looks—he hadn't seemed to have a problem with her weight, but her hair, her face, her clothing were still fair game—hadn't mattered when he could make her feel like the most beautiful woman on the planet with one look. His suggestions as to how she should act, what she should say, how she might do better had been irrelevant when he was treating her to fancy dinners, to expensive gifts.

'What do you want to know?'

Jacques was watching her, and her face heated even at the thought of him knowing what she was thinking.

'How'd you get the scar?'

He frowned, as though he wasn't sure what she was talking about. And then his hand lifted and he rubbed his thumb over the scar. Lily was hit with the desire to do the same, and she clenched her hand, determined not to be caught in this attraction between them.

'I was in a fight.'

'Kyle?'

He smiled, though his eyes were hooded.

'He didn't land a punch that night. No, there have been other fights.'

His eyes glinted dangerously, and her knees nearly went weak.

What is wrong with you, Lily?

'Next question. What do you do?'

'I own a sporting goods company.'

'What does that entail?'

'Well, there's a shop where the public can buy sporting equipment, but mostly we do bulk and international orders.' He slanted a look at her. 'You've never heard of Brookes Sporting?'

'Hard to believe, isn't it?'

He smirked. 'Just a little.'

'And that's what you chose to do after your rugby career ended?'

There was a beat of silence before Jacques asked, 'How did you know I played rugby?'

She only then realised she wasn't supposed to know that.

'You expected me to know your company, but not that you played a popular South African sport? Besides, I'm sure Nathan mentioned it a while ago...' She trailed off when she saw he wasn't buying it.

'Really? The brother who didn't think I was going to come to his engagement party told you I used to play rugby?'

'Would you believe me if I told you I used to watch you play?'

'No.'

She sighed. She was going to have to tell him the truth.

'I overheard your conversation earlier, Jacques. I'm really sorry.'

That explained how she'd known he would follow her lead when they'd spoken to Kyle, Jacques thought. It also meant she had heard Jade and Riley's suggestion, which put his plan to convince her to be involved at risk.

'Is eavesdropping a hobby of yours?' he asked slowly.

'I didn't mean to,' Lily replied primly. 'I was upstairs because I saw—'

'Kyle and the cheater?'

She nodded. 'And when I walked past the room you were in I heard the whole marriage thing...'

So she *had* heard it, he thought, but soothed the faint trickle of panic by telling himself that she didn't suspect he wanted *her* involved. She wouldn't have agreed to his suggestion to continue the charade of their pretend relationship at the party if she did. And then Jacques would have lost the opportunity to ensure that all the wealthy people who formed part of his brother's social circle—including Lily's ex-fiancé—saw him and his 'new girlfriend'.

The rest of his plan had originally involved them leaving together at the end of the night. It would have just been for coffee—though the party attendees wouldn't have known that—and he would have suggested their pretend relationship continue for just a while longer. But this new information meant he needed to speed up that plan...

'Why don't we get out of here?'

Her eyebrows rose and her cheeks took on that shade of red he liked so much.

'Together?'

'Yeah. We can grab a cup of coffee.'

'Why?'

'I like you, Lily.' Though he'd meant the words to convince her to have coffee with him, he found that he genuinely meant them. Something tightened in his stomach at the knowledge. 'I also think there's nothing more you'd like to do than to get out of here.'

Her face had changed when he'd said he liked her, and though he couldn't quite read it he thought there was a trace of uncertainty there. As if she didn't believe what he said. The tightening in his stomach pulsed, and for the first time he considered how manipulative his plan was. Sure, it wouldn't hurt Lily—but it wouldn't benefit her either. It was entirely for *his* benefit.

But you helped her, too, a voice in his head reminded him. That made him feel better, and because he couldn't afford to dwell on why he should reconsider he chose to focus on that.

'You're right.' Lily's expression was unreadable. 'And buying you a coffee is probably the least I can do to say thank you.'

She was setting boundaries, he realised. Letting him know that she was only accepting his offer because she wanted to say thanks. He wasn't sure why that bothered him, but he didn't have time to ponder it.

'Are you sure you want to leave, though?' she asked.

She looked inside to where Nathan and Caitlyn were standing.

'I don't think Nathan expects me to stay longer than I already have,' he said, ignoring the guilt.

'Do you want to say goodbye?' she asked softly, and he looked down to see a compassion he didn't understand—and didn't want—in her eyes.

'I don't want to interrupt them.'

She watched him for a moment longer, and then nodded.

He reached for her hand, thinking about how easily he could feign affection with Lily and yet struggle with women he was much more familiar with. His skin heated when her fingers closed around his, warning him that his plan might have complications he hadn't considered.

But as he made his way through the crowd of people with Lily he knew that those complications would be worth it when the Shadows Rugby Club was his and he could help place them in the international league. If he could do that it would make up for the fact that he'd *cost* them their place in that league seven years ago.

When he felt like being kind to himself he told himself his actions that night of the championship game that should have determined that place had come from anger. From pain. That night had been the last time he'd seen either of his parents, too. Not a coincidence, considering that *they'd* been the reason he'd got into a fight with a player who hadn't deserved Jacques's attention. Who wouldn't have got it if he hadn't uttered those same words his father had before Jacques had arrived at the game...

'You're such a disappointment.'

The memory of that night still plagued him—still scarred him—but if he could pull off his PR company's ridiculous plan maybe he would finally find some peace.

Maybe he would finally be able to put it all behind him and move on.

'Do you have somewhere specific you'd like to go?' Lily asked once they were outside.

He watched her pull her coat tighter around her, saw her look out around the private estate his brother's house was on, and realised she was nervous.

'I'm not going to kidnap you, Lily.'

She looked at him. 'I know. And I'm going in my own car.'

Smart girl, he thought, even though disappointment lapped at him for reasons he didn't understand.

'My office is pretty private.' He saw something in her eyes, and said, 'You'll be safe, Lily. I promise to behave myself.'

My future depends on it.

She tilted her head, as though she was considering his words. 'So let's have coffee somewhere more neutral, then. I know a place…'

CHAPTER FOUR

'THIS IS *NEUTRAL* for you?'

Jacques joined Lily in front of her store, and looked pointedly at the sign that said 'Lily's' above the glass entrance.

'Relax,' she replied, though the way her heart was beating told her she was probably saying it to herself.

'We're just stopping here for the coffee—then we can take a walk down the beach. It's not too busy this time of night.'

'I usually let a woman take me out for dinner before I do romantic walks on the beach, Lily.'

Her hand froze on the door at his words, and it took her a moment to hear the store's alarm beeping. She hurriedly entered the code, trying desperately to come up with something to say. But her mind only formulated excuses—not the sassy comeback she'd hoped for.

You should have known it wouldn't last, a voice mocked her.

And though she wanted to deny the words she couldn't. She'd thought it was a *good* idea to bring him back to her store and then to walk on the beach. She'd feel better in a familiar place, she'd told herself.

But being in that familiar place had snatched her from the fantasy world she'd been in for the past few hours.

The world where she'd flirted as though she were in a thinner body. As though she had all the confidence in the world. As though she wasn't trying with all her might to value herself.

'This is nice,' he said, breaking the silence. 'It's a coffee shop and a bookstore?'

'Yeah. I love reading and I love coffee, and a lot of the people I know do, too. So I thought it would be pretty great to have a place where you could relax and do both. And, of course, there's the view.'

She was rambling, she knew. A combination of nerves at Jacques being there and the defensiveness she always felt when she spoke about her store.

Her parents' warnings echoed in her head—as did their urges for her to do something more *respectable* than being a store-owner—and she shook it off. She had more pressing things to worry about at the moment.

'Do you have any preferences for coffee?'

'Black, no sugar.'

She busied herself with the task, and for a few moments there was silence.

'You have good taste.'

The milk she was pouring spilled onto the counter. 'Wh…what?'

'I assume you decorated the store yourself?'

She nodded mutely, refusing to look at him in case he wore that amused expression again.

'It's the perfect décor for a shop like this.'

She'd gone with a blue and white colour scheme, to complement the view of the sea that stretched endlessly through the glass entrance. White bookshelves held as many books as she could fit in them—old and new—and lined the walls on either side of the shop. The wooden tables and blue-cushioned chairs were homely, comfort-

able—exactly what she'd been going for when she'd decorated, though she knew she'd spent hopelessly too much
on them.

But she only worried about that when she did her accounts and saw how many negative numbers they had.

'Thanks,' she said, making quick work of the clean-
up before handing him his coffee in a takeaway cup. She
cleared her throat. 'We don't have to...to do the walk. I
just thought it made sense...'

'I was teasing, Lily.'

The smile on his lips made her stomach flip. And then
there were even more gymnastics when he lifted her chin.

'You know—that thing I do so I can see you blush?'

She took a step back. 'You mean the thing I shouldn't
let fluster me?'

'Exactly.'

She couldn't help a smile at his quick answer. 'How
about we take this to the beach?'

She left her coat and her shoes in the store, and a few
moments later they were walking on the sand together.

'It's beautiful, isn't it?' he said, looking out to the
water.

Waves crashed against the sand at his words, and the
reflection of the full moon on the water shimmered, as
though thanking Jacques for the compliment.

'Yeah, it is. I remember going on holiday to Johannes-
burg when I was younger. I refused to go again when I
realised there was no beach.' She shrugged. 'Something
about a beach just—'

'Calms you?'

'Yeah.' She glanced over. 'Did the same thing ever
happen to you?'

There was a bark of laughter. 'That would have involved my parents actually *taking* us on holiday, so no.'

The words surprised her, and if his silence was any indication they had surprised him, too. She wanted to press him—for reasons she didn't want to think about—but before she could Jacques jogged a few paces ahead of her. Lily watched as he threw his empty coffee cup into a nearby bin, and in a few quick movements climbed onto a large boulder.

He grinned down at her when she reached him. 'Join me.'

'Up there? In this dress?' She shook her head. 'I'll pass.'

'How about that one?' Jacques nodded at the boulder next to the one he was on. It was smaller, but she still didn't see herself up there.

'I don't think you understand, Jacques—'

She broke off when he jumped down next to her, threw her coffee cup into the same bin—despite the fact that hers had only been half-empty—and took her free hand.

'Come on—it'll be a good place to talk.'

Helpless to do otherwise, she let him lead her to the next boulder, but stopped when they reached it.

'I don't see how this is going to work.'

'Like this.'

She felt his hands on her waist, and realised his intentions too late—he was already lifting her.

'Oh, no, Jacques,' she gasped. 'I'm too heavy—'

But she didn't get a chance to finish her sentence since her feet were already on the smooth, cold granite of the boulder.

A few moments later, Jacques joined her. 'Did you just say that you were too heavy?'

He barely sounded winded, and it took Lily a while to find her words. She was too busy wondering whether she'd overestimated her weight or underestimated his strength. Since she didn't live in a world where the former was ever a reality, she settled on the second.

'I guess not,' she finally answered him.

'You think you're heavy?'

'I…well… Kyle wasn't as strong as you are,' she finished lamely.

He gave her a strange look, but didn't say anything. Instead he offered a hand, gesturing that they should sit. She ignored the spark that zipped through her at the contact, and snatched her hand back as soon as she was sitting.

'Thanks for agreeing to have coffee with me,' he said when he settled down beside her.

'It was the least I could do after you helped me with Kyle. Even if you *did* throw most of mine in the bin.'

'Sorry…'

Jacques smiled apologetically, but something on his face told her there was more.

He confirmed it when he said, 'I actually wanted to talk to you in private because…'

He took a breath, and she felt a frisson of nerves deep inside.

'I was hoping you would do a little *more* than just have coffee with me.'

'What do you want?' she asked stiffly, hearing a voice mocking her in her head.

Did you really think he was being nice to you because he liked you?

'Nothing we haven't already managed to pull off.' He paused. 'I'd like you to pretend to be my girlfriend.'

CHAPTER FIVE

It SOUNDED SILLY even as he said it—more so when he saw the look on her face—but he ignored the feeling. *This* was the point of continuing the charade for so long. This was the point of asking her out for coffee.

It shouldn't matter that the easiness they'd shared this past half an hour—the ease responsible for that slip about his parents—had dissipated.

'Are you sure you just want me to pretend to be a *girl-friend*?' she asked quietly.

'Yes. We've done a pretty good job at convincing Kyle. A few more people wouldn't hurt.'

'"A few more" isn't quite the number, though, is it?'

Wondering how she knew, he answered, 'Fine, it's a lot more than a few. But you won't actually be *on* television. I just need the people at the studio to know you exist, so when I mention you on air it'll be believable.'

'What are you talking about?'

'*Latte Mornings*. I have an interview on the show tomorrow morning.' He frowned, realising now that they weren't on the same page. 'What are *you* talking about?'

'I heard your conversation, remember?'

She looked straight at him, and if her words hadn't surprised him he might have acknowledged the way his stomach tightened in response.

'You need a wife, right? Someone who will make you more…palatable to the public for some business deal you're working on?'

'Hold on.' He took a deep breath. 'You don't get to make assumptions about things you overheard—out of context, I might add—in a private conversation.'

Her cheeks flushed, and the spirit that had had her looking him in the eye earlier faded as she averted her gaze. 'I'm sorry that I eavesdropped, Jacques, but I… I can't be your *wife*.'

'I'm not asking you to *marry* me, Lily.'

'Then what *do* you want from me?'

'I just want you to pretend to be my girlfriend. You may have overheard that I'm not entirely willing to marry someone to get the public to like me.' *Not if I don't have to.* 'But you gave me the idea tonight that I could pretend to have a nice, respectable girlfriend and that might have the same effect.'

'And that's the real reason you wanted coffee?

'Yeah. It isn't that much to ask, considering that I did the same for you tonight.'

He shouldn't feel bad about this. He shouldn't have to defend himself.

So why was he?

'And maybe if you'd asked me straight I would have agreed. But instead you just told me to continue the charade for a bit longer—which *now*, of course, I realise is because you wanted to test whether it would actually have an effect, and not because you wanted to annoy Kyle— and then "coffee".' She lifted her hands in air quotes. 'You manipulated me.'

'And what *you* did wasn't manipulation?' he snapped back at her, guilt spurring his words. The picture she had painted reminded him too much of his father.

'I didn't manipulate you,' she answered primly. 'I told you why I did what I did. I was honest with you as soon as I had the chance to be.'

He shrugged, pretended her words didn't affect him. 'And I'm a businessman. I know how to capitalise on opportunities.'

'This isn't an *opportunity*,' she said coldly. '*I'm* not an opportunity.'

'Of course not.' He said the words before he could think about how they might undermine the cool exterior he was aiming for.

'Then stop treating me like one.'

She was right, he thought, and then remembered that she'd said if he'd been straight with her maybe she would have agreed.

'You're right—and I'm sorry for the way I went about this.'

She gave him a look that told him she didn't entirely trust his words. That look combined with the wounded expression just behind the guard she was trying so desperately to keep up, made him feel a stab of guilt.

He *had* manipulated her. And he should know, since he'd witnessed his father manipulating his mother for his entire childhood. Somehow the man had made his wife believe that telling their children they were disappointments, failures, was normal. That raising them without the love and support parents were supposed to give was acceptable. And his mother, so desperately in love with a man who had only wanted her for her money, hadn't believed she'd deserved more.

That her children had deserved better.

When Jacques had finally managed to convince his mother to kick his father out it had only taken his father a few minutes to change her mind. And now Jacques regretted it. The trying. The hope. The fact that he'd done it on the night of the championship.

It had been the reason he'd been so easily provoked into the fight that had got him suspended for three years. That had lost his team their chance to be a part of the international league they had fought so hard to play for.

It was why buying the Shadows now was so important. And why he needed to make amends with Lily.

'Would you give me another chance to ask you to be my girlfriend? My pretend one, of course.' He wasn't sure why he clarified it, but it made him feel better.

'If you tell me why you need a pretend girlfriend, yes.'

He nodded, and forced himself to say the words.

'Seven years ago I was suspended from playing rugby.' It took more strength than he'd thought it would to say the words. 'I got into a fight that cost my team a championship game and the chance of playing in the highest league they could play in.'

She interlaced her fingers and rested her hands in her lap. 'What was the fight about?'

'It doesn't matter,' he answered, because it was true.

'The scar?' she asked, tapping at her lip.

He wondered what intrigued her so much about it, but only nodded. There was a beat of silence before she spoke again.

'It must have been important if it cost you something that clearly meant so much to you.'

Maybe it had been important to him once—the chance of a family without his father. Now Jacques thought he'd been fighting over something that hadn't been worth nearly as much as it had cost him.

'It doesn't matter," he said again. 'It's only the effect the entire thing had on my reputation that does.' He paused. 'I heard recently from a few business associates that my old rugby club is going to be sold soon, and I want to be the one to buy it. Except I've been told that some of the club's biggest sponsors will pull out if it's sold to me. The only way to prevent that, it seems, is to build a more…*positive* reputation.'

She stared at him. 'You're seriously telling me that people care that much about your reputation?'

'Apparently.'

'And the only thing you did to get this negative reputation was have a fight?'

'One that lost my team the championship *and* an opportunity.'

'Yes, of course—but that's *it*?'

He hesitated. 'Well…'

Jacques really wasn't interested in rehashing the details of the year when he'd spiralled into the depression that had damaged his reputation even more.

'Well…?' Lily repeated, a single brow arching in a way that made him forget the tension of the conversation they were having.

'The year after I was suspended I spent a lot of time… Well, I spent some time on a self-destructive path,' he said once he had steadied himself.

'What does *that* mean?'

'I…' He'd hoped his explanation would be enough. 'I told myself that I didn't care what people thought about me, and I did exactly what I wanted to.'

And yet, ironically, it had been caring about what people thought that had *made* him act that way in the first place.

When she didn't speak after a few moments, he found himself asking, 'Why aren't you saying anything?'

'What did that entail?' she said in lieu of a reply.

He tried to formulate an answer, but nothing he could say would make him look good.

'I can't help you if I don't know the truth, Jacques.'

'Parties. A lot of swearing at journalists. Women.' He ran a hand through his hair, wondering how telling her all this intimidated him more than tackling the largest of men on a rugby field. 'What more do you want me to say?'

'So you were a bad boy?' she asked.

He cringed. The term brought memories he would rather ignore.

'I thought people *loved* bad boys.'

'Maybe,' he conceded, and then considered her comment. 'I think people only love bad boys as an idea. Something or someone far away from them. But they definitely do not when a bad boy, say, wants to date their daughter.'

She tilted her head, and one of her curls sprang over her forehead.

'So you're saying that people don't want you to buy a rugby club because they love the club too much?' She looked at him. 'They don't want you to "hurt their child"?'

He opened his mouth to protest, thinking her over-simplified explanation couldn't possibly be the reason he was in his current dilemma. But after a few moments he realised that that was *exactly* what was going on.

'Pretty much, yeah.'

'And if you have a girlfriend...?'

'If people see that I have a respectable girlfriend—a steady one—maybe they'll like me enough to trust me with the Shadows again.'

She frowned, and he waited as she processed his words.

'You really think that would work?'

No, was his first thought, but he said, 'I trust the people who work for me. If they say having a wife—or a girlfriend—people like will make them see me more favourably, then I believe them.'

There was another pause, and then she asked softly, 'How do you know people will like *me*?'

The hesitancy in her voice scratched at the protective instincts he'd locked away seven years ago.

Look where that had got him with his mother.

'Because you're likeable.'

Her curls bounced as she shook her head. 'No, I'm not.'

'Based on whose evaluation?' When she didn't reply, he said, 'Lily, you asked me to be honest. How about you do me the same courtesy?'

She looked down at her hands and he saw another glimpse of that other side of her. The side he'd seen when she'd claimed to be too heavy for him to lift her onto the boulder. It hit him harder than he might have anticipated, and he clenched his fists to keep himself from comforting her.

He barely knew the woman, and even if he did there was no way he wanted to get involved with her troubles. He'd purposely steered away from relationships to avoid being lured into protecting someone as he'd had to protect his mother. And Lily's insecurities reminded him a little too much of the woman he hadn't seen in seven years.

And yet when Lily answered him he found himself forgetting his own warning.

'I had a…a difficult time growing up. Didn't have that many friends. And then a failed relationship…'

The vulnerable look on her face twisted his heart.

'I mean, *that* must say something about my likeability.'

He watched her face change into an expression that

told him she'd said more than she'd meant to, and then the guard slipped back up again. It took him a moment to figure out how to respond.

'You have Caitlyn. And Nathan. They love you.' He paused. 'And *I* like you, Lily.' He said it again, to make her see that someone who didn't know her as well as Caitlyn and Nathan could like her too. Again, he found that he meant it. 'And you can't blame yourself for what happened with Kyle.'

She tilted her head. Didn't meet his eyes. 'Actually, I can. I didn't see him for what he was. I *let* him treat me poorly. I—'

'Stop!' he said harshly.

Seeing the surprise on her face, he forced himself to calm down. But Lily was doing exactly what his mother had done with his father—blaming herself, making excuses. It had always made his blood heat, just as it did now.

'Don't make excuses for him.'

'I'm… I'm not,' she stammered. 'I just meant that—'

She broke off when she looked at him, and he realised he hadn't schooled his face as well as he should have.

'I'm sorry. I just—'

The tone of her voice sucked all the anger from him. 'You don't have to apologise,' he said softly, unable to help himself as he took her hands into his.

She nodded, and the colour that had seeped out of her face started to return. His stomach turned, and he realised Lily wasn't the right person for his plan. She was too vulnerable…too fragile for him to bring her into the public light.

It had nothing to do with the fact that she awoke feelings in him that he had buried the night he'd written his parents off. Feelings that reminded him of when he'd fought for his mother. Feelings of protectiveness, of tenderness—feelings that had no place in what he wanted to achieve…

'*I'm* the one who should be apologising,' Jacques said, his decision made. 'I shouldn't have asked you to do this.'

'What?'

'You're not the right person for this, Lily.'

He saw her face blanch, was about to comfort her, but then thought better of it. He moved his hands from hers, immediately missing the warmth, and stood.

'I don't think that being in the public eye together is right for either of us,' he finished lamely, but he could tell that under her stony expression she was upset.

'Okay,' she said hoarsely, and then cleared her throat. Her voice was much stronger when she spoke again. 'You're probably right. No one would believe we were together anyway.'

She pulled her legs up and he could see she was contemplating how to stand without his help. He offered it anyway, and she accepted reluctantly—and again, so she could get off the boulder.

With each step back things between them grew more tense. Something inside Jacques grew more unsettled—so much so that he sighed in relief when they reached the pathway leading to her store.

'Thank you for your help with Kyle today,' she said primly, and each stilted word had his chest tightening.

'I was happy to help.'

It sounded strange to him to be so formal after what they'd just spoken about, but he didn't know how else to respond. He didn't even know why her words left him with an ache in his chest.

Silence stretched, making it feel as though there was more distance between them than the few centimetres from where she stood on the pathway and where he stood in the sand. The silence was heavy with disappointment, and it shook him more than he cared to admit. Perhaps because he'd lived with it hanging over his head his entire life. The disappointment that he would never live up to expectations he didn't know.

Like when he'd been hailed as the best player the Shadows had ever had and it hadn't impressed his father.

Heaven only knew what the man wanted from him—or from Nathan, for that matter, since even Nathan's law career had made but a blip on Dale Brookes's radar. But even disappointment implied caring. It implied that his father felt enough for his children to *want* them to achieve certain things. Since Jacques was sure that wasn't the case, maybe it was his own disappointment that his father didn't love them that was bothering him…

He shook his head. *Where had that come from?*

'Jacques?'

'Yeah?'

'I think I'm going to kiss you.'

He barely had time to process her words before her lips were on his.

Heat seared through him and his lungs caught fire.

He heard her intake of breath, realised that she felt the same.

Except that while his reaction had been to deepen the kiss hers was to pull away.

They stood like that for a moment, his hand lightly on her waist, both of hers on his chest. He felt them shaking against him and only then realised that his body was shaking too. Her eyes were wide, and the flush on her cheeks was caused by an entirely different reason than his earlier teasing.

'I'm so sorry,' she breathed, aiming her striking eyes at him.

Stealing his breath. Stoking his desire.

'I didn't mean to—'

This time he interrupted her with another kiss.

His arms went around her waist and he pulled her closer, lifting her from the path until she stood with him on the sand. Somewhere in his mind it registered that the romance of taking a walk on the beach that he'd teased her about earlier shrouded them now—that their first kiss was now on a beach in the moonlight. But then he stopped thinking, consumed by the magic of her mouth.

She tasted like strawberries just ripened. Smelled like a warm day in spring. Something inside him softened at the sensations that came with her kiss. She responded hungrily, deepening it. He heard a groan and realised that it had come from him. Because she was making him forget where they were—who he was and what he had to lose—he fought to slow the kiss. He hoped it would lessen the tension, the urgency, that had built between them.

But his attempt was a vain one, only succeeding in making him want more.

In making him *need* more.

He pulled away from her, his breathing as shaky as hers, and forced himself to take a step back. Forced himself not to be charmed by that just-kissed look on her face. He ignored the fact that her expression was like that because *he* had kissed her—deeply and thoroughly—and reined his emotions in.

'We shouldn't have done that.'

She looked up at him, her hand freezing midway to touching her lips, and he watched her fingers curl into a fist.

He felt as though his heart was right in the palm of that hand.

'No, we shouldn't have.'

She bit her lip, and his body yearned to go back to what they had been doing. It took him a moment to realise that she was doing it to keep herself from saying anything.

'We probably won't see each other after this, so it doesn't matter.' He felt like an absolute jerk saying it—even more so when he saw her flinch. Her words about no one believing that they would be together played in his head again, and he wondered at them. Wondered why he thought his words now had proved the truth of that to her somehow.

'Good luck with the TV show tomorrow. I'm sure everything will work out.'

She turned her back on him and hurried down the path before he could respond. And because he wanted to give her—and himself—some time to process events, he waited before following.

But that time wasn't nearly enough for him to process everything that was going on in his mind. To figure out why his actions that night had shamed him. Especially since they weren't actions he would have been ashamed of at any other time.

Or with any other person.

It was Lily, he realised. Something about her made his actions feel…unethical. *Manipulative.* He hadn't thought he was being manipulative. Or perhaps, more accurately, he hadn't cared. At least not until she'd called him on it. And that kiss had only complicated things between them. He worried that it would affect the self-confidence she had so much trouble with.

Which was why this was for the best. He didn't need to

worry about someone else's self-confidence. He needed to focus. He'd worked too hard to make up for his past to be distracted by a woman. Besides, as much as Lily intrigued him, she needed someone who would take care of her. Someone who would be patient with her insecurities, who would appreciate the spirit that covered them.

Someone who didn't have a million hoops to jump through before people saw him as decent.

And that wasn't Jacques.

It was for the best, he thought again, and didn't examine why it didn't feel like it. Or why realising that he wouldn't see Lily again any time soon made him feel more empty than the task ahead of him.

CHAPTER SIX

LILY TOOK A shaky breath as she walked into the *Latte Mornings* studio. She still wasn't sure why she was there. When she'd got home the previous night she'd convinced herself that she would forget all about Jacques. Especially since she still felt raw because his interest in her—his kindness *to* her—had all been a ploy to get her to help him.

She'd told herself she should have known. *Kyle* had been nice to her once upon a time. It was why she'd fallen for him—and the way she'd learned that niceness was never simple.

But still, it stung.

Jacques's dismissal felt like confirmation that she wasn't likeable. And even though he'd claimed otherwise his actions had shown her the truth. They had amplified all her insecurities and she'd been determined to escape them. She'd been determined to show Jacques she was as right for his plan as anyone else.

So she'd kissed him.

It had been impulsive. It had been hot. It had been everything she'd expected from a man with Jacques's undeniable sexiness and charm. But there had been something more, too. She remembered the scar above his mouth again, the fight he'd said he'd had with Kyle, and realised it had been *dangerous*.

It both thrilled and terrified her that she seemed to be attracted to the danger she sensed in Jacques. And, though she wanted to, she couldn't deny that it was part of the reason she was walking into a television studio at six in the morning to pretend to be his girlfriend.

She knew this plan was a form of redemption for him. She'd read articles about what had happened during his last game. Watched the footage. She'd seen the absolute anger on his face. Felt the danger of it settle in her throat when she hadn't been able to tear her eyes away.

Her instincts told her that that fight *had* mattered, despite Jacques's claims otherwise. And the more digging she had done, the more she'd become convinced of it. The internet was full of what had happened after that fight. His red card...the suspension. The year he'd said he'd been 'self-destructive'. The pictures.

She didn't know Jacques very well, but she knew the man in those pictures wasn't the same person she'd spoken to the night before. The man in those pictures was broken. Completely so. But the man *she'd* met hid that brokenness well...

It had all fuelled her urge to help him. And in an effort to avoid the thought that she wanted to help only because she was attracted to him, she'd realised she could do with *his* help. She *needed* it if she wanted to save the store she'd opened six months ago from going under. And she *had* to save it—or the guilt that anchored her heart to the soles of her feet most days would be for nothing.

Pretending to be Jacques's girlfriend would give her a platform where she could market her store from. To get more customers, to get more income and pay more bills. *That* had been the real reason—at least the biggest one—

she'd got up at four-thirty, got ready and driven almost an hour to the television studio.

Because she couldn't fail with her store. She couldn't fail at her dream. And she sure as hell couldn't prove her parents right and fall even further short of their expectations.

But her steps faltered when she saw the two security guards at the entrance of the studio. How was she going to get past them?

If she tried to talk her way through—told them she was Jacques's girlfriend—she would just seem like some crazed fan. In fact *all* her options would make her seem like that. And even if they did believe her, how would she verify it? She couldn't call Jacques, since she didn't have his number. The only thing she had of him was the memory of the heat their lips had sparked when they kissed. And she highly doubted *that* would get her through...

Her courage failing, she turned to leave.

'Lily?'

She turned back at the sound of her name, her heart beating so fast it might have been sprinting to win a race. Jacques stood just behind the security guards, a cup of coffee from the barista next to him in his hand. Her eyes greedily took him in, which in no way helped to slow down her heart-rate. She'd managed to underplay her attraction to him in her memories, convincing herself that she'd exaggerated his good looks. Even the pictures she'd seen on the internet hadn't swayed that conviction.

Now, though, she was forced to admit that she couldn't have exaggerated Jacques. She had never seen someone look *that* good in jeans and a T-shirt, though the black leather jacket escalated the look. Along with the mussed hair, she saw another reason for his bad-boy nickname...

But the confusion on his face distracted her.

'Hey, babe,' she said, and wondered if the 'babe' was too much. But when she saw the way his eyes widened, she decided to commit.

'I'm *so* sorry I'm late. Can I go in?' she said to the security guards, and after getting a brief nod of confirmation from Jacques they let her through. She walked up to him, steeled herself against the attraction, and gave him a quick kiss.

'I didn't think you were coming,' Jacques said, the slight shock in his eyes at her presence and at the kiss almost immediately cloaked.

'I changed my mind. I didn't want you to go through this alone.' She took the coffee from his hand and sipped. It was strong, without any milk, and she had to force herself not to spit it out. 'Do you think we could get another?'

Amusement crept into his eyes, and he nodded. A few moments later he was back, this time with a coffee that had milk in it—he'd taken note the night before, she thought—and two sachets of sugar.

'Let's swap, *honey.*'

The drawl he used made her lips twitch.

'I know how much you like hot coffee.'

She thanked him as they exchanged their coffees, and then forced herself not to react when he put an arm around her shoulders and the smell of his cologne filled her senses.

'You want to tell me what you're *really* doing here?' he said under his breath as they rounded the corner to where they shot the morning show.

'I'm paying back a debt,' she responded in the same tone.

'You didn't have to.'

They were in the main studio now, and she was briefly

distracted by the busyness of the set. She had never been on one before, and it was a little overwhelming.

She forced her attention back to Jacques, moving in front of him to make it look as if they were talking intimately. In reality, she just wanted to be out of his arms.

'I know, but this is important to you, right?' He gave her a wary nod and she continued, 'So let me do this. It's not like it's real. What's the harm?'

He studied her for a moment, and then he said, 'Thanks.'

'No problem.' When their gazes locked and something sparked she took a step back and looked at her watch. 'What time are you going on?'

'Seven-thirty.'

She nodded, stayed still for a moment. And then, when the silence grew a little awkward, she said, 'It wasn't until I got here that I realised I wouldn't be able to get in. So... thanks for getting yourself some coffee.'

She smiled thinly at him, and turned away before she could become ensnared by his magnetism.

'Mr Brookes? We're ready for you in Hair and Make-up.'

Lily watched as the young woman tucked her hair behind her ears when Jacques directed his attention to her.

'You can follow me,' the girl said quickly, and turned. But then she realised that Jacques wasn't following. 'Is there a problem?'

'No...not unless my girlfriend has to stay out here?'

The girl's eyes widened, and her black hair whipped from side to side as she looked at Lily and then back to Jacques again.

Though it was strange hearing Jacques call her that, something fluttered inside Lily at the thought. Something that was lined with pride, with satisfaction. With a thrill.

She tried to ignore it.

'Um…sure, you can both follow me.'

Decidedly less confident, the girl led them to a room that looked exactly like the rooms Lily had seen in movies. Jacques was settled into the chair in front of one of the mirrors, and she sat herself on the couch opposite the chair. The man who was doing Jacques's make-up was tall and lanky, with bright green spikes all over his head. There was barely an introduction—though she did learn the make-up artist's name was Earl—before he began putting foundation on Jacques's face, and she couldn't hide her smile.

'Something amusing you, Newman?'

She met his eyes in the mirror and found her smile broadening. 'Why would you think that, Jacques?'

'Maybe because of that ridiculous smile on your face?' He closed his eyes as he said it to allow Earl to put foundation around them.

'Fine—you caught me. But I was only thinking how wonderful it is that I don't have to do your make-up for you today. Thanks so much, Earl.'

Earl glanced over at her, his expression amused before he schooled it and got back to work.

'You're ruining my reputation, Lily,' Jacques growled, and Lily felt a thrill go up her spine.

She loved the banter, the easiness of the conversation they were sharing. It seemed that having a conversation with Jacques as his pretend girlfriend was a lot easier than having one as his friend. Although, to be fair, she could hardly call whatever she and Jacques shared a *friendship*. Perhaps 'alliance' was a better word.

'Are you going on with him?' Earl asked as he put some wax on his hand and vigorously rubbed it through Jacques's hair.

'No, no,' she said quickly. 'I'm just here for moral support.'

'And you're doing a great job, babe.'

She shot Jacques a look that she hoped told him he was laying it on a bit too thick, but Earl didn't seem to notice.

'You two are quite sweet. Not who I would have pictured you with, Bad-Boy Brookes, but maybe that's a *good* thing.'

Earl pulled at a few more strands of Jacques's hair, then nodded. 'You're as ready as I can make you. I'll go check how long it'll be before you have to go on. I'll be right back.'

He had barely walked out of the room before Lily spoke.

'That nickname has quite a ring to it.'

Jacques got out of the chair and came to sit next to her. He knew just as well as she did that he was too close, but since he seemed to want it that way Lily refused to indulge him by moving away. She just shifted her weight so that she was leaning to the other side.

'It's not one I'm proud of.'

'Nor should you be, if all the articles I read last night were true. Particularly the one that had the headline: *Bad-Boy Brookes's Year of Debauchery*.'

He turned towards her, the look in his eyes dangerous. 'I'm not sure what's more disturbing. The fact that you looked me up, or that you've mentioned that horrible headline.'

She flushed, but refused to look away.

'I had to know what—or who—I was agreeing to support. And I'm glad I did it. I now understand why you need me.' She paused, sensing the tone of the conversation would change if she continued talking about the things she'd learnt the night before. Unwilling to lose the easiness between them, she said, 'Besides, now I'm pre-pared if some woman tries to gouge my eyes out.'

'It's not *that* bad,' Jacques said, hoping his blasé attitude would mask his embarrassment.

'Yeah, you're right. I mean, the articles didn't make it sound bad *at all*,' she teased. 'Only about ninety per cent of them used the name "Bad-Boy Brookes" when refer-ring to your personal life—the other times they used it to refer to your willingness to do whatever it took to win a match. And it was also *only* used if you were seen par-tying with more than one woman over a single weekend. So you're right,' she said again. 'It really wasn't that bad.'

She stood, and Jacques's eyes moved over her. The jeans she wore highlighted the curves of her hips, and he stood quickly so that his eyes wouldn't be drawn to them any more. Not that it made him uncomfortable. He had always been the type of man who appreciated the fe-male body, and he wasn't afraid to show it. Except that Lily… Well, she wasn't the kind of girl who inspired the lust he was used to.

His eyes travelled over her body one more time, and he felt the result of it in his chest, his gut, and then his body. No, he thought again, not the type of lust he was used to at all…

'But then, of course, there was that photo shoot.'

Her eyes widened, her cheeks glowing with that won-derful colour he'd grown to like so much the night be-fore, and he grinned.

'Which one? My agent at the time had me do quite a few.'

'The underwear one,' she said in a high-pitched voice , and avoided his eyes.

His smile grew broader. She hadn't intended telling him she knew about that, he thought. So why had she?

'Yeah, that was at the peak of my career. One of my favourites. Body didn't croak then like it does now.'

'Are you fishing for compliments?'

She still wasn't looking at him, and he took a step closer.

'Only if you have them.'

'Somehow I think your ego can handle it if I don't offer them to you.'

'Maybe my ego, but not my heart. I need to hear my girlfriend compliment me. Just once.'

Her lips twitched, and she brought her eyes back to his. 'You *know* you look just as good now as you did then. Even though I haven't seen you in your underwear recently.'

'We could change that.'

The joking air between them immediately turned into a sizzle. He hadn't intended to say the words, but he hadn't been able to stop them when she'd spoken. And damned if he didn't mean them. He could see it as clearly now as he had during their kiss last night. The chemistry, the attraction… He wanted it more than he could say. It was almost as if he…*needed* it.

The thought jolted him, and he took a step back. Forced himself to take control again.

'Is it going to be a problem for you?' he finally said, to change the subject.

'What?'

Her voice was a little breathy—just as it had been after their kiss—and he had to steel himself against the desire.

'My dating history?'

She shook her head quickly, causing the curls she had tied up at the base of her skull to bounce.

'Of course not. It's not like we're *really* dating. I have no emotional investment in this whatsoever.'

Her face had gone blank with the words, and for the first time since he'd seen her that morning he wondered why she was there. *Was* she paying back a debt?

He searched her face for a clue that there was more, but saw nothing.

And that had his instincts screaming.

There was something else—something more—but he wouldn't know what until he asked her.

Before he could, they were interrupted.

'Mr Brookes, they want to go through your questions one last time.'

Earl had come back, and with one last look in Lily's direction, Jacques walked out through the door. He forced himself to focus on what he was there to do, and went through the questions he'd previously been emailed with the producers one last time.

He knew his PR firm had given the studio those questions, which was why he'd agreed to this appearance in the first place. It was also why neither Jade nor Riley was there yet. He was confident enough about his answers—answers they had coached him through—to have them there only for the interview itself.

He knew the questions off by heart by now: how was his business going? Particularly his international expansion? Did he have any news about his personal life?

He hadn't had much of an answer for that when they'd first spoken about it, but now he would casually mention his relationship with the lovely Lily Newman, and send her a loving look on camera, after which the host would go on to talk about his past rugby career.

Did he miss it? Did he regret the way it had ended?

Since he did, he would say so, and the sincerity of

his words—according to his PR firm—would be a great segue into his plans for buying his old club. Hopefully seeing him in a stable new relationship, doing a popular family show would boost his image enough that the club's sponsors wouldn't pull out if he bought it.

But he didn't want to spend any more time thinking about the hoops he had to jump through to get people's approval. When he was finished with the producers he walked out of the room—and paused when he saw Lily.

Her arms were folded over a loose red top, a patterned white and red scarf perfectly accessorising the effortless look. She looked a little out of place, he thought, and watched her brush one of her tight curls from her face. It didn't seem to matter that the curls were tied at the nape of her neck. They found a way to frame her face regardless.

She turned to him, smiled , and his heart slowed, nearly, *nearly* stopping. His lungs constricted and he felt as if he'd been kicked in the stomach.

It took a moment for him to recover. The smile on her face disappeared and she took a step forward, but he raised a hand and waved her away, not sure he could have spoken to her if she had come to face him.

What just happened? an inner voice asked, but he shook his head, unable—unwilling—to answer that question. He couldn't afford to. Not minutes before his interview.

And yet when he was called on to the set he had to actively *force* himself to focus on what he was about to do.

He dismissed the insecurity that threatened, reminding himself that he was good at playing games. He'd made an entire career of it, hadn't he?

He could pretend to have a girlfriend, and he could pretend to be someone the public wanted him to be. The way he played only mattered if he didn't score the try, he reminded himself, and no matter what happened he *would* be scoring this try. He *would* be the one to buy his club.

It had saved him from the anger he'd felt at home—had given him an outlet for the frustration he'd felt with his family. But when he'd realised his family wasn't worth it he'd let that anger control him. He'd let it ruin the thing that had always given him meaning. Purpose. But he would make up for it—for the mistakes he'd made before he'd known any better.

'Welcome back to *Latte Mornings*!' David, the host of the television show's sports segment, spoke the moment the producer gave the signal. 'Today's guest needs no introduction. He is one of our biggest rugby legends, who earned respect during his rugby career because of his phenomenal talent. Mr Jacques Brookes. Thanks for being here, Jacques.'

Game on.

'Thanks for having me.'

David went through the questions Jacques had prepared for, only going off-script to make a joke or to comment about something Jacques had said. He didn't once mention Jacques's suspension, which was a relief, since Jacques had worried about that before the interview. Now, though, Jacques was more concerned about the questions regarding his personal life. He wasn't sure he wanted to know why that was the case...

'So, Jacques, tell us about what's going on in your personal life? Are you still breaking hearts?'

David laughed, and for a moment Jacques wanted to wipe the smile off David's face. *Why* would the man remind people of one of the things Jacques wanted them to forget?

'Well, actually, I've been dating someone I think may

be the one.' He looked over at Lily, smiled, and watched as a pretty flush covered her cheeks.

He was still astounded at the fact that something that simple—that natural—could wind his insides with attraction.

David raised his eyebrows. 'That wasn't the answer I was expecting, but that's great. How long have you two been together?'

His mind blanked for a moment, and his accelerated heart-rate suddenly had very little to do with his attraction to Lily.

'Er...six months?' He glanced at Lily, and she nodded and smiled.

He felt steadier. He'd remembered that six months was how long she'd told Kyle they had been together, so the timing would be consistent in their world of pretence.

He realised that his answer had sounded unsure, so he laughed and looked back at David. 'I was just making sure I got it right.'

'Of course. We wouldn't want you to get into trouble.'

David smiled at the camera, and Jacques resisted the temptation to roll his eyes. He didn't care much for David's sometimes over-the-top media personality, but he knew it got the ratings, so he ignored it.

'Tell us a little more about your girlfriend...?'

David's eyebrows rose again, and Jacques answered, 'Lily.'

'Lily. What a beautiful name.'

David smiled over at Lily, and when Jacques's eyes followed he saw her return it with a shy smile of her own.

'Tell us more about her. What does she do for a living? How did you two meet?'

Jacques wasn't sure how long he sat there, his brain telling him that he should have anticipated this line of questioning *before* he'd mentioned her. Suddenly he realised he knew nothing about her except the little she'd offered—and that wasn't nearly enough to maintain the pretence.

Gears shifted in his head, and he forced steel into his gut as he tried to resist the decision his mind had already made. He *had* to do this, he thought. It was the only way he wouldn't destroy his plan with his faux pas.

'I'd love to tell you more about her, but actually I think this would be a great opportunity to introduce her to the public. Lily, could you come over here, please?'

CHAPTER SEVEN

PLEASE TELL ME I'm dreaming, Lily thought when Jacques called her over. It certainly seemed like one of those horrible dreams—going on a live television show that almost the entire South African population watched, unprepared. Especially with everyone on set looking at her expectantly.

She felt someone touch her back, and then the coat that had been in her hands was replaced with a microphone and her feet were moving, one at a time, until she was under bright lights and next to Jacques.

Up close, she could see something in his eyes that she couldn't place her finger on, but it didn't matter when she was pretty much living her worst nightmare.

'It's *lovely* to have you with us, Lily.'

David broke the silence, and his eyes told her he was as surprised—possibly even as annoyed—as she was at her being on camera.

'Thank you,' she said softly, and it took Jacques moving the hand that held the mike for her to realise she hadn't spoken into it. Feeling the heat in her face, she cleared her throat and repeated the words into the mike.

You have to stay calm, Lily, she told herself. *Be confident. This is your chance to do exactly what you came here for.*

'Am I in trouble?' Jacques asked, breaking the tension her little fumble had caused, and he casually put his arm around her waist, pulling her closer.

She couldn't deny that it calmed her—which she might have appreciated if *he* hadn't been the one to put her in this position in the first place.

'Definitely!' she answered through numb lips, and resisted looking around when she heard a chuckle go through the studio.

'Is this the first time he's done something like this, Lily?' David asked her, and she idly thought that he must have recovered from *his* shock.

'Yes. And the last time, too, if I have anything to say about it.'

Another chuckle went through the studio, and she felt herself relax slightly. She *would* survive this, she thought, and then she would take her time and enjoy killing her pretend boyfriend.

'We've been pretty private for the most part.'

Jacques spoke up, and she looked down at his smiling face. Noted that the smile was more apology than amusement.

'Which is why there hasn't been anything on social media? Or in the gossip columns, for that matter?' David asked, and drew Lily's attention to the fact that in the world that they currently lived in, relationships were all over social media. And, since Jacques was a public figure, there should have been *some* sign of their relationship somewhere.

Jacques's hand around her waist tightened, and she wondered whether he could tell that she was beginning to panic.

'I think when you have something this special you don't really want it to be in the public eye.'

It would have been a sufficient answer, but Lily found herself saying, 'And since I knew that Jacques was a public figure, and I'd heard about his…his past, I wanted to take it slow and keep it between us for as long as possible. I guess that will end after today.'

David smiled at her, and then sobered. 'And his past doesn't bother you?'

'We all have pasts, David. They make you the person you are. But they aren't the entirety of what defines you. Jacques is one of the best people I know. He works harder than anyone. His business ethic is impeccable. He does so much for the people he cares about, and his charity work—' which she'd read about only a few hours ago '—clearly shows that he doesn't need to know those people personally. If I had let whatever had happened in his past affect my answer the day he first asked me out I wouldn't ever have got to know the other sides of him.'

There was a long pause after she spoke, and she looked down at Jacques to see warmth in his eyes. Her cheeks grew hot again.

'Well,' David said eventually, 'it really does seem like you know a different Jacques to the man we're used to. But that might not be a *bad* thing.' David winked, and then continued, 'We have to go to an advertisement break now, but when we come back we'll talk to Jacques a little bit more about that past we've just touched on.'

When they were off the air Lily's legs began to shake. A delayed reaction, she thought, and was incredibly grateful that it hadn't happened while they were still live. Before she knew it Jacques's arms were around her, drawing her into a hug while keeping her steady, and she wondered if he had sensed her instability.

'Thank you,' he said.

His sincerity sent a shiver through her, and she folded

her arms around him so that their display of affection didn't look strange.

But she didn't respond, unsure of whether the mike he still had pinned to his top was on and if anyone would hear her say what she really wanted to. She drew back after a moment, her body prickling with awareness even though she wanted to kill him.

'All this attention has made me a little shaky. I think I'll wait in the make-up room, so you can't call me back on air again.'

Lily made sure that there was a lightness to the tone she used as she spoke, making it sound teasing and not like the warning it really was. But when she looked at Jacques she saw acknowledgement of her real intentions.

She took a deep breath and walked to the make-up room, aware that people were now watching her. She pretended not to notice, and breathed a sigh of relief when she saw that no one was in the room. She closed the door behind her, locked it, and then sank onto the nearest couch.

Her hands were shaking, she realised, and curled her fingers into her palms to stop them from making her seem like she wasn't calm. Even though no one was there, and even though no one would see her panic, she still felt the compulsion to pretend not to be vulnerable.

It was a defence mechanism she had developed to survive the bullying at school. And it was one that had kept her from seeing the person Kyle had really been. From seeing what their *relationship* had really been. Because if she could pretend everything was okay, even to herself, then surely it would be. It *had* to be.

But that had never been the case. For her younger self being overweight had meant bullying from her peers. And being an introvert who didn't know what she wanted for the longest time had meant her parents had never understood her. How could they when they were extro-verted, successful professionals who'd always known exactly what *they* wanted?

Her solution had been to pull back, to be someone no one would notice. That was why Kyle's attention had been so flattering. But then he'd tried to make her believe that who she was wasn't enough. And because it had been so easy to believe him, it had taken seeing him with another woman to realise that she *was* enough.

No, she thought, that wasn't true. It had taken see-ing him with another woman to make her realise that she *should* be enough, and that *she* needed to believe it.

She'd been doing a pretty good job of it, she thought, until she'd gone on live TV unprepared and all the inse-curities had come rushing back. Now everyone would be watching her, judging her. She looked down at the clothes she was wearing and started to shake again. They made her look even frumpier than she usually did, and the con-fidence she'd had when she'd chosen them washed away.

All the reasons she'd had for pretending to be Jacques's girlfriend didn't seem to matter any more. Especially when she realised she hadn't even had the chance to pro-mote her store when she'd been on air. All she had done was boost Jacques's ego even more.

But wasn't that the reason he'd brought her on the show in the first place?

She took a few more deep breaths to calm the anger pumping through her veins and walked to the door, avoid-ing the mirrors in the room so that she didn't have to be reminded—*again*—of how terrible she looked. When she opened the door Jacques was standing there, hand in the air, ready to knock. She plastered a smile on her face, not wanting the sacrifices she'd already made to be undone, and brushed a kiss on his cheek.

'How did the rest of the interview go?'

She forced cheer into her voice and slipped her hand into Jacques's, gently pulling him towards the exit. She assumed since he was there that his interview was done, and she didn't want to stay any longer and pretend she loved a man she wasn't even sure she *liked* at that moment.

'Great.'

Jacques walked with her, though she could sense the resistance in him. They didn't speak for the rest of the short walk to the exit, but Jacques stopped before they could walk past security.

'I have to stay and meet with Jade and Riley. The PR firm reps.'

She nodded, remembering their conversation last night—though it seemed a longer time ago—and brushed another kiss on his cheek as goodbye.

Hopefully for ever.

'Will I see you for dinner later?' he asked, threatening her hopes of never seeing him again. But then she realised that she *wasn't* really his girlfriend, and that this was his attempt at seeing the non-girlfriend Lily again.

And *that* she could refuse.

'I'm working late tonight, honey—remember? You can call me later.'

She waved at him and walked out of the studio, knowing full well he didn't have her number.

CHAPTER EIGHT

'YOU ARE SO lucky I had a deadline this afternoon or I would have called earlier.'

Lily briefly closed her eyes at Caitlyn's irate voice on the phone and locked the front door of the store. It was just before seven, and normally Lily would have taken the store's accounts outside and enjoyed the sound of the sea lapping against the pier and the laziness of Friday evening as she worked.

But today she'd exposed enough of herself to the public.

'I'm not sure I would use the word "lucky",' Lily replied, gathering her things. She just wanted to get home, soak in the bath and forget the mistakes she'd made that day.

'Oh, trust me, you're definitely lucky,' Caitlyn disagreed. 'But that luck has run out and now I want to know exactly what's going on with you and my future brother-in-law.'

'There isn't anything going on with me and Jacques.'

'Really?' Caitlyn demanded. 'Because I'm watching a clip of you defending his past right now. It currently has four hundred thousand views.'

'Cait,' she said wearily. 'Please. I can't deal with snippiness today.'

Lily wasn't surprised her friend had called, demanding answers. She'd already had to deal with her mother's hurt because Lily hadn't told her she was dating again. And by 'deal with' Lily meant 'lie to', since she couldn't possibly tell her mother it was all a charade. She'd managed to talk around it, but that conversation alone had taken up a substantial part of her energy.

But then she'd had to conjure up more for her work day. Because as soon as she'd walked in Terri and Cara, her staff, had demanded why *they* hadn't known. And then people had begun to recognise her, and the store had grown busier than it had ever been before.

'I'm sorry, Lil. I'm just worried about you. You barely know Jacques. Hell, *I* barely know him.'

'I know. I *know*,' Lily repeated more definitely. 'I'm sorry for snapping. It's just been a…a long, long day.'

'Don't apologise.'

Lily could almost see the hand her friend was waving her apology away with.

'At least not to me. Besides, I keep telling you that you don't have to say sorry for bringing the fire. I love it when you do.'

She paused, and Lily sensed her hesitation over the phone.

'Will you tell me what's going on now?'

Lily sighed, and quickly explained everything that had happened in the past twenty-four hours. The only thing she left out was the kiss—she didn't need Caitlyn to remind her of how much she had messed up, and that was the part she was most embarrassed by.

Caitlyn didn't say anything when Lily was done, and her heart pulsed. Her silence was out of character, which meant that Caitlyn wanted to say something she knew Lily wasn't going to like.

'Cait, just tell me what you're thinking.'

'I don't want to…' Caitlyn sighed. 'Fine. Look, I just want you to be careful, okay? I don't really know that much about Jacques, and even when I pressed Nathan about him last night he wouldn't tell me any more than he already had. I just… Well, I don't think he's the person you should move on with. Especially not after Kyle.'

Lily felt annoyance, but pushed it aside. She didn't know why she'd felt it in the first place.

'I'm not moving on with Jacques. This…it's pretend.'

'Are you sure?'

She waited a beat, and then answered, 'Yes.'

'And if you go on with this pretence you'll be fine with all the attention?'

Lily knew Caitlyn wouldn't be her best friend if she didn't know everything about her—well, mostly everything, she corrected, thinking how she'd never told Caitlyn about the way things had really ended with Kyle. But it irked her that her friend knew just where to hit.

'Actually, I take that back. You *have* to be fine with all the attention. You're in this now. You have to keep this illusion going until Jacques's deal is signed, and perhaps even after that.'

Though she desperately wished that Caitlyn was wrong, the feeling in the pit of her stomach told her that her friend was right. She'd known it the minute she'd got that call from her mother.

'I'll figure it out,' Lily breathed, and heard Caitlyn sigh again.

'Just be careful.'

'I will be. Thanks.'

There wasn't much to say after that, and when she'd said goodbye Lily locked up and made her way to the parking lot. She kept her jersey tight around her, despite the early summer heat, and kept her head down. She didn't want to be recognised. Not only because she'd had enough of it that day, but because she didn't know what to expect if one of Jacques's more devoted fans found her.

'Lily.'

Her first instinct was to grab for the pepper spray in her handbag. But though it took her a moment, she recognised the voice.

Jacques was leaning against the car that was parked next to hers. He'd changed his T-shirt from white to blue, abandoned the leather jacket. She felt a flash of disappointment, but shook it off.

'Hi…'

His deep voice rumbled, and her train of thought was derailed. And for that reason, she said, 'No.'

'No, what?'

'No, I'm not interested in whatever you're here to say.'

'Give me a chance.'

'No.'

She shook her head and walked past him to the driver's side of her car. A hand closed over her arm.

'Can we go somewhere private to discuss this, before we draw an audience?'

She knew he was right—that people would recognise him and then perhaps her sooner or later—but she couldn't bring herself to agree.

'We don't have anything to discuss. I did what you asked. Debt paid. Now we can move on.'

'Lily, please. I just need a few minutes. *Please.*'

Her heart softened, though her mind urged her to stay strong. For a minute she struggled between the two. But one look at his face had her sighing.

'My flat is twenty minutes away.'

'Mine is ten.'

She frowned. How had he always been that close to her and yet had only now managed to disrupt her life?

'Fine, I'll follow you.'

Lily was grateful for the short drive, since it didn't give her enough time to indulge her feelings about going to Jacques's flat. So she ignored the slight churn of panic in her belly. Ignored the rapid beat of anxiety in her chest. She'd experienced them often enough with Kyle to recognise the signs of anticipating an argument.

Instead she focused on her breathing. And as she parked her car in front of the sophisticated building in Jacques's secure estate she gave herself a pep talk. But she didn't speak in the elevator they took up to his flat. She didn't comment when he let her in and the first thing she saw was Table Mountain. When the first thing she heard was the crashing of waves.

Jacques put on lights, though it was only just beginning to grow dark then, and she got a better view of the glass that made up one side of his flat. Part of it was a sliding door, she realised when he opened it, and took a step closer. It looked out onto the beach, and the steps leading down from the balcony of the flat went directly to the sand. Having specifically rented her shop at the beachfront for its calmness, she appreciated Jacques's choice. Even though he probably didn't really live there, she thought, looking at the inside.

Grey laminate floors stretched across the open-plan room. Soft white furniture was arranged in the living room to face the spectacular view, with a light brown carpet and white dining room set just behind it. The kitchen was next to that, designed in white and grey to match the colour scheme of the entire flat. Lights beamed softly in the roof above the living room and kitchen, and an intricate fixture hung over the dining room table, illuminating it intimately.

It looked like the homes she'd seen in magazines—visually beautiful, glossy, and so very perfect. Except it didn't *feel* like a home. It didn't have the cosiness a home with a view like his should have.

'You're upset because of the interview today.'

It wasn't a question, and she braced herself for the inevitable.

'You already seem to know the answer to that.' She saw the confirmation on his face. 'Why am I here, Jacques? For you to point out the obvious?'

'No, I wanted to…to apologise.'

The way he said it made her think that wasn't the real reason she was there. She thought about Caitlyn's words, thought about her own reservations, and *knew* he didn't only want to apologise.

'I shouldn't have ambushed you this morning. I just… I didn't know what to do when they started asking questions about you.'

'*And* you thought having me on camera with you could only help your aim to buy the club.'

'Yes.'

He was watching her closely and she shifted.

'But that doesn't mean I don't feel bad about it.'

'*Do* you?'

'I do.'

'At least you're being honest.' And sincere, she thought, looking at his face.

'I'm sorry if I upset you.'

The words seemed more genuine now.

'I also wanted to thank you.'

He took a step forward, and instinct had her moving back. Then, because she didn't want it to seem as if she was afraid of being close to him—he *didn't* affect her that much, she assured herself—she stepped out onto the balcony.

The fresh air immediately eased some of the tension in her chest.

'Why do you want to thank me?' she asked when she heard him step out beside her.

'Our interview has gone viral.'

Ah, there it was. The real reason she was there.

'Yes, I've heard,' she said dryly. 'So you're saying thank you because we're all over social media?'

She could feel him watching her, and her heart hammered.

'Yes,' he answered, leaning against the railing as he'd done the night before at Nathan's. 'But more because the comments people have made are positive. My PR firm is very happy.' He paused. 'People really like you, Lily. And because of that they're starting to really like *me* again, too.'

She almost laughed. 'I'm glad it's working out for you.'

'You don't believe that people like you?'

'It doesn't matter what I believe.' But he was right. 'You got what you wanted.'

Jacques pushed himself up, his face revealing no emotion. 'Why don't you just say what you really want to say, Lily? Say what you mean.'

She looked at him. 'You used me.'

'*You* were the one who showed up at the studio today.' His voice was low. 'I didn't ask you to. In fact I'm pretty sure I remember telling you that you weren't the right person for it.'

His words sent a jolt through her.

'I know that. And I realise now that it was a mistake.' She forced herself to calm the anxiety pumping through her at the confrontation, told herself she was doing the right thing.

'But I showed up there because I chose to—which means I actually had a say. You took that away from me when you called me on to *live television* without checking with me first.'

A flash of regret crossed his face, but Lily refused to be swayed by it. She might as well say everything she needed to now.

'I would have never agreed to that if you'd asked me, and in my book that means you used me.'

The regret was gone from his face now, replaced by a stormy expression that she might have been wary of if she hadn't expected it.

But instead of the fire she knew he was capable of, he simply said, 'You knew what this would entail when you agreed to do it.'

She waited for more, but there was nothing. She shook her head.

'Why can't you just say that you shouldn't have done it? And then you can apologise sincerely—not because what you did *upset* me, but because you did it at all.'

He still didn't reply.

'I know the real reason you wanted to talk is because you need me,' she said. 'And because I'm already in two minds about helping you, it would probably be best if you stop with the silent treatment.'

CHAPTER NINE

THERE WAS A part of him that appreciated her temper. It was so different from the insecurity he could sense just beneath the surface, and the honesty was refreshing. But a bigger part of him was disturbed that Lily's words were describing his father.

Again.

From the moment he'd met her he'd been treating Lily as his father had treated his mother. Manipulating her, using her. But, unlike his mother, Lily had called him out on it both times. She wasn't as similar to the woman who'd raised him as he'd thought, Jacques realised. But did that matter when *he* was acting like his father? Someone he'd fought all his life *not* to become?

'I'm sorry I used you.'

'Thank you,' she answered softly, and he had to take a moment to compose himself. To protect himself against the emotions—the memories—he'd always managed to keep far, far away from his daily life.

Until he'd met Lily.

'So, will you help me now?' he asked when he was sure he had control of himself again.

'If we're being honest, I really don't want to.'

She looked at him, and his heart ached at the vulnerability he saw on her face.

'So I apologised for nothing?'

'No, you apologised because you want to be a decent human being.' She shot him a look that had him smiling and shook her head. 'You were kidding. Okay, well… A sense of humour.'

She shook her head again, and looked out to the beach.

'When you get over your surprise, how about you tell me what's going on?'

'I told you—I made a mistake this morning. And now I realise how big.'

'Because people are recognising you?'

'Yes, but more than that, too.'

She angled her shoulders so that he couldn't see her face. Again, his heart pulsed for her.

'My parents called this morning. They wanted to know why I hadn't told them we were dating.'

She turned back to him now, and his heart's reaction became harder to ignore.

'What did you say to them?' he asked, to distract himself.

'I lied.' She shrugged. 'What *could* I tell them? That I was pretending to be your girlfriend for a business deal? They would be so disappointed in me. And I've disappointed them enough.'

The words to ask how were at the tip of his tongue, but he stopped himself. He didn't want to become more invested in this woman. Not if he could help it.

'We're in this now, aren't we?' She looked up at him. 'We have to keep this going until the deal's done. Until people lose interest.'

Since it was exactly what he'd wanted, he thought he should confirm it to her with excitement. But instead, he found himself saying softly, 'Yeah, we do.'

She crossed her arms, sucking in her bottom lip in

such a defeated way that he couldn't help it when his words came tumbling out.

'Why did you do it? I'm not talking about the reason you already gave me.' He brushed off the explanation he knew she had ready. 'Sure, maybe you *did* come through this morning because you wanted to thank me or pay off a debt. But that wasn't the only reason.'

She tightened her arms around herself, and he knew he'd been right.

'You're *invested* in this somehow.'

Her face paled, but barely so. If he hadn't been so enthralled by the colour of her skin, by the features of her face that were so effortlessly breathtaking, he wouldn't have noticed.

Stop.

'No, I'm not.'

'Yes, you are.'

'If there *was* another reason, Jacques, why would I share it with you?'

She had straightened her spine, and he felt satisfaction pour through him. *This* Lily he could handle.

'So there *is* another reason?'

'Oh, for goodness' sake.' She threw her hands up, and then put them on her hips. 'If I tell you, you'll just use it as leverage to force me to keep the game going.'

Guilt burned in his stomach, but *that* he could easily ignore.

'You were the one who said that we have to go through with this. And telling me might remind you why you decided to do it in the first place. It might even give you the motivation you seem to need.'

Her eyes fluttered up to his, and he felt a punch in his gut at the emotion there. At the fire that sparked between them for the briefest moment.

Her hands fell from her sides—defeat, he thought—and her expression softened. And something gleamed in her eyes that made the voice in his head which was so concerned about his feelings when it came to Lily shout all the louder.

'What do you see out there?' she asked, gesturing to the beach.

He frowned. 'People?'

'Exactly. It's a Friday evening. People are going home from work after a hard week. They come to the beach to relax, enjoy a cocktail. Maybe read a book and unwind. And yet here *I* am with you.'

It took him a moment, but he got there.

'Your shop...?'

'Should be open—yes. I should be using the opportunity. Capitalising on it.' She paused. 'I used to. For a few months. But then keeping the store open at night took more money than I had.'

He waited for the rest, though he'd begun to put two and two together.

'I *was* at the studio this morning because I owed you. But I was also there because of that.'

She looked at him with a quiet strength he wondered if she knew she had.

'I've put more into this place than you could possibly imagine. I've sacrificed so much.'

She took a deep breath.

'My store is failing, Jacques,' she said in a voice that broke, and the expression on her face told him she thought *she* was failing, too. 'I'm barely staying afloat being open during the day. If I don't get more customers I won't be able to afford to pay the rent, or the electricity bill, or the rates. Not to mention pay my two staff members and the millions of other things small business owners need to pay.'

She shook her head, looked him in the eye, and he saw the fatigue. But then she straightened her shoulders again.

'So I thought if you mentioned my name, my occupation, it would drive more people into the store during the day, which might let me pay for keeping the store opening during the evening. I thought pretending to be your girlfriend would help my business.'

'So you were using *me*, too?'

'No!' she said sharply. 'I didn't trick you into doing anything you didn't want to. *You* were the one who wanted me there, and I saw how that might benefit the place I love so much. But I would never have done what you did to me.'

He knew he shouldn't have said those words the moment they'd left his lips, but he hadn't been able to help it. And now he wondered why he couldn't just let it go. Why he couldn't admit he'd been wrong.

'You didn't tell me any of that before I did the interview. *You* didn't even mention it when you were on TV.'

'I know.' She sighed. 'I didn't think it through properly. If you hadn't gone to get coffee I would have probably realised that and gone home before I embarrassed myself. And then I was on TV and I couldn't think straight. It was like a nightmare come true.'

'But you managed to defend me so well that people are saying I'm lucky to have you.'

'That's why I was there.'

Suddenly he remembered how struck he'd been when he'd seen her just before the interview. And how much what she'd said during the interview had meant to him. There was something about Lily—about the two of them together—that took Jacques completely out of his comfort zone.

And into a zone that forced him to *feel*.

'I don't always make the best decisions.'

Her words dragged him out of his thoughts. 'I'm glad you made this one.'

'I don't know if I can say the same,' she admitted softly.

'Well, you made the decision.' He stepped closer to her. 'And you were more prepared than I was when you did. Reading up on me, however creepy, shows me your decision wasn't entirely rash.'

Her lips curved, and the tension in his shoulders slackened.

'The things you said…they really helped. No one has ever said something like that about me.' Her eyes fluttered up at him and he quickly added, 'Not in public, I mean.'

'Yeah, I figured that when people kept asking me, "Is Jacques really the way you said he was on TV?" Mostly girls with hearts in their eyes, but it's something.'

'So you had more people in your store today?'

She sighed, gave him a look that told him she knew what he was doing.

'Yes.'

'It can keep being like this, Lily.'

'Yes, I *know* if I pretend to be your girlfriend some more my store will be a lot busier,' she said flatly. 'I know I don't really have a choice, Jacques. You don't have to keep trying to convince me.'

'Thanks for the confirmation. But I thought… Well, I was thinking about more than that.'

He wasn't sure why he'd faltered when his idea was actually a good one.

'I can help you use the momentum of this publicity to get regular customers. I can help with your business plan, with the accounts—with pretty much everything your shop needs to stay successful when this is all over. I can even give you a loan—'

He broke off when she stepped back abruptly.

'I don't want your money, Jacques. You can't *pay* me to do what you want me to.'

CHAPTER TEN

'I'M NOT PAYING YOU,' Jacques answered with a frown. 'I'm just offering you a loan to help get you on your feet again.'

'And would you have offered me that loan if you didn't need my help?'

Her breathing was much too rapid, and she forced herself to inhale and exhale slowly.

'No, I suppose not. But—'

'Then don't do it now,' she snapped, and turned away from him so that he couldn't see the tears in her eyes.

She suddenly felt incredibly tired. The interview, the store, the public, and now this conversation... She'd told him things she hadn't intended to because—well, because he'd *listened*. Maybe he even cared.

But that was just an illusion, she thought, and *she* was the magician, weaving a world where she believed in things that didn't exist. Like someone who was genuinely interested in her worries, her cares.

And his offer of money... It reminded her entirely too much of the way her relationship with Kyle had ended. If she accepted money from Jacques, as she had from the Van der Rosses, all the regret she'd felt since then would have been a lie. She would have been lying to *herself*. It would make her just as bad as she already thought she was for taking that money in the first place…

'I'm sorry, Lily, I didn't mean to offend you.'

'No, *I'm* sorry. I shouldn't have…' She took a breath. 'It's just been…so lonely. Who'd have thought starting a store would be lonely?'

She'd meant it as a joke, and was horrified when her eyes burned. Because it *had* been lonely. And carrying the burden of the store's fate alone…

She couldn't turn to her parents—they'd just say *I told you so* and try to make her see where she'd gone wrong. Because in their minds *she* would be the one in the wrong.

As she always was.

When she had complained about being bullied at school they'd asked her what *she* had done. When she'd broken off her engagement they'd asked her what *she* had done.

There was constant disapproval from them. A constant expectation of failure. Especially when the things she wanted were so different from what *they* wanted.

'I don't want your money, Jacques. But I *will* accept your help with my business skills. I want you to train me, show me where I'm going wrong. But that's all.' She paused, watched his face for his agreement. When she saw it there she nodded in response.

'Is the money thing…? Is it because of Kyle?'

Her insides felt as if they'd been dipped into an ice bucket. 'What?'

'He had money. I thought maybe you didn't want to be reminded of it.'

The ice defrosted, but her body still shook.

'You're right. I don't want to be. I just want that part of my life to be over.'

He was quiet for a moment, and then he said, 'It's been bothering me for a while. You and him together.'

His face was clear while he spoke, but something in his eyes made her belly warm.

'I can't see it.'

'Because he's rich and handsome and successful and I'm just okay-looking with a struggling store?'

'Stop that,' he commanded. 'I don't want to hear you talk about yourself like that any more. And I sure as hell don't want to hear you make him sound like he's some kind of prize.'

She felt a flush stain her cheeks. 'I'm sorry.'

'And stop apologising. You have nothing to apologise for.'

He walked towards her, and her heart sped with each step he took.

'I'm going to say this once, because you need to hear it.'

He lifted her chin with a finger, forcing her to look into his eyes.

'You are the most…*captivating* woman I have ever met. Your hair makes me want to slide my fingers through it so I can see the curls bounce back.' He pulled at one, as if to illustrate his words. 'Sometimes when I look into your eyes I feel like you're looking through me. And that doesn't scare me—even though it absolutely should. And those lips…'

He brushed his thumb over them, making her tremble.

'They make me regret stopping last night. Every time I see them I want to taste them again, to check whether they're really as sweet as I remember.' He lifted his eyes to hers. 'Don't tell me you're "okay-looking" when you have that effect on me. When I have eyes, Lily.'

There was a pause while she tried to catch her breath.

'We have an audience.'

His fingers grazed her chin again, tightened slightly when she tried to turn her head to look at what—who— he was talking about.

'This won't look nearly as genuine if you check to see where the cameras are,' he murmured, tucking a curl behind her ear and moving so that there was no more space between them.

Any hope she had of catching her breath again disappeared. Not because of the cameras—though somewhere at the back of her mind she *was* worried about being photographed after a hard day's work. No, that didn't bother her as much when she was still recovering from the seduction of his words. From the proximity of his body.

The fresh, manly smell of his cologne filled her lungs. The easy way he touched her made her see only him, hear only him. She wanted to shake her head clear, to beg the logical part of her mind to take control again.

But all her senses were completely captivated by him.

His hand wrapped around her waist, lightly at first, and before she knew it she was pressed against his body.

'Is this what our arrangement is going to look like?' she managed to ask, and his eyes darkened.

'I really hope so…'

It was as if he had no control over his body, and his lips had touched hers before he had finished speaking.

She *did* taste as sweet as he remembered, and it made every regret he knew he'd have when he could think again worth it. He fought against the heat that demanded passion and slowly explored her mouth, relishing every feeling, every thrill that went through his body.

His hands made their way up over the back of her waist, loving how the curves of her body felt under his touch. Loving the quiver that it sent through Lily's body. His right hand moved further along, brushing the side of her breast and making them both shudder. The sane part of him—the one that reminded him they were being watched—was the only thing that kept his hand from lingering there, and it finally made its way to its intended destination.

He slid his hand through her curls and tilted her head to give him better access to her neck, pulling his lips from hers so that they could memorise the feel of her pulse against them. The moan that he heard in return made him abandon his resolve to take it slowly, and when he took her mouth this time their kiss was more passionate, more dangerous.

He would never have his fill of her, he thought, and his hands gripped her hips to pull her even tighter towards him.

The shock of desire his action brought made him break away, and he took a step back, fighting to control his body. And when that didn't entirely work he just wanted to control his lungs.

'You are...'

Lily looked rumpled and it made him feel better when he saw the way her chest heaved just as his did.

'Dangerous, Jacques. You make me...'

She didn't continue her sentence, but her words helped sober him from the drunkenness of passion.

'Feel?' he finished for her. 'I make you feel, don't I?'

Her shake of the head didn't matter when he knew it was the truth. She did the same thing to him.

'I'm sure we've given those watching more than enough to talk about,' she said, instead of answering him, looking at the small crowd that had gathered behind the fence around his property. 'How did they even know we were here?'

'We're standing on a balcony, Lily,' he replied dryly. 'And we were talking for the better part of an hour. It wouldn't take much for people on the very busy beach to notice us.'

'Okay, fine. Let's go back inside, then.'

They walked back into his flat, and he closed the door so their audience would lose interest.

And then he watched her gather herself, and found he was utterly taken by her.

By the simple green dress she wore that flared out at her waist. By the hair that was tied to the top of her head in a bun, curls spiralling out wherever they could manage it.

She didn't look like any other woman he knew, he thought. And *damn* but she drew him in like no other woman ever had.

'Would you like to have dinner with me?'

'No, no, no,' Lily said quickly. 'There is no part of me that wants to do that after that kiss.'

'It was just pretend, Lily. It wasn't real.'

'I'm not interested in trying to convince you that you're fooling yourself if you want to believe that. But I *will* say that we need to draw a line if I agree to go through with this.'

'I thought you'd already agreed?'

'I can change my mind.'

She watched him for a moment, and Jacques wondered how now, during the most important deal of his life, he'd found the only woman who stood up to him.

'Look, I'm not going to pretend like there isn't an attraction between us, because clearly...' She waved a hand between them and his lips curved. 'But I don't want to pursue it. And I don't want you to either.'

The seriousness of her tone faded the remnants of his smile, and for the first time he heard the plea in her voice.

'Those are my conditions,' she said after a pause, and when she looked at him his heart stuttered at the confirmation of her plea. And although there was a part of him that wanted to tell her he couldn't accept those conditions, he nodded.

'That's fair.'

'So you agree?' she asked, eyebrows raised. 'Anything that happens between us from now on is strictly business. We can't complicate things by letting pleasure cloud our judgement.'

He was surprised by how much he didn't want to agree with her, but he nodded.

'If that's what you want, yes, I agree.'

'It is what I want,' she confirmed, though her tone made him think she wasn't as convinced as she wanted to be. 'Then I will have dinner with you. Because you're not calling me on to live television again just because you don't know enough about me.'

'That's why I suggested it.'

At least it should have been.

'Could I just have a moment to freshen up?'

'Sure.'

He showed her to the bathroom, and then tried to gather his thoughts. He needed to focus on his task. It hadn't left his mind once in the few months that he'd been trying to secure the sale, and yet with Lily he constantly needed to remind himself of it.

It was just too easy to get caught up in getting to know her. In wondering how she could afford prime retail property with modern and expensive décor on Big Bay Beach in Cape Town when she didn't have the money to sustain her store. She must have got the initial money *somewhere*. And after her reaction to his offer of a loan he thought it had to be connected.

And then there was her plea to keep things professional. After the way she'd dodged his question about Kyle, Jacques knew he was the reason why she'd asked.

Maybe he would have reacted the same way if his fiancée had cheated on him. But he'd never had a relationship last long enough for him to know what being in one felt like. He'd never wanted to be responsible for another woman's feelings. He'd had a lifetime's worth growing up with his mother. It was just a bonus that avoiding relationships meant he never needed to worry about how much of his father he had in him. About whether he was as cold, as oblivious to his partner's feelings.

And since Lily now had him suspecting that there was a little *too* much of his father in him, it was for the best that he just focus on business. On the deal that would help him make peace with his past.

He'd made progress. The TV interview that morning had had an incredibly positive influence on his image. But he didn't know if it was enough. So he would spend more time with Lily, and then hopefully Jade and Riley would tell him his reputation had been restored and the sponsors had changed their minds.

And if they hadn't…

You'd marry her?

His gut turned at the thought, and the strength of his resistance stunned him. There was immediate panic because of it, and he forced himself to breathe. Told himself it was only because marrying her would go against what they'd agreed on. It had nothing to do with the fact that marrying her would definitely be manipulative, knowing what he knew now. Their attraction. Her vulnerability. The protectiveness she inspired in him...

He turned when he felt a hand on his back, his heart thudding at his thoughts.

'Are you ready?'

'Yeah,' he answered, and cleared his throat when he heard the rasp of his voice. 'There are still a few people outside, though, so maybe we should stay here. I'll pour some wine.'

He wasn't suggesting it because he needed to compose himself. And he wasn't heading to where he kept his alcohol because he needed it to help him do that.

If he needed to marry Lily, he would. It was business, after all. But because of their agreement he'd talk to her first. That was fair, wasn't it? And it wouldn't be manipulative then, would it?

It made him feel calmer, that decision—until a voice asked him what had changed. He hadn't liked it when Riley and Jade had suggested marriage, but he'd believed he would have done it if he'd had to. And definitely without reservations over *who* he was marrying.

So the question wasn't *what* had changed, but who had changed *him*.

And really, he thought as he looked at Lily, should he even bother answering that question?

CHAPTER ELEVEN

'YOUR FLAT IS LOVELY, by the way,' Lily said to break the tension.

Tension she'd thought had started to subside before she'd freshened up.

'Thank you. Though I don't know if I should believe you, based on your tone.'

Something in *his* tone told her something had changed. But she was determined to keep things civil between them, and she wasn't sure if she could if she asked him about it.

'It really is lovely,' she insisted, settling on the safe subject. 'It just doesn't feel like you live here.'

'Why not?'

'You don't have a table on your balcony,' she said, and her pulse picked up—just a little—at the attention he aimed at her. 'That would have been the first thing I would have done when I moved in. I would eat my breakfast there, my lunch... Actually, I'd probably use any opportunity I could to appreciate that view.'

'I can appreciate the view fine from here,' he responded in a low tone.

She turned, saw that he was looking at her, and blushed. 'We had an agreement.'

'We still have the agreement. But I don't think it would

do any harm to flirt.' He grinned, but something felt off. As if he was saying the words on autopilot.

'Maybe not for you,' she said, and then closed her eyes. She hadn't meant for that to come out.

She held her breath, waiting for him to respond, and then sighed when he just said, 'You're right, though, I don't live here.'

She turned back at the proximity of his voice, took the glass of wine he handed her.

'Where *do* you live, then?'

'Near the office. I spend more time there than at home anyway.'

'Because you have nothing to go home to?'

There was a pause. 'Maybe.'

He gestured for her to take a seat, and she did, nearly groaning when the couch enveloped her aching body. It reminded her that she should be at home, soaking in a bath and drinking a glass of wine *there* instead of with Jacques.

She realised then that he hadn't really answered her question. It *had* been a little invasive, she considered. But it had fallen so freely from her lips because it was true in her own case. When she was at home her mind had nothing else to do but think about how she had failed in her life. How her parents had been right…how she should have never thought she was good enough to run a successful store. How running a business required business acumen, not the creative mind *she* had.

And when it was done with that her mind would start on how she should have just left Kyle without a backward glance, instead of accepting money so that she felt as if she'd paid with her soul.

'Maybe we should start with something a little…

less…' she suggested when her thoughts made her chest tighten.

'I think that would be for the best,' he answered, and sipped from his wine glass. 'Tell me about your family.'

It was an innocent question, but she felt a wall go up around her heart. She had to tell him *something*, though.

'There's nothing out of the ordinary there,' she said slowly. 'My mom used to be a paediatrician. She's retired now, but she still helps out at the local hospital three days a week. My dad's a couple of years younger than her, so he's still working. He's an engineer.'

'What kind?'

She tilted her head, a smile tickling her lips that he'd thought to ask.

'Civil.'

He nodded. 'Siblings?'

'None. I'm the only child.'

He frowned. 'It doesn't sound like you're happy about that.'

She'd heard that, too. The slight dip in her voice that had tainted her words. But what could she tell him? That her parents, with their engineering and medical degrees and professional stability, had expected her to follow in their footsteps from a young age? That when she'd proved to be different from them they hadn't been able to adjust? That instead they'd just tried to apply to her the mould they were used to and hadn't seen how it had eroded her confidence, her self-worth?

'No,' she answered him. 'My parents have…' She stopped herself, and cleared her throat. 'It's nothing.'

A single raised eyebrow sent her heart jumping.

'It's something.' There was a pause. 'Lily?'

His tone was a mixture of forced patience and genuine curiosity, and she knew if she were talking about anything else it would have made her smile. Now, she chose her words carefully.

'They just…their expectations of me are a bit high.'

'Why?'

She lifted her eyes at the softness his voice had now, felt the warmth in his gaze right down to her toes.

'They're very…rigid. Things are straightforward for them. Simple. Do you want to be a doctor? Study for a medical degree. Engineer? Study engineering.' They were simple examples, but she saw that he understood what she meant. 'I'm not straightforward.'

'And they can't understand that.'

'No, they can't.'

'I understand not living up to your parents' expectations.'

She looked up to see Jacques staring out at the beach. When he looked back at her she once again saw that stormy expression in his eyes.

'But the more important question is whether you've lived up to your expectations of *yourself*?'

She'd never thought about it, she realised in surprise. *Had* she lived up to her own expectations? Did she even *have* expectations of herself? Her mind scrambled for an answer and she bit her lip. She had goals and dreams. Why were they so difficult to remember now?

Because they're so closely tied to other people's expectations of you.

She frowned. Was her store failing because her parents had expected it to so she did too? Did she believe that she could do better, that she could *be* better, because that was what Kyle had expected of her? What did the money she'd accepted from Kyle's family—the first decision she'd ever made for herself—say about her expectations of herself? What did it *make* her?

'Have *you*?' she asked, desperate when she looked at Jacques and realised he saw too much. 'Lived up to your own expectations?'

Though his expression gave nothing away, she saw the hand holding his glass of wine tighten, and she realised the answer was no.

It made her feel better—a little less vulnerable—and because it did she said, 'Fortunately no one will be asking us that question.'

She nodded at the relief she saw in his eyes.

'But they might expect you to know that my parents live about an hour away from here, in Langebaan. And they'll expect me to know about *your* family. I already know Nathan. How about you tell me about your parents? Other than their ridiculous expectations of you, of course.'

She'd said it lightly, but his face hardened, a light going out in it.

'Neither of my parents work. They have money—a lot of it—that my grandfather made in the mining business. They keep busy, of course, but they don't have jobs.'

'Oh,' she said slowly, processing this new information.

It reminded her that Nathan worked for the Van der Rosses not only because he was a good lawyer, but because he had the connections to get into the biggest law firm in the Western Cape. It made his humility, his good nature, so much more appealing.

'Where do they live?'

'Somerset West.'

'And since you live on the opposite side of Cape Town that puts a nice distance between you and your parents,' she said, and saw confirmation in his eyes before something else eclipsed it…guilt? Because she thought it was, she added, 'I'm not judging. It's the same with my parents.'

'Distance helps. You don't have to constantly be reminded of how you've fallen short.'

He understood, she thought.

'Not that it matters in my case, since I haven't seen them in seven years.'

'*Seven* years?' He nodded, but didn't meet her eyes. 'That's when…'

'When I destroyed my career?'

Now he looked at her. 'Yes.'

The admission was difficult for him, she saw, and felt a little relief at that. They were on the same page, then, sharing difficult things with each other. She still worried that she had told him too much. But it felt good finally to admit that she couldn't be what her parents wanted her to be. It felt good finally to talk to someone who understood. Caitlyn didn't, and since she was Lily's only friend there hadn't been any other options.

Now there was Jacques.

She didn't quite know how to feel about that. So she settled on something a little more familiar.

'So, how about we get to that dinner you promised me?'

Jacques's lips curved into a smile. It broke some of the tension he felt about his surprising admission. The tension that had started when he'd realised she was changing him.

And he'd only known her for two days.

'I usually have my housekeeper prepare meals for me when I know I'll be staying here,' he said, and took her wine glass from her as she tried to get out of the hole the couch had created for her body.

He'd bought the piece of furniture specifically because it had that ability, which felt like heaven after a tough rugby practice or match. But watching her struggle now gave him a new appreciation for it. Her cheeks were flushed as she tried to scoot her way to the edge of the seat. Though it helped to get her feet closer to the ground, it made her dress ride up, exposing her thighs.

A ball of fire dropped in his stomach, turning his amusement into something more serious. Something more dangerous. It rooted his feet to the ground even as it woke every nerve in his body. She hadn't noticed this new development, and the more she moved the higher the dress went.

Eventually she sighed and, without looking at him, lifted a hand for his assistance.

It took him a moment to move—to force his body to behave—and then he set their wine glasses on the table and quickly took her hand, pulling her up without paying attention to the force he used. Though it helped her out of the seat, it also made her lose her balance—and before he could totally comprehend what had happened she had fallen against his chest.

His arms went around her, steadying her, but when she looked up at him, the colour of her skin still tinged with pink, rational thought flew out of his mind. Their eyes met, and the heat that always simmered between them turned into a boil. His arms tightened, pulling her closer to his body. Her curves fitted perfectly there, he thought, and the air in his lungs thickened. Her eyes had widened, but she hadn't protested at their proximity. Instead her arms had wound around his neck, and those full lips of hers had parted.

He remembered their taste from that afternoon, when he'd kissed her for what he'd told her was the public's sake. But it had really been because he'd had to know whether the attraction, the pull he felt for her was real. And now that he knew it was—now that he could acknowledge that despite all his playboy-like dating years he'd never wanted another woman as intensely as he wanted Lily—he wondered how their kiss would be.

Whether now that they were in his flat, away from the public, their kiss would turn into something more. Something that would sate the nagging need he felt for her...

'Jacques!' She interrupted his thoughts in a hoarse voice. 'You...*we*...we promised.'

Somewhere at the back of his mind it bothered him that she'd had to remind him—*again*—of that promise, that agreement they'd made only a few moments earlier. It seemed vague, faded—just like the goal that had consumed his mind from the moment he'd learned the Shadows Rugby Club was for sale.

The realisation made him step back, put some distance between them.

But still his body yearned.

'I'm sorry.'

'Me, too,' she answered, and something in her voice—her eyes—made him wonder if she was apologising because they had stopped things before they got...*interesting*.

There was a long pause, and then he heard her release a shaky breath. The sound revved him into action. 'So. Food?'

'Yeah—what do you have?'

He forced his mind to focus and picked up his wine, downing it even as he wished for something stronger.

'I didn't tell my housekeeper I was coming,' he said, only then realising that he didn't have much to offer her.

'I think there's some lasagne left over from when I was here last week.'

'Did you invite me to stay here for dinner without having dinner to offer me?'

Embarrassment stirred beneath the desire he'd felt just a few moments earlier.

'Yes. But to be fair I wasn't exactly expecting this. I thought we'd go out.'

'Do you have any ingredients to make something?'

He walked to the kitchen, checked in cupboards that held only cutlery, crockery and the few items he needed to make coffee.

'I'm afraid not.'

She stared at him for a while, and then a smile crept onto her lips.

'What?' he asked, as his mouth twitched to mirror hers.

She shrugged. 'It's just nice to know you don't think things through sometimes either. You know—like the rest of us normal people.'

He smiled at her, but her words had scratched at a wound he'd thought he had buried a long time ago. He'd always wanted to be *normal*. Normal children had normal families. Normal families had fathers who cared about their sons and didn't brush them aside for something—anything—better.

He pulled the fridge open with enough force that the door swung from his hand, hitting the counter and then his arm. Since there was nothing in it there was no damage, but he had to close his eyes to control his anger. To control *his* damage.

'I was only teasing,' Lily said from behind him, and he turned, his heart softening when he saw the uncertain look on her face.

'I know. I was just thinking that I should have something for you other than this.'

He gestured to the fridge. It held only a half-empty bottle of orange juice. It was a lame excuse, and they both knew it, but Lily didn't call him on it. Instead she watched him, the look of uncertainty fading, leaving only a shadow of vulnerability on her face.

He could see that vulnerability every time he looked at her, he realised. It was the reason he hadn't wanted her to take part in his plan in the first place. And it was the reason she was the *best* person to take part in his plan. She was *real*—with real feelings, real emotions.

She had the same concerns he did—that she had fallen short of the expectations her parents had of her. And while he was sure that was because she hadn't had the courage to tell her parents to adjust those expectations, his concerns were a result of years and years of trying but never succeeding.

Once he'd realised nothing he did would ever mean anything to Dale Brookes—would ever make his father *love* him—he had stopped trying. But he hadn't given up on his mother until the night of the championship game. He hadn't been able to believe that after everything Dale had put her through—after everything she'd seen the man put him and Nathan through—she'd stayed with him after he'd promised her for the umpteenth time that he would change.

Not even the taunts his father had aimed at him after his mother had decided not to leave had given her a clue that he wouldn't *ever* change. And after that night—after the subsequent events that had ruined his career—he had cut ties with his parents. He'd put away those protective instincts he'd felt for his mother. Had vowed never to apply them to another woman.

Except Lily.

'How about that lasagne?'

She interrupted his thoughts and he frowned as he tried to remember what they were talking about.

'Let me check.' He checked the freezer, saw there was nothing in it, and closed it again. 'I'm sure there aren't any people outside any more. We should go out.'

'Because there's no food in your freezer?'

'Are you mocking my hosting abilities?'

'Who? Me?' She fluttered her eyelashes. 'I would *never* do that to my oh-so-gracious host.'

He eased with the banter. 'What do you feel like eating?'

'What's the closest place?'

He frowned. 'It doesn't have to be close. We can drive somewhere nice—'

'No.' She cleared her throat and pulled the jersey she still wore tightly around herself again. 'Let's just get something at the closest place.'

It took a moment for him to put all the pieces together.

'You don't *want* us to be seen in public?' When she looked away, he shook his head. 'Lily, that's not a realistic expectation for this whole plan. We're—'

'Just not tonight, okay?'

It was a plea that went straight to his heart.

'I've given people enough of me today. And I look fa—' She stopped, looked at him with uncertainty and then finished, 'I look frumpy in this dress.'

'No, you don't,' he said immediately. 'And you weren't going to say that.'

'What?'

But she'd walked into the living room, away from him, and he realised she knew exactly what he was talking about.

'Yesterday you said you were too heavy for me to lift you.' He was talking to himself mostly, but when he saw her face he knew his gut had been right. 'Lily, were you going to say *fat*?'

CHAPTER TWELVE

'No,' SHE ANSWERED QUICKLY. 'Of course not.'

'Why on earth would you think that?' he asked her, dismissing the obvious lie.

She wanted to be flattered by the incredulous tone he used, but her embarrassment was too much for her to think of anything else.

'We should probably get going.'

Please don't push, she thought, and while the minutes passed repeated the plea in her mind.

'There's a place we can walk to from here. It's secluded...intimate. Something only the residents around here know about.'

Relief pummelled the reply from her mouth. 'Yes, that sounds perfect.'

He nodded. 'We can go down there.' He gestured to the balcony stairs.

She followed him down the steps, through the gate he'd opened in the fence that no longer had to keep out a crowd. Her feet felt heavier with each stride. It didn't take long for her to realise the weight had nothing to do with the sand they were walking on, but guilt.

Guilt for avoiding his question. For lying to him. She didn't *want* to tell him, but she felt compelled to and she wasn't sure why. Though she wanted to ignore it, his silence made her feel as if he was pulling back. It sent waves of panic through her that soon took control of her tongue.

'I was overweight for a very long time.' Her insides shrivelled at the words, but she knew it was too late to stop. 'I lost some weight when I started university, and then a little more while I studied. It was hard.' She cleared her throat when her voice suddenly went hoarse. 'I've been struggling to keep it off since then.'

He didn't respond, but gripped her hand. The warmth from it spread through her body.

'You still feel like you're overweight?'

'I…' She took a deep breath and was grateful for the slight pressure from his hand. 'I'm not perfect. I'll never be a supermodel.'

'And in your mind that means you're fat?'

She flinched at the word, just as she had the first time he'd used it. But it was her own fault. She'd thought it first—had almost said it—and she couldn't shy away from it now because it offended her But it brought back such memories—hurtful ones that made her want to fade into the background.

Before she could respond, he stopped, and put a hand around her waist, pulling her in to his side.

'We're here.'

She'd been so lost in thought, so lost in the difficulty of their conversation, that she hadn't seen the beach torches that led to a small wooden deck. The deck seated four tables of two and four, then led into a beach cottage that had been renovated into a restaurant. Paraffin lamps lit the deck, lining the two steps that led up to it and the wooden banister that surrounded it.

Jacques's hand still held hers as they walked up the steps and she saw the beach-themed green and blue interior of the restaurant. A stocky young man greeted Jacques with enthusiasm, with recognition, and seated them at the only free table on the deck.

'This is… Wow, it's beautiful.' She looked out to where the moon lit the sea, and only then saw the small dance floor just beyond the deck. 'Do people actually *use* that?'

He shrugged. 'I've never actually been here to see that.'

'But you *have* been here before. With other women, of course, considering the waiter is now discussing you with his friend over there.'

She nodded her head to where the man was animatedly speaking to another waiter, gesturing in their direction.

'He might just be a fan of mine.'

'He might be,' she agreed. 'But since the other waiter just sent me a knowing glance I suspect I'm right.'

He smiled, but didn't meet her eyes. 'You are.'

Though she wasn't surprised, she *was* a little annoyed—too much for someone who supposedly didn't care about Jacques's past.

And then he said, 'But you're the first I've brought here at night.'

'And that's important because…?'

'Because night-time dates set the tone for the rest of the evening. This kind of place…it's intimate.'

Her heart pounded at the implication.

'And the waiter you pointed out just took a picture of us. He'll probably post it to all his social networks.'

That's more realistic than thinking he wants to be intimate with you, Lily.

'So "secluded" and "intimate" don't necessarily mean private?'

'We aren't supposed to be private, Lily,' he reminded

her. 'But I can ask him not to post it. To delete the picture, even. I doubt his boss would want him taking pictures of the restaurant's patrons anyway.'

'You'd do that? For me?'

He didn't meet her eyes. 'For both of us. We still have a month until the club's sale is finalised, and I think we've had enough exposure for today.'

But she knew he'd just given her that reason because he couldn't admit he *would have* done it for her. It had her insides glowing.

'It's fine—let him post it. What harm could it possibly do after all we've already done today?'

He nodded his thanks, and then called the waiter over to order wine.

It gave her time to think about why his words had warmed her so much. They shared an attraction, yes. And if she hadn't lived the kind of life she had perhaps that would mean something. But attraction didn't last. Reality would soon catch up with them—just as it had with her and Kyle. And Jacques would soon realise—just as Kyle had—that Lily simply wasn't enough.

She'd thought about it a lot after she'd broken off their engagement.

Lily knew she would have made Kyle a decent wife. She'd passed her degree—a Bachelor of *Arts*, much to her parents' chagrin—at one of the top universities in the country, so she'd have been able to engage with his peers without embarrassing him. She had lost weight, so she'd looked fine, she supposed, but not good enough that she'd threaten any of the supermodel wives of the business acquaintances Kyle would have to charm. And she had been easily manipulated—which had probably been a huge part of her appeal. Easily bullied.

Lily would have done almost anything Kyle had asked because—well, because he'd asked her.

She could remember the times when she hadn't responded favourably and had had him pressuring her. She'd given in so quickly, terrified he would leave if she didn't. And yet despite all that Lily had clearly still lacked *something*. And that something had been significant enough that Kyle had turned to another woman to get it.

No, she thought again. Jacques's interest in her wouldn't last for very long. Not once he found out she wasn't anything more than a prop in his charade.

But she could enjoy the present. She could enjoy the fact that she was in a restaurant—a beautiful one she would never have discovered otherwise—with a man she liked. And, being in the present, Lily didn't have to think about the context that word 'liked' was being used.

'You're perfect, you know,' he said when the waiter had left, so sincerely that she regretted that he wouldn't want her soon. 'Your body, your weight… You don't have to worry about it.'

'Thank you,' she said softly. And then, because the way he was looking at her gave her gooseflesh, she continued, 'Like I said, I've lost a lot of weight. Now I try to keep what I eat appropriate, so that I don't gain it again.'

'That isn't the only thing you do.' Jacques's voice was low. 'You wear clothes you think hide your body. And even then you pull at them so they don't cling where they aren't supposed to.'

He paused when the waiter arrived to pour their wine. As soon as he was gone, Jacques continued.

'You worry about what people think about the way you look. So much so that you put a jersey on during a warm evening just in case someone sees you. Am I right?'

Her vocal cords wouldn't work. Not that there were any words for her to say after Jacques's little speech. It stunned her—shook her—that he was so perceptive. That he'd seen things she hadn't paid much attention to. She cringed that she hadn't been able to hide them. Felt the mortification balling in her stomach coated by anger.

'The judgement in your voice… Is that because you think I shouldn't care what people think?'

His brow furrowed. 'I wasn't *judging* you, Lily. But I do think you could worry a little less about it.'

'Because that's worked so well for *you*?'

It was a low blow—one she'd made deliberately, out of anger. But when she saw him recoil she immediately felt ashamed.

'I'm sorry. I shouldn't have said that.'

'But you were right.'

He shrugged, and she could almost see the weight that lay heavy on his shoulders. It made her feel even worse.

'No, *you* were right. I… I said that because I *know* you're right. And yet somehow… Well, some scars just don't go away.'

'Kyle?'

Again his perceptiveness was disturbing.

'Yes. But he was in a long line of others.'

'Then *why* did you date him, Lily?'

Because his tone was pleading with her, and because he was asking her for the second time—third, if she counted the night they'd met—she told him.

'He was interested in me. After years of no one wanting me, of feeling like I wasn't enough at home or at school, this successful, attractive man wanted *me*. So I ignored all the signs that told me he was just like the people who had bullied me in my childhood. It took catching him cheating to finally open my eyes.'

She didn't blame him for the silence that followed. But that didn't help her feel less exposed.

'I didn't realise…'

She lifted her glass to her lips, saw that her hands were shaking. 'Why would you?'

'I never liked him.'

He said it in a gruff voice, and it made her smile.

'You have good instincts.'

'And you blame yourself for *not* having them?'

Her fingers curled around the stem of the wine glass. 'No, I don't. My gut knew all along that he wasn't the right person for me. I just didn't listen.'

Because she'd already told him too much, she told herself there was no point in holding back now.

'I blame myself for believing that I couldn't do better.'

'But you know now that you can.'

It was a statement that told her he wouldn't accept any other.

'Yes.'

'Lily, you have to *mean* it.'

'I *do* mean it.'

'No, you don't. You may believe it in part, but something's keeping you from believing it fully.'

She felt a door slam shut in her heart.

'Let's order.'

CHAPTER THIRTEEN

It took Jacques a moment to realise he'd been shut out. Another to deal with the rush of emotions that realisation brought. The anger was there, and the frustration. As was the curiosity. But the feeling that was strongest was the desire to make her *believe*. She didn't have to be defined by people's opinions. By one decision.

You're trying to convince yourself.

He shook it off. He didn't need to indulge thoughts that came from nowhere. But he *did* need to say something—this *one* thing—so that he wouldn't have to think about it over and over that night when they'd parted.

He waited for her to order, knowing she would use that as an excuse if he didn't, and placed his own. When the waiter had left, he said, 'You're a strong woman, Lily. Even if you don't believe it right now, some day you will and I'll have told you first.'

He'd wanted to reach out, to lay a hand over hers, but the look on her face had his hand sticking to his thigh. Her eyes were glossed with emotions that he felt in his own chest, her face a picture he didn't think he would ever be able to forget.

There was surprise, yes. But there was also hope. Pleasure, too. All because he had seen something in her that he now realised had been whittled away after years of being bullied.

What he wouldn't have given to see that look on his mother's face just once...

'Thank you.'

He nodded, unable to find words when his mind, his heart, were in turmoil.

'So, the flat...' She cleared her throat. 'Why did you buy it if you don't spend enough time there to have more than half a bottle of orange juice in your fridge?'

Grateful for the change in topic, he answered, 'I bought it after my first big rugby pay-cheque. The club is based down the road from here. It made sense to live close by. I could walk to and from the daily practices, and I was able to leave my car behind when we had away matches.'

'But you don't spend much time there now. So why do you still have the flat?'

'Because...because it reminds me of the happiest times of my life.'

There was another beat of silence, and then Lily said, 'That's why you want the club, too? Because it represents something good in your life?'

'Are we going to spend the whole evening talking about things that make us uncomfortable?'

He reached for his wine, drank it in one gulp. When he set it down he saw that she was watching him. She gave him a small, comforting smile.

'Seems like we can't get away from it.'

'We could if we just stopped now. If we talked about something innocuous like the weather.'

'It *is* a lovely evening,' she agreed, lifting her wine in a mock toast.

He smiled, then sobered. 'What do you want to know?'

His own words would have surprised him if he hadn't felt the shift that was happening between them. And, though he'd resisted it from the moment he'd first felt it, it still seemed to have power over him.

It still seemed to compel him.

'I want to know what really happened the night of that game,' she said, as he had known she would.

'I got into a fight, got a red card—my team lost and I got suspended.' It sounded crass, but it was the only way he could tell her.

'I know. I read all that in the papers. What I want to know is *why*?' she said softly. 'It's clear how much that time in your life meant to you. How much it *still* means to you. What could have happened to make you give it up?'

He took a deep breath, opened his mouth, and then shook his head.

He tried again. 'I told you my grandfather was in the mining business?'

She nodded.

'That was my mother's father. He spent years building his business, and the family name grew with it. By the time he retired he was a millionaire, with his name appearing on every rich or most successful list in South Africa.'

He paused and ran a hand through his hair.

'It meant people knew the family name—who they were. Here and overseas, since my grandfather had started trading abroad. If you aren't careful, having that kind of money and power tends to make people take advantage.' Another pause. 'My mother wasn't careful.'

He stopped, tension tight in every part of his body. He didn't look at her. He didn't want to see the empathy he knew would be there.

'She was an only child—my grandmother died during

childbirth—and my grandfather sent her overseas to live with his sister while she went to school.'

He took another breath.

'She got pregnant with me there. My grandfather was furious. She'd just finished school. With his connections, my mother would have had the world at her feet.'

He lifted his eyes to hers.

'He made it clear that she couldn't come back here. Not when she was unmarried and pregnant.'

She nodded, making him see she was familiar with the inflexible values of past generations.

'My mother decided to get married to spare my grandfather the embarrassment. It wasn't too bad for her, considering how much she loved my father. He just didn't love *her*.'

Anger still heated his blood at the thought.

'But he loved her money. There's no proof that he planned the whole thing, but I *know* he did.'

He could almost taste the bitterness on his tongue.

'We moved back to SA and my grandfather died a few years later. My mom had just fallen pregnant with Nathan, but my father's lack of interest in us become clear when my grandfather was no longer around. He didn't have to pretend to be a family man any more. My mother had inherited most of the money—the rest was in a trust fund for us—but since they were married her money was his, too.'

He shook his head when he realised he was saying too much.

'You didn't ask to know all this.'

'No,' she agreed. 'But since you've told me there must be a reason.'

He nodded, and tried to build up his nerve to tell her the rest.

'I watched my father treat my mother—and us—poorly for most of my life. I tried to get her to leave him, but she was clinging so hard to the memory of the man he had been when he was wooing her—when he was pretending to be someone he wasn't—that she wouldn't. Until she found out he'd been lying to her about the money he was spending. She could take his uninterest and harsh words, but lying about money was too much for her.'

He shook his head, still not quite believing that *that* had been more important to her than her children's well-being.

'I got her to consider making him leave, and on the night of the championship we packed his bags. We were kicking him out. But when he found out it didn't take long for his charm to soften my mother's defences. A few words, compliments, promises, and she took him back. Not even my begging was enough to make her reconsider.'

He felt Lily's hand over his, and looked down to see it was covering his clenched fist. He forced himself to uncurl it and took a deep breath. He wasn't done yet.

'He turned on me that night. Said things I don't want to remember but can't forget. No matter how much I try.'

He took another breath as the memories flew through his mind.

Failure. Disappointment. Useless.

'I wasn't fighting the opposing team that night, Lily...'

There was a beat of silence before she said what he couldn't bring himself to.

'You were fighting your father.'

Lily's heart broke when he nodded, and she entwined her fingers with his, squeezing. But the moment was interrupted when the waiter brought their food, and she pulled her hand away, grateful for the break in the tension.

A small wave of guilt flowed through her when she looked at the burger in front of her, but since it was accompanied by a salad—and she hadn't eaten since lunch—she figured it was okay.

'Why did you never go back?'

'It was too late. I got suspended for three years—the maximum for what I did. Even if a team had wanted me, being out the game that long meant I wouldn't have had the same skills.'

'I'm sorry.'

He shrugged. 'It doesn't matter now.'

'But it *does*,' she said, wondering why he was pretending it didn't after everything he'd told her. 'Isn't that why you're doing this? Because of how much it means to you?'

She could see he was considering it, so she gave him time and dug into her meal. The burger was juicy, soft, and for the first time in a long time she found that she was enjoying a meal without feeling guilty.

'It does matter,' he said as she bit into a piece of lettuce. 'Because that loss—my red card—set the Shadows back years. In the past seven years they haven't made it to another championship. They lost their chance at playing in an international league because of me. If I buy the club I can change that. I *will* change that.'

'Yes, you will,' she said, seeing the determination in his eyes.

But it made her worry about what her part in his plan would cost her.

'Knowing what you know about my past...' She cleared her throat. Reached for her wine when the action didn't do anything to help the sudden dryness that was there. 'About my…insecurities, would you have still called me on to live TV today?'

A mixture of emotions played over his face. 'I… I don't know.'

There was a long pause.

'Why not?'

'Because there's a part of me that wants to protect you. But there's another part…'

'That wants this so badly you can't afford to protect me.'

It wasn't a question, but disappointment still soaked through her heart when there was another pause.

'I've wanted to prove myself for as long as I can remember. I've been working *seven years* for it.' He took a breath. 'I'll do everything I can to make sure you don't get hurt during this, Lily.'

She nodded, but couldn't reply.

'Lily, please.' Regret filled his voice. 'I'm sorry.'

'Don't apologise,' she answered, once the ache in her chest had subsided. 'You've been honest about your intentions. At least you have been this evening.' She exhaled shakily. 'I know this is important to you. And since you've been working so many years for it, it seems selfish to expect you to sacrifice it when you've only known me two days.'

'That's not…' He sighed. 'I don't know what to tell you, Lily. Except that it feels a hell of a lot longer than two days.'

He was struggling, she realised. It sent a shiver of hope through her. But then her mind offered her a look into the future.

She'd continue the charade with Jacques, convincing herself that he had feelings for her—developing feelings for *him*—deeper and more intense than anything she'd felt for Kyle. And then Jacques would get his club and he'd no longer need her.

And she would have to nurse the pain of the worst heartbreak of her life.

No, she thought, her heart aching even at the prospect of it. It was better to stop that hope from developing into something more dangerous now.

'Don't worry about me,' she said into the silence. 'I can look after myself.'

She could—and she would.

'You…you still want to do this? Even though—?'

'Yes,' she interrupted him. 'I'll still help you, Jacques.'

'Why?'

'Because it's time I faced my fears. And…because you need me to.'

She said nothing about reminding herself that there could be no hope for them.

'Have I told you how amazing you are?'

It was a line, she knew, but when she looked into his eyes she could almost believe it was true.

'Now, *darling*, there's no need for flattery. We're already dating, aren't we?'

CHAPTER FOURTEEN

AND SO THEY WERE.

For a month Lily dated Jacques Brookes. She went to charity events. Corporate events. She was wined and dined in Cape Town's most expensive restaurants. Showered with public displays of affection. Treated like royalty.

It was so similar to what she'd experienced with Kyle that she knew she should have pulled back. And if she'd *felt* anything similar to what she had when she'd been with Kyle maybe she would have.

But she didn't. Because there was one significant difference: Jacques.

The conversation they'd had the night they'd had dinner at the beach had clarified things. Lily knew what Jacques expected of her—knew why—and that made it easier to focus on their professional agreement. To lock away all those strange feelings that had been stirred the first two days they'd known each other.

She also couldn't deny that the attention their relationship got contributed to her focus. The pictures of them kissing on Jacques's balcony had been in the papers the day after they'd been taken. The photo of their 'intimate' dinner had been shared more than a hundred thousand times on social media after the waiter had posted it. Their interview snippet now had over a million views.

Their relationship had been sealed in public.

She didn't have time to think about personal feelings when she was dealing with all the interest in her. Customers now wanted pictures, signatures—though heaven only knew why they wanted them from *her*. She was just the girlfriend, not the actual celebrity.

When it became too much she reminded herself that she was facing her fears. She reminded herself that growth was never without pain. And she repeated that to herself when people began to poke into her past. When people who had never been her friends came forward to testify about how wonderful she'd been to them.

And, worst of all, when they discovered that she'd once been engaged to another of Cape Town's most eligible bachelors. The media had hounded her on that one, and more than one outlet had questioned the sincerity of her interest in Jacques.

Since that wasn't the kind of attention Jacques was hoping for, she'd expected him to step back. To tell her that he couldn't afford to be with someone who gave him negative press.

But he hadn't.

Instead he'd had his PR firm release a statement defending their relationship. He shut down any questions about her past when they were together, and held her tightly against him as he did so. As if he knew that she needed the comfort, the reassurance. And each time he would check that she was okay, Lily found that she was. Because although she would be shaking, Jacques would be holding her hand. Protecting her.

He'd said he would, and he'd kept his word.

And *that* was the real reason she was okay.

Jacques had even asked Jade from his PR firm to coach Lily when she could. So Lily knew what she shouldn't say in public—anything about Kyle except that they'd once been engaged and it hadn't worked out—and she knew what she should post on social media.

Those posts were strictly about Lily's, though, since Jade handled anything regarding Jacques and Lily's personal lives and their relationship. Still, Lily had seen an influx of 'likes' and 'follows' on the store's different accounts, and she knew that she would have to utilise them to keep momentum after her and Jacques's fake relationship ended.

That thought had caused a strange twinge in her heart lately, but she told herself it was because of the friendship she and Jacques had settled into. They'd got to know each other better over the dinners they'd shared, and Lily had got to see different sides of Jacques at different events. And sometimes after the events, Lily would watch his old games, his old interviews, and realise just how much he'd given up when his career had ended.

And then there were his business skills. Her respect for those grew whenever she saw him in action, and sky-rocketed with everything he taught her about her own business. He'd taken her accounts, her business plan, and each time she saw him he gave her notes and guidelines. He pointed out where she had been going wrong—sometimes shockingly so.

It embarrassed her, and told her she shouldn't have opened a store before she had known all that, but never once did he make her feel like a failure. Even when her own thoughts mocked her—even when she would have fully understood if he called her that—he didn't. He just patiently told her where she should adjust, and how she should do so.

With those adjustments, and the increased traffic the store was getting, things were going surprisingly well. Despite the attention her relationship with Kyle had got, and despite those who called their relationship fake for the sake of Jacques's interest in the Shadows—those who saw through them—Lily was okay. Going out with Jacques was a little less intimidating every time she did it, and the clothes Jade would send her for events didn't scandalise her quite as much any more. Lily even found herself amused that for every one of those who doubted their relationship, ten others praised her for taming Bad-Boy Brookes.

So she ignored her worries. She ignored how, every time she spoke to her parents, she was reminded of the backlash she needed to anticipate when things with Jacques ended. How, every time she spoke to Caitlyn, she had to repeat that she didn't feel anything for Jacques other than friendship.

Because she didn't.

The niggle left behind after each of those conversations didn't mean anything.

And friends did sometimes pitch up at their friend's flats at five-thirty in the morning, Lily told herself as she did just that.

She hadn't been able to sleep the night before, and she suspected it was because she and Jacques would be attending one last event together that night, before Jacques made his bid for the club.

It had made her anxious—more than it should have—because she didn't want to lose her friend, she assured herself. So she'd got up at four, got ready for the day, and grabbed two coffees on her way to Jacques's flat. If she couldn't sleep, she could at least enjoy the sunrise.

With a friend. Who happened to have the perfect view to do that from…

She used the key he'd given her when he'd told her she could stay at his place on the nights she was working late. Between that and the events they were attending she was sometimes too exhausted to make the twenty-minute trip home. And, since Jacques's was less than half that time away, she'd found herself taking him up on his offer. But only the nights she knew he wouldn't be there. Lily wasn't sure she could handle staying in the same flat with him yet.

Yet?

She shook her head, forcing the thought away as she walked down the passage to Jacques's room. He was hosting the charity event that evening—for a Shadows-affiliated charity—at a venue in Big Bay, and had been staying at his Blouberg flat for the past week to see to the final arrangements.

When she got to his room, she pushed the door open softly.

And her heart just melted, pushing thoughts of friendship far away.

He lay on his back, one hand cushioning his head, the other on his bare chest. Though she appreciated the strength of his body—the defined chest, the chiselled abs, the full biceps—the unarmed expression on his face undid her. There was no guarded expression now, no worry lines, no indication that he was thinking about a million other things while he spoke to her.

Now he was just a man who slept. It made her realise, not for the first time, how much his plan required from him. And, while she understood the importance, she worried that it was going to break him in the process.

When she felt her chest tighten and her heart burn—

when she felt that neat little box she'd put her un-friend-like feelings about Jacques into tearing open—she took a shaky breath and walked towards him. She took no more than two steps before he shifted, turning his head in her direction. And though she stilled completely at the movement he opened his eyes, the sides of them crinkling with his smile when he saw her, as though her appearance was perfectly normal.

'Hi,' he said huskily, and her skin turned to gooseflesh.

'Hi,' she responded, and heard the hoarseness of her own voice—felt the intensity of her attraction for him edged with something more—and cleared her throat.

'I'm sorry I woke you, but I want to show you something.'

Now he frowned, and turned his head to the clock next to him.

'Lil, are you *kidding* me? It's not even six a.m. yet.'

Warmth spread through her body at his use of the nickname.

'No, I'm serious. Come to the living room.'

She turned to leave, eager to escape the tension that was rife in her body. It subsided—but only slightly—when she stood on his balcony, with the sight of the waves crashing on the shore and the salty air filling her lungs.

She handed him a coffee when she felt him next to her, saw that he had pulled on the shirt she assumed he'd worn the night before but hadn't closed it all the way, and cleared her throat again.

Forcing herself to focus on why she was there, she nodded her head in the direction of the sun. They didn't speak as they watched the sun slowly rise.

Lily wished she could spend more time appreciating the beauty of where she lived instead of worrying. Instead of feeling the constant fear of failure. She watched as the yellow and orange colours spread over the ocean, bringing light and warmth. And when the sun rose high enough that a ray lit over them she sighed, heard Jacques sigh, too.

She felt him move closer to her and she turned, tilting her head back to look up at him.

If she thought her heart had melted when she'd seen him asleep, she had no words to describe what was happening to it now.

'Is it wrong for me to want to kiss you?' he asked, taking the coffee from her hand and setting it on the table he'd added after her suggestion.

One of many things he'd done for her that made her heart melt a little more each time.

'Are there cameras around?' she replied softly, forcing herself to think of what was *real*.

'No.'

'Then why do you want to kiss me?'

He took her face in his hands gently, and it began to feel very real.

'Because you're beautiful. You're kind. You're just… you're amazing.'

She opened her mouth to deny it, but his lips were on hers before she could.

And then she was lost in the romance of kissing a man entirely too handsome to be interested in her.

On his balcony.

With the sun rising behind her.

And then she was lost in the kiss.

His lips felt as if they belonged on hers as they nudged. As they teased. As they sent warmth flowing through her body. And then his tongue joined hers, and she tasted the mint from his toothpaste, the coffee on his lips. She felt the temperature rise, the warmth now heat.

She put her hands on his waist, under the shirt he'd thrown on, and let them skim the sides of him. Her body responded when she felt his shudder, and she closed the distance between them so that she could memorise how those muscles would feel against her. So that when he realised he didn't really want her she would remember what it had been like to feel him against her.

To feel what it was like to have a man like Jacques want her.

He angled her so that she was pressed against the balcony railing, moaning when her hands slid over his abs and back down again. She couldn't think, couldn't breathe with his hands on her. She moved one of her own hands from where it explored his body, so that she could slide it through his hair as she'd wanted to do from the first night they'd met.

And then, when she felt him press even closer to her, she moved that hand to the base of his neck, wanting to taste more, to give more. A deep sound came from his throat, and pleasure thrilled her body at the thought that *she* was the one making him moan. That *she* was the one he was so greedily taking in.

He pulled back, and with fire in his eyes rasped, 'Stop me. Stop me now before we do something neither of us will be able to forget.'

'I don't want to stop,' she said, before reason could kick in.

Desire flared in his eyes as he dipped his head down towards her again.

His mouth was just a breath away when they heard a crash.

Jacques immediately shoved her behind him, but she

moved to see what the sound was, her heart beating hard for an entirely different reason now. At first she saw only a short man with dark hair, sprawled across a bin on the beach. The cause of their interruption. Then, when he pushed himself up, she saw the camera around the man's neck.

'He's taking pictures of us...' she breathed, and shock planted her feet to the ground before she willed herself to move.

She was in the house in the seconds it took for Jacques to take the steps down to the beach. A moment later she heard another crash that she wasn't entirely sure she wanted to know the cause of. She wrapped her jersey tightly around herself, stuffing her hands under her armpits to stop them shaking.

It was still strange to have someone take pictures of her. She was growing used to it at public events, but this kind—the kind that she couldn't prepare herself for, the kind that had photographers climbing fences to get their shot—still felt as if someone had told the world all her secrets.

And it succeeded in reminding her that real intimacy was out of the question for her and Jacques. She wasn't there to make memories she'd never forget. Memories that would probably haunt her for the rest of her life. She *had* to face reality, and that reality was that she was just a prop for Jacques. It made her wonder if he'd known about the camera. If he had kissed her *because* of it.

The hurt stunned her.

'Are you okay?' Jacques said when he walked into the house a few minutes later.

He slammed the doors shut, locked them, and pressed a button that tinted the clear glass.

'I'm... I'm fine.'

'Lily.' He took a step forward, and then stopped when she took one back. 'I took the memory card from his camera. He doesn't have any pictures of us.'

The words told her that he *hadn't* only been kissing her for the camera. And even if her mind still doubted it, her eyes saw that he held a small square memory card in his hand. She wanted to feel relief at that—should have—except that the fact that she'd doubted Jacques told her that she didn't quite trust him.

Was it because she knew those pictures would benefit him? Was that thought even fair? Jacques's actions over the past weeks had shown her that he was willing to protect her. That he was willing to risk losing publicity to do so. So why didn't she trust him?

Because the last man she'd trusted had hurt her, she thought.

And just as quickly she realised that she was scared the man she now loved would, too.

'I... I have to go. The shop...'

She couldn't say any more, too raw from the realisation.

'Okay...' Jacques replied slowly. 'Lil, can we just talk—?'

'No,' she said quickly.

The responding coolness in his eyes had her stuttering through an explanation.

'I'm... I'm already late. I have to go. I... I'm sorry.'

She didn't wait for him to speak. Instead she fiddled with the locks on the door and, when it opened, checked that there was no one else waiting to take her picture. When she was sure, she ran to her car.

She ran because more than anything else she wanted to stay.

And that terrified her.

CHAPTER FIFTEEN

I'll pick you up at seven.

THAT WAS IT. That was all Jacques's message had said. But it was seven now, and Lily had to stop herself from looking at the text message again to check whether she'd read it correctly. If she hadn't she would feel like an even bigger fool, standing there in her store—in front of its glass wall—in the scandalous dress Jade had sent her.

She and Jacques had decided—before the fiasco of that morning—to meet at her store, since the charity event's venue was around the corner from it. But as she looked down at the tight plunging neckline that pressed her breasts together, exposing more of them than the world had ever seen, she wondered if that had been a good idea. It seemed even worse when she considered the way the white dress hugged the curves of her body, barely brushing her knees and leaving nothing to the imagination.

Lily couldn't deny that the dress would draw attention to her and Jacques that night. And, while she had grown to be okay with Jade's other dress choices for that very reason, this one was the worst.

She smoothed at the non-existent creases, and then sighed. She was thinking about the dress because she didn't want to think about that morning. Just as she'd kept busy all day to avoid it. Lily was happy to brush her feelings under the carpet—maybe if she didn't pay attention to them they would go away.

Love doesn't just go away.

A rap on the door brought her from her thoughts—thankfully—and her throat dried when she saw Jacques. He was in a slim-cut navy blue suit, a white shirt open at the collar, his hair swept back in that untidy way she liked. His broad shoulders wore the stylish look effortlessly, his handsomely rugged features making him look so much more masculine—though she didn't know how that was possible.

Her body reminded her about the chance she'd missed with him, and she had to take a moment to compose herself before she opened the door for him.

'Hi,' she said, her knees going weak at the smell of his cologne.

'I'm sorry I'm late. Things were a bit busy today.'

His words were stilted. Clearly that morning wasn't going to be as easily forgotten as she'd hoped.

'That's fine.'

She turned away from him, letting him close the door behind him as she grabbed her handbag. When she looked at him again he was staring at her. Her face flushed.

'Jade was right.' His voice had softened. 'That dress does look amazing on you.'

'Thanks.'

She lifted a hand to her hair, and then brushed at her dress again.

'It's perfect,' he said. 'Lily, you're—'

He took a step forward and she moved back.

'Jacques, no.' She drew a breath. 'Please.'

'You're running.'

She lifted her eyes to his.

'From what? There's nothing to run from here,' she reminded him. *Herself.* 'We're just two people with an agreement, right?'

His eyes flashed. 'Where is this coming from? Things were fine—good, even—until—'

'Until this morning, when we kissed and almost did something to make things a little too real for the both of us?'

She could see that he hadn't expected her to verbalise it, but panic didn't give her a choice. And when he didn't answer her dread took its place, followed by something else that had her eyes burning.

'Let's just go,' she said, when she'd composed herself. 'It doesn't seem like we have anything to talk about anyway.'

She was pushing him away. And for the life of him he couldn't understand why.

Or why it bothered him so damn much.

Jacques grabbed two flutes of champagne from the nearest waiter as he walked into the venue where his charity event was being held. The room had a stunning three-hundred-and-sixty-degree view of the beach and the city through its glass walls—save for the end of the room that held the foyer. Still, it was a design unique to that hotel, which was precisely why he had chosen it.

He handed Lily a glass, and she smiled her thanks. But it wasn't her real smile. Over the past month he'd grown accustomed to the pretend smile she gave to photographers, to the public. He'd seen the smile she reserved only for people she cared about. The one where the skin around her eyes crinkled just a little. He'd seen it because in their private moments she'd aimed it at him.

The fact that she wasn't aiming it at him any more set him on edge. And that edge was quick to turn into anger. Because anger was easier than the longing he felt after their kiss that morning. Or the disappointment at her reaction to it.

Lily shifted next to him, reminding him of where he was, and he realised that she was uncomfortable. Public events weren't enjoyable for her, and unlike him, she wasn't accustomed to pretence.

The things he knew about her past made him realise there was more to it than that, of course, and though he'd already said it that night he repeated, 'You don't have to worry about how you look, Lily. You're gorgeous.'

She gave him an annoyed look.

'You *have* to say that, since your people sent me this ridiculous dress.'

His eyes moved over the white dress that clung to her body, desire trembling through his own.

'I approve of it.'

'Yes, you would. Your plan is more important than my insecurities, after all'

His focus on his plan had been dwindling because of her, so he said, 'That's not fair. You know it isn't.'

Vulnerability settled in her eyes. 'Maybe not. But it should be.'

'Jacques?'

He turned at the voice that interrupted his reply, and forced himself to greet Jade and Riley civilly.

'We're the first to get here,' he said, though it was through clenched teeth. 'I don't think I need to work the party just yet.'

'You *always* need to work the party,' Jade answered, and there was something in her voice that put his back up.

'What's going on?'

'I...er—' Jade glanced at Lily, and then back at Jacques. 'Actually, do you mind if I borrow Lily for a moment?'

His eyebrows rose, but he answered, 'Sure.'

Jade gave him a quick smile, and then hooked an arm in Lily's. Her height put her head barely at Lily's shoulders, making them a strange couple. He watched until they'd disappeared through the doors that led to the foyer and the bathrooms, and then turned back to Riley.

'What was that about?'

'She was trying to get Lily away from you,' Riley answered, and shifted his weight between his feet. 'We got news today that some of the sponsors still aren't convinced. About twenty per cent of them—the ones who aren't coming this evening—aren't prepared to stay on.'

'So?' he asked, refusing to let the panic settle in his chest. 'That's twenty per cent. We have the majority on our side.'

'They're the twenty per cent who contribute sixty per cent of the club's sponsorship.'

Riley named names, and Jacques swore under his breath. He knew exactly who they were—knew the club would take a huge knock if they pulled out.

'So what do we do?' he asked flatly.

'Well, we did some digging, and we think we can get some of them over to our side. They're family companies, and maybe if they see you as a family man...'

It took Jacques a moment to realise what Riley was saying.

'You want me to propose?'

Riley nodded. 'That was always our original suggestion. Of course we didn't anticipate all the good Lily would do to your reputation. People genuinely *like* her. Maybe if we had a bit more time...'

He trailed off, watched Jacques closely. And who could blame him? Jacques thought. He hadn't been open to that suggestion when they'd first made it. *And now you are?* an inner voice questioned, but he shook his head, refusing to dwell on it. Or on the panic about a possible marriage—even a fake one—that had his head spinning.

'How would I even *do* that? I mean, there's no time to arrange a proper proposal…'

Jacques stopped when Riley handed him a small blue box.

'You got a *ring*?' Jacques narrowed his eyes, his heart speeding up. 'How long have you two been planning this?'

'We only got the news today. But we thought tonight would be the perfect opportunity.'

The box felt heavier than anything he'd ever carried, and the weight of it sat on his chest. He stuffed it into his pocket, but that did no good either. He could still feel it there, throbbing against his thigh.

He had to talk to Lily about it. He couldn't do this to her after everything they'd shared. She didn't deserve—

His thoughts halted when he saw Kyle walk into the room.

'What's *he* doing here?' Jacques growled, and Riley shifted next to him.

'I… I don't know.'

'You and Jade *arranged* this event, Riley. How the hell don't you know?'

Anger had him clenching his fists as his eyes flitted between the space where he'd last seen Lily and Kyle.

'He must have bought someone else's ticket. His name wasn't on the guest list.'

'You'd better hope that's true.' Jacques turned to Riley.

'Because if I find out this was a scheme to get more money for this event...'

'It isn't,' Riley said quickly. 'We wouldn't do that.'

'I know that if this event is a success it's more likely that the club will come to me,' he said in a low voice. 'And that your firm will get a bonus for helping me secure it...'

'I promise, Jacques. This wasn't us.'

Though his colour was pale, Riley's voice was firm. It told Jacques he was telling the truth.

'I need to find Lily. Excuse me.'

'There's one more thing, Jacques.'

He was already on his way to find Lily, but he turned back impatiently.

'What is it, Riley? I don't have the luxury of time, here.'

His eyes were searching the room for Kyle, but with Riley's single sentence everything in Jacques's body froze.

'Nathan called us a few hours ago to let us know he'll be bringing your father as his plus one.'

CHAPTER SIXTEEN

'WHAT ARE THE chances of us meeting like this?'

Lily thought she was imagining his voice at first. She'd escaped from where Jade had been introducing her to guests in the foyer to the bathrooms. But on her way there, she'd realised it wouldn't have given her the privacy she'd hoped for and had headed to the conference room instead.

But now she turned and saw Kyle, and realised two things. One, he must have followed her, and two, his voice hadn't been her imagination.

'I think the chances were always going to be pretty high, since you must have seen me come in here.'

'I see you've worked on that confidence problem since I last saw you.'

Warning coated his tone, but Lily braced herself against the inevitable fear. And, though it wasn't easy, she found she could do it.

'Why are you here?'

'To see you.' He took a step closer and her breath almost caught. 'To remind you of your place.'

'Don't you have someone else to remind now?'

The bravado was a farce, but it was her only defence.

'I don't have to remind Michelle of her place. She knows exactly what I need from her.'

'I still don't understand,' she said a little desperately. 'Why are you here?'

She wanted him to get to the point. Because the sooner he did, the sooner she would be able to escape.

'I've seen pictures of you and Jacques together,' Kyle spat. 'You're disgracing yourself. And making *me* look bad.'

'That's not true.'

'You were *my* fiancée, Lily. And everyone knows that now. So start acting like someone worthy of being associated with my name.'

'No one cares about me and you, Kyle,' she said, unable to help herself. 'All they're interested in is Jacques. If I need to act appropriately for the sake of anyone's name it would be Jacques's and not yours.'

There was a pulse of silence, and then Kyle closed the space between them. Instinct had her moving back, every brave part of her fading into the fear that had her heart in her throat. A part of her mind was telling her she could simply escape the event if Kyle bruised her, another was formulating the apology she would have to give to Jacques if someone saw her leave.

But she didn't have time to think about it any further. The door opened and in a few quick movements Jacques was in front of Kyle.

'You should leave. Before I remind you of what my fist feels like.'

Lily didn't think she'd ever heard anything sound as menacing. And, considering the look on Kyle's face, she didn't think he had either.

'She's after your money. Just like she was after mine.'

The air in her lungs quite simply froze. But Jacques didn't respond to Kyle's words. Instead he said, 'I'm going to say this one more time, and then I'm going to act on it. And, no, I *don't* care if people speculate about it when they see you leave with a bloody face.'

Jacques sent Kyle a hard look.

'They're all aware of my reputation.' There was a short pause, and then Jacques repeated, 'Leave—before I make you leave.'

Kyle didn't stay any longer to tempt fate, and when he was gone Lily's knees went weak. In one quick movement Jacques's arms were around her, steadying her.

'It's okay,' he said softly. 'He's gone. And he won't be back.'

'How do you know?'

'Because I told you I would protect you. And that means making sure Kyle never gets to you again.'

At his words, she rested her head on his chest and for a brief moment closed her eyes. She wished they could stay like that, away from the realities of the world. But she knew they couldn't. Not when Kyle's presence had reminded her of something she'd managed to avoid thinking about in the past month. Not when she knew Jacques would ask her about it.

She took a step back, asked a question to delay the inevitable. 'How did you know where we were?'

'I saw him arrive, and then I got distracted.' A shadow passed over his face. 'When I couldn't find him again— or you—I began to look for you. And then I found you.'

'Thank you.'

'What was he talking to you about?'

She turned her back towards him, needing the time to compose herself. She told herself she needed to do this—not because Jacques had asked, but because *she* needed to tell him.

She needed to do this for herself.

When she turned back, he was watching her with expressionless eyes.

'When I found Kyle cheating on me I was devastated. Not because I loved him—which I realised after a few weeks—but because it gave my insecurities more grounds than they'd had in a long time.'

Her voice faltered with those words, but she cleared her throat.

'And although Kyle begged me to go back to him— though he told me that he'd just made a mistake—I couldn't believe him. You don't make a mistake like that when you love someone.'

Get to the point, she told herself.

'When he realised I wasn't coming back he began to buy me things. And when I sent them back he told me I could have whatever I wanted. That it would be my "choice".'

Bitterness washed over her tongue.

'And when *that* didn't work he threatened me.'

She saw the fist Jacques made in response to her words, stifled the hope that flared inside her. It didn't mean anything.

'I told him if he didn't stop I would go to the police, and I was on the way there when his family's lawyer called me.' She took another breath—for courage. 'He wanted a meeting. He told me that the Van der Rosses wanted to "solve" the situation without involving the police, and that he would ensure Kyle stayed away from me. By then I just… I just wanted it all to go away.'

She still cursed her naiveté.

'So I agreed to the meeting, and when I got there Kyle's parents were there, too. They were never…fond of me. They thought I was beneath their son, that I was too dowdy, too…common.'

And she'd proved them right, she thought with a pang.

'Though they were perfectly nice to me. Told me they were so sorry about how everything had ended with me and Kyle.'

The rest came out as a rush. She couldn't bear the silence, the tension that pulsed from Jacques.

'And then they told me that they'd give me whatever I wanted if I signed a non-disclosure agreement. I just had to agree never to speak about Kyle's philandering ways—especially since his father was pitching to an important client with solid family values—and I could ask them for anything.'

'And so you asked for money?'

The flat tone broke her heart.

'I didn't. Not at first. I asked them why they thought it was necessary. Whether they really thought I would ruin their business because Kyle had broken my heart. And my self-confidence, which was really the case.'

She closed her eyes, and then shrugged.

'Though they only actually said something about "covering all their bases", I realised that it was because they didn't think much of me. The look on his mother's face... I knew what they thought of me, and it made me feel so...*worthless*.'

She bit her lip, tried to stop the tears from coming.

'So I asked for something that would make that feeling go away.'

She paused now, and looked at Jacques's face. His expression made her attempts not to cry useless, and she brushed at the tears.

'My store,' she continued when she'd cleared her throat, 'was something I'd been working on for years. I knew I would never have enough money to start it if I didn't take the money from them. So we agreed on an amount and I signed the document.'

So now he knew, she thought, and folded her arms as she waited for him to respond.

'That's why you didn't want to take the loan I offered you?'

'Yes.'

There was a pause.

'I have to propose to you.'

'What?'

He shoved his hands into his trouser pockets. 'I don't have the Shadows' most important sponsors on my side. Riley told me that they might be swayed if I propose to you.'

'And you…what? Want my permission?'

'Yes.' His tone was clipped. 'I didn't want to put you on the spot again.'

Her heart wanted to soften at his words. At the confirmation that things between them had changed. That *he'd* changed. But how could it when he couldn't even look her in the eye?

'I appreciate you asking me. And…and I know this is important to you. So of course I agree.'

'Thank you.'

He nodded and then turned away.

'Jacques, please. Say something. Anything. Tell me you're disappointed in me. That you can't stand it that I took money from them.'

He turned back. 'Is that how you feel about yourself?'

A sob escaped from her lips. *'Yes.'*

'Would you do it again?'

'I didn't even want to take a loan from *you*, Jacques. You know the answer to that.'

'Why not?'

'Because taking that money has stripped away my confidence, my self-worth.' She was purging herself now, she thought. 'Because I've belittled my success by taking it. Because the lack of success in the months before I met you eroded every belief I'd had that owning my shop would make me feel better. That it would make me feel like I was more than what other people thought me.'

It would have felt *so* good if she'd finally been able to make a success of something. If she'd finally been able to prove her parents wrong. The engagement had been the only thing they'd approved of in her life, and she'd disappointed them once again when she'd told them it had ended.

She hadn't told them Kyle had cheated on her. It wouldn't change the fact that they saw her as a failure. That she saw *herself* that way…

'Oh, here you are.'

Jade popped her head into the room, and her smile faltered as she looked from Lily to Jacques.

'I'm sorry, I've interrupted something…'

'What do you want, Jade?' Jacques asked tersely.

'I was actually checking to see if this room was free, not looking for you. Yet. But there *are* a few people…' She trailed off. 'I can stall them if you like?'

'No, that's fine,' Lily said. 'I'll go.'

She avoided Jacques's gaze as she walked out of the room, too embarrassed by her confession to look at him.

She spent a few minutes in the bathroom, composing herself and freshening up.

When she returned to the event she thought she could fake her way through trivial conversation. Until her eyes settled on Nathan and something inside her sagged with relief.

'It's nice to see a familiar face here.' She kissed him on the cheek.

'I know how you feel,' Nathan answered, but when he gave her a smile it seemed distracted. 'It's almost like old times.'

His eyes shifted over the room and she remembered that Caitlyn wasn't with him. That she wouldn't be for the rest of the night.

'I didn't think you would come without Cait. She told me she had a deadline for tomorrow morning.'

'I wasn't going to. But I changed my mind last minute.'

'Did you bring Kyle?'

'What?' Nathan's attention was now on her. 'Kyle's *here*?'

'He was.'

'Are you okay?'

'Yes,' she answered, and found that it was true. 'Your brother helped.'

And that was the reason she was okay.

'Is Kyle still alive?'

She smiled, though she could tell Nathan was only half-joking.

'He is. But he won't be bothering me again.' She was pretty sure of that.

There was a moment of silence and then Nathan closed his eyes. 'Lily, I didn't bring him, but I think he was here tonight because of me. I mentioned it to him earlier today. I'd just decided to come, and was telling him I couldn't work late on a case. I'm so sorry!'

'It's okay.' Her heart was beating at its normal rate again. 'It worked out in the end.'

And she needed to find the man who'd ensured that. They needed to talk.

'Will you excuse me, Nate? I have to find...'

Her voice stopped working when she saw a man walking towards them. Dark skin, dark hair peppered with white, a strong, muscular build. If it hadn't been for the fact that he was clearly years older Lily might have thought she was looking at Jacques. And then, when he stopped in front of them, she saw Nathan's face.

Her heart began to thrum uncomfortably in her chest.

'Dad,' Nathan said, confirming her suspicions. 'This is Lily. Caitlyn's best friend and—'

'Jacques's girlfriend.'

His deep voice held a hint of an accent—British, she thought—and it reminded her, again, of Jacques. But there was something beneath the tone that sounded off to her.

You're bringing your feelings for Jacques into this, an inner voice told her, but she shook it off. It was too complicated a thought to consider before introducing herself.

She smiled and offered a hand. 'Yes. It's lovely to meet you, Mr Brookes.'

'Please, call me Dale,' he said, and brought Lily's hand to his mouth.

A shimmer of discomfort went down her spine, but again she shook it off.

'Does Jacques know you two are here?' she asked pleasantly, directing her question at Nathan.

She saw something that might have been shame pass through his eyes—he clearly knew she was actually referring to whether Jacques knew his *father* was there—before he shook his head.

'I don't think so, no. I haven't seen him yet.'

Suddenly it made sense to Lily. Nathan had been looking for Jacques. To warn him? No, she thought. He could have called him to do that. This was some kind of…*ambush*, she thought, and anger simmered through her veins.

'I should probably find him, then,' she said, and heard the coldness in her stilted tones.

'Are you looking for me, my love?'

An arm snaked around her waist, pulling her closer until she was moulded to Jacques's body.

'Yes, I was.'

She brushed a piece of hair away from his face and he looked down at her, just as she'd intended. He smiled, but by now she knew when it wasn't genuine. Even if she hadn't been able to tell she would have known it by the hard glint in his eyes.

'Well, I'm here now.' He turned his head to the two men in front of him. 'And I see Nathan's introduced you to my father.'

There was a pause.

'Why are you here, *Dad*?' He said the word in a mocking tone.

'I heard you needed some help with your...*investment*.'

Dale had used the same tone as Jacques, and Lily felt Jacques's arm tighten around her.

'You told him that?' Jacques asked Nathan after a moment.

Lily saw Nathan's slight nod, saw the apologetic look in his eyes. It told her that maybe Nathan hadn't meant to ambush Jacques. Maybe he'd wanted a reconciliation. But that didn't seem to be the direction their conversation was going in.

'Well, I don't need your help. Haven't needed it in a very long time, if I recall.'

'Yes, the success of your rugby career tells me how *well* you're doing in your life.'

The muscles under Lily's hand hardened, coiled, as if she was touching an animal that was about to pounce.

'My rugby career may not have ended in the way I

had hoped for, but it made me into a much better man,' Jacques replied in a measured tone. 'I'm going to buy my club—without your help—and I'm going to turn it into something I never could have while I was just playing for it.'

Determination fortified every word, sending pride bursting through her body.

'Trying to convince me, son, or yourself?'

'That's the trouble with you, Dad. You never really got to know me,' Jacques said easily. 'If you had, you'd know I never say things unless I believe them. It's called *conviction*—though you wouldn't really be familiar with the word.'

His arm dropped from Lily's waist, and he took her hand instead.

'You'd also know that I no longer feel the need to convince you of anything.'

With those words, Jacques pulled at her hand and they walked away.

CHAPTER SEVENTEEN

THERE WAS NO time for him to process his thoughts. There hadn't been since Jade had interrupted his conversation with Lily. And now he had his feelings about Lily's revelation and seeing his father again swirling through his head—all before he needed to speak to the people who held his fate in their hands.

'Stop.'

Lily tugged at his hand, stopping him in a relatively empty corner of the room.

'I have my speech soon. And the proposal…'

She drew in a breath at his words, but shook her head and then angled him so that his back was to the crowd.

'I know. But you have to take a moment to breathe. Pretend you're stealing an intimate moment with the woman who's about to be your fiancée.'

She was right—he needed to breathe. He needed to deal with the rush of emotions that was making him feel nauseous *before* he spoke to the crowd.

Suddenly he became aware of the way his chest was heaving, and because he didn't want to be he focused on Lily. 'I heard the way you said "fiancée". It scares you.'

'Of course,' she answered breathily. 'Doesn't it scare you?'

'No.' *Yes.* 'It's not real.'

'Someone should tell my heart that,' she murmured. Her eyes widened and she quickly followed that with, 'It's beating so fast at the prospect.'

Focusing on her words—on the possibility of what they might mean—was helping to distract him. 'Mine is, too.'

'You don't have to say that to make me feel better.'

'I'm not.' And he realised he wasn't.

'I thought you weren't scared?'

'I'm not. But that doesn't mean I'm not nervous.'

As he said it he realised that there was more to his confession. That it coated something he didn't fully understand yet.

'I'm sorry for the way things turned out tonight,' she said.

'It's okay,' he answered, and looked down at her.

As he did so, he realised that he'd been avoiding it since she'd told him about accepting money from Kyle's family. His heart immediately softened—he worried that it had weakened—and he felt the disappointment that he'd felt at her words disappear.

That was why he'd avoided looking at her. Because though her confession should have made him doubt her—he had experience with people who thought money was the most important thing, after all—he didn't. He *couldn't*.

And he found himself feeling even more for her.

'Is it really okay?' She shook her head. 'Kyle pitches up here, and then your father. It's like the past is trying to make sure we remember it.'

She gave him a small smile.

'For what it's worth, I'm really proud of you. I was worried at first. I saw your face when you joined us. But then you *spoke* and I could tell it was just occurring to you. I was so proud.'

He felt as if her words had switched on a light in his body. It warmed him even as it pulsed in his chest, and he realised that the desire to hear those words from his father had driven him through most of his life. Even when he'd been convincing his mother to leave he'd still wanted to hear it.

And though he'd realised long ago that it wasn't going to happen he hadn't accepted it. Not until he'd heard Lily say it and felt that desire go free inside him.

'It looks like you're up,' Lily said, nodding her head to where Jade was trying to get Jacques's attention.

He gave Jade a quick nod, and then tried to formulate something to say to Lily. But he found he couldn't. His brain was a mess from the things he felt, and from those he thought he should feel but didn't.

So he focused on his responsibilities. They'd become too vague for his liking, and the urgency of the plan he had been so set on had faded into the background over the past month. But tonight would change that, he told himself a little desperately. He would put all the distractions aside and charm whoever he needed to.

Starting with that proposal.

'Thank you, Tom,' Jacques said, when the MC handed him the mike after his introduction. 'Let's all give Tom a hand. He's doing a terrific job, hosting this evening's proceedings.'

Applause rang out and Jacques's eyes moved over the crowd. His gaze settled on Nathan, who was standing alone on one side of the room, shoulders hunched. Though Jacques was still angry with him, he knew his brother had just wanted to help.

But, considering that Jacques no longer saw his father, he also knew that Nathan's attempt at reconciliation hadn't worked. Just as Jacques had always told him.

He went through the formalities, thanking everyone for attending and introducing the charity they were supporting that evening. While a representative for the charity said her thanks, Jacques's heart started beating faster. As he handed the woman a large cheque and posed for the required photos his lungs felt heavy. And when he finally held the mike in his hand to end his speech his entire body shook.

But he ignored all of it, and focused on the face of the woman he was about to fake propose to.

'I know many of you here remember me as the man who ended the Shadows' path to the internationals. The man who threw away his career in a fight that shouldn't have happened. It's shaped your opinion of me. And *that* has shaped my opinion of myself.'

His heart thudded for different reasons now.

'It has also driven me. Because I wanted to prove...'

He trailed off, thinking about how he'd wanted to prove that the public's opinion of him was wrong. How he'd wanted to prove his father wrong.

'I wanted to prove that I was more than the mistakes I'd made. That those mistakes didn't define me. That desire has allowed me to build a successful company. It's given me a perspective that's helped me support charities like the one we're here for this evening. But, most importantly, my journey in not letting the past define me has led me to my girlfriend, Lily.'

The first thing he saw when his eyes rested on her was that colour on her cheeks that had drawn him in the first time. The second was the smile she sent him. Though the uncertainty, the traces of fear, were visible to him, it was the sweetest, most encouraging smile he'd ever seen.

And the words that came from his mouth no longer seemed to be pretence.

'There have been times when I've focused so much on *wanting* to be a better person that I haven't actually *been* a better person. And she has helped me see that. Her calling me out on my bad behaviour has given me no choice but to learn from the past. Which is probably why you have all seen a better-behaving Brookes instead of Bad-Boy Brookes.'

He waited as a chuckle went through the crowd.

'But perhaps more importantly is the fact that she's *shown* me how to learn from my past.'

He thought about how she'd refused his money—taking it would certainly have been easier than the training she'd asked for instead—and about how it made sense now that he knew about Kyle.

'I wish you could see yourself the way I see you.'

He walked down the stairs towards Lily now, taking the microphone with him.

'You would be able to see your strength, your beauty.'

A path opened up as he walked towards her, and when he stopped in front of her he could see the hope shining through her uncertainty. It scared him, and something urged him to stop. But he couldn't. Not yet.

'And you'd know that you've exceeded any expectations I had of you or our relationship.'

He knew how much those words would mean to her, but when her hope shone even brighter it glossed all his feelings with a deep fear he couldn't understand.

'I can't imagine my life without you, Lily,' he said, almost automatically now, refusing to hear the truth of the words.

Instead he pulled out the box Riley had given him earlier and went down on one knee.

'Will you marry me?'

CHAPTER EIGHTEEN

IT WASN'T UNTIL that moment that Lily realised just how much she wanted him to be saying those words for real.

The desire for it shook her, but she didn't let it distract her. She breathed a 'yes' and applause erupted around them. Jacques smiled at her, but there was a storm in his eyes that made her heart hurt without her even knowing why.

He slid the ring onto her finger—a simple stunning solitaire—and pulled her into his arms. Heat pricked at her eyes when she felt the stiffness of his arms, the tightness of the muscles in them, but all the years she'd had of pretending to be okay when she wasn't helped her smile and accept the kiss he brushed on her lips.

The rest of the evening went by in a blur of congratulations and a tension that she knew she wasn't imagining. Not when she could sense Jacques pulling away from her. Not when she recognised it because she'd done the exact same thing herself earlier. And while a part of her wanted to hope that they were doing it for the same reason—that he was in love with her, too—Jacques's behaviour was edged with a coldness that warned her against hoping that.

The thought troubled her so much that she escaped the party as soon as she saw an opportunity to do so. Her opportunity came when Jade and Riley whisked Jacques away to speak to a sponsor they apparently needed on their side who'd arrived unexpectedly. The crowd had thinned by then, and no one seemed to notice as she slipped out of the hotel to the beach just beyond it.

When she was far enough away that no one would see her—when she was sure that she hadn't been followed—she closed her eyes and accepted the truth that she'd been running away from since that morning.

She was in love with Jacques Brookes.

Panic gripped her throat, and when she opened her mouth to breathe a sob escaped. She laid a hand on her throat, forced air into her lungs. Forced herself to think. Why was she afraid of falling for Jacques? Because she'd told herself that she needed to stay away from him? That she needed to love herself?

Perhaps, but she knew those resolutions had come from the Lily who'd been treated so poorly by her ex-fiancé. By the Lily who'd thought she deserved to be treated that way. Who had *expected* it because she didn't think she deserved more. But that Lily had slowly been whittled away. She'd been replaced with a Lily who hoped that she *did* deserve more. She'd been replaced with a Lily who had experienced what it was like to be treated well. Who had experienced a good relationship for the past month.

Yes, it had been a pretend relationship for the most part, but Lily thought that their *friendship* hadn't been pretend. The respect they'd shared, the way Jacques had treated her, the things he'd said to her, about her—those hadn't been pretend.

Or had they?

Didn't Jacques deserve more than her? Didn't he deserve someone who was proud of her body, of herself?

Someone with all the confidence that *she* struggled to muster? Someone who felt as if she were enough? Someone who could actually live up to his expectations?

Someone who could live up to her *own* expectations?

She was reminded of when Jacques had asked her about those expectations. She'd realised she didn't *have* expectations of herself—not her own. She only had those that had been invented by those around her.

But now she knew she wanted to be successful. For herself and not just to prove someone else wrong. She wanted to think more of herself. It would be a process, but at least now she believed that she deserved more than an emotionally abusive fiancé. She wanted someone who saw her as more than who *he* wanted her to be. She wanted someone who saw her for who she was.

She wanted Jacques.

And if she ignored her uncertainties—if she looked at the facts, at the evidence—she thought that he wanted her, too.

But he didn't want to.

'Lily? I've been looking all over for you.'

She turned to the man she loved. Saw the look on his face, saw the confirmation of her suspicions, and her heart broke.

'I'm sorry. I needed some air.'

The words sounded distant—as if she was pulling away again—and the door he'd hidden his feelings behind opened.

He slammed it shut.

'Did things go well with the sponsor?'

'I think so. They asked about my plans for the club.'

'Which is a *good* thing, right? It means they're considering your business aptitude and not your personal life.'

'Yeah, probably. But Jade and Riley think my personal life is the reason they were interested. They think the sponsors caught the proposal.'

'That was the plan, wasn't it?'

'Yes, it was.'

So why was he annoyed by her response? By her sudden aloofness?

'It's all there is, isn't it?' Jacques said through a clenched jaw. 'This plan of ours. This *agreement*.'

She tilted her head, and it stole his breath how much he wanted to tuck those curls behind her ear. How he wanted to pull her in and melt that coolness.

'Are you trying to bait me, Jacques?'

'What could I possibly achieve by doing that?'

'My temper? I could lash out at you and give you a reason to deny those feelings you've realised you had for me.'

'I don't… There are no…'

'No feelings?'

'No.'

She laughed. 'Of course. There were no feelings when we kissed this morning. Or when you said those things tonight. No, that kiss actually *was* for the camera. And tonight—that was just for the audience, right?'

'Now you're trying to bait *me*.'

'Is it working? Because I'd really *love* to talk to the man I've fallen in love with instead of whoever *you* are.'

It took him a minute to process what she'd said. Another to think up a response. 'How…? You can't…'

'I don't blame you for thinking that.' She folded her arms, looked out to the ocean. 'I've been trying to deny it since this morning, when I realised it.'

'Since this morning?' he repeated.

Now he knew why he'd felt her pulling away. She didn't like her feelings any more than he liked his.

Why did that upset him?

'We always knew about the attraction between us,' he said steadily.

'The *attraction*?' she scoffed. 'I *wish* this was just an attraction. That would make things *so* much easier.'

'What do you want from me, Lily?'

'I want you to admit that there's more between us than an "attraction". I want you to admit you feel something for me.'

That door he kept those feelings behind vibrated again, and he was having trouble keeping it shut.

'You don't want that, Lily. You're just confusing all of the…the show with real emotion.'

You're making up excuses for yourself.

'Don't do that.'

Her voice was measured, but he could hear the anger.

'Don't belittle my feelings. I've spent my life trying to convince myself that I have a right to them.'

'I wasn't trying—'

'Do you think I *wanted* to tell you the truth about my store? About Kyle? Do you think that I told you how it made me feel because we're *friends*? Because we're attracted to each other?' She shook her head. 'No one knew about that. And not just because of the papers I signed.'

'Then why did you tell me?'

'Because I thought you would understand. You know what it's like to think about your past with shame. This whole charade has been so that you could make up for it. I wanted your help with my store for the same reason.'

She drew a ragged breath.

'And I told you because I wanted you to know. To love me despite my mistakes.'

The door was flung open at her words, and he knew that he *did* love her. He knew that he'd known from the moment they'd kissed. That he'd had it confirmed while he'd been proposing.

But still he couldn't bring himself to say the words.

Instead he said, 'I meant it when I said you've shown me how to not let the past define me.' He exhaled. 'I don't judge you for accepting the money. I can't because…because I *do* understand it. The shame. The determination not to let a mistake define you.'

'But?'

'But…you've distracted me from it.'

'I've distracted you from what?'

'From my *plan*,' he said desperately. 'From showing the world that I'm more than my mistakes. Than my failures. Than the disappointment.'

'Showing the world or your father?'

He didn't respond. He couldn't. Because she was right.

'Seeing him tonight reminded you that you've been doing all of this for *him*, not the world. That all those things—mistakes, failures, disappointment—are things you're trying to convince *him* that you're not. And maybe even yourself.'

'Stop!' he said sharply, feeling her words piercing his heart.

'I understand it, Jacques.' She moved closer to him. 'I'm trying to convince myself that I'm not those things either. That *I'm* not a failure.'

'You're only a failure because *you* keep telling yourself that, Lily.'

The words were harsher than he'd intended, but he just wanted her to stop. To stop reminding him of the pain he'd managed to avoid for so long. He didn't listen to the voice telling him that it wasn't Lily, that it was seeing his father that had unlocked the pain. All he knew was that he *felt*—and *she* was making him feel.

He couldn't distinguish between the feelings. Not any more.

'You keep thinking about the things you've failed at. But have you looked at what you've *succeeded* at? You had problems with your weight, so you lost it. You had a relationship that you realised wasn't working for you, so you left. The shop you opened was struggling, so you found a way to make it work for you. Yes, you've failed. You've made mistakes. We *all* have. But we need to look at how we've dealt with the failure and mistakes. *That's* what defines us.'

There was silence after his little speech, and he realised his chest was heaving. He used the time to gain control of his breathing again—to gain control of *himself* again.

'Are you going to look back at this night and think it's a mistake, Jacques?' Her voice was soft. Deceptive. 'Because if you can't give me a reason to stay, to listen to the things you're saying, you might find something else to define yourself by.'

CHAPTER NINETEEN

LILY DIDN'T KNOW what she expected after her words. All she knew was that she didn't have to stay—not any more—if there was nothing to stay for.

But she knew she hadn't expected a kiss.

He was standing in front of her before she could register what was happening, and then he slid a hand behind her neck and pulled her in until his mouth found hers. Heat immediately flared at the touch, but the greed their kisses had held before had been replaced by emotion. She didn't know what it meant—didn't know if he was telling her he had feelings for her or if he was saying goodbye.

She pulled back. She didn't need any more memories of him if it was goodbye.

'I need you to *say* it, Jacques.'

'I... I can't.'

He rested his forehead on hers, but she stepped back, unable to stand being near him any more.

'Why not?'

She hated the heat that prickled in her eyes. Hated it even more that her heart softened as she saw the battle on his face. But she *had* learnt from her mistakes. And that meant she could no longer hope for things in a relationship that she would never get. She could no longer stay with someone who couldn't be honest with her. She deserved more.

So when he didn't answer she didn't make any excuses. She just cleared her throat and said, 'We'll have Jade leak a story that we've gone away to celebrate our engagement. Just for the two days before you make your bid for the club. I'll let Terri and Cara know, and they can take care of the store for me. And then you can make your bid, get your club, and people will see us less and less. An appropriate amount of time will go by and we'll announce our break-up.'

'Lily, please—'

'No, Jacques. I know better than anyone what you're willing to do when you really want something. And if that something was me, you'd be able to say so.'

It hurt, the truth of that realisation. But she needed to face it.

'It's the least I deserve after doing all this for you.'

Because she had to believe that, she walked away from him. She only stopped to slip her shoes back on in front of the hotel, and then climbed into the first taxi she saw. She kept her composure until she reached her flat. Until she stripped off that ridiculous dress, kicked off those ridiculous shoes and climbed into the shower.

And then she let the tears come.

They turned into heart-wrenching sobs too quickly, but they helped steady her. And when the water turned cold she *felt* steadier. She let the water wash the tears from her face and then focused on the rest of her body. When she was done, she made herself a cup of tea, gripping the mug for the warmth and comfort it provided.

She was proud of herself. There was an ache in her chest that grew more painful with each beat of her heart, but she was proud. From the moment she'd met Jacques she'd told herself she couldn't be interested in him—in anyone, really—until she knew her self-worth.

It was the only way she knew how to survive what she'd been through with Kyle.

How to ensure that it would never happen again.

She couldn't be treated the way Kyle had treated her again. She couldn't be manipulated as she'd been by his parents. She wanted to think of herself without shame, without disgust. And the only way she knew how to do that was to stand up for herself.

Jacques hadn't treated her the way Kyle had. And after that night at the beach he'd no longer manipulated her. But in her heart she knew that if she'd accepted the little that Jacques had offered her she would have been undermining her worth again. She wouldn't have been standing up for herself, or for the love she now believed she deserved.

So she was proud of herself.

Even when a voice taunted her that she'd failed at *this* too she stayed proud. And she banished those thoughts by remembering the way Jacques's face had glowed with something he didn't even know when he'd proposed.

It had made her almost believe he'd meant all those things he'd said to her. That she *had* been showing him how to learn from the past. That maybe her determination to do that *had* been an example to him. Even if she hadn't always succeeded, she'd tried. And wasn't that something?

And maybe she could believe that he thought she was strong—something she'd never thought of herself before. And that she was beautiful—something she'd never given herself a chance to believe before. But what had meant the most was what he'd said about her exceeding his expectations—something she'd never, ever experienced before.

She hadn't even cared that everybody had been look-ing at her. The only thing she'd seen was that look on Jacques's face…

She stilled.

She hadn't cared that everybody had been looking at her.

That was in such stark contrast to what she'd felt only a month ago at the television show. Then, she'd *hated* the thought of people looking at her in normal clothing. But tonight she hadn't cared that everybody had been look-ing at her in a tight dress. She hadn't been thinking about what anyone might have thought about how she looked in it. She hadn't cared about her weight.

It was a victory she'd never thought possible. A victory that she knew had come from the time she'd spent with Jacques. His easy acceptance of her, his compliments, the way he'd forced her to see herself as he did—even if it had been harsher than she would have liked, she thought as she remembered what he'd told her that night—it had all been part of the reason she was in love with him.

It was the reason she'd laid everything on the line and told him how she felt.

Though she'd thought them all gone, another tear fell down her cheek.

Had she given up the man who'd shown her how to love herself?

Were the reasons she had worth the sacrifice?

She didn't know. But when things had ended with Kyle she'd promised herself she would learn from the expe-rience. And she knew she had. But, as Jacques had told her, she needed to stop dwelling on the past. She needed to learn from it and move on.

She could no longer expect to fail. She could no lon-ger accept others' expectations of herself as her own. She

needed to stand firm in her confidence, in her newly discovered self-worth. She needed to stop letting her past
mistakes define her.

She would pay back the money, she told herself. It
didn't matter that it might take years. What mattered
was that paying it back would allow her to take back the
integrity she'd lost. What mattered was that she would
finally be able to appreciate her hard work, her success,
if she did.

What will you learn after Jacques? an inner voice asked.

Lily closed her eyes. What she'd learnt *during* her time
with Jacques was easy, she thought.

But all she had for after was a pain in her chest, mocking her for thinking she could move on to 'after' at all.

Jacques wondered if he would ever forget how it had felt
when Lily had walked away from him on the beach. How
it had felt to know he had feelings for her but being unable to say it.

It had been two days and he hadn't forgotten it.

Hell, not even the news that he'd got the club had banished the memory.

He'd given it time. He'd thought that maybe the mis-
ery of the past two days had just delayed the excitement,
the happiness. But it had been nearly five hours now, and
the satisfaction of getting everything he'd always wanted
was still missing.

Because it was only what you thought you wanted.

He pushed up from the table he'd put on his balcony
after Lily had suggested it to him. It was true. He'd *believed* he'd wanted the club. He'd believed it so much
that he'd resisted his feelings for Lily because she'd distracted him from it. Because she'd distracted him from

the plan that had driven him for *seven years*: to ensure that he wasn't defined by his failures, by his mistakes.

Or by the man who loved money more than his own children.

Jacques's fingers tightened on the balcony railing he was leaning against.

He'd spent so much of the past seven years trying to prove his father wrong. But the truth was that Jacques had also been trying to prove that who his father was didn't define *him*. That the man who would tell his son he could never mean as much to his mother as *he* did— who would call his son a failure and a disappointment— didn't dictate who Jacques would become.

When he'd realised he had treated Lily in those first two days when they'd met like his father had treated his mother, something had shifted inside Jacques. And he'd seen a change in himself over the past month. He hadn't cared as much about his plan as he had about Lily. His wish for the world to see him as someone better than he'd once been had become less important than him being better for Lily.

And then he'd seen his father, and he'd been able to stand up to him. He'd been able to set aside his feelings for the parent who'd dismissed him—who'd been the reason his mother had dismissed him, too—and he'd bought his club, just as he'd told his father he would.

He'd thought it had been possible because he'd changed so much over the seven years since he'd last seen the man. But the real reason had been the change he'd experienced over the past *month*.

With Lily.

For Lily.

Because although she'd thought she wasn't good

enough for him, *he* was the one who had needed to work to be good enough for *her.*

His actions two days ago had shown him he still wasn't good enough for her.

Now, he didn't know why sticking to his plan had been so important to him. Of *course* he still wanted the opportunity to make up for his mistakes. Rugby—the Shadows—had been there for him when he hadn't had anything, and he would do all he could to show his gratitude for that. But since the night they'd spent at the beach restaurant he'd been resisting his feelings for Lily.

He hadn't been acknowledging it, but he'd changed—and that was because of his feelings for her. Feelings he now knew had grown with every moment he'd spent enjoying her company and her uncertain feistiness.

Her point of view had always given him something to think about. And he had genuinely enjoyed seeing how her mind, eager and quick to learn, grasped the aspects of business that he'd taught her.

He'd never been interested in relationships. When he'd discovered rugby—when he'd discovered he was *good* at it—it had become all he'd been able to think about. It had been easier to focus his attention on work than on relationships. Than on love.

Part of him realised now that it was because of the fear witnessing his parents' relationship had instilled in him. And maybe that was why he'd clung to his plan instead of opening up to Lily. It had *still* been easier to focus on work, on things that didn't force him out of his comfort zone.

But Lily had forced herself out of *her* comfort zone to take part in his plan. She'd put herself in the public eye despite her insecurities for *him.* Before she'd really known him. Just because it had been important to *him.*

And he didn't even have the courage to admit that he loved her.

He didn't deny it any more. He was in love with Lily. It still terrified him, but the past two days had shown him something even more terrifying—a life without her.

The fear of that thought had been eclipsed by excitement now. By hope.

She'd always seen a side of him that no one else had bothered to see. He'd known that the moment she'd said those things about him on the talk show. And he knew that was something special. He'd fought for years for the world to see something *she* had seen within twenty-four hours.

Lily had told him she knew how hard he fought for the things he wanted.

It was time he showed her that he wanted *her*.

CHAPTER TWENTY

LILY FLUCTUATED BETWEEN the devastation that had her
spending hours in bed and a busyness that had resulted
in a spotless house and a fridge filled with food she knew
she would have to share with Caitlyn and her parents—
as soon as she'd built up the courage to see any of them
and explain what had happened with Jacques.

She hadn't heard from him since that night on the
beach, but whenever the phone rang her heart jumped
with the hope. And then she would see that it wasn't his
name or number—like now, when her display showed
Caitlyn's name—and she would sink back into the devastation.

'Hello?'

'Wow, you sound terrible.'

'Thanks, Cait.'

'Not in the best of moods, are you?'

Caitlyn's cheery voice grated on her, and Lily clenched
her jaw.

'Aren't you supposed to be engaged or something?'

The annoyance turned into devastation once more.

'Yes,' she hiccupped.

'I know it wasn't real, but I saw a clip of it on television
again this morning—it's been on about every hour since

it happened—and it looked really sweet. Not as sweet as *my* proposal, of course, but then, mine was real—'

'It *was* really sweet,' Lily interrupted, not in the mood for her friend's energy. 'Listen, Caitlyn, I'm not feeling—'

'Actually, Lil, I'm calling for a reason.' There was a pause. 'I'm worried about Nathan. He hasn't been… Well, he hasn't been himself for the past few days. And I know it has something to do with him wanting to smooth things over between his father and Jacques.'

'Yeah, their dad was at Jacques's charity event.'

Caitlyn sighed. 'I know. He wouldn't tell me anything about it.'

'Probably because it didn't go well.'

'I thought so. I heard Jacques was staying at his beach flat so I came by, hoping we could talk, but he isn't here. Could you…? Could you please come by and open up for me? I don't want to wait outside his flat and risk the chance of being branded as "the other woman" if a photographer sees me.'

'You don't know when he'll be back?' Her heart thumped at the prospect of running into him.

'No…please, Lil.' Caitlyn's voice had gone hoarse. 'I'm really worried about Nathan.'

Lily's resistance melted. She couldn't leave her friend in the lurch. 'I'm on my way.'

She clicked off the phone and dragged herself to the bathroom. She showered, shoved her hair into a bun on the top of her head, and stared at her clothing options.

She was engaged, after all. She couldn't look the way she felt. The thought had her selecting a pretty white and pink floral dress and adding a pair of pink button-shaped earrings.

Twenty minutes later she was walking towards Caitlyn at Jacques's flat.

'You're a life-saver,' Caitlyn said as soon as she saw Lily.

'Sure,' Lily answered, and handed her friend the key. 'You can let yourself out.'

'I won't need the key. Jacques can let me out.' Caitlyn frowned. 'Besides, don't *you* need it?'

'I…'

She'd wanted to give Caitlyn the key and escape as soon as she could, but she couldn't answer Caitlyn's question without telling her the truth. She didn't quite have the energy for that.

'Yeah, of course. I'll just let you in, then.'

She took the key back and pushed open the door.

And froze when she saw Jacques.

His gorgeous face was set in a serious expression, his muscular body clothed in fitted black pants and a light blue shirt. He held a gift-wrapped box in his hands, and she idly wondered if it was for her.

And then she began to put the pieces together. Caitlyn's cheerful tone at the beginning of their telephone conversation, the fact that she didn't look nearly as upset as she'd sounded earlier.

'You missed your calling,' she told her friend.

'I'm sorry, Lil.' Caitlyn had the grace to look chagrined. 'It was a favour. For family.'

With one last apologetic look she left. Leaving Lily alone with Jacques.

She closed the door behind her, not wanting anyone to witness whatever was going to happen between them.

'Thank you for staying.'

'Did I have a choice?'

'I… I didn't know if you would have come if I'd asked.'

'I don't know if I would have either.'

Everything inside her was coiled and twisted. She didn't know what to do to make it go away.

'I was hoping we could talk,' he said, and took a step closer.

'About what?' Then she realised what the day was. 'You made your bid today.'

When he nodded, she set her handbag on the couch.

'How did it go? Or are they still making their decision?'

'I got it.'

'Congratulations.'

'Thank you,' he answered, but something in his tone sounded off. 'I really mean that. None of this would have been possible without you.'

'Then why don't you sound happy? It's everything you've ever wanted, isn't it?'

'I thought so. Until I got it and it didn't make me feel the way I thought it would.'

'I don't understand.'

He set the gift down on the coffee table and took another step towards her. She took a step back, unsure whether she would be able to handle it if he came any closer.

His eyes dimmed at her movement, and he shoved his hands into his pockets.

'When you got your shop…did it make all the trouble you'd gone through worth it?'

'You already know the answer to that.'

'Humour me.'

She took a deep breath. 'It felt like it was worth it at first. When I signed the lease on the property…when I decorated it. It was mine. But then… But then reality set in, and I couldn't escape what I'd done to get it.'

'And then it didn't seem worth it any more?'

'For a while. But since I met you things have been

going better. I've told myself I'll pay back the money, and that's made it a little easier to live with myself.'

'When did you make that decision?'

'Two nights ago.'

His eyes searched her face, as though he was looking for something there, and she shifted her weight. Tucked a curl behind her ear.

'Do things…not seem worth it any more to you?' she asked.

He smiled, but she could see the touch of sadness behind his eyes.

'Not so much, no.'

'Why not?'

'Because I sacrificed something much more important to get it.'

Though her heart-rate spiked, she asked, 'What?'

He didn't answer her for a moment, and Lily thought she'd been foolish to ask.

'I told you…you distracted me from my plan. And I meant it. I'd spent years fixated on making a name for myself other than the bad one the world had given me.' He paused. 'When I heard the club was going to be sold I was sure that it would be my chance.'

'I know all of this.'

'Yeah, you do. But you don't know that the reason I was successful in the end was *you*. Not because you helped my reputation—I think we could have chosen anyone else for that and my reputation would have improved.'

This time she didn't move back when he took a step forward.

'I succeeded because *you*, Lily Newman, showed me how to be someone I've been trying to be for years in one month.'

Speechless, she watched as he walked back to the table and picked up the box. She took it from him wordlessly.

'What...?' She cleared her throat when she heard the hoarseness of her voice. 'What is it?'

'Open it. Please.'

It was a plea, and though there was a part of her that was still in shock she was helpless to resist it. She tore the paper open with shaking hands, opened the box and felt the pieces of her heart that were already broken turn into a million more.

He'd given her a beautiful picture frame—wooden and hand-made. She recognised Caitlyn's artistry in it, and knew her friend had created it with Lily in mind. But it wasn't the frame that had Lily choked up. It was the picture it held.

It was a photograph of the exact moment she'd told herself to focus on for the past two days. The moment she recalled when she wanted to think of something happy. When she was brave enough to face what she had lost.

It was a picture taken at the charity event, of when Jacques had proposed to her. He was on his knee, looking up at her with an emotion on his face that was similar to the one it held now. She traced his face, and then looked at her own. Looked at the light, at the hope that shone in her eyes. She saw her eyes focused only on him, though there were so many people looking at her.

When a sob threatened, she put the lid back on the box. 'Why would you give me this?' she rasped, shaken.

'I told you that night that I wished you could see yourself the way I saw you. This picture *shows* you how I see you.'

'I don't know what you want me to see, Jacques,' she said desperately. 'I can't tell what that look on your face is.'

He lifted her chin, forcing her to look at him.

'It's love, Lily. I love you.'

And he kissed her.

He'd thought saying the words would be hard. But once he'd seen her they had come effortlessly. He'd kissed her because he'd been able to tell she didn't believe him. And he'd thought maybe if he could show her…

The moment his lips touched hers there was no more thinking. No more rationalising. He should have known that by now, and yet he was constantly surprised by the way her kiss could consume him.

By the way her *taste* could consume him.

After days of uncertainty—of wondering if he'd ever be consumed by that taste again—he felt more urgency, more greed than he would have liked. For a moment he considered allowing it. He considered letting passion dictate the kiss. But he wanted to show her more than passion. He wanted to show her that there was more than the attraction he'd claimed had always been between them.

She already knew about that. What she *didn't* know about was his love for her. What she didn't know was the intimacy he craved to have with her.

Slowly he deepened the kiss, and with each movement he showed her. With each stroke of his tongue, with each caress of his hands, he opened his heart to her. He showed her that he was hers, and only hers.

And for the first time he discovered that love was more potent than any attraction.

'Stop!' she said breathlessly as she pushed him away.

Somehow they'd ended up against the wall, and when he moved back he wished *he'd* had it behind him to steady him. 'What's wrong?'

'What's *wrong*?' she repeated. 'Jacques, you've had my best friend trick me into coming here. You tell me you got your club, but that it hasn't made you happy. And then you give me this gift, tell me you love me, and kiss me until I don't know who I am…'

Her chest heaved, but he couldn't tell if it was from their kiss or her words.

'You've got what you wanted and it hasn't made you feel the way you wanted it to. So…so maybe you're just moving on to the next thing. What happens if this—if I—don't make you happy? Do you just move on again? Because that…well, it won't work for me.'

'We weren't even a real couple and you made me happier than I've ever been, Lily.' He took her hands in his. 'I know you're worried that this is a rash decision for me, but it isn't. I haven't been able to stop thinking about you.'

He could see that he wasn't convincing her, and panic gripped his heart. But he took a deep breath and reminded himself that he always did whatever it took to get what he wanted. That meant that he needed to fight for Lily.

And *that* meant laying it all on the line.

'I resisted it from the moment we had dinner on that beach and I saw the person you really were. I resisted it through every dinner after that, through every event when I saw you fight against your insecurities. When I saw you overcome them.'

He took a deep breath.

'I fought it because I'd seen what a terrible relationship looked like. I was terrified that I would be like my father—that whatever relationship I was in would turn out to be like my parents. So I stayed away from them.'

'And had multiple partners instead?'

He winced. 'Yeah.'

'So what changed?'

He could tell he had her attention now, and the panic began to subside. 'I met you.'

'As simple as that?'

'As *complicated* as that. I've told you that you changed me, Lily. I mean it. Fear kept me from telling you this before, but I love you.'

Her eyes shone with tears, and her voice was hoarse when she asked, 'And this is not because you're looking for the high you hoped to get when you heard you'd got the club? I'm sorry it didn't feel the way you wanted it to, but…but that can't be the reason you've realised you love me.'

'Not that alone, no,' he agreed. 'I realised I loved you when you called me out on the beach.'

'You love me,' she repeated.

'I do.'

Her eyes began to shine with that hope he'd seen when he'd proposed to her. So he took the box from her hand, opened it again, and handed the frame to her.

'What do you see in that picture?'

'You're proposing.'

'What do you see on my face?'

Tears gleamed in her eyes when she looked at him. 'Is it…is it love?'

He set a hand under her chin, brought her head up to look at him. 'Tell me what you see on my face now, Lily.'

'You mean it?' A tear ran down her cheek. 'Don't do this if you don't mean it.'

'I *do* mean it,' he said quietly, and lowered his hands to her arms. 'Do you want to know what *I* see in that picture, Lil?' He didn't wait for an answer. 'I see a beautiful, kind, caring woman. One who sacrificed her own insecurities to help someone get what they thought they needed.'

He pulled her closer to him.

'I see a woman who has fought to overcome all the things life has thrown at her. Who has used her failures, her mistakes, as lessons. Who showed *me* how to do that too.'

His arms went around her waist, and he closed the distance between them until she was gently pressed to his body.

'I don't want to make *this* mistake, though, Lily. Because I don't know how I'd come back from it. I don't know how I could learn from it when it would be the worst mistake of my life.'

'I didn't know how I could learn from it either,' she whispered. 'I told myself that I could use it as a lesson to be better in the future, but I didn't know how.'

'So we won't make this mistake?'

'No, we won't.'

She looked at him with those beautiful eyes, more piercing now after her tears.

'I love you, Jacques.'

He rested his forehead on hers. 'I've never heard anything that's made me happier in my life.' He took another moment to appreciate it, and then he said, 'I could never imagine being married to someone after seeing what my parents went through. But that's because I'd never loved anyone. And then I met you—I fell in love with you— and I imagined it all so easily. In fact I can't *stop* thinking about it.'

He held his breath, hoping she understood what he'd meant.

'Me either.'

It wasn't the answer he'd hoped for, but the words sounded like trumpets in his ears.

He had a chance.

'I think about a future with you,' she said. 'I look at this gorgeous ring—even though it's pretend—and it undoes every resolution of mine to move on. It undoes every thought of mine that I *can* move on.'

She paused.

'I always thought I didn't deserve the good things in life. And I'd accepted it.'

'You didn't accept what I offered the other night.'

She smiled. 'That was *your* fault. You showed me that settling for anything less than what I wanted wasn't right. Every time I thought something demeaning about myself I heard your voice telling me to snap out of it. Or reminding me of all the things I've achieved. I wouldn't have been able to survive with just a part of you, Jacques. I wanted *all* of you.'

Her eyes flashed with uncertainty, and then the look was replaced with boldness.

'And I think maybe I *deserve* all of you.'

'You do, my love,' he said in relief. 'I'm the one who doesn't deserve *you*.'

'No, Jacques. We're stronger than that now. Together we're stronger. And we deserve each other.'

'Say it again, Lily. Tell me you love me again.'

'I love you.'

She'd barely said the words before his lips were on hers again. This time there were no reservations. This time there was passion. There was greed. There was urgency. But there was also love and intimacy. He gave just as much as he took, his passion fuelled by their acknowledged feelings. By their love.

And then he pulled back.

'I love you too.'

With those words all the turmoil inside her was calmed. All the insecurities faded. And she believed that she deserved this happiness. She deserved this happiness with the man she loved.

'You're a pretty lucky man, Mr Brookes,' she said, looking at the picture again. Now looking at it didn't hurt. 'Some people would say you have it all.'

'Those people would be right,' he replied, grinning. He pulled her in for a hug, his head resting on hers. 'Though you have to admit *you're* pretty lucky too.'

Her cheek rested on his chest, the picture still in her right hand, and she smiled. 'Oh, I know I am. Haven't you read the papers? *I'm* the one who tamed Bad-Boy Brookes.'

He chuckled. 'Yeah, you did. And I'm looking forward to a lifetime of it.'

Her heart sped up and she pulled back, setting the picture on the table.

'Do you mean…?'

'You can't possibly be surprised.' He smiled. 'How do you like that ring?'

'I'm pretty in love with it.' Her heart bursting, she asked one more time. 'Do you *really* mean it?'

'With all my heart, Lily. I can go down on one knee again if it would convince you?'

Lily looked at the picture again, saw the expression on his face. The real one since the emotion she hadn't been able to identify before now had a name. And then she looked at her own face again, and her eyes filled with tears.

'It was real, wasn't it?' she whispered.

'It was, but I'd like to ask you again anyway.'

She smiled when he went down on one knee, this time holding her hand with the diamond ring on it instead of inside its box.

'I love you, Lily. You will *always* be my real redemption. Will you marry me?'

'I can't imagine wanting anything else more.'

He grabbed her, twirled her around. And when they kissed Lily knew that the only thing that would define them in future would be their love for one another.

* * * * *

COMING SOON!

We really hope you enjoyed reading this book. If you're looking for more romance, be sure to head to the shops when new books are available on

Thursday 11th July

To see which titles are coming soon, please visit

millsandboon.co.uk/nextmonth

LET'S TALK
Romance

For exclusive extracts, competitions
and special offers, find us online:

 facebook.com/millsandboon

@MillsandBoon

@MillsandBoonUK

Get in touch on 01413 063232

For all the latest titles coming soon, visit
millsandboon.co.uk/nextmonth

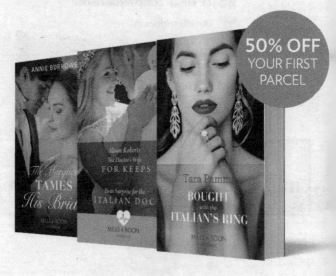